THE SCARLET DRESS

LOUISE DOUGLAS

Boldwood

First published in Great Britain in 2021 by Boldwood Books Ltd.
This paperback edition first published in 2022.

1

A CIP catalogue record for this book is available from the British Library.

Paperback ISBN: 978-1-80280-846-9

Ebook ISBN: 978-1-83889-284-5

Kindle ISBN: 978-1-83889-283-8

Audio CD ISBN: 978-1-83889-280-7

Digital audio download ISBN: 978-1-83889-281-4

Large Print ISBN: 978-1-80048-853-3

Boldwood Books Ltd.

23 Bowerdean Street, London, SW6 3TN

www.boldwoodbooks.com

MIX
Paper from
responsible sources
FSC® C171272

For the Hot Tub Girls, with love x.

PROLOGUE

The next time the child wakes, darkness has fallen. Through the chink in the curtains she sees the moon shining, a milky light behind the clouds. It's quiet and still; an atmosphere as if thunder is gathering. The child listens to the rasping of her own breath.

Inside the room, nothing moves. On the wall, plaster Jesus, caught in the moon-glow, looks down from between deep shadows, one hand raised in blessing. The child wants her mother, but her mother is dead. All the child has is the locket that she keeps beneath her pillow, small and heart-shaped; a secret.

'Dad?' she calls, tentatively. There is no answer. She listens hard but hears nothing, not her father's snoring, nor the tapping of the paws of his little terrier, Trip, on the lino downstairs.

She is completely alone.

The child pushes herself up, untangling her limbs from the damp sheets. Her throat has been cross-hatched by razor blades; the glands in her neck are plum-sized, hard as pebbles. Her glass is at the side of her bed but the bottle of lemonade that Mrs deVillars brought over earlier is on the chest of drawers against the opposite wall, Jesus watching over it. Slowly, carefully, the child slides her legs out of bed. The floorboards creak, warm and warped beneath the soles of her feet. She's so hot she will melt like candle-wax, but at the same time she's shivering with cold. Her nightdress sticks to her, drenched with sweat.

She moves to the window, which has been open for weeks to try to draw in any passing whisper of cool air, and puts her hands on the ledge. Outside, the night is black, with the texture of treacle. It tastes like the weed washed up on the mud and dried in the sun; the feathers of gulls. Distantly, ship lights glimmer on the estuary.

The moon is emerging from its hiding place amongst the clouds: a good half-moon chalked onto a humid sky with the distant Welsh mountains like inkblots below. In the moonlight, the child sees a movement on the mudflats at the shoreline. Someone is down there. For a moment, in her feverish state, she believes it is her mother and her heart lifts even though deep down she knows it can't be. She watches the person as they go to the edge of the sea, and hold back their arm, and fling something far out; a silent splash as it makes contact with the water. Whoever it is stands for a moment, staring out over the sea until the moon retreats and then they turn and disappear back into the shadows.

1

THURSDAY

A lively wind danced across the estuary flatlands, shimmying the feathered heads of the reeds that lined the rhynes. Marnie Morahan headed back down the track with the dogs: her own beloved Tessy and the foster dog, a monstrous-looking animal that Jenna at the rescue centre had named Mister. He had short legs and a chest so barrelled that he waddled rather than walked. His head and neck were covered in scars and old wounds from his days as a bait dog, one ear almost completely gone, the other with chunks missing like a leaf got at by snails. His grizzled snout was encased inside a *Silence of the Lambs*-style muzzle designed to protect him from himself. If another dog came too close, Mister might try to kill it and he was already on his final warning. His next aggressive bite would be his last.

Marnie loved all animals, even difficult-to-love ones like Mister; *especially* ones like him. It was people she struggled with. It was a two-way street. Marnie didn't trust people and most people thought she was weird with her old black clothes and boots, her piercings and tattoos, her hair shaved close to her skull, her sullen expression and downcast eyes; her reluctance to be involved with anyone except for her immediate family, Jenna and her dog-training clients. Her muteness. Marnie knew people called her a misfit, and worse. It didn't hurt because she was used to it; she'd been the odd one out all her life. Sometimes she worried that her oddness would become an embarrassment to her daughter, Lucy, or worse, that bullies might target Lucy because of her, but fortunately Lucy was a sunny, friendly girl, popular at school. She accepted Marnie as she was and expected others to accept her too. Lucy understood that Marnie could no more change than the sun could rise in the west: she didn't need to be close to people and people didn't need to be close to her.

The track was stony. Gritty puddles had formed in the potholes. The grass that grew in shabby green strips was submerged in the wet. The hedgerows on either side had lost their leaves months earlier and were black and twiggy, and the branches of the wind-worn trees above were jagged, mistletoe growing like ragged hair in the pits of their joints. Deep ruts made by ploughs in undulating stripes across the fields were full of water that reflected the light.

Clouds raced across a high, wintry sky that morning; a flock of lapwings banked steeply into the air, flashing white then black. Tessy stopped to sniff at a pile of dung and Mister looked up at Marnie with bloodshot, prize-fighter eyes, confused because he did not understand the joys of sniffing.

Marnie put her hand in the pocket of her ancient coat and pulled out a handful of dried pilchards. She offered one to Mister through the muzzle, but the dog backed away, believing it to be a trick, expecting to be punished. Marnie dropped the treat on the ground. Mister stared at it, but made no move to eat it.

What have they done to you? Marnie wondered. What did they do?

Mister clamped the stub of his tail between his back legs and shivered.

They walked on, Tessy running ahead to flush out a partridge that was hiding in the foot of the hedge, wagging her spaniel-flag tail. The partridge squawked and flapped clumsily into the air, trailing red feathers. The small group stepped carefully over the railway sleepers laid across a drainage rhyne, silvery reeds growing tall along its length and walked to the end of the track. Marnie put Tessy back on the lead before she opened the gate and they went through together.

To their left, now, was the old wall that surrounded the gardens of the deVillarses' house, a three-storey Gothic villa with the official name of Blackwater but known to the residents of Severn Sands town as the Big House. To their right was the old Channel View holiday park where Marnie's father used to be caretaker and where she had spent all her free time growing up. It was no longer a holiday park. Now it was a building site.

For almost a month bulldozers had been churning up the fields where the caravans used to be ranked, breaking the foundations of the old amusement park and funfair. The ancient hedgerow that used to encircle the park was gone, replaced by interlocking metal barriers and signs warning people to keep out. Piles of bricks and plastic piping were stacked over what had once been Marnie's playground. The old apple tree that only last week she'd made the builders swear they wouldn't touch lay on its side, roots exposed like a great muddy scab, branches reaching out helplessly. Marnie had wished a curse on those builders when she saw what they'd done to the tree. She used to scramble up its trunk and hide amongst its leaves when she was little. She knew every branch, each knobble and handhold. The tree had been a friend to Marnie and she didn't have many friends.

'It was dying anyway,' the foreman, Gabriel Romanescu, had said when she'd challenged him. 'If it had been healthy it wouldn't have gone so easily.'

Marnie had stared at the tree, the branches that used to cradle her snapped like bones.

'I'm sorry you're upset,' Gabriel had said, filling in the spaces left by Marnie's silence, as people invariably did. 'I don't like it when we have to remove trees but sometimes there's no choice.'

Now, as Marnie drew closer to the old entrance to the holiday park, a weed-infested shingle drive that ran beneath a dilapidated arch with the name of the park above it, she realised something was different. The jaws of the great earth-moving machines were motionless, their engines silent. The contractors in their high-vis protective workwear were gathered around a part of the site where the funfair used to be and there was an atmosphere of uncertainty, exacerbated by the quiet.

Marnie clicked her tongue and the dogs stayed close. Gabriel Romanescu, clad in high-vis workwear and a hard hat, mud clagging his boots, was standing next to a police car parked by the exit. A roll-up burned between his lips, one eye narrowed against the smoke. He was using both hands to compose a message on his phone. He looked up as Marnie approached and then looked down again.

Marnie stopped a few feet away from Gabriel. She didn't have to speak for Gabriel to know that she was wondering what had happened, and why work had stopped.

'I can't tell you,' he said, without taking his eyes off the phone. 'It's confidential.'

Marnie waited. Gabriel glanced at her, then back at the phone. He removed the cigarette, examined it and dropped it on the mud.

'We've found some bones buried in the old funfair area,' he said. 'We think they're human.' He paused a moment, then corrected himself. 'We can see that they're human. But we're not supposed to talk about it. All communications have to go through head office.'

Marnie was silent. The breeze blew cold from the estuary. She narrowed her eyes against it.

'Let's hope they are old bones,' said Gabriel. 'Let's hope they've been there for hundreds of years. We've dug into burial grounds before. Once we found a prehistoric graveyard. The universities were all over it. We had to stop work.'

Marnie gazed past Gabriel into the holiday camp, and she could see it as it used to be: full of people, colour and noise; children playing cricket between the caravans, smoke puffing from barbecues, music singing out from transistor radios; laughter, screams and splashing from the swimming pool. She could see the young woman from Caravan 49, Alice Lang, walking towards her, wearing her lemon yellow sundress, the blonde hair with the dark roots pinned back from her face, the ribbons of her espadrilles making diamond shapes on her calves.

Gabriel was still talking, but Marnie was no longer listening. Behind him, Alice was smiling, waving at Marnie and Marnie couldn't wave back because she was carrying a plastic laundry basket full of Alice's clothes. The heat that day was intense, the sun beating down, shining on the sequins sewn onto the scarlet dress that was folded on top of the laundry, and it was a day in late August, almost twenty-five years earlier. Marnie Morahan, aged ten years and two months was sick, and even though she didn't know it yet, she was about to betray Alice. And she'd never have the chance to make it up to her, because this was the day that Alice Lang would disappear.

2

Will Jones was the only passenger on the single carriage connection from Bristol Temple Meads to Severn Sands. He sat by the window, jiggling his feet, feeling headachy and raw.

He didn't want to go back to the town where he'd grown up but he owed it to Alice. He'd once told her he would do anything for her, and he'd meant it. He meant it still. When it came to Alice, he had never had a choice. For two and a half decades he'd been powerless to do anything, but now he had a task: to make sure the man who had killed her was brought to justice.

He stared at his own ghostly reflection staring back at him from the surface of a grimy window, the countryside flattened as it unscrolled behind. Alice was dead. There was no avoiding it now. If he was honest, deep down he'd known she was never coming back, but for as long as there was no concrete proof of her death there could still be a tiny thread of hope that she might return. Until today, he'd allowed himself to daydream, to look for her face amongst the commuters on the underground, to imagine a chance encounter in a restaurant, or a park and to write the script of the exchange that would follow – 'Alice?' 'Will? Oh my God, is it really *you?'* – to picture the two of them going forward into a future together. Now that thread had been severed. Alice was dead, gone in the cruellest way: murdered. What was left for Will was an over-whelming desire to make Guy deVillars pay for his crime.

Because Guy had killed Alice.

Will had always suspected; now he knew.

It was Tony Costello, an old university friend of Will's, who told him that Alice's remains had been found. Tony, a detective with the Avon and Somerset Police, knew about Will and Alice; like all Will's friends, he'd heard the story of their summer a hundred times. He knew that Will had, for a while, been suspected of doing Alice some harm. Even after a witness came forward to say they'd seen Alice walking alone towards the sea the night she disappeared, fingers still pointed towards Will. When the police investigation was dropped, Will tried to get on with his life. But the shame of being suspected of having hurt the girl he loved and the bitterness he harboured towards his accusers had never dissipated. Neither had the sorrow that she was gone. Tony knew full well that Will's career and his passion for unsolved crime were rooted in his obsession with the mystery of Alice.

There was no easy way to break the news, and during their phone call earlier that morning, Tony hadn't tried to sweeten the pill.

'I thought you'd want to know,' he'd said to Will after a few basic pleasantries, 'that human remains have been found buried in Severn Sands.' He paused a moment then added: 'The remains of a young, slightly built female.'

Will's mouth had gone dry. He'd licked his lips, tried to slow his breathing.

'Will? You still there?'

'Yes. Yeah. I'm still here. Have they... has *she* been identified?'

'Not yet.'

'So you don't know...'

'We can't be one hundred per cent certain that it's Alice Lang but everything points to it being her.'

There was a long silence.

'Where?' Will had asked at last. 'Where in Severn Sands did they find her?'

'The old holiday park. Funfair, to be specific.'

Will groaned. He reached out his free hand to steady himself.

'I know it's hard for you, buddy, hearing this,' said Tony gently, 'but at least now she can be laid to rest. Now there can be resolution.'

Will's palm was flat against the black tiles of the kitchen wall. He was imagining Alice's body curled in its grave; her moonlit skin pale against the dark soil.

Tony was still talking.

'There was a silver chain in amongst the neck bones. One of the charms is a letter "A". The other is a little silver swallow. Do they mean anything to you?'

Will remembered that little metal bird resting in the hollow of Alice's throat beside the "A", its outline defined against her brown skin, glinting in the sunlight. He remembered her fingers touching it; she turning to him, smiling, saying: 'It's perfect, Will!'

'Will?' Tony had asked. 'Will? Are you OK, buddy? Are you OK?'

* * *

Will had been at home when Tony Costello called; making an espresso for his girlfriend, Saoirse. Saoirse worked in publishing – that was how they'd met – and mostly she commuted to an office on the other side of London. The previous day, though, she had come down with what felt like the flu, and had decided to work from home. Normally Will would have been able to go away without having to answer any questions, but because Saoirse was there, in the apartment, he had to tell her that he was packing because he was going back to Severn Sands.

'Why?' she asked croakily, clutching a handkerchief to her nose as he stuffed his laptop charger into a side pocket of the rucksack. 'What's the point in going back? You can't *do* anything.'

'I need to be there, where it happened, so that I can write about it.'

'Why can't you write here?'

'Because it wouldn't be authentic.'

Saoirse looked at him doubtfully. The rims of her nostrils were pink.

'I owe it to Alice to be there,' said Will.

'You owe it to Alice?'

'Yes.'

Saoirse bit her lip, literally, to stop herself saying something unkind about Alice. She, like Will's other girlfriends before her, believed Will should put Alice behind him and move on, but given the unfurling tragedy she could hardly say anything snarky. Instead she stared at Will in a sorrowful way. She didn't look great, to be fair, wan and watery-eyed. The coffee steamed on the window ledge. Will knew it would never be drunk. It was one of the annoying things about Saoirse: she was always making drinks, or asking for drinks, and then not drinking them. He was forever pouring half-cups of cold coffee into the sink.

'Alice isn't the real reason you're going away. You want to get away from me, don't you, Will?' she said.

'What?'

'You're going to do what you always do when things get tough; you're going to walk away rather than deal with it.'

'Jesus, Saoirse, this has nothing to do with you.'

'I know things have been difficult lately but...'

'Saoirse...'

'... every couple has ups and downs. Why don't you stay and we can talk and try and work things out, find a way forward.'

'Saoirse, *please*! How can you even say that? Alice is dead!'

There were a few moments' silence. He heard the wheezing in her lungs. He continued packing, shoving things into the rucksack.

She tried a different tack. 'What if I get really ill?'

'You have a phone. Ciara and Finn are ten minutes away.'

'I can't believe you'd leave me when I'm like this.'

'You'll be OK,' said Will.

Saoirse turned and left the room, closing the door loudly behind her and Will felt guilty for a moment but not guilty enough to go after her. They'd been together for eighteen months, which was towards the top end of the length of any of Will's relationships. Lately, Will had developed the suffocated feeling he always had when heading towards a break-up. When this feeling manifested itself, there was little point prolonging the agony. Will and whoever-she-was may as well get it over and done with, go their separate ways. And right now he absolutely needed to prioritise his emotional energy for Alice and Alice's murderer. He didn't want his feelings for Saoirse, or anyone, to get in the way of that.

* * *

In a heartbeat, Will's mind flipped back to Alice.

She was gone, but she still felt so present that she might have been sitting beside him on the train, a small, fidgety presence, with her bangles and her earrings, her Lennon sunglasses, her ankle chain, her tattoo. What would become of this ever-present, pestering, laughing little ghost now? Would she disappear? And if she did, what would be left for Will? What would be left *of* him?

3

After the scarlet dress was found at the side of the estuary it seemed that the theory that Alice had drowned was correct. Marnie believed it too.

She had gone down to the shore many times as a child and thrown flowers into the water. If she closed her eyes and concentrated, she was certain she could feel Alice close by. Occasionally, she even caught glimpses of Alice's face in the mist shape-shifting over the estuary, or the reflections echoed across its expanse. Often, she dreamed of Alice, and in her dreams the sea and Alice were the same entity. It had mostly been a comfort. If Alice was part of the estuary, then she still existed; she was not wholly gone.

But none of it had been true; not the feelings, not the glimpses, not the dreams. Alice had never left the holiday park. She'd been abandoned there like a piece of rubbish, as if she meant nothing.

Marnie had almost reached the junction with the lane that would take her and the dogs home when a chunky maroon car pulled up at the roadside. The passenger-side door opened and a blonde woman climbed out.

'Excuse me,' the woman called, 'can I have a quick word?'

Marnie felt the usual panic about how to convey the fact that she couldn't talk. She and the blonde had made eye contact so she couldn't pretend she hadn't noticed. She waited for the woman to catch up. She was glamorous, heavily made-up. Strands of hair kept sticking to her lips. She brushed them away and smiled but at the same time her eyes moved up and down over Marnie's body, taking in her appearance, categorising her; labelling her what? Goth? Bumpkin? Weirdo?

'I am *so* sorry to bother you,' the woman said, widening her eyes to emphasise her sincerity, 'but I'm Xena Wills from the TV news. I'm trying to find someone who's willing to be interviewed about the old Channel View holiday park. Do you know anyone?'

Marnie shook her head.

'Oh...' The woman's smile faltered, but soon returned. 'You're walking your dogs; you must be local! Are you local? Yes? Fantastic! Well then, wouldn't you like to be on TV? Honestly, it'll take five minutes, simple questions and we'd be terribly grateful.' She smiled as persuasively as she could. Marnie took a step backwards. Her throat was tight, as it always was when strangers tried to talk to her. She touched her lips and shook her head, hoping the woman would understand.

'What is it?' the woman asked. 'What's the matter? Don't you understand English? Oh! Are you deaf?'

Marnie nodded, because it was easier that way, then she turned and walked away, the dogs at her side. The woman gave a brief, disbelieving laugh and said something to her colleague. Marnie caught only one word, 'inbred'.

Good luck finding anyone who will talk to you round here, Marnie thought.

Stories still circulated in Severn Sands about what happened when the press piled into the town in the wake of Alice Lang's disappearance and the headlines that ensued.

Tina Truss, who worked part-time as a cleaner at Channel View, had given an interview to a personable young man who had taken her out for cocktails and who said he was freelance but turned out to be working for the *News of the World*. In the interview, Tina had put forward every rumour she'd ever heard about Alice Lang, and the holiday park. The stories that followed were of wife-swapping and pop-up bordellos, prostitutes renting caravans so they could 'entertain punters' during the summer season. People in the town still hadn't forgiven Tina for the things she'd said, even though she claimed her words had been taken out of context and that she'd been duped.

Marnie's sympathy for Tina was limited. After the interview was published, the Trusses had new windows put in and the front of their house had been re-cladded in mock stone so that it stood out from the pebble dash on the rest of the street. Every time Marnie walked past, even though the Trusses had long since moved, she was reminded of the awful things Tina had said about Alice and the shame her betrayal had spread through the town.

4

The closer Will came to Severn Sands, the more dread he felt. He would have done anything to give Alice's story a happier ending. He would have given up the rest of his life for a single day, a single hour, even another single minute with her.

If only he'd behaved differently back then. If only he'd been able to control his jealousy.

Will knew this was his last chance to make things right. This was not the time for wild accusations; he needed to focus on the facts. Forensic evidence would be long gone so he would have to find another route to prove that Guy deVillars was responsible for the death of Alice Lang.

It wasn't as if Will hadn't had plenty of time to think about his strategy. He had been planning to write a book about Alice for more than two decades. He had a title, *The Girl in Caravan 49*. The morning's discovery was the obvious starting point and the end would be an account of the trial of Guy deVillars. Will would be there, in the court to watch Guy being found guilty of murder. *Then* there would be resolution.

But first, work must be done. In the absence of concrete

evidence, and with the police starting from scratch, it would be up to Will to build a case. Others had known Alice while she was in Severn Sands. Mr and Mrs deVillars, Guy's parents and owners of the holiday park, were hardly likely to say anything that might implicate their son, but Will's mother, Angharad, had a memory that was still razor sharp. Angharad was in Majorca now, only a phone call away.

There were two other key witnesses: the park's caretaker, John Morahan, and John's daughter, Marnie.

Marnie.

Thinking of her gave Will an uncomfortable sensation. *Two* uncomfortable sensations. Shame and guilt. He really didn't want to have to face Marnie Morahan again.

To distract himself, he read the headlines of the newspaper stories he'd clipped and saved over the years.

Young woman missing from holiday park.

'Raised voices' heard near caravan where pretty Alice was staying.

Our troubled daughter: Alice's parents speak out.

Alice talked of suicide: schoolmate's revealing claims.

And most recently:

Holiday park mystery: What really happened to Alice Lang?

a story inspired by a medium who claimed Alice had faked her own death in the estuary and gone off to live with a group of travellers. It was a theory that had done the rounds before.

There'd be more headlines in tomorrow's papers, more speculation. Picture editors would juxtapose images of the building site with the crowded hedonism of the holiday park in its heyday.

They'd use the Second Severn Crossing looming in the background as a metaphor for life's journey. People who hadn't known Alice would search the internet for pictures and information. They'd post comments about her, some sympathetic, some critical, some cruel. They'd make assumptions and judgements. They'd behave as if she belonged to them but Alice didn't belong to anybody. Only Will Jones had truly understood the kind of person she was.

A copy of his favourite picture of Alice was saved onto his phone. She was sitting on the step outside the door of Caravan 49 with a colander between her knees. She had been hulling strawberries that John Morahan had given her, picked from his garden. She was looking at Will over the top of her sunglasses, a playful expression on her face, bangles on her arms. She was wearing her tangerine bikini. It showed off her deep tan and her neat, little figure. Will didn't like the picture because it was sexy – although it definitely was – but because it summed up Alice. Playful, vivacious, happy.

They were lovers by the time he took that photograph. Alice and Will. They were in love. And that afternoon, the afternoon of the strawberries, Will had watched Alice licking juice from her fingertips and had wondered how it was possible for a person to be as happy as he was without exploding like a firework. For ever after he would remember the sunlight falling on Alice's cheek, she tucking her hair behind an ear, the sweet, sweet taste of the strawberry that he stole.

It was perfect; how it always was when they were together, until Guy deVillars started coming between them, spoiling things.

For three weeks, from the day Alice arrived in Channel View holiday park, almost until the day she disappeared, Will had existed in a state of beautiful tension. He hardly slept, tossing and turning under the sheets in his bed in the chalet that he shared with his mother, while she, Angharad, snored on the other side of the wall. He went out to run in the moonlight because the days were too hot, and swam illicitly in the park's pool. During the days he dug over Mrs deVillars' flower beds, although the soil was dry and hard, then he stood at the side of the estuary throwing stones into the water, doing anything he could to alleviate the pressure building inside him because of Alice, trying to wear himself out so he could sleep. For three weeks she was all he thought of, all he dreamed of. She filled his every waking moment with a longing like a thirst that couldn't be quenched, like an itch, a pain, an earworm. For three weeks he'd existed in a state that veered between blissful agony or agonising bliss, that was either heaven or hell but never anything in between, and all the time the only stain on Will's happiness had been Guy deVillars and the way he watched Alice, the way he tried to insinuate himself into her company and come between Will and the girl he loved.

It was Guy's fault that Will and Alice had argued that last evening; Guy's fault that they'd ended on a bad note.

Will had never truly believed that Alice had drowned herself, not even after Mrs deVillars found Alice's scarlet dress at the side of the estuary. Alice wouldn't have done that. It was easier for him to believe she'd left with the travellers. He could acknowledge that Alice had more than her fair share of personal demons but Will knew that at heart she was an optimist. She believed she had a good future ahead of her; she loved life more than anybody he'd ever known. With every atom of her being, Alice Lang had wanted to live and that was what made her murder even more cruel.

It was what made it crucial that the person responsible was brought to justice.

5

The cottage where Marnie Morahan lived with her daughter, Lucy, and an assortment of animals was on Holm Chapel Lane, on the outskirts of Severn Sands town. It was a narrow lane, hedgerows on either side, the dark, uneaten winter berries on the blackthorn wizened and gnarled. That afternoon, a tractor was slowly moving in the gloaming, flattening the tops of the hedges with a mechanical arm to make them tidy before the birds began nesting. In the field to one side, a herd of bullocks grazed: to the other, sheep were fattening with the spring's crop of lambs.

Marnie went into the cottage, turning on the lights, putting a log into the stove. She shut Tessy in the kitchen while she attended to Mister, who was being housed in the feed room of the stable block to the back of the cottage. Before Mister was rescued he'd only ever lived in cages. He found the domestic environment overwhelmingly complicated and frightening and preferred the plainness and predictability of the feed room with its bare walls and barred window. Marnie was happy to let him rest where he felt most comfortable. She had put a heater in the room, and covered the concrete floor with carpeting and blankets. She was settling him when the phone rang in her back pocket. It was Jenna.

'Hi, Marnie, you OK, love?'

Marnie pushed the feed-room door closed with her hip, and bolted it from the outside. She texted a thumbs up and walked back towards the cottage. Tessy was standing with her front paws on the window of the back door, muddy streaks down the glass. When she saw Marnie, she scrabbled at the window, bouncing on her back legs, her whole body wagging with joy.

'I heard what they found down the holiday park,' Jenna said. 'I wanted to make sure you were all right. It must've been an awful shock for you. You knew the girl, didn't you?'

Marnie was reunited with Tessy. She kneeled down so that the dog could lick her face. Her body circling Marnie's was the best comfort. Jenna was still speaking.

'Oh, my days, it's so *horrible!* I mean, if she was buried, that means she was actually murdered, doesn't it? They'll have to re-open the investigation. Do you think the press are going to descend on us again? My mum said before you couldn't move for reporters going through dustbins and that. That's all we need, isn't it? Holiday park closed down, bulldozers and tipper trucks spreading mud everywhere and now a load of bloody journalists snooping about. What if it turns out that it *was* someone local that killed her? What then, Marnie?'

Marnie went into the kitchen, tucked the phone between her shoulder and her ear and filled Tessy's water bowl from the tap.

Jenna rarely waited for a response from Marnie. She continued: 'Your dad worked there, didn't he, at the holiday park? They would've questioned him at the time, wouldn't they? He must remember everything that happened. You'd better warn him about the journalists. They'll be after him, Marnie, you mark my words, as she was buried *there*, and him being the caretaker and all. They'll be after everyone who might remember something, especially the men. I mean, it's bound to have been a man, isn't it? Unless it was a woman. And it's usually someone the victim knew. Almost always it is. I've read about these things. They'll be trying to find someone to blame. They always need someone to blame.'

There was a silence then, during which Marnie could hear Jenna's breathing and her footsteps. She deduced from nearby whinnying and distant barking that Jenna was at the rescue centre, crossing from one building to another.

'Anyway,' said Jenna, 'please say "no" if it's too much, but we had this dog come in today, a little lurcher bitch found in the Catbrain pillbox. She's in an awful state, Marnie. I'm standing outside her kennel now and she's sat in one corner pressed up against the wall absolutely trembling, God love her. I can't take her home because of the cats and Mina's got the baby. I mean, she *could* stay here, but it's breaking my heart to see her like this. You'd love her, Marnie, I know you would, and she'd be absolutely fine in the house with Tessy. She's such a little sweetheart but I know you've already got Mister, and if it's too much…'

Marnie texted a thumbs up.

'You'll take her? Oh, fantastic! Are you free now? No? Later then. Seven?… Eight? Half eight?'

Smiley face.

'OK. Half past eight. Thanks, Marnie. Thanks *so* much. You're a star. I knew you wouldn't let me down. I'll see you later. You'll love her, I promise you will. You'll want to keep her. You won't want to give her back.'

Marnie disconnected and put the phone down on the counter. She gazed about her kitchen, light and cosy. The cottage walls were painted a dusty blue, apart from the dining room, which was primrose yellow, and the rooms were full of colour and things that Marnie had collected for good luck: fir cones and pebbles, pieces of driftwood from the estuary, sketches of the different dogs she'd owned and fostered, trophies she and Tessy had won at agility competitions, and others that Lucy had won with her pony, Scrumpy, at gymkhanas and country shows. A framed picture of Marnie aged about four, with her mother, Denise, was on the ledge above the stove. Marnie, skinny in a white dress, sandals and ankle socks, hair held back with a plastic clip, was smiling shyly, leaning against Denise, who was crouched on her heels with her arm round her daughter. Marnie's dad had taken that picture. It was one of the few things Marnie had left that was of Denise, along with her memories, a box she kept in the bottom of her wardrobe and the locket that Marnie found hidden beneath her own pillow the day her mother died.

John Morahan had burned most of the pictures of Denise. He'd burned them with her clothes and books, in the incinerator in the back garden of the caretaker's cottage, one day not long after the funeral. He'd have burned everything if Angharad Jones hadn't come along and stopped him.

'Come on now, John, what are you doing? What if one day you need those things to comfort you? Or,' with a significant nod towards Marnie, 'she wants to know about her mother? What then?'

Angharad had packed away what was left of Denise's belongings: her shoes, her make-up bag, the bottle of perfume on the bathroom window ledge; the few books left on the shelves. She'd put them in a box and taken the box back to her chalet. 'You want anything, lovey, you just come and ask your Auntie Angharad, all right?' she'd said to Marnie, tweaking the child's chin.

Marnie didn't terribly mind that the photographs were gone. Denise never managed to be herself when she was being photographed; she was too self-conscious. Marnie preferred to remember Denise when she was happiest, which was when she was reading. She used to lose herself completely in whatever book she had on her lap, her fingers twining the silver chain of the locket as her eyes moved to and fro across the pages. It used to annoy Marnie's father, as if he was jealous of the books and the time that Denise spent with them, but Marnie liked to sit beside her mother and read with her. Sometimes she'd look up from her own book to see that Denise had stopped reading, and instead was staring out of the window.

'Oh don't mind me!' she would say if she noticed Marnie watching. 'My mind's wandering! I'm miles away.'

But when she didn't notice Marnie's eyes upon her, Denise's face truly seemed distant as if she was literally far away and not just in her mind.

* * *

The cottage was Marnie's sanctuary. It was small and bright with no dark corners and nothing to remind her of the situations and people she feared. She didn't let anyone inside unless she knew and trusted them, so there was never any sense of bad feeling or unease.

Angharad had explained to Marnie the importance of keeping bad vibes away from the places where she wanted to rest and feel safe, like the living room and bedrooms. 'Even a thought,' Angharad had said, 'a single dark thought can leave a tiny stain, like a smear, and once it's there it will cause trouble. You can't paint over it. You can't bleach it away. It's there for ever.'

'What about a fight?' Marnie had asked, this conversation taking place back in the days soon after her mother's death when, although a painfully shy child, she could at least bring herself to talk a little.

'A fight? Like an argument, you mean?' Angharad had tutted and shaken her head. 'Oh, no, bless your heart, you don't want to try to relax in a room where people have been arguing. Even if people make friends again, they can't take their ugly words back. They last for ever.'

Marnie had been nine years old when Denise died. Denise had been a gentle and attentive mother, quiet and kind. The trouble was, all the good memories had been tainted by knowing what came after. Marnie couldn't look back at a time when Denise and she were together, without knowing that soon after, Denise had died.

So Marnie managed her history by keeping it at arm's length. Her mother was in the graveyard, and Alice, she had believed, was in the sea. The two women she had loved best were gone but they were close enough for her to call on if she needed them: distant enough not to disturb her equilibrium. But the past was like water. Once the tide turned, you couldn't hold it back.

Human remains had been uncovered at the old Channel View holiday park and people who had forgotten the name, Alice Lang, were remembering it again. They were remembering the blisteringly hot summer, the days of hosepipe bans and parched grass, of sunscreen and sunburn; the summer when the dreadfully intimate photograph of Alice's bedroom inside Caravan 49 had been leaked to the press, the impression of her body on the bed, the sheets rumpled, her underwear on the floor. They were remembering that the young woman had gone missing and Will Jones had been blamed. Then someone came forward to say they'd seen Alice walking down to the water and her dress had washed up at the side of the estuary. After that everyone said she must have drowned but no trace of her had been found.

Until now.

6

Will Jones stood on the platform at Severn Sands station, his ruck-sack hooked over one shoulder, and looked about, seeing himself as if he was watching a film.

To Will, the present was black-and-white arthouse, but the past was in full colour like an old Super 8 video, the definition turned up too high, oranges and bright pinks, a blinding golden backlight, the film shakily unspooling, a juddering projector throwing images onto a wall.

The first time he saw Alice properly he had been clearing the drainage rhyne at the edge of the holiday park. The water levels were low and the rhyne had stagnated and was beginning to stink. He'd spent the afternoon pulling out reeds, irises and weed, and was pushing a wheelbarrow full of wet foliage along the service alleyway behind the hedge that ran behind the caravans. The contents of the barrow were heavy and they stank, steaming as they wilted in the heat. Midges drifted in the miasma.

Will's chest and arms were muscular and he had a good tan from working outside. Girls looked at him now, which they'd never done before. When the holidaymakers arrived at the park, as they unloaded their cars, the teenage daughters sometimes offered him a smile, or stared at him blatantly, chewing gum. Little Marnie Morahan, always alert to what older girls were doing, had nicknamed him 'Diet Coke man'. He told her to shut up but secretly he liked it. He didn't have a girlfriend. Well, he kind of did. A local girl, Daisy Bradshaw, had taken to calling by the holiday park every afternoon when she finished work in the chemist's in Avonmouth and sometimes they walked to the kiosk for an ice cream or a bottle of pop, but Will didn't feel anything for her except mild irritation. Daisy had a long, sorrowful face and moony eyes. Her hair was pulled back into a tight ponytail, accentuating her neck, which was the same width as her face. Her conversation was mainly limited to her work, her attempts to deal with the disgruntlement of elderly and afflicted customers, and people complaining about the cost of prescriptions. Her voice was dreary and monotone.

That afternoon – the afternoon Alice arrived – after Will had been clearing the rhyne, sweat was running down his back and the top of his head was burning. He was thinking about getting back to the chalet he shared with his mother and putting his head under the cold tap and then drinking from the tap; he was so thirsty he could drink a bucketful, but he stopped when he saw a movement through the leaves of the hedge and heard a female voice singing along to a song piping from a tinny radio. He knew exactly where he was, behind the rank of smaller caravans reserved for the holiday park's seasonal staff and single occupants. This rank was on a spur, away from the family caravans. It was quieter here, less hectic.

Will didn't make a habit of spying on the holidaymakers, but this young woman's voice was so sweetly out of tune, so cheerful, that this time he did. Whoever she was, she was on the other side of the privet, only a few feet away. He let the handles of the wheelbarrow down carefully, so as not to alert her to his presence, and he crept forward to look through a gap in the leaves. Alice was hanging her swimming things on the wire rack attached to the caravan window frame, dancing to the beat of the music. The colours of the memory were so bright they were almost blinding. Will saw Alice wring out her lime-green towel, twisting it from both ends and shaking it, the drops of water catching the sunlight and sparkling before they disappeared. She flapped the towel straight and then folded it over the rack. Then she picked up her tangerine bikini, and squeezed it in her hands, water dripping onto her bare feet, before she pegged the two pieces onto the rack. She had her back to him. She was wearing a strapless, splashy yellow dress, that held itself up just above her breasts and a different towel was wrapped around her head like a turban. Wisps of damp hair had come free around her ears and at the back of her neck. There were delicate, paler vertical stripes between her neck and her shoulders where the straps of her bikini had protected her from the sun. Will, hot, parched, sunburned, had looked at her through his peephole of dark green leaves and it was like looking into a pool of clear water. She was dazzling.

The memory brought a lump to the adult Will's throat. He squeezed his free hand tightly shut, digging his fingernails into the flesh.

Alice. Alice. Alice.

The most alive person he had ever known; she was like the wind gusting over the hilltops, or a snowfall, or a sunrise, something as immense and intense as the moon drawing the great tides or as small and vital as a swallow darting through the summer skies. She was such a part of the world and she was dead. She would never come back and it was all because of that pathetic, weak, privileged coward.

Will Jones unclenched his fist, stretched out his fingers, straightened his shoulders.

He looked around him. Apart from the train driver, who had exited his compartment and was now walking towards the public lavatories, Severn Sands station was deserted.

It hadn't changed. Weeds were growing through the cracks in the concrete, litter had accumulated on the sharp grey stones that lay between the tracks and there was some half-hearted graffiti behind the bumpers. Once, Daisy had asked Will to meet her here after work; she'd asked in a way that he couldn't refuse. When she'd stepped off the train, her face had been flushed, her blouse crumpled, dark stains under the arms. Together they'd walked down to the seafront and he'd bought ice creams and they'd sat for a while on the wall and watched the sea come in. Daisy had talked and Will had tried to be interested but he wasn't. He didn't care about the pricing of sunscreen, he didn't care about two-for-one offers, or that some elderly woman with a cut had bled all over the staff room; the thought of it made him feel sick.

'This has been so nice,' Daisy said, when it was time for them to go home. 'Let's do this again tomorrow!'

She had taken hold of his hand. Hers was warm and damp.

'You will come and meet me, won't you, Will?'

'Yeah,' he said, 'sure.'

'You'll be waiting on the platform like you were today?'

'Yep.'

'Promise?' Daisy had asked, wheedling. Wheedling didn't suit her. She was big, broad-shouldered; good-looking but not in a feminine way. 'Promise me? Pretty please?'

'I said so, didn't I?' Will replied tersely.

The promise had been worthless. He hadn't gone back to the station the next day. That was the day he watched Alice hanging up her swimming things from his viewpoint behind the hedge and he forgot about Daisy altogether, as if she'd never existed.

Daisy. How long had she waited here, at the station before she realised that Will wasn't going to turn up? If he concentrated hard enough, would he be able to see her, twenty-four-and-a-half years earlier, checking her watch and the station clock, wondering where he was?

Will Jones took his phone out of his back pocket and made a video sketch of the station, zooming in on the great, metal bumpers at the end of the track, designed to stop trains making contact with the wall. It had become habit to make little videos during the course of his research, to publish on social media when his latest book was released. Normally he enjoyed it but today it was nothing more than a displacement activity.

He put the phone back in his pocket, walked along the deserted platform, and crossed a metal footbridge that gave a view of a sprawling old lorry park. He exited the station and turned through a narrow brick alleyway, littered with rubbish, bramble tendrils creeping over the walls. He came out into the town, his footsteps a lonely sound on the pavement, and walked towards the coast road. The air smelled of seawater, of mud, of wind, a smell he'd long forgotten. The long stream of traffic crossing the closer of the two main Severn Bridges murmured high above. From this distance, it looked too slender a structure to be real, like an optical illusion or a trick.

As he drew closer to the seafront, Will could see the great expanse of water of the miles-wide estuary, the darkness at its far edge marked by a trickle of flickering lights emerging along the coast on the Welsh side. The tide was in and the estuary reflected the lights of the bridges and the roads on either side. A faint, ghostly mist was suspended just above the water's surface. It was the gloaming hour, midway between day and night. Will had forgotten that strange light-catching quality of the water, myste-rious and compelling. He'd forgotten how it moved all the time; fierce currents beneath the surface, dragging tides, deep, vast channels and hills of mud and sand. He used to imagine the estuary-bed as a secret landscape, uncovered twice a day before being submerged beneath depths of seawater. It had been a fantastic canvas for the imagination until Alice was feared drowned and then it became something sinister and cruel.

7

Lucy was thirteen and Marnie didn't normally meet her from the school bus, but she was catching a later bus than usual because she'd stayed on to help make lanterns for the school's forthcoming parade of light and Marnie was consumed by a deep, nagging anxiety that something awful might happen if she wasn't there to walk her daughter home. She knew rationally that just because human remains had been found in the holiday park, it didn't mean this small, windswept town was suddenly full of murderers, that it was no more dangerous now than it had been the day before or the day before that, but she didn't want to take any chances. Angharad Jones had imbued her with a strong bent towards caution. Best not to give fate any opportunity to trip you up.

It was the bones that were bothering Marnie: cold and lonely and hidden for so long. Alice was a creature of warmth and light and energy, of freedom and open spaces, not dankness and darkness and the sightless, creeping organisms that lived in the dirt underground. The loneliness of those bones was heartbreaking.

And so was knowing that she, Marnie, must have walked close

to, or even over Alice's quiet grave thousands of times, the soles of her feet compacting the soil. How could Alice have been so close and Marnie not have realised? How could she not have known?

The funfair had been where John Morahan spent most of his time, and consequently was the part of the park Marnie knew best. It was old-fashioned by modern standards, colourful and kitsch, like an advert for the 1970s, the rides surrounded by gardens, everything brightly painted, from the little white picket fences around the flowerbeds to the candy-striped inverted cone roofs on top of the kiosks. It was almost always noisy and crowded; and did not seem like the kind of place that might be hiding a terrible secret.

Where had Alice been exactly, Marnie wondered, walking the funfair in her mind, trying to remember the details.

There used to be four main attractions: the carousel itself, a valuable antique Bordelaise; the rickety flume, which Camille deVillars' parents, the founders of the park, had had built to their own bespoke specifications; the fun-house and the dodgem cars, together with a kiosk where customers could exchange cash for tokens to ride, and another that sold drinks, ices and snacks. The structures were surrounded by established gardens, flowerbeds and lawns, which wove in and out of the rides, making a kind of wonderland. There were benches where people could sit and rest and watch the fun, while bees buzzed and birds sang in the trees, encouraged, always, by a prolificacy of feeders. There was even a pond, a little stream, an island, a wishing well, goldfish and ducks.

The bones must have been discovered beneath one of the garden areas, because the rides were, of necessity, built on solid bases.

The funfair had been enclosed by a high fence, meant to resemble a Wild West stockade. Inside the fence were borders designed by Mrs deVillars. These were twelve feet wide in places, with a narrow space behind for the gardeners – Marnie's father aided by Will – to attend to the tall plants and trees at the back without having to walk through the medium-sized and shorter flowering plants at the front. The gardens used constantly to evolve, as old or diseased trees were removed and straggly bushes replaced. In the last few years, before she became too ill, Mrs deVillars had begun to turn the gardens into a wildlife haven, slowly replacing all the non-native plants and letting the lawns run to meadow, but back then they were more manicured and organised.

Wouldn't someone have noticed if a grave had been dug?

Clearly nobody had looked hard enough.

Marnie didn't blame the police for giving up their search for Alice when the details of her past came to light. She had lived a chaotic life. She was one of those young people who attracted trouble, choosing the wrong friends, making bad decisions, lurching from one difficult situation to the next. Her teachers, friends and colleagues at the numerous places where she'd worked said she was kind, loving and generous, but a drama queen. She flirted with danger: not waiting for the lights to turn before she crossed the road; jumping from the bus before it stopped. Walking down to the sea in the dark of night was exactly the kind of thing she would do.

Most people favoured the theory that she hadn't meant to kill herself, but had walked out too far, underestimating the power of the currents in the estuary, and been carried away by the tide. Alice was not one to pay attention to the signs along the seafront warning of the dangers and telling people not to attempt to swim.

Marnie remembered watching the police from her bedroom window, those eyes-down officers with sticks in their hands, searching the mudflats.

'What are they looking for?' she'd asked her father.

'Shoes,' her father had replied.

He meant Alice's shoes. Marnie didn't know this. She didn't

know that people believed some harm had come to Alice. She understood that Alice was missing, but in her childish way, believed she was lost as somebody playing hide and seek might be lost. Nobody had thought to explain the situation to her; all she had were dribs and drabs of information.

Before Alice came to Channel View holiday park, things had been difficult for Marnie. Her mother was gone, her father was enmeshed in grief. Mrs deVillars wanted to help but was reticent, as if she was afraid of interfering or upsetting John. Marnie believed there must be something repellent about her. Her father didn't like touching her and other people literally moved away to avoid her. Angharad, the one person apart from Mr deVillars who wasn't scared of John, did her best, but John wouldn't let her do much. Marnie's hair hadn't been cut in months. She could feel the tangles knitting together but didn't know what to do about them. She knew she was dirty. She knew that she smelled. She knew she was a disgrace. She was ashamed.

She developed a way of walking, with her chin down and her shoulders hunched, which meant she never had to catch anyone's eye, never had to see the expression on anyone's face. The holiday-makers called their children away from her. 'Leave her alone,' they'd say. 'She doesn't want to play.' Sometimes the kids called her names. If Alice hadn't come along when she did, the whole summer would have been terrible. But Alice came and she saved Marnie.

When she found out that Alice was missing in a way that meant she was never coming back, ten-year-old Marnie had felt her heart breaking all over again. The pain of her mother's death revisited her with a vengeance and she retreated into her carapace of silence, this time for good.

As she walked towards the bus stop on the main road to meet Lucy, Marnie let down her barriers and gave vent to the grief she felt at the loss of Alice, grief that was shot through with guilt. Old guilt because of how Marnie had betrayed Alice's trust and new guilt because she hadn't realised where she was. She'd been talking to Alice in the wrong place, imagining her all wrong, she who was so sensitive, who was supposed to know these things intuitively. Marnie Morahan was struggling to come to terms with how very wrong she had been about everything.

8

In the old days the narrow streets around Severn Sands seafront had been peppered with signs advertising accommodation, but things had changed. Will had to walk the residential neighbourhood for a full fifteen minutes before he came across a Bed and Breakfast 'vacancies' sign hanging outside a Victorian villa on the Aust road. He rang the bell and after some time the door was opened by a tall, long-faced man in his seventies wearing slippers, a grey cardigan and spectacles on a chain around his neck. *Antiques Road Trip* was playing on the television in a room to one side of the corridor behind him. The smell of fried chops mingled with the perfume of the floral air freshener plugged in beneath the hall table. The stairs led steeply up one side of the hall. On the other was a large photograph in a fancy frame of a heavily built woman with sunglasses pushed back onto the top of her short-cropped white hair, tanned skin; posing in a bright, dramatic landscape that Will recognised.

'Snowdonia?' he asked, nodding towards the photograph.

'Last year,' said the man. 'Do you know it?'

'I did the Three Peaks when I was at university.'

A pair of walking boots had been placed on the shelf beneath the picture and tucked behind the boots was what looked like an order of service for a funeral: a makeshift shrine to a not-so-long-gone wife. Will tried not to be unsettled by the woman's eyes, small and blue beneath dark, heavy brows that were incongruous with the white hair. Her cheeks, like her husband's, were hatched with broken veins.

'Are you looking for a room?' the man asked with an undertone of suspicion.

'I need somewhere for a couple of nights.'

'I don't usually get people turn up in February. I don't suppose you're here on holiday, not at this time of year.'

'I'm a writer,' Will said. 'I need somewhere to hole up while I'm working.'

'A writer, eh?'

'Yes, I used to live in Severn Sands. I grew up here.' The man still seemed unconvinced. 'My mother used to work at the holiday park.'

'What was her name?'

'Angharad Jones.'

There was a glimmer of recognition. 'Bonny woman? Used to run the bar?'

'That's her, yes.'

'I knew Angharad. And you're her lad? William, isn't it?'

'Yes.'

'You used to go out with our Daisy.'

No, no, no, fucking no! Too late Will recognised him: Dave Bradshaw, Daisy's father; something to do with the town council, a pillar of the community, a point Angharad had stressed over and over when Will gave Daisy the cold shoulder.

It played back to Will, the débâcle of Daisy turning up at the holiday park, tearful because Will wasn't at the station to meet her as he'd promised he would be and she wanted to make sure that no terrible accident had befallen him. Mr deVillars had been standing helplessly beside Daisy, afraid of touching her, and Guy was watching, smirking like a cat with his green eyes and his milk-coloured hair, face shaded by a straw boater. A couple of hours earlier Will had watched Alice hanging up her swimming things and all he wanted to do now was think about Alice, be with Alice, stand guard over Alice, make sure Guy deVillars didn't get anywhere near her.

Will had been obliged, that afternoon, to do the decent thing and walk Daisy home, not to this house, but a 1960s semi in a different street. They'd hardly said a word to one another during the walk. Daisy kept sniffing, asking what she'd done wrong and trying to hold Will's hand but he couldn't bear her touch so he'd walked most of the distance with his hands tucked under his armpits. When they reached the house and Daisy's father opened the door, Daisy had pushed past him and run up the stairs and moments later a bedroom door had slammed.

Mrs Bradshaw – the same woman as in the Snowdonia picture, only back then she'd been a heavy blonde, flushed and freckled – had been hovering behind her husband. She asked Will if he'd like to come in for a cup of tea and Will knew that it was expected of him, but all he could think about was Alice, alone, back at the holiday park and so he'd said, 'No, thank you, I have to go.' He knew he would be blamed for treating Daisy badly, but he didn't care about the Bradshaws' opinion. He literally could not have cared less, so desperate was he to get back to the girl in Caravan 49.

Will wondered, now, if he should turn and leave the guesthouse, but he wasn't sure he'd find anywhere else to stay at this time of the evening on a miserable February Thursday. So he stood his ground, keeping his expression neutral.

'How is Daisy?' he asked.

'She's all right. Done well for herself, all things considered.' Mr

Bradshaw sniffed. 'You're a writer then, are you? What sort of books do you write?'

'True crime. Unsolved mysteries.'

'Well, I know what's brought you back here then.' The old man tugged at his earlobe. 'Talk of the town it is. I've got a single room available. It's at the top of the stairs.'

'That sounds ideal.'

'It's seventy pounds a night.'

'Seventy?'

'You heard me.'

'Does that include breakfast?'

'As long as you're up at half past seven.'

Will had no choice but to concur.

'Follow me,' said Mr Bradshaw, and he headed off up the stairs, shoulders hunched, holding onto the banister, struggling but trying to give the impression of being fully fit and strong. There was a small landing on the first floor. The light was dim, the carpet busy, and it clashed with the wallpaper, its pattern being floral and the wallpaper geometric, although both were in various shades of orange and brown. Framed photographs of Daisy smiling unconvincingly as a child were hung on the wall, each a little lower than its neighbour, echoing the stepping of the stairs.

Mr Bradshaw took a deep breath and set off up the next flight. At the top, he stopped again to catch his breath then straightened up.

'Here we are then,' he said, turning a ceramic door knob and pushing open a door that sloped at the top to accommodate the pitch of the roof. 'It's not the height of luxury but I've had no complaints.'

Will stepped into a small attic room. The door to the connected bathroom was ajar. The predominant smell was pine toilet cleaner with an undercurrent of damp.

'It's great,' said Will.

'The décor was Eileen's choice. She was very fond of flowers.'

'So I see.'

'Yes,' said Mr Bradshaw, surveying the room. 'It's all very Eileen.'

He took off his glasses, took a handkerchief out of his pocket with which he wiped the lenses, then he replaced them on his nose.

'Right,' he said. 'There's one more thing we need to get clear from the offset. I want you to understand that I don't want you writing anything about this establishment.'

'What do you mean?'

'I know what they found up at the old holiday park this morning and I know that's why you've come back. I understand the kind of books you write and I don't want my guesthouse featured in any of them. I don't want to see my name in print. I don't want to be quoted without my permission. I don't want any funny business.'

'Of course not.'

'I don't want you mentioning our Daisy either. That poor girl's been through enough as it is.'

'You have my word, I won't mention her.'

'Right. Well, then. That's it. I'll leave you to it. You'll find me downstairs if you need me.'

With that, the old man pulled the door shut behind him, and left.

9

Last summer, when Lucy was twelve, Marnie had ironed her daughter's jodhpurs and a cotton polo shirt and polished her riding boots, brushed her hair and fastened it into a bun at the back of her head and the two of them had walked to the Big House. Marnie stood back while Lucy knocked on the door. Mr deVillars had answered, and Lucy had asked politely if there were any jobs she could do at the holiday park during the school holidays. He'd asked if she liked animals and when she said she did, he'd winked at Marnie over Lucy's head and said: 'Fantastic! Our pets' corner is short of a keeper and frankly I was wondering how we were going to manage!'

So Lucy had spent the summer caring for the park's rabbits, guinea pigs, two lambs and a goat; cleaning out their pens and enclosures, feeding them, and talking to the visiting children who asked questions about their care. With Mr deVillars' encouragement, she'd taken her own pony, Scrumpy, to the park, and given rides to young holidaymakers, leading the pony around the park's perimeter while the children sat on top holding onto the pommel of the saddle, their parents hovering nervously at their side.

Scrumpy had been bored witless but enjoyed the carrots, apples and polo mints with which he was liberally rewarded. By the end of the season he resembled, more than ever, one of the pot-bellied ponies in the Thelwell illustrations Lucy liked to copy and pin to her bedroom walls. Marnie had been proud of her daughter and it was an easy summer for her, knowing where Lucy was and that she was doing something constructive and safe.

Marnie's father, John Morahan, had retired from his position as caretaker the previous year, but still spent most of his days at Channel View, pottering around the funfair in his overalls, hoping some small mechanical issue would arise that required his attention, or chewing the fat with Edward deVillars. Nobody understood the machinations and the temperament of the antique carousel better than John, and Mr deVillars liked having him around, ostensibly in case of a problem but really because he enjoyed John's company. Although there was a wide disparity in their backgrounds, education and social standing, the two men were of a similar age and shared a passion for cricket.

They both liked to tell the story of how they first met many years earlier. John, living in a static caravan parked on farmland with Denise and baby Marnie, was working as a mechanic for a haulage company. He had spotted Mr deVillars on the farm track when he was driving home from a late shift in the early hours of a dark winter's morning. Mr deVillars' told him that his car had broken down and he'd been stuck for hours. It had been a stroke of luck – or fate, perhaps – that John happened to be passing.

John, tired as he was, had taken Mr deVillars back to his car and looked under the bonnet. He tweaked a couple of wires, told Mr deVillars to turn the key and, miraculously, the car had started. John had refused to take any money, so Mr deVillars had returned to the farm the next day with a crate of beer to show his gratitude. John had accepted the gift on the condition that Mr deVillars came into the caravan to enjoy a bottle with him. From these tentative beginnings a warm friendship had sprung that culminated in Mr deVillars offering John the caretaker's job at the holiday park, along with the opportunity to move his little family into the grace-and-favour cottage, a huge step up from the static caravan in the farm-yard. It was an arrangement that suited everyone. The Morahans had a proper home in which to live, John had a steady job that he enjoyed, and Channel View had a highly qualified and motivated caretaker with engineering skills. Mr and Mrs deVillars had been looking for someone exactly like John Morahan for months. Marnie's father never tired of commenting on how the two men's paths had been destined to cross.

John would never have admitted it, but he and Edward deVillars were as close to being best friends as it was possible for men like them to be. And for all that her father was a difficult, grumpy old sod, Marnie was glad he was at Channel View that summer to keep an eye on his adored granddaughter and to lend a hand, if a hand was required.

Lucy was more confident, even last summer at twelve years old, than her mother had ever been. It made Marnie proud to hear the stories she told when she came home after a day at the holiday park. Marnie would put food in front of Lucy, who was invariably starving hungry, her hair tangled, her skinny arms strong and brown, clothes stained and covered with animal hair, and desperate to recount the day's adventures. Lucy was not afraid to scold children older than herself if they didn't show what she regarded as adequate respect to the animals, and despite, or perhaps because of, her bossiness, attracted an ever-changing fan club of younger children who used to trail around the park behind her, copying everything she did. Some of them sent her drawings and letters after they'd gone home.

Last summer had been a good summer, a peaceful and happy

one. But then in the first week of September, everything suddenly changed.

Lucy was already back at school when the last batch of holidaymakers left Channel View holiday park and no new ones arrived, even though the park usually stayed open until after the winter half term holiday. Now it was empty, a ghost park. The remaining staff were laid off. The swimming pool was drained and the power to the club house disconnected. The bar was emptied of liquor and locked, and shutters were fastened over the doors to the kiosks and the launderette. 'Keep Out' signs were erected. Pets Corner was ominously empty.

There was confusion in Severn Sands, contradictory stories circulating about what was going on. Someone had spoken to someone who said the animals had gone to one of Bristol's city farms. Someone else said they'd heard the park was going to be refurbished and brought up to date. Mr and Mrs deVillars hadn't been seen out and about in weeks; perhaps they'd moved away. And then the news came. Marnie heard it from her father, who had it from Mr deVillars himself. It transpired that the progress of Camille deVillars' dementia had been accelerating over the past year. Her husband, knowing he was losing her, and wanting to devote his time and energy to his ailing wife, entrusted the park to their son, transferring control and ownership of the entire business. Part of the agreement was that Guy would keep the park open at least until after his mother's death. One of the few things that still gave her pleasure was looking out of the windows of the Big House and watching the holidaymakers enjoying themselves. Guy had not honoured the agreement. He'd shut the park down at the end of the lucrative summer season, and put the antique carousel and any other assets that could be sold up for sale. What was worse, he'd gone behind his parents' backs to seek and gain outline planning permission for the redevelopment of Channel View while the park was still open, increasing the land's value fourfold. He had, according to John Morahan, stitched Mr and Mrs deVillars up like kippers.

Now there would be no more Saturday or holiday jobs for Lucy and the other teenagers growing up in Severn Sands. The last thing that gave the town its personality and its *raison d'être* was being dismantled. New people would come to live in the new houses. They would commute to work in Bristol or Cardiff, they would walk their dogs in the fields that used to be Marnie's queendom; everything would change.

Perhaps new people would revitalise the town and the changes would turn out to be a good thing, but the existing residents weren't used to the idea yet. They were still grieving for the loss of the holiday park. The finding of Alice's remains felt like an omen; a sign that things should have been left as they were. And whoever it was who had killed Alice, if they were still in Severn Sands, must be feeling afraid and vulnerable. And if that was the case, didn't that mean they would be dangerous?

Marnie would be extra careful with Lucy. She wouldn't take any risks.

She walked to the bus stop, Tessy beside her. The temperature had dropped as the wind grew stronger. A dark van with blacked-out windows drove slowly past in the direction of Channel View. Marnie wondered if it was the undertaker's van, sent to collect the bones. Behind it was a sleek saloon that might have contained the coroner, both vehicles trailing death like exhaust fumes.

She shouldn't be so morbid. Lately, her mind's tendency to veer towards the bleak had been troubling Marnie. She'd had a strong sensation that something malevolent was approaching, often feeling uneasy for no good reason. A few days earlier, walking along the estuary path, she'd been convinced someone was following her. She'd kept looking over her shoulder, but nobody had been there.

She'd tried to summon some essence of Alice from the sea to keep her company, but Alice wouldn't come. And she wasn't sleeping well. She was having night terrors. If it wasn't for Tessy waking her before she reached the screaming, soaked-in-sweat stage she'd have been a wreck by now. Another thing: Marnie hadn't thought much about Denise in years, and had considered herself completely over whatever grief she'd felt at the loss of her mother. But in the past few weeks, every now and then she'd been overwhelmed with a longing for her mother so intense she could hardly bear it.

Marnie was almost at the bus stop. She glimpsed the estuary, moonlight shimmering slick on the surface of the water, and had a sudden longing to be out there, to feel the damp wind in her face, the spray against her skin. When she was a child, Mr deVillars had had a boat, the *Starling*. During fine weather, he and John Morahan had taken the boat out fishing, and sometimes they'd taken Guy and Marnie with them; Will Jones too. Marnie and Will had loved those excursions, but Guy wasn't a natural-born sailor. He'd used to sit at the back, his chin pressed into the swell of the life-vest, pale and ill-tempered. Occasionally he'd leaned over the side of the boat to be sick, and then sat back up wiping his chin. Marnie would pretend she hadn't noticed but Will used to smirk. He'd always hated Guy. Will had been like his mother; no compromises. And he could be terribly jealous.

The boat used to reveal the magic of the estuary. The water at the shore-line was murky, full of silt. Yet out deep, close to the islands, it was perfectly clear and glassy. You could look down and see the life beneath the surface, seaweed, fish, shellfish, the glorious colours of the underwater world. It was this that Marnie used to think of when she thought of Alice in the estuary; this beauty and calm and wild peace.

10

Will put his rucksack on the bed, switched on the bedside lamp, crossed to the little window in the eaves and looked out over the town. He could just make out, through the chimney-pots and rooftops, the flat expanse of the estuary in the distance and the bridge.

A tiny kettle had been provided, which he filled with water. A couple of teabags and some sachets of dried coffee lay in a dusty saucer next to an upturned mug. Will made himself a coffee, took out his laptop, placed it on the table beneath the window, sat on the chair, and rolled up his shirtsleeves.

He did a quick internet search. News about the holiday park discovery was already in the public domain. He skim-read an article and discovered something he hadn't known: Channel View holiday park had been sold for development, not by Edward and Camille deVillars, but by Guy.

Guy. Bloody Guy.

Will had known him all his life. The two boys had been at Severn Sands Primary School together, although Guy was a couple of years older. He was one of those children who never got into trouble. Effortlessly clever, well-mannered and conscientious, he had been every teacher's pet. This was irking for Will, who was noisy and clumsy, inclined to forget or lose homework, and constantly being scolded for one thing or another. Guy was sent away, aged eleven, to a boarding school in Sussex, St Aubin's. Will moved up to the comprehensive with his peers and their lives followed different paths. St Aubin's alumni graduated into an established old-boys' network. Guy and his friends moved in a sphere of privilege: favours were reciprocated, money changed hands; influence was imposed; careers made; scandals suppressed. It was a different world and one that represented everything Will despised.

During his early teenage years, Will had been wary of the older boy but had little to do with him. Guy was away during term times and in the holidays he surrounded himself with friends he'd made at school and invited back to stay at Blackwater House. The deVillarses didn't hold shooting parties or hunt balls but the house was large enough to accommodate the sons and daughters of the well off; it had its own lovely gardens, tennis courts and a pool. The girls who came were the sisters of Guy's school friends: slender, willowy creatures who hid their faces beneath the rims of wide sunhats, wore flimsy clothes and laughed a great deal; girls who never seemed to eat and who stayed away from the holiday park. Will always had the feeling that they pitied the people who holidayed there, mocked them even, and this made him feel humiliated and his humiliation caused him to distrust Guy and his friends and avoid them as far as he could.

By the time of the Alice summer, Guy was in his second year at university and had been away for most of the year. Will's mother filled him in on the gossip. Guy had been seeing a French girl, he'd fallen heavily for her and had been spending his free time in the Loire Valley. But the girl had moved on and Guy had come home to lick his wounds. Camille was anxious that her son mix with some young people; she wanted him to have some uncomplicated fun.

It was awful timing that Alice had turned up at the exact same time as Guy was in Severn Sands on his own and in search of distraction. It was unusual for a young woman to come to the park without a partner, family or friends, and Guy had honed in on her straight away. Alice insisted it was Camille who was trying to throw her and Guy into each other's company, but she was wrong. Guy had designs on Alice from the moment he first set eyes on her.

Will, preternaturally aware of anything to do with Alice and conscious of whenever another man so much as glanced in her direction, had spent hours watching Guy watching Alice. He'd seen how Guy hung around the swimming pool, an area he normally avoided, hoping for the chance to talk to Alice and to charm her. This was more than a flirtation for Guy; more than a way to pass the time. Will had seen him come to Alice's caravan with gifts: supplies from the Big House's kitchen garden, a bottle of local cider, a book about the history of the deVillars family, a bottle of sunscreen because he'd noticed her shoulders were burning.

As a teenager, Will believed his dislike of Guy was justified because Guy was inherently a slimeball. Now, with the benefit of maturity, Will acknowledged that he had been jealous too. Guy had inherited his mother's fair hair, her well-defined eyes and wide smile. He was tall and slim; naturally approachable. The young Will would have described Guy as creepy and effete; the older Will could see that Guy had been good-looking in his own way, gentle-manly and charming. He was good with compliments; he under-stood how to talk to people as if he was genuinely interested in them; an attentive listener, a good asker of questions. And, of course, Guy had money. He wore his wealth modestly, but it was there, like a subtle brand of aftershave.

Guy plied Alice with attention. Wherever she was in the park, he would materialise beside her, like a shadow. Will warned her that he was on the rebound from the French girl and that he was only using her, but she had laughed at his warnings.

'Using me for what? We're not *doing* anything, Will! We're only talking.'

She had been too naïve to realise that Guy's intentions weren't innocent; that he was playing a long game. It was obvious to anyone with eyes in their heads that he wanted Alice and that he'd do anything to get her.

While he was working in the gardens, Will saw the two of them together at the side of the swimming pool: Alice in her bikini and sunglasses, lying on a lounger with its back propped up, her knees bent, a paperback at her side, and Guy sitting on the lounger beside hers, in an open-necked linen shirt, cotton shorts, loafers; he leaning forward so that he could listen to what she was saying, seemingly entranced by their conversation.

'What did you talk about with Guy?' Will asked Alice later, back at her caravan, after they'd made love, when he felt calm enough for the words to come out in a reasonable tone, not angrily, not possessively.

'Nothing,' she said.

'Obviously it wasn't "nothing". You were talking to him for the best part of an hour.'

'I didn't realise there was a time limit on the conversations I'm allowed to have with other people'

'I didn't mean...'

'Yes, you did. Stop being jealous, Will. There's no need and it's not nice.'

'I'm not jealous of Guy deVillars.'

'No?'

'No.'

There was a pause.

Then he'd asked: 'So what *were* you talking about for almost an hour?'

Alice insisted there was nothing between her and Guy, but she spent so much time with Guy that Will believed she must like him. Mustn't she have been at least a little impressed by Guy's money and the fact that he, one day, would inherit Channel View holiday park? Why else was she so fascinated with the book he gave her? Will had seen it at the side of her bed, and when he'd opened the page marked with a hair grip he'd found a photograph of Guy as a child, standing beside his father outside the Big House. Had Alice imagined herself standing in that same position, outside the Big House as Guy's future wife?

Despite Alice's protestations, Marnie had confirmed that Guy was the 'special' date Alice had arranged for the evening of her disappearance. A romance of some kind had been on the cards between them – at least that's what Guy hoped. It was hard to imagine softly spoken Guy being roused to the kind of violence necessary to kill a person, but Will had written enough crime books to know how explosive repressed feelings could be. There was some truth in the cliché that it was the quiet ones who were the most dangerous. And Guy was the kind of person who might do something terrible to cover up a perceived humiliation; a narcissist who would do anything to avoid shame, especially the shame of rejection.

11

In the old days, buses and trains used to run until all hours. Now, if you were in Severn Sands and didn't have a car you were, as John Morahan liked to say, buggered. Marnie did have a car, an old Ford estate, but it was on its last legs, held together by rust and duct tape. She worried about it giving up the ghost and only drove when she had no alternative. If Lucy had missed the bus, then Marnie would have to walk home, collect the Ford and drive into Bristol to pick her up. Lucy would be alone at the school in the dark, and what if the car broke down en route? What then?

Marnie stepped from one foot to the other, her feet cold despite two pairs of socks and her stout boots, her breath clouding in front of her, a knitted hat pulled down close over her bare head. Tessy looked up, checking in, concerned, and Marnie smiled to convey that she was all right.

A seagull called mournfully from the sign at the entrance to the service station, glowing from the light within. Marnie looked for the bus, her eyes straining to see along the road. A blue VW rounded the corner, slowed and turned into the service station. It used to be Mrs deVillars' car, but her nurse, Zoe, used it now. The woman parked and climbed out, hurried across the concourse, light on her feet. She was dark-skinned, large-boned, tall with short, bleached hair. She had a daughter, Maya, who went to the same school as Lucy and the two girls had become friendly.

Two minutes later the bus chugged round the corner. The driver nodded to Marnie as she pulled up at the stop and opened the doors. Lucy thanked the driver and climbed down, a thin adolescent in black tights, a knee-length skirt and a coat, swamped by her uniform. Her feet, in their big clumpy shoes, seemed too big for her body. Marnie's heart clenched: Lucy was a tough little thing, but still she was so vulnerable. Behind her was Maya; her socks around her ankles, the buttons on her coat fastened in the wrong holes, the paper stick of a chew-lollipop sticking out of the corner of her mouth.

Lucy looked tired, but she always looked tired in winter. The season didn't suit her and school wore her out. She never complained, but she found it an ordeal. Like her mother, she would rather be in the open air, in the company of animals. In her heart, Marnie would have liked to take Lucy out of school and let her run free at home. Only if she did that, Lucy might never escape Severn Sands. She might be stuck for ever, like Marnie.

Lucy crouched to make a fuss of Tessy, holding her face between her hands and kissing her snout. The other girl stood behind her, chewing her lollipop and gazing around to avoid having to make one-sided conversation with Marnie.

'I'm starving,' Lucy said. 'Can I get something from the garage?'

Marnie put her hand in her pocket and pulled out a couple of coins amongst shreds of tissue and fragments of dog treats. Maya made a small sound that sounded like: 'Ugh'.

Marnie, fishing further, found the note that she'd known was there somewhere, folded into a small square. She unfolded it, eyes down so as not to see the expression on Maya's face and gave it to her daughter.

Lucy said: 'Thanks,' and put her arm round Marnie's waist in an expression of solidarity. Marnie held onto her, the two of them rocking together for a moment, Marnie's lips pressed into the top of her daughter's head. Lucy was perfect, in Marnie's eyes; perfect in every way. She loved the bones of her daughter and was deeply grateful that her child had turned out to be nothing like her at all. She pulled away first, overwhelmed by Lucy's affection and made a pushing motion with the back of her hand. *Go on then. Off you go.*

The two girls disappeared inside the service station. Marnie waited outside with the dog, basking in the glow of Lucy's affection, trying to remember if she had ever embraced her own mother so generously. She didn't believe that she had.

Once, when Marnie was seven or eight, she'd won a prize at primary school for a drawing she'd made of Trip Hazard, her father's dog. Mr and Mrs deVillars, who'd recently paid for the refurbishment of the school hall, had been invited to present the prize. Denise had made sure Marnie was dressed up like a little princess, clean socks, clean sandals, a ribbon in her hair and she'd stood back to look at Marnie and said she'd never been prouder. But she wouldn't come to watch Marnie receive her award, she said she was too busy.

She wasn't busy. Marnie knew she was going to stay in the cottage and read.

Her father, who really was busy and who never took a day off work if he could help it, had taken off his overalls and put on his wedding jacket, spat on his good shoes and buffed them with a rag, and then walked to the school with Marnie. He'd waved at her from the back of the hall as she climbed the steps to the stage to collect her prize. He'd given her the thumbs up and taken a photograph.

He'd stopped at the shop and bought her a KitKat on the way home.

Marnie's father had come good but who was she to judge her mother? She was no better, hiding away from Lucy's school, staying in the shadows.

After a short while, Maya and Zoe emerged from the brightness of the service station, the nurse carrying a bag full of shopping. Maya was now eating a packet of cheese and onion crisps.

Zoe said 'hello,' to Marnie. 'You heard the news about the park? Shocking, isn't it?' Her voice was tired. Maya paused, her fingers inside the crisp packet, and looked from Marnie's face to her mother's, trying to work out what was going on.

'Poor Camille,' said the nurse, 'she doesn't understand. We've tried to keep the worst of it from her but it's hard with the sirens going up and down the road and the journalists... And on top of everything, the police were at the Big House earlier talking to Mr deV. He's upset too, of course. Guy is on his way back from London.'

'What's happened?' Maya asked.

Zoe ignored her daughter and continued: 'Mr deV doesn't want to tell Camille the truth but it's heartbreaking to see her so upset. I think it would be better if she knew. God knows what's going through her mind. Don't you think we should tell her? At least then we wouldn't have to keep making up stories. I swear she knows when she's being lied to. I'll have a word with Guy, when he arrives.'

The door to the service station swung open and Lucy emerged clutching a greasy bag and a bottle of lemonade.

'The man in there said they found a dead body at the holiday park,' she said. 'He said it was a girl. Is it true? Who is it? Who's died? Is it someone we know?'

Maya's eyes widened dramatically. 'Someone's *died*?'

The nurse and Marnie exchanged glances.

'The police think it's a young woman who went missing a long time ago,' said the nurse, 'before either of you girls was born.'

'She went missing? Didn't people look for her?'

'They looked, but they didn't find her. The body had been hidden.'

'Somebody hid her?' asked Maya. 'Who? Why? The person who killed her? Was she *killed*?'

'We don't know. Probably. The police will investigate.'

'They'll find out who did it and arrest them?'

'Yes.'

'Why didn't they do that before?'

'They didn't know a crime had been committed. They didn't have the body.'

Maya processed this information then looked at her mother again.

'So whoever did it might still be in Severn Sands?'

'It's possible.'

'It might be someone we know?'

'Come on, Trouble,' said the nurse. 'We need to get back.'

'But, Mum...'

'We'll talk about it later.'

12

Will trotted down the guesthouse stairs, averting his eyes as he passed the pictures of Daisy, making just enough noise so that Mr Bradshaw wouldn't be taken by surprise when he tapped on the living-room door.

'Come in,' Mr Bradshaw called. Will pushed the door open.

The old man was sitting on an armchair in front of the television, watching *The Chase*.

A three-bar electric fire was blazing and the room was very warm. Like the rest of the house, it was fussy, overfull with furniture. Will noticed a desk in the alcove in one corner, a filing cabinet beside it. On the cabinet was a tray with two decanters, each half full and an old, framed photograph of the councillors, including Mr Bradshaw, standing outside Severn Sands town hall. Other photographs around the room were family shots: Mr and Mrs Bradshaw, and Daisy in various stages of growing up. In one of the pictures Daisy was wearing a wedding dress: a big, meringue-type affair. Beside her was an older, bald-headed man, smaller in height and stature than Daisy, his chest puffed out with pride.

'They're divorced now,' said Mr Bradshaw without looking up. 'It didn't work out.'

'Sorry to hear that,' said Will. He rubbed his hands together. 'Anyway, I'm going out for something to eat. I won't be long.'

'You do as you like,' said Mr Bradshaw. 'You don't have to answer to me.'

* * *

Outside, the air was cold. Will walked to the seafront and headed down the promenade, looking for a chip shop or a takeaway. Where there used to be a string of cafés and restaurants now there was nothing save one place, the Dolphin café, that still had tables and chairs in the yard outside. Its walls were painted bright green. A weather-worn plastic dolphin with a napkin tied around its neck, clutching a crude hot-dog beneath its flipper leaped grinning over the 'Dolphin' sign. The café was still functioning, but it was closed for the night.

The wind was blowing off the sea. Will shivered and pulled up the collar of his jacket.

Severn Sands had been fading when he left but since he'd been away its decay had accelerated. The lights that used to be strung along the seafront had disappeared. The Paradiso lido was derelict, graffiti covering the concrete terraces where people used to lay their towels and slather their shoulders in sun cream; the American ice-cream parlour had been demolished, although the small wall that used to encircle it remained. All that was left of the children's play-ground were empty beer cans and discarded crisp packets. The road was pot-holed; weeds grew through cracks in the pavements. The only sign of life anywhere was a dim, floating glow from the control room of a massive cargo ship moving slowly and distantly down the channel on its way back to Japan, and the constant stream of car and lorry headlights coming over the bridge.

The ship, tall as a block of flats, was a familiar sight. Will recalled how he used to fantasise about stowing away, sailing out to sea. Camille's father, Lord Mills, had been in the navy and, when he was visiting, used to tell good sea-faring stories, about waves big as skyscrapers, whales breaching against the horizon, icebergs, sea frets a hundred miles deep; the melancholia of making landfall.

It was a good job, thought Will, that the old Lord wasn't around to see the state of Severn Sands now.

He walked on, hands in pockets, feeling like a stranger and at the same time feeling like he'd never left this place. He breathed the estuary air, walked out of the town, passed the community cricket pitch, its grass still mown, the pavilion still standing. That, at least, had survived. John Morahan and Edward deVillars had enlisted Will to play for the local team. Will recalled being bowled out after one game, and, walking back to that same pavilion, finding Marnie doing handstands against the wall, bracing her elbows, arching her spine, her T-shirt falling down over her face. Her mother was still around then, although she never came to the cricket, and Marnie was an ordinary child, chatting to Will, pestering him to hold her hands and swing her round.

Will's mother never came to the cricket matches either. She refused to get involved on the grounds that why should she give up her Saturdays to make food for people she made food for all week, if she wasn't being paid to do so? Guy deVillars sometimes came to watch the games, but never joined in, even though he was, according to his father, one of the stars of the school team. There was a picture displayed in the Big House: two rows of floppy-haired young men, one row standing behind their seated team-mates in front of a far grander pavilion than the one in the village. Guy was in the middle of the front row, holding a cricket bat, elbows on knees, his fringe falling over one eye, squinting into the sun. That was typical Guy, playing cricket for his fuck-off expensive school but refusing to lift a bat for his home town team.

That memory linked to another, a late summer's evening, the year before Alice came. Will had been helping Marnie clean out the animals in Pets' Corner. She was a hard worker but so small that it took her ages to fork the soiled straw into the barrow. After that it had to be pushed to the dung heap on the park's far perimeter, behind a copse of trees and at a distance where its odours and the flies they attracted were unlikely to inconvenience the holidaymakers. Will had been manning the wheelbarrow, his hands hot inside a pair of leather gauntlets. Marnie was wearing a T-shirt with the cartoon of the holiday club's motto, a cheerful piglet, the Severn Boar, on the front, and straining to carry a bucketful of water to top up the trough in the goat meadow. After her mother's death, she became scruffy and unkempt but at the time of the memory Denise was still alive. Marnie's hair was in pigtails and she'd been holding the handle of the bucket with both hands, her elbows locked, shoulders braced against the weight. In this awkward position she waddled, rather than walked, the bucket bumping against her knees and splashing water into her boots. The barrow wheel squeaked with each rotation and the straw smelled of ammonia and ponies. In the half-light, they spotted Guy de Villars coming out of the storage shed and hurrying across the mown grass towards the Big House.

Marnie and Will stopped to watch Guy ducking and diving into the shadows. 'What's he doing?' Marnie had asked.

'He's been looking at his dirty magazines again,' said Will.

'His *what*?'

It was true that there was a stash of copies of *Playboy*, *Penthouse* and *Men Only* inside the shed. They'd been there for ages but Will had no idea who they belonged to or who had put them there. For all he knew, John Morahan might have found them around the camp and put them up on the high shelf out of reach, intending to burn them at some later date.

'What's a dirty magazine?' Marnie persisted.

'Nothing,' said Will. 'It's nothing.'

But now he wondered about those magazines, wondered if they had belonged to Guy, if Guy did have some kind of perverse addiction, a distorted attitude towards women. He wondered if Guy had gone to Alice's caravan that August evening all those years before and if his attempts to seduce her had gone wrong; if Guy had put a hand over Alice's mouth to stop her screaming, if he'd held it there too long and then panicked when he realised what he'd done; if he had hidden her body and then made it look as if she'd drowned in the estuary.

After supper, Marnie decided to go to see her father. She didn't know if he knew about the discovery at the holiday park, and whether he did or he didn't, she needed to make sure he was OK.

Lucy was curled up on the sofa with Tessy, watching a teenage drama on her phone. She blew her mother a kiss goodbye.

Marnie's cottage sat in the centre of a plot of land, an orchard of ancient apple trees, a pond with a willow praying over it, and a small paddock where Marnie kept her agility equipment. The stable where Scrumpy lived, together with a companion donkey called Seashell, opened into the orchard. Marnie checked on the animals before she left. Mister was asleep beneath the heater in the feed room.

Marnie set off alone, walking the empty roads to her father's bungalow. She kept her eyes down, her hands in her pockets, moving quietly and lightly, like an animal that doesn't want to draw attention to itself. Behind the curtains of the houses and bungalows in Severn Sands town, lamps glowed and television screens flickered. People were eating dinner off trays on their laps while they watched the news, hungry for details about the discovery at

Channel View. *Do you think it's the girl who vanished? Who else could it be? Who would have thought such a thing would happen here?* They were disinterring the old stories and rumours, dusting them off, hoping their pet theory would turn out to be the right one.

The night was clear and cold. The wind had dropped. There'd be a frost later. The ground would be hard and the puddles would freeze, making the tracks Marnie walked slippery as glass. Distantly, the traffic sang as it crossed the Severn Bridge, a string of moving lights, and Marnie's mind drifted back to the afternoon before Alice disappeared and how they'd encountered one another outside the service area in the holiday park. Alice had been leaning against the small brick wall. Behind her trailing pelargoniums, alyssum and petunias tumbled from planters, the colours of the flowers painfully bright. Alice was wearing her yellow dress. She had kicked off her flip-flops and had bent one knee so that the sole of her foot pressed against the wall behind her. She was smoking a roll-up and talking to Guy deVillars who was standing beside her. Her eyes had brightened when she saw Marnie, then darkened with concern.

'Are you OK, poppet?' she'd asked. 'You're ever so pale.'

Marnie nodded although she didn't feel OK, she felt unbalanced and sick.

'Look,' said Guy, 'I'll, er...' he pointed back towards the Big House.

'Sure,' said Alice. 'See you later.'

Guy had left. Alice reached out her arm and touched the soft inside of her wrist against the side of Marnie's neck. 'Oh, sweetheart, you *are* hot. You need to get out of the sun.'

That was what Mrs deVillars had told Marnie a little earlier. She'd found an old straw hat for Marnie to wear. The rim kept the sun out of Marnie's eyes but other than that, it wasn't helping, only making Marnie's head even hotter.

'You need to sit down,' said Alice. 'Why don't you go into the laundry room and wait for my drier to finish and then bring my stuff back to the caravan? You can read the magazines. That way you'll be out of the sun *and* doing me a favour. What do you think?'

Marnie had always found Alice lovely, but that day, in that bright light, she had seemed more magical than ever.

'OK,' Marnie had answered. 'I'll wait for your clothes.'

Alice had taken hold of Marnie's hands and leaned forward to kiss her, smelling of cigarettes and perfume and sun lotion.

'You're a darling, Marnie,' Alice said. 'You're a little angel. And tomorrow I'm going to tell you a secret! A really good one! The *best* secret you've ever heard.'

Alice was fond of sharing secrets. It was something Marnie also enjoyed.

'Tell me now,' Marnie begged.

'I can't,' said Alice. 'Tomorrow! I promise!'

If Marnie hadn't been feeling so sick, she almost certainly would have made more of it but that afternoon she simply didn't have the energy.

14

There was a pub in between the town and the holiday park where Will and Angharad used to go on special occasions, a sprawling roadhouse pub that showed sport and was popular with families in the early evenings and serious drinkers later on. The food had always made up in quantity for what it lacked in sophistication. Will quickened his pace, anticipating the pleasure of drinking a cold beer as he waited for a meal to be served: something old-fashioned and greasy, gammon, pineapple and chips perhaps. Saoirse was vegan and he hadn't had a meat meal for ages. The thought of it made his stomach grumble with guilty anticipation. From a distance he could tell there were no lights on inside the pub and as he came nearer, he saw that it too, had closed, its windows hidden behind protective metal covers, the lawns in the beer garden turned to weed and litter.

That was a blow. There was nowhere else in Severn Sands to buy a meal that Will knew of. He'd have to make do with a snack from the service station. He stood for a while, looking about him. The road he was on led to the holiday park, and then doubled back behind it, like a lasso, enclosing Channel View and the Big House.

He was so close now, Will reasoned, that even though the thought filled him with dread, he might as well continue to the holiday park. To re-familiarise himself and to pay his respects. To get the most difficult part of his return over and done with.

The night was dark, flimsy clouds veiling the moon. The blades on three distant wind turbines sliced through the night. A frost was settling on the grass. Will inhaled and felt the cold in his lungs.

It was a long time since Will had felt cold like this. Country cold. Bone cold.

He had forgotten how the low, flat land held onto the rawness here, how the darkness was darker, somehow, how the chill of the water spilled over onto the plain, wrapping itself around you. 'Proper countryside' was how he'd described it to Saoirse; a wild, forgotten place cut off from the world by the Levels to one side and the sea to the other. A place where nobody without a reason to be there would ever go.

'You'll have to take me there one day,' Saoirse had said, but this wasn't the place for her. She liked her countryside sweet and verdant: the rolling hills of Devon; the hollyhocked cottages and country pubs of the Cotswolds. She wouldn't see beauty here, especially not at this time of year, when there were no leaves on the trees, no flowers, no birdsong, nothing but flatness and water and mud.

The wind lifted Will's hair; he felt its icy breath on his neck.

He had expected to feel nostalgia as he drew closer to the old holiday park, but he didn't expect the grief, crushing and physical, that assaulted his body, slowing his footsteps, filling him with the kind of horror he'd heard described by the families of murder victims, but never experienced directly himself. The missing of Alice, his sadness, was a burden heavier than anything Will had carried before. What a terrible waste of a life!

Over the years, Will had had counselling, hypnotherapy, even psychotherapy to try to get Alice out of his head and heart. He knew his obsession with the young woman he'd loved for three weeks during his nineteenth summer was the darkness at the root of his tendency to drink too much, to work too hard, to be unfaithful, to stay up too late, to say things that shouldn't be said, to go too far because he never knew when to stop. The therapists had tried to needle Alice out of Will's psyche. They'd poked at her like a cockle in its shell, but they couldn't move her. She was so deeply rooted that she was part of Will, integral to him. In any case, he didn't want to be rid of her. He was like an addict. He knew his passion for Alice wasn't healthy, but the thought of it being taken from him was unthinkable. He honestly didn't think he could exist without it.

Will walked until the concave wall protecting the town from the sea gave way to the small cliffs where Marnie used to hunt for fossils and where she had her secret cave. This was a lonely and strange place. If it wasn't for the distant traffic on the bridge, Will could have been alone in the world.

The coast wall was shored up with rocks. Further on, the road veered away inland, and there was a bulge of land facing the estuary that housed a straggle of odd little factories and lock-ups, a good half of them empty, behind a stretch that used to belong to the Ministry of Defence. This was Catbrain Point, the place where the travellers used to come in their rickety old trucks and converted ambulances. This was where they hobbled their shaggy ponies and tied up their whip-thin dogs, where they lit their fires and sat huddled, talking, or sang to the accompaniment of tinny guitars. Will's mother hated the travellers. He remembered her shouting at the nut-brown women, with their tattooed arms, babies carried in slings wrapped around their bodies. She hated the bearded men, their slow way of speaking, their constant hanging around smoking pungently scented cigarettes, looking for cash work in the summer season. Channel View relied on them but Angharad called them vultures and she wouldn't allow them into the bar. There must have been some reason for the bad blood. A psychologist Will was seeing once mooted the idea that his father might have been a traveller who abandoned Angharad when she fell pregnant. It was possible – Angharad refused point-blank ever to discuss the circumstances of Will's conception – but it could have been something less significant that triggered her dislike. She was a woman without compromise. 'Either you're with me, or you're against me,' she used to say. If you were with her, she would love you unconditionally. She would see you right in any way she could. But if you were against her, then you'd better watch out.

The travellers had come under suspicion when Alice disappeared, along with the men who were building the Severn Bridge, hundreds of workers, many from overseas who lived in their own village ten miles from Severn Sands. The local press had been full of speculation but no link between either the travellers or the builders and Alice was ever found.

15

John Morahan had moved out of the caretaker's cottage opposite the holiday park and into a retirement bungalow on a complex on the outskirts of the town. As she approached, Marnie could hear music blaring: 'Layla'. Her heart sank. 'Layla' was John's song of choice when he was feeling sorry for himself. For it to be this loud, he must be feeling really low and almost certainly drunk. The sound grew louder as she approached the bungalow, and she noticed the twitching of curtains. One of the neighbour's doors opened and a flossy white head appeared above a pink housecoat.

'I can't hear the television,' the old woman complained shakily, 'and the cat is too scared to go out. I was going to call the warden.'

Marnie held up a hand in apology and approached her father's door, conscious that she was being watched from all sides. She knocked briskly. When there was no sign of her father having heard, she moved across and banged her fist on the living-room window. After a moment, the curtain moved back and her father's face appeared so close to Marnie's on the other side of the glass that she stepped back in alarm and almost fell. John's face was blurred by condensation as he exhaled. The curtain dropped back, and a moment later the door opened, a blast of guitar music accompanying a fug of tobacco smoke. John's little Jack Russell, Trip Two – 'TT' for short – wagged around Marnie's ankles, yapping enthusiastically.

John was stooped, dishevelled, the button on his trousers undone to accommodate his swollen belly, his jumper on back to front and inside out, his face wrinkled and sallow beneath a tangle of hair, still raven black. 'Come in,' he said, wafting the cigarette between his fingers, the action described by a lingering swirl of smoke. Marnie could feel his loneliness like a drop in temperature. His face was ravaged, his eyes wet and swollen. She couldn't tell if he'd been crying or if it was the drink, or a combination of both. She had only seen him this distressed once before and that was after her mother's funeral, when he'd given in to his grief. The broad-shouldered hero of a man Marnie remembered from her childhood, the man her mother used to tell her was the handsomest man on the planet, was gone.

'What are you doing here?' John asked gruffly. 'It's not Friday, is it?' He looked her up and down, checking to see if she had a bag containing the traditional Friday fish supper.

Marnie turned sideways and stepped past her father into the bungalow. She shut the door behind her, so she could no longer feel the eyes of the neighbours upon her, put her hands over her ears and scowled.

Ungraciously, John went into the living room and reduced the volume of the record player. He didn't make way for Marnie. Instead they stood almost nose to nose in the claustrophobic hallway and neither was capable of saying any of the things that needed to be said. Marnie went into the kitchen, small and beige, kitted out for one elderly person. Dishes were piled in the sink. She filled the kettle, fighting the urge to tidy because she knew her father would take it as a criticism and become angry.

'If you've come because of what they found at the holiday park you didn't need to,' said John. 'Edward deVillars already told me. He brought a bottle of Scotch. He said: "John, old chap, I'm afraid I have some rather bad news..."'

John was a good mimic. Marnie could hear Edward deVillars speaking as her father spoke, she could imagine the old man's apologetic, faltering manner.

'He said one of the diggers had been uprooting a tree,' John continued, 'the body was beneath it. The roots had picked the bones apart so it's a job to find them all. And he doesn't think they'll be able to tell what happened to the lassie, not now.' John scratched his stomach viciously. 'Poor kid,' he said bitterly. 'Poor kid. Twenty-three, she was. Twenty-bloody-three. She's been dead longer than she was alive.'

What kind of tree, Marnie wondered, her mind focusing on this detail as the kettle began to puff behind her. She hoped it was a silver birch, or one of the ornamental cherries; something pretty and vibrant, a tree suitable for Alice.

John was still talking. 'At least there'll be no more nonsense about her walking into the estuary. Someone took that dress down to the river; someone led us all down the garden path.' He pointed his finger at Marnie and wagged it. 'My money's on Angharad's boy. I used to catch him outside that caravan all the time. I should've told the police. I didn't, because of Angharad, but I should have.'

Marnie rinsed two mugs under the hot tap and placed them next to the kettle. Her father's words were bringing back uncomfortable feelings. John Morahan wasn't the only one who had lied.

She took a jar of Co-op coffee from the cupboard, spooned the granules into the mugs, filled the mugs with water.

John was still ranting. 'Angharad, God love her, she's a good woman, but she thought the sun shone out that lad's arse. Even when I told her what he'd been doing that night, she was all: "Oh, well, boys will be boys,". Truth is, he was so out of his mind he might've killed the girl and not even realised.'

Marnie thought of Will, sitting on her bed in the caretaker's cottage, making her promise not to tell what he'd done.

John stubbed the end of his cigarette on the edge of an ashtray, tipping it, spilling old ash and crumpled fag ends on to the floor. Immediately he shook a new cigarette from a packet on the counter, put it in his mouth, struck the end of a tar-stained thumb against the wheel of a disposable lighter. Marnie closed her eyes. Take yourself away, she'd learned, when her throat became tight and breathing was difficult; go back to a time and a place when you were happy. When she was a child she used to collect lighters discarded in the holiday park. She liked their jewelled colours. She'd kept them in her secret cave, along with Alice's tin.

John lit his cigarette and turned away, heading back towards the living room. As the door opened, Eric Clapton's voice became louder. God, Marnie hated that record. Denise had hated it too, so much so that the child Marnie had learned to associate the music with her mother laying down her book and saying: 'I'm going for a walk.'

Denise preferred to walk alone.

Marnie used to trot upstairs and look out of her bedroom window, watching her mother diminish in size the further she walked along the side of the estuary. John had always been a noisy man, a turner-on of radios and televisions, a banger and clatterer, a laugher, a singer, a snorer and shouter. Denise was the opposite, and Marnie... Marnie was the quietest of them all.

Marnie picked up the mugs and followed her father into the living room. John dropped heavily into his reclining chair. The arms were filthy, black and greasy, stuff that he'd brought to the chair and discarded piled on either side. The television was playing, some cricket match or other, the commentator's voice drowned by the music. Marnie cleared a space on the occasional table for the mugs. She picked up a printout of an article taken from the internet that featured a photograph of Alice Lang with her parents, and a separate picture of a piece of jewellery.

'Mr deVillars brought it,' said John. 'See that necklace? The police want to know where it came from. Alice's parents had never seen it before.'

Marnie had forgotten the necklace and the little silver swallow. Her fingers went of their own accord to her throat. She remembered when she had worn that same necklace, Alice's fingers at the back of her neck gently fastening the clasp, and then Alice turning her by the shoulders to look at her and saying: 'Oh, that's lovely, Marnie! We'll have to get one for you, the same, but with an "M".'

She put the sheet of paper back on the table.

John was staring at the television. Trip Two went over to him, reached up his hairy snout and pushed it into John's hand, until the man relented and scratched the top of the dog's head. Trip whined. 'Tell you what, Marnie,' said John. 'Now you're here, make yourself useful and take TT for a walk, would you? He hasn't been out at all today.'

16

Will stopped at the archway at the park's entrance. The word 'WEL-COME' was spelled out in large plastic letters. Overshadowing the arch were two tall poles, each bearing a marketing sail-flag with the name: 'Loxtons' and a banner saying: 'Coming soon! A bespoke development of three- and four-bedroom executive homes!' The homes were illustrated on a great, flat board, brick-built, steep-roofed houses with artfully depicted happy families relaxing in the gardens.

Security lights had been mounted on towers around the perimeter of the park, illuminating new warning signs: 'Danger!' 'Keep out!' Light spilled across the pavements and the roads, lighting up the trenches and holes already dug in the field where the caravans used to be ranked. It was like a high-security prison. Moths flitted around the bulbs, drawn by the brightness of the false moons.

Will stood there alone. He stared into the glare, and saw how much of the park had already been destroyed. This wasn't the world he had known and it didn't feel right. Things should have stayed as they had been. It should still be summer and the park should be full of families, and Alice Lang should be there, sitting cross-legged on a towel spread on the grass beside her caravan, practising her yoga. Will saw her there in her tie-dyed harem pants and bikini top, the bangles clattering down her arm as she held it up to him, inviting him to take her hand and join her. Her arms were slender, her wrists slim. She had a tattoo on the inside of her right forearm, a Celtic trinity knot, which she told him meant 'family'. Will liked to turn over her arm and tilt it so he could trace the never-ending line of the knot with his fingertip, making Alice shiver.

She'd been here all the time. She'd been here and he'd gone as far away as he could go. He'd left her alone in the cold and the dark.

He should have stayed.

He had never felt so wretched.

Will stepped into the shadows to avoid the TV crew who were setting up ready to broadcast during the ten o'clock bulletin. He overheard a conversation, confusion over Alice's surname – 'Long? Lane?' – and his phone pinged. A message from Saoirse. Will deleted it. He couldn't be distracted now when he was focused on Alice, when he was so close to where her body had lain hidden; his sweetheart, his love. He could almost feel her presence, hear her laughter; see her beside him, a full head shorter than he was, so that when he looked down he could see the parting of her hair, the stripe where the dyed blonde was growing out to reveal the darker hair at the roots, something he found heartbreakingly endearing. So close that he could see the precious curl at the top of her ears and the studs glinting, the balls of honeyed skin that were her shoulders and the cups above her clavicles, small hollows that stretched over the fine bones. He imagined his arm round her, the feel of her body against his, the sweet, clean smell of her hair, her absolute femininity.

Why had Guy killed her? What made him do it and how, then,

did he find the cynicism to take off her dress before he buried her body, and then the wit to throw the dress into the estuary, knowing that when it was found people would believe Alice had drowned?

Guy was a coward, that was for sure. If he had killed Alice accidentally, he wouldn't have owned up to it. Once, when they were kids, Will had seen Guy attempt to leapfrog one of the illuminated Severn Boar bollards that directed holidaymakers around the park after dark, and he'd knocked it over and broken it. When John Morahan saw the damage and asked what had happened, Guy, looking straight at Will as if daring him to tell, had replied: 'No idea.'

Will heard footsteps and turned to see a small, scruffy woman, bundled up in boots and a long coat, coming towards him. She was holding a leash attached to a small dog that trotted beside her, its short legs moving fifteen to the dozen. The woman was staring at the ground, not at what lay in front of her so as she approached, Will said: 'Hi,' so she wouldn't be alarmed by his unexpected presence.

The dog immediately started yapping. 'Sorry!' said Will. 'I didn't mean to make you jump!'

The woman was a silhouette against a sky that glowed with moonlight trapped behind a veil of clouds, but something about her chimed with something in Will. Everything about her and her demeanour felt like a warning to stay away from her, an invisible barrier. But Will knew who she was. Of all the people he could have encountered, she was the one he least wanted to see.

'Marnie? Marnie Morahan?'

She looked as she always had, older obviously, but with the same determination on her face, wary-eyed and lips set in a defensive line. Her expression was neutral but Will detected fear and he remembered how, after her mother's death, Marnie had been like a small, wild animal, always expecting to be chased away. He hadn't thought about her much in years. For long swathes of time he'd forgotten she existed, but now she was here, in front of him, he remembered all she'd been through and Angharad telling him she'd become completely mute after Alice disappeared; that psychological trauma could do that to a sensitive child. He remembered how he'd used and then discarded her and felt a rush of shame. She'd been very young. Perhaps she'd forgotten.

'It's me, Marnie,' he said, 'Will Jones.'

She held up a hand to warn him against coming closer and a terrible tension began to wrap around the two of them. God knows where it would have ended if they hadn't been startled by a thin noise behind them, a ghostly wail coming from the holiday park. Will turned to see a pale figure moving amongst the machinery. It was a woman dressed in white, and the white caught the glow from the spotlights when she walked through their spill and then faded into the dark. Will's heart raced, unsure if what he was seeing was human or spectral.

'Alice?' he murmured, wondering if it could be true, if his love was so powerful that her spirit had somehow been summoned from death itself. For a few moments he was entranced, giddy with hope. He was distracted by a pressure on his arm. Marnie was giving him the dog's lead to hold; he took it. Marnie turned to the metal fencing that surrounded the park, she took a run at it and then, agile as a cat, she scrambled up and over, dropped down the other side, and ran across towards the ethereal figure. Will snapped himself out of his reverie. The woman in white, disappearing now into the darkness, was no ghost.

Will looked down at the dog, which panted and wagged its tail hopefully.

'What the fuck is going on?' Will asked.

He watched as Marnie followed the white woman into the gloom beyond the light cast by the security lamps and soon he couldn't see either of them although he could still hear a faint crying.

Will could not climb the fence, certainly not with the dog in tow, so he retraced his footsteps, past the camera crews to the entrance to the park, ducked under the barrier and went inside, pulling the little dog on the lead behind him. He kept to the shadows to avoid the scrutiny of the assembled media and made his way to where the big earth-moving machines were parked, the buckets resting on the ground, the place where he'd last seen Marnie. He spotted her at last and slowed his pace.

Close up he saw that the figure in white was a tall, bone-thin woman with masses of long, silver hair, wearing a nightgown and slippers. Marnie had taken off her coat and wrapped it round the woman's shoulders and now was reaching up, attempting to put her own knitted hat on the woman's head. Will switched on the torch on his phone to give them some light and he saw that Marnie's head was shaved, that her ears were rimmed with studs, that there was a tattoo of a Celtic knot, like Alice's, at the base of her hairline at the back of her neck. The other woman was no longer crying but talking to Marnie in a quivering voice, flapping her hands, her fingers long and white, like feathers.

As Will approached, she turned to face him and he recognised her: Camille deVillars. Last time he'd seen her she'd been a beautiful woman in early middle age. Now she was a wraith in a nightdress.

'Who are you?' she asked.

He turned the torch towards himself, so she could see. 'It's me, Mrs deVillars,' he said, 'Will Jones.'

'Angharad's boy?' Her voice was shaky. 'Why have you got John Morahan's dog? Did it run off again? Did it kill one of the guinea pigs? I told him he should keep it tied up. It's not the dog's fault. You can't expect a dog to tell the difference between a rat and a...'

Will stepped forward. He took the hat from Marnie, gave her the lead, and pulled the hat gently onto the old woman's head. He removed his own scarf and wrapped it around her neck. He could feel how cold she was. Her slippers were caked in mud.

'May I help you?' Will asked. 'Would you mind if I carried you back to the Big House?'

'What about the girl? Alice?'

Will glanced to Marnie. She wouldn't look at him.

'She's out here on her own,' said Mrs deVillars. 'She's been out here for such a long time and it's so very cold.'

'It won't help her if you fall ill,' Will said gently. 'May I?'

He bent to lift the old woman into his arms. She didn't fight him, rather relaxed and put her arms round his neck to help him. She was nothing but skin and bones, cold as ice; her weight barely registered with Will.

Marnie took Will's phone and she set off with the dog, pointing the light towards the ground so Will could see where he was treading. They walked together through the building site, heading back towards Blackwater House, keeping to the shadows.

17

There was an arched gate set into the stone wall that surrounded the gardens of the Big House. This was the way Camille deVillars must have come into the holiday park and this was the way they left it. They followed a paved pathway to the back door, which was ajar.

It opened into the boot room. Will placed Mrs deVillars gently into an old armchair. Her head, with its mass of white hair, fell forward. Her skin was grey and she was shaking. Marnie tied TT's lead to the door handle.

'Will you stay here while I go and find help?' Will asked. Marnie nodded and he disappeared into the house.

Marnie turned on the electric radiator and directed it towards the old woman. Then she took a towel, knelt on the tiled floor and lifted Mrs deVillars' feet into her lap. She took off her slippers and patted her feet dry with the towel. They were long and thin, icy cold. Marnie remembered all the kindnesses Camille deVillars had heaped on her as a child; the hours she had spent trying to counsel Marnie out of her muteness, and then, when that didn't work, teaching her the basics of sign language.

'You're a good girl, Marnie,' Mrs deVillars said now in her frail, old woman's voice, as if she was remembering the same times as Marnie. 'I was always very fond of you. Poor little thing, losing your mama. You didn't deserve that.'

Marnie kept her face hidden, cleaning carefully around a scratch on Mrs deVillars' heel.

'She didn't deserve it either,' Camille deVillars continued. 'It wasn't good for Denise being here. I used to say to Edward that it would be better if the Morahans went somewhere else, but Edward thought the world of John and...'

Footsteps were approaching, voices. TT stiffened and stared at the door, a growl in his throat. The door swung open. Mr deVillars swept into the room with the nurse and, behind them both, Will Jones.

'Oh, Camille, my darling girl, whatever have you been up to?'

Mr deVillars leaned over Camille so that Marnie was obliged to shuffle out of the way. He took his wife's hands in his, held them to his lips.

Marnie, close as she was, saw expressions chase across Camille deVillars' face before it settled on confusion. The old woman tried to pull her hands away from her husband's, but he held them tightly. Only Marnie witnessed the small, urgent struggle. 'You silly girl,' Mr deVillars continued, 'wandering off like that in your nightie! Look at you! You're perished! It was the police that upset you, wasn't it? I should never have let them through the door.' Camille was still trying to free her hands, but she was too weak. Surely, thought Marnie, Mr deVillars could feel that his wife didn't want to be constrained like that? Still he held onto her. He lowered his voice and asked the nurse in a stage whisper. 'Should we call the doctor, Zoe?'

'I don't think that's necessary,' the nurse said. 'What Camille needs is to be warmed up.'

'You take her upstairs then. Will you help her, please, Marnie?'

Marnie pushed herself off the floor and went to one side of Mrs deVillars, taking her arm. As the women left the room, she heard Mr deVillars' tone relax as he wondered aloud how on earth Camille had managed to get out and then offered Will a small glass of something to thank him for his trouble.

A lift had been installed in the hallway of Blackwater House, enclosed in a column of glass. It was large enough for a single wheelchair; without one the three women could squeeze in together. As soon as the door clicked shut Marnie became breathless. She felt as if she was trapped in a transparent coffin that travelled upwards painfully slowly. It seemed to take for ever to reach, and then go past the first-floor landing.

'Camille can't have come down in the lift,' said Zoe. 'You need a code to operate it. She must have gone down the stairs all on her own. Why did you do that, Camille? Why did you take yourself off out?'

'She must be so cold,' the old woman said in a trembling voice, 'and so lonely. I wanted to find her to tell her I was sorry. I...'

'She heard about the remains being discovered on the news, didn't you, Camille?' Zoe said. 'Which wasn't great. We should have found a gentle way to tell you ourselves. Finding out like that was a shock. It's upset you something awful, hasn't it?'

'She's been out there all on her own.'

'I know, dear, but not any more.'

'She's somewhere warm now?'

'Yes.'

'They're looking after her?'

'Yes.'

The old woman's distress was difficult to witness, but Marnie didn't know what she could do to comfort her.

The lift reached the attic floor and juddered to a stop. It opened onto a narrow, windowless passageway, the ceiling sloping above.

'This is where the servants used to live,' said Zoe. 'They're small rooms but just what we need, aren't they, Camille? This way.'

They went into Camille's bedroom, at the far end of the attic. The bed had been placed against a partition wall with a bathroom converted for an invalid behind. On the opposite wall was a barred window that Marnie recognised as the one beneath the large gable at the front of the house. The room was warm, hot air pumping through vents.

The nurse took off the coat and hat, helped Camille sit down in an easy chair, and unwound the scarf from her neck. 'There we go,' she said, 'that's better. Let's check you over.'

Marnie stood back, hovering, waiting to be told what to do.

Zoe talked to Camille as she examined her. 'That husband of yours, what are we going to do with him?' She turned to Marnie. 'I'm forever telling Mr deV to make sure he takes the keys out of the doors and puts them up somewhere where Camille can't find them, but does he listen? No. It's almost as if he wants her to go wandering. He says he's worried about locking the doors in case of fire, but I'm always here, and Maya too. We wouldn't leave you to burn, Camille, would we, dear? We'd never abandon you.'

The warmth of the bedroom was oppressive. Marnie's eyes felt itchy and hot. They were drawn to a painting of the young Camille sitting on a daisy-speckled lawn.

'It's a lovely picture, isn't it?' said the nurse. 'Camille's father commissioned it for her eighteenth birthday. You like to look at that one, don't you, Camille? It brings back happy memories.'

'It was before Edward,' Mrs deVillars said.

'That's right.'

'When my parents were alive.'

'Yes.'

'Those were such lovely times.'

'I know, dear.'

The nurse directed a thermometer to the old woman's forehead and looked at the reading.

'OK, that's not too bad. I'm going to run you a bath. Can you stay a few more minutes, Marnie? I won't be long.'

She went round the partition behind the bed and moments later Marnie heard the splashing of water and the thrum of a boiler firing up.

'Just need to warm some towels!' Zoe called from behind the partition. 'Two ticks!'

Marnie pulled up a chair and sat facing the old woman.

Mrs deVillars looked at her. 'Is that you, Marnie? Come closer so I can see you properly.'

Marnie did as she'd been asked.

The old woman looked around, then leaned forward, lowering her voice. 'I knew this was going to happen. Denise wrote me a letter.'

Denise had been dead long before Alice came; and why would she write a letter when she could so easily walk over the road and talk to Camille if she had something to say? Mrs deVillars was confused. Marnie took her quivering hand and cupped it between hers, trying to convey reassurance.

'It was a long time ago,' the old woman continued, 'but these things don't go away. The truth always finds a way. You must be on your guard. Promise me you'll be careful?'

Marnie raised Camille's hand to her lips. The old woman clenched her fingers. She was becoming agitated.

'You're not listening, Marnie! You need to listen! I'm not stupid! Everyone treats me like I'm stupid but...'

The nurse came back into the room. 'Are you ready, Camille? There's a lovely warm bath waiting for you.'

Mrs deVillars said: 'No, I haven't...' She tailed off. She looked around her as if she didn't recognise where she was. Then she looked back to Marnie and the confusion deepened. She gazed down at her own lap, took her hand from Marnie's and first dusted, then picked at some imaginary stain on the fabric of her nightdress, her eyes avoiding Marnie's.

Whatever it was that had been troubling her had passed.

Marnie took back her hat and coat and Will's scarf. Then she leaned down and kissed Camille gently on her cold cheek, held a hand up to say goodbye to the nurse and left the room. As she went down the narrow stairs that connected the attic to the first-floor landing, she heard the key turning in the lock of the door behind her.

18

When Marnie came into the living room, Mr deVillars offered her a drink, but she declined. Will drained his glass, they collected the dog and left the same way they'd come in, through the back door. They walked round the house to the drive, gravel crunching beneath their feet. At the gateway, Will looked back. He saw the nurse watching from the top window beneath the gable. Marnie didn't follow his gaze. She put her hands in her pockets, the dog's lead looped over her wrist and set off, walking fast; Will had to jog to catch up.

'Wait, Marnie!' he called. 'I'll walk you back. There are things we need to talk about.'

Marnie strode on.

'I need to tell you, I saw something in the Big House...'

She turned to face him; one hand held up like a police traffic officer.

He stopped. The little dog growled. Will took a step backwards. Marnie turned and began to walk away faster now, almost running.

'Marnie!' Will called. 'Look, I know why you're angry, I don't blame you, but...'

She hurried away from him and he felt a surge of emotion and frustration. He needed Marnie. He needed to tell her what he'd seen because out of everyone, Marnie Morahan was the one who best knew how the world had been during the summer of Alice. She was the one who would understand.

He ran after her.

'Marnie!'

He put a hand on her shoulder. She gave a gasp of fear. He could hear the panic in her breathing.

'Marnie, it's me, for God's sake, Will Jones. We're buddies, remember? Scooby and Shaggy, Dumb and Dumber... shit, sorry, I didn't mean... Look, I'm not going to hurt you! I didn't come back to cause trouble. I want to make things right. I want us to be friends again.'

She was struggling. Her lips were parted a little, he could see the sharp edges of her teeth but she couldn't get the words out. Then she held up her hand again, to make him take a step away from her and give her more space. She took her phone out of her pocket and she tapped in a sentence, turned the screen to show him:

You asked me to lie for you and then you went away.

Will read the sentence once. Read it again. He scratched his head, playing for time. So she did remember. Bollocks.

He could not excuse himself for implicating the child that she had been in his guilt so he took a different tack, ignoring the first part of her accusation and dealing with the second.

'I had to go away, Marnie. It was university. The term was start-ing, I couldn't *not* go.'

She looked at him and her eyes were the eyes of the child who'd been betrayed. He remembered holding her hot hand as she lay in her bed in the caretaker's cottage, and how he'd made promises to her: a promise that he'd write every week *without fail*, a promise that she could come and visit him when he was settled in university, a promise she could stay in his room. He'd make a little bed for her on the floor and they'd drink Coca-Cola – proper Coke, not the treacly brown fizzy pop they sold at Channel View – and later he'd get a flat of his own and she could come and live with him there. She'd have her own room and they'd play cards every night and watch videos on TV and eat popcorn. All this but only if she would promise, swear on her father's life, that she'd never tell anyone about him and Alice.

'Marnie,' he began, 'look, I know what you're thinking and I—'

The hand was raised again. *No!*

'Marnie, I'm sorry. I was a dick, I admit it. I always meant to reply to your letters, I always intended to...'

He trailed off, remembering too late that he'd never even opened the letters Marnie had painstakingly written to him, care of Durham University, never read a single one of them, never attempted to reply. It hadn't been that he didn't care, it was that he cared too much, that he was ashamed.

'God, Marnie, I'm so sorry, I...'

She typed another message into the phone; held it up to him.

My dad thinks you killed Alice.

'What? Jesus! No! No, Marnie, I swear I never... Guy was with her that night, you know it was Guy, I...'

She shrugged. It was meant to be a dismissive shrug, but it was too panicky for that.

She reached down, lifted the little dog into her arms, and hurried away.

If she hadn't been so obviously frightened, Will would have

19

Back at her own cottage, after Jenna had dropped the new dog off, a dear little lurcher called Luna, and when Luna was contentedly curled in a crate in the dining room, Marnie checked that all the doors and windows were locked and then herself settled amongst the cushions on the living-room settee, beside Lucy. The lamps were lit, the room was cosy, but the evening's events had disturbed her greatly. She was anxious about what Camille de Villars had said. She felt as if the spirit of her mother's unhappiness had been invoked by the old woman's ramblings, confused as they were. She wished Will hadn't come back.

She picked up her phone and, feeling as if she were somehow betraying Alice, searched for news. She found headlines, plenty of them, about the discovery of the bones, and a link to a report featuring the blonde journalist she'd met earlier. That link led her back to a copy of the original television broadcast of the appeal by Alice's adoptive parents for information about the whereabouts of their daughter made after Alice went missing.

Marnie clicked on the link. There they were, stuck in the amber of a television report twenty-four and a half years earlier, in their old-fashioned clothes, Mr and Mrs Lang: Cynthia in a drab beige, belted dress, her frizzy brown hair permed in a style that must have been out of date even then, and Adrian in a loose shirt and trousers, a creased linen jacket, the pair of them being ushered, shuffling, into a room where a desk had been set up with microphones. As the couple made their way to their allocated seats, there was a barrage of clicking and flashes and Mrs Lang raised her hand to shield her eyes.

Marnie had watched this same footage as a child on the television in the living room of the caretaker's cottage where she was confined with the fever. She'd been sitting on the woolly orange rug with her dolls, two Barbies that had been left behind at the holiday park and a Tiny Tears that her mother had given her. The Barbies only had one outfit each, so Marnie had to improvise with scraps of fabric and safety pins. Her mother's locket was open on the floor beside her, the twin pictures of Marnie as a tiny baby and as a toddler gazing up out of their frames.

She'd been alone in the cottage. John was probably over the road at the caravan park. But even if he'd been there, he would have let her watch the news. He hadn't bothered to try to shield his daughter from the coverage of Alice's disappearance; it never occurred to him that it might affect her. It wasn't that he didn't love her – Marnie had never doubted that – but rather that he was so wrapped up in his own emotional turmoil that he had no capacity left to consider anyone else's.

Marnie had stopped playing with the dolls to watch the broadcast. Because of what Alice had told her about the Langs and the ways in which they used to discipline and try to control her, Marnie was predisposed to dislike the couple.

I wouldn't put it past them to have kidnapped her themselves, one of the Barbies said to the other.

No, the second doll replied, *it would be exactly the kind of thing they would do!*

Watching the broadcast again as a parent, Marnie was more sympathetically disposed towards the Langs. They looked tired and distressed. What, as a child, she'd assumed was callousness in the stiffness of their demeanour, she now interpreted as shock. They were private people. Alice had told her as much. They didn't like being the centre of attention. Their primary concern was to conform; to be seen as conscientious pillars of the Church and community in the rural Lincolnshire village where they lived. And here they were, thrown into the epicentre of a drama and a crisis, having to listen to a police spokesman report to the assembled journalists that there was evidence that sexual activity had taken place inside Alice's caravan in the hours before she disappeared and that cannabis had been smoked. They hadn't gone into the details of Alice's troubled past then, but the Langs must have known it was coming. It was humiliating for them, and for Alice too, and for Alice's memory. Marnie reached out her hand and took hold of Lucy's warm foot. Lucy turned and smiled at her mother sleepily from behind a curtain of silky hair.

Marnie looked back to the phone's small screen.

Mrs Lang was asked if she had a message for Alice, and the woman raised her head and looked straight into the camera.

'Alice,' she said, 'whatever trouble you're in, we can sort it out together. You're not on your own.' She had hesitated, composed herself, then spoken again. 'We miss you. We want you safely back. Wherever you are, remember that God is with you. He'll forgive you, as will we, whatever it is that you've done.'

20

FRIDAY

Marnie was up before dawn the next morning, lighting the range to heat the boiler to warm the house. The plumbing in the cottage was old and cranky; she must ask her father to check it over.

Once the boiler was rattling and gurgling, and the kettle on, she drew the dining-room curtains and let Luna out of her crate and into the cold winter garden. The new dog was scared of everything. She skittered, surprised by a gust of wind, the soft crunch of the iced grass beneath the pads of her paws, and the sound of a van trundling down the lane. Her eyes were wide, her ears moved between the two positions of either pointing straight up, or lying flat against her head. At first, she kept looking to Marnie and Tessy for reassurance but after a while she relaxed enough to have a little sniff and then she went into a corner of the garden and hid behind a bush to toilet.

After that Marnie made a mug of coffee and filled a hot-water bottle, which she tucked between her jumper and her jacket and then she went to see to the animals in the stable. She let Mister, muzzled, potter round the garden while she attended to the donkey and pony.

It was heavy work forking the dirty bedding into the barrow, hard to breathe the icy air, but the radio was playing and Marnie sang along to the old songs in her head as she worked. Soon, the hot-water bottle had been abandoned, and even without it she was warm despite the chill. The damp straw stank of ammonia and was clodded with manure. The breath puffed in steamy clouds from the animals' nostrils, the two of them nudging at Marnie for attention. She loved them. She loved being in the stables with them and she never minded being there without human company. She enjoyed the early morning solitude, the contented animals mooching with her. She leaned on the stable door while Scrumpy nibbled at the sleeve of her jumper. The robin was perched on the arm of the wheelbarrow; everything was as it should be. This was the place where, if she had considered it, Marnie would say she felt happiest in the world: away from people and with her animals.

When the work was done, she scratched Seashell's woolly forehead while she watched the dogs. Tessy had scented something at the edges of the hedge and was tracking the nocturnal progress of a fox or badger. Mister stood gazing out towards the direction of the sea, head held high, sniffing the air. The sun announced its progress with a paler patch in a charcoal sky, like a rubbed-out piece of a drawing. Marnie imagined Alice being here with her, standing behind her, out of sight.

I'm tired, Alice, she told her.

I know you are, sweetpea. I know.

I couldn't sleep for thinking about you.

I know.

Marnie had been woken in the night by the sound of barking, not one of her dogs but a dog from the town, and then she'd heard a distant siren – an ambulance, perhaps, making a dash from the motorway – and once she was awake she knew she wouldn't sleep again. She'd lain in bed, her body supported by a nest of pillows, with her bedside light on, Tessy curled beside her, and she thought of Alice being dead and she cried quietly. When she ran out of tears, she made tea and thought how strange it was that Will was somewhere nearby. At one time she'd have been overjoyed to know he was back in Severn Sands. Now she felt unsettled. He shouldn't be here. He didn't belong any more.

What was he doing in Severn Sands anyway?

Why had he come back?

And why had he been sneaking around the holiday park on his own, in the dark?

Then she thought of Alice leaning on the wall outside the launderette, pursing her lips as if she was about to blow a kiss, but instead puffing a stream of blue cigarette smoke into the sky. Guy had been watching her as if he'd never seen anyone smoking in his life.

'Cigarettes taste best on dry summer days,' Alice told Marnie once. 'Don't bother with them in the winter when the air's cold and wet. All you get then is a mouthful of smoke that'll make you cough. But on hot days...' she'd narrowed her eyes and pulled an expression of rapture, '... honest to God, there's nothing better.' Marnie had never smoked but if she had, she would have rolled her own cigarettes using her thigh as a table, as Alice had. She would have picked strands of tobacco from her tongue. She would have had a little red tin, like Alice's, for her resin.

Oh, Alice, I miss you.

I'm sorry.

Marnie stood in the concrete yard outside the stables, filling water buckets from the tap that jutted out from the wall, trying not to splash her legs. How hot it had been that summer of Alice, how relentless the heat. She remembered how, a few days before Alice disappeared, her throat had become sore. It wasn't too bad at first, but she kept pressing her fingers against her glands, trying to press them down. She remembered, one afternoon, spotting the familiar shape of her father at the far end of the holiday park. He was holding a hose and the water was arcing from its mouth, painting a silver half-moon against the deep blue sky. Children were playing, running around, screaming. The pitch of their voices became muddled with the white-hot dazzle of the sunlight on the hose-water and Marnie couldn't differentiate between sight and sound, she felt so dizzy.

And the next moment, the ground fell away from beneath her feet as she was gripped by big hands, swooped into the air. It took only a moment for her to realise what was happening, but before that moment came she was panicked and the panic hadn't left by the time she realised it was Will; that he'd grabbed her from behind and was swinging her around. She tried to kick him, but it was hard to kick backwards. She was too big for such horseplay now, but all her protest amounted to was an indignant croak.

Will eventually dropped her and she gathered herself together, and dusted herself down. Idiot, she was thinking, and worse; he was still laughing. If they hadn't been on the holiday park, Marnie would have attacked him with her feet and fists. She enjoyed a good play-fight with Will, but there were holidaymakers around and it had been imbued in her since she was big enough to understand that she had to behave herself in front of the paying guests.

'I want to show you something!' Will had said, a big, good-looking teenager in his baggy shorts and scruffy T-shirt. He'd beckoned her off the main site into the service alleyway which ran behind the hedges. There were signs saying: 'No Entry' to keep the holidaymakers out so they didn't see the staff moving laundry, gas bottles and waste bins, and using the alley as a shortcut around the park. He'd led her into the patchy shade beneath the old apple tree, where the air was a little cooler and she'd flopped onto the dusty yellow grass. Will had taken a box from his pocket and put it into

Marnie's hands, a white cardboard box with a pink silky bow on the top.

As she hefted the water bucket into Seashell's stable, Marnie remembered that delicate, square box even though she hadn't thought about it in years. She remembered because of the joy she'd felt when Will passed it to her because she had believed it to be a present for her. Her tenth birthday had been and gone a few weeks earlier, the first birthday since her mother's death, and although Angharad had sent a card and a gift of a cardigan from her Free-man's catalogue there'd been nothing from Will. 'I'll buy you something later,' he'd promised.

Now, with the box in her hands, Marnie looked up at him hopefully, he was swimming in the haze of the heat like a mirage. He'd nodded. 'Go on,' he'd said, his eyes bright, grinning broadly, 'open it!'

Marnie had prised open the lid with her thumb, leaving a dirty smear on the box, but never mind. Inside the box, nestling in a cleft of pale pink silk, was a necklace: a silver chain threaded through the link attached to the top of a small silver swallow charm and next to the swallow, a silver letter 'A'.

Marnie hooked a grubby finger under the silver chain and it trickled over her skin, sending fragments of light dancing. It was light as air; the prettiest thing Marnie had ever seen.

But 'A'. Marnie looked at the letter, trying to work out what it represented. 'A?'

'For Alice!' Will leaned forward, his eyes bright. 'What do you think? Do you think she'll like it?'

Marnie Morahan, aged ten years and two months, had had to use all her resources not to let the disappointment show on her face.

Twenty-four and a half years ago it was. All that time gone, all that water flowed under the bridge, and now the necklace that had been lost with Alice had been found and Will Jones was back in Severn Sands. Had he come to watch and listen, to find out what people were saying about Alice's death? To see what they knew?

Or had he come to check on Marnie? To make sure that she had kept his secrets. To make sure she'd keep them still.

21

Will had stayed up late, writing down his experiences of the evening: meeting Marnie, seeing the ghostly figure of Camille deVillars in the holiday park, going back to Blackwater House, and every detail that he could remember of the photograph he'd noticed tucked amongst dozens of other family pictures on the bookshelves in the living room.

Because of this and also because of the vodka he'd bought at the service station on the way back to the guesthouse, he slept well despite the excessive warmth of the little room in the eaves. When he was woken by the ringing of his phone the next morning, the grief for Alice and guilt about Marnie, from which he'd been relieved whilst unconscious, returned. He tried to slip straight back into sleep, so he wouldn't have to face the day, but the phone kept ringing and in the end he pushed himself up on his elbows, leaned back against the flowery pillows and looked at the screen.

It was Saoirse's sister, Ciara, calling and, knowing that if he answered his voice would give away his drowsiness and his hangover, and not wanting to talk to Ciara anyway, Will diverted the call to voicemail and sent a message saying:

Sorry, I can't talk right now.

He could tell from the ensuing accusatory ping that Ciara had left a voicemail in reply. He felt a shiver of anxiety. What if Saoirse was seriously ill? No, of course she wasn't. It was the flu, that was all, nasty but not dangerous. She'd be OK. She was young and fit. They weren't expecting him to return to London, were they?

No, of course they weren't. And he wasn't going to start feeling guilty about Saoirse.

Well, maybe a little guilty. Perhaps he should call Ciara's partner, Finn, to find out how ill Saoirse really was. Finn was as laid-back as Ciara was uptight and wouldn't exaggerate or pile on any emotional pressure. But Finn was under Ciara's thumb, and if they spoke, he would be certain to tell Ciara and that would only cause more trouble.

Best to do nothing and trust that Saoirse would be fine.

Will knew without looking that he was already too late for Mr Bradshaw's breakfast. Instead he made and drank a cup of black coffee that contained three sachets worth of stale granules and still tasted disgustingly weak while he reread what he'd written about the events of the evening before.

Mr deVillars had left Will alone in the living room of the Big House while he went to fetch ice from the kitchen for the whiskies. Will had wandered over to the bookshelves where the framed photographs were displayed. His eyes had skimmed over a dozen family groupings before they spotted Alice. There she was, his darling girl, in the back garden of the Big House, part of a group of about twenty people standing loosely together. There were lanterns in the branches of the trees, a banner saying 'Happy Birthday Camille', a stack of wrapped gifts. Will knew Alice had been to the party. She'd told him she wouldn't be available that evening because Mrs deVillars had invited her to join the celebrations.

'Mrs deVillars invited you?' Will had asked, jealous on many levels.

'Yes.'

'Why would she do that?'

Alice had rolled her eyes. 'Because she feels sorry for me being here by myself and thinks it would be nice for me to meet some new people.'

'She didn't invite me.'

'She probably asked your mother if you'd both pop by and your mother probably said: "No," because she doesn't like rubbing shoulders with Mr and Mrs deVillars in her spare time.'

This could have been true.

'It's OK,' Alice had said, 'I won't be there long. I'll have a couple of vol-au-vents, a couple of drinks, then I'll come back. I'll meet you later. Mrs deVillars will be upset if I don't show.'

'It wasn't Guy who invited you?' Will persisted.

'No.'

'Honestly?'

'Honestly.'

That was what Alice had told Will. But the photograph told a different story. Alice had taken care of her appearance for the party. She was wearing a white dress that Will didn't remember, those wedged sandals with the ribbons that tied around her calves, and her hair was straighter than normal, hanging to her shoulders, with a flower pinned above her right temple. Standing beside Alice, so close that their arms were practically touching, was Guy. Alice was looking towards the camera, smiling, holding a champagne flute, but Guy, Guy was staring, unashamedly, at the young woman beside him. He was looking at her as if they were a couple; with desire. He was looking exactly like someone who had invited the young woman he fancied to his mother's birthday party as his date.

Even the memory of the photograph displayed so boldly was

enough to make Will feel bad-tempered. He was convinced, now, that Alice had lied. It *was* Guy who had invited her to his mother's party and she had agreed to go with him and she'd taken trouble with her clothes and her appearance for the event. She'd tried to look the part of Guy's girlfriend and she had fitted in. What she'd said about Angharad turning down Mrs deVillars' invitation had been nonsense; an attempt to appease him. None of the staff were at that party, not even John Morahan.

Will got up, brushed his teeth vigorously and took a dismal shower, the water trickling from the eyes of a scaled-up shower-head, before drying himself with a scratchy towel too small to fasten around his waist.

He wished he hadn't seen the photograph, wished it hadn't triggered these particular memories. He didn't want to think of Alice lying to him. He didn't want to remember her choosing to spend time with Guy deVillars when she could have been with Will.

Will had only met Guy once since he left Severn Sands.

It was a chance encounter at a party in London: some publishing do, a fancy affair at a restaurant beside the river. Will had gone with his partner at the time, a journalist called Emily Richards, a birdlike woman who main-lined black coffee and smoked too much. They were outside, on the terrace watching the tourist boats and river taxis puttering along the wide, brown water. The terrace was done up with bunting and clashing pelargoniums in trendy metal troughs. Uniformed waiting staff circulated with trays of canapés and drinks. The sun was beating down, that strong, dusty, London sun, the music was too loud and the champagne was sour in Will's stomach, the sound of other people's small-talk grating inside his head. The initial alcohol buzz had passed and he was at the stage of drinking heavily to fend off melancholia. Emily was wobbling on ridiculously high heels and chain-smoking stinky French cigarettes that made Will dizzy. It was in this condition that he suddenly found himself staring into a pair of feline eyes.

'Good grief,' Guy deVillars exclaimed, obviously forgetting how much he and Will used to dislike one another, 'it's Will Jones, isn't it?'

Guy had aged well. He was still slim, well-dressed, well-groomed. He smelled expensive. His hair was slightly long, still fair. He wore a linen jacket, a hat, designer glasses. He looked chic and cool and sober.

Will, at that dishevelled stage of drunkenness where his shirt was probably sweat-stained and his hair rumpled, was at an immediate disadvantage.

'Oh my God, do you two know one another?' Emily exclaimed, bouncing forward, the smoke from her cigarette causing Guy to shrink backwards. 'Guy used to write a finance column for the *Indy*, didn't you, Guy! It's wonderful to see you!'

There followed some catching-up between Emily and Guy. Guy kept a small flat in London but mainly he lived in South Gloucestershire with his wife and children. They'd bought an old country house near Wickwar, at the foot of the Cotswolds, which they were renovating. Emily brought Guy and Will up to date with one another's careers – Guy did something in the City to do with money – after which Will had enquired after Guy's parents.

'My father's well,' Guy said, 'but Mother has become rather absent-minded lately.'

Will recognised the euphemism for dementia.

'But they're still running the holiday park?'

'I keep trying to persuade them to call it a day, but they won't let it go.'

'It was their life,' Will said. 'As I recall, it meant everything to them.'

'Yes,' Guy said, 'but...' he paused, 'it's not like it used to be.'

Guy's face was lowered, tilted towards the drink in his hand and now he looked up at Will from over his glasses but beneath his brows. 'It was never the same after that summer,' he said, and Emily interjected: 'Oh? What summer?'

'The summer a young girl went missing. I don't recall her name.'

'Alice,' said Will. 'Her name was Alice Lang.'

Had Guy really forgotten?

'Intriguing,' Emily said. 'What happened?'

'She drowned,' Guy had answered. 'She walked into the sea.'

'She killed herself?'

'I'm afraid so. Nothing like that had ever happened at the holiday park before. My mother never got over it.'

Anger was making Will's ears sing; everything was becoming hazy. He leaned a little closer to Guy, so close he could see the pores on his nose.

'Alice's body was never recovered,' Will said. 'Nobody saw her go into the estuary. We don't know for sure that she drowned.'

'That was what the police said.'

'But they didn't *know*.'

'Why would she kill herself?' Emily asked.

'Do you have any theories, Guy?' Will asked. 'You were always watching Alice. You must have had some idea.'

'I hardly knew her. I mean, she was an attractive young woman but...' Guy ran out of steam. 'It was a tragedy,' he said to Emily. 'Will's right, nobody saw her going into the water but that's what happened. They found her dress at the side of the estuary.'

'Your mother found her dress,' said Will.

'Ah, yes,' said Guy, 'you're right, she did.'

Emily was drawing to the end of her cigarette. She put it between her lips and fished in her handbag for the packet. 'Awful,' she mumbled.

'Terrible,' Guy agreed.

Will couldn't let it go.

'You must have been one of the last people to see her, Guy,' he said.

'What do you mean?'

'You were with her that evening, weren't you? You were in Caravan 49 the evening she disappeared? You were on a date with her. A "special" date. She'd bought a bottle of champagne.'

'Listen, old chap, I don't know what you're getting at, but I never went on a date with Alice, not in the way you mean.'

'Are you sure? Was her disappearance really nothing to do with you, Guy?'

'Will! For God's sake!' Emily had tossed her cigarette over the balcony, laughed in a brittle way and put her hand on Will's arm. 'Stop it!' she'd hissed.

Will couldn't remember what happened after that. He'd been blinded by rage. Emily must have calmed him down; perhaps they left the party. There couldn't have been a scene because there had been no repercussions. All he remembered for sure was the conviction he'd had that Guy was keeping his face low, not looking directly at Will because he was hiding something, because he didn't want to inadvertently reveal the truth.

And he had been lying, Will knew that for sure. He'd said, 'I hardly knew her,' said he'd never been on a date with her, but Will had now seen the photograph in the Big House. Guy had been with Alice at Camille's party. If Guy had nothing to hide, then why would he have lied?

As Will was dressing, the phone rang. It was Ciara again. Saoirse's older sister was a lawyer, a formidably intelligent woman who didn't suffer fools. She had a way of narrowing her eyes when she spoke that made Will feel deeply uncomfortable, as if she could see straight into the darkest chasms of his soul. Will followed Finn's example and was careful about what he said to Ciara, aware that any inconsistencies would be noted and used against him at a later date. He picked up the phone, intending to divert the call to voice-mail but accidentally answered. He stared at the screen, horrified. Distantly, Ciara's voice chirped: 'Will? Will?'

Will raised the phone carefully to the side of his face as if afraid it might bite him. 'Hi, Ciara,' he said tentatively. 'How's the patient?'

'Not great,' said Ciara, her voice terse. 'She's sleeping. I'm calling so we can talk frankly.'

Will said: 'Oh.' He paced the length of the room, three whole steps, and back again.

'Is it over with you and her, Will? As far as you're concerned, is it over? Because if it is, stop messing her around and say so.'

Will would have liked to explain himself to Ciara. He'd told Saoirse from the offset that he was difficult, that he found commit-ment difficult, that he didn't have a great track record with women. Saoirse had been so confident in herself she'd believed she could overwrite Alice's story, but, of course, she couldn't. Will hadn't set out to hurt or humiliate her. He'd tried to love Saoirse, but his heart was never truly in it. How could it be, when it still belonged to Alice?

'I've never messed Saoirse around,' he said, echoing Ciara's phrase. 'I have never told her a lie. I've never cheated on her.'

'But you shoot off to the West Country when she's sick...'

'It's my work. I've been working towards one particular book for a long time and there's been a significant development.'

'Do you want Saoirse to move out?' Ciara asked. 'Is that what you want, but you don't have the backbone to say?'

Actually, what Will wanted was for Ciara to hang up and leave him alone, but this was an opportunity being offered to him. If Saoirse *was* going to move out it would be far less hassle if she did it while he wasn't there.

He liked Saoirse. No, he more than liked her. She was fun and sassy, and mostly it was good having her around. When Will was working on a book, he used to look forward to Saoirse coming home from work, and to hearing her stories. But he couldn't cope with her becoming needy, or, as appeared was happening, her sister becoming needy by proxy. He wouldn't be pressed into making promises he'd never be able to keep.

'I know things haven't been great lately,' he said carefully. 'If Saoirse thinks we're over then—'

'She doesn't want it to be over. God knows why, but she still wants to—'

Will couldn't cope with this. Not now.

'Look, Ciara, I'm sorry but this isn't a good time.'

'Then when is a good time?'

'I don't know.'

'OK. If you don't call back in the next twenty-four hours, I'll help her pack up and leave. It's up to you, Will. Your choice.'

He cut off the call.

22

Marnie Morahan had perfected a system of training agility dogs without using verbal commands. Word had spread about the silent teacher and her gentle, intuitive methods and she had ended up with more clients than she could manage. Now she was established and her services were in such demand that she was in the position of being able to limit the numbers in her classes and charge more accordingly.

Dogs didn't need language to understand what was required of them. They read the subtlest movements, the slight shoulder-lean to left or right, a transference of weight from one leg to another that meant a turn was imminent, even the movement of an eye that signalled intent. Dogs were more than capable of understanding what their human partner wanted them to do without verbal commands. Not having to shout whilst running made life easier for the humans, too.

What Marnie taught was how to strengthen the natural bond with a dog, how to communicate at instinctive levels, how to create mutual trust and understanding that went beyond the normal constraints of reward-based training. She worked with her friend,

Jenna, Jenna giving verbal instructions and feedback where necessary to the human clients.

Marnie and Tessy were dancing partners in the arena, and when a course was run well the high was addictive. Only those who had experienced it could understand. The times when she was working with her dog were the only times when Marnie felt completely fulfilled and totally, unconditionally happy.

It wasn't that she didn't love Lucy. She did; she loved Lucy more than she had ever loved anyone, but with the loving of her daughter came concern and self-doubt. In Marnie's eyes, Lucy was the most wonderful, precious child ever born, and because Marnie knew she was far from the most perfect parent, she had a persistent, nagging fear that she wasn't giving Lucy the upbringing she deserved. She could not help but worry, all the time, that some harm might come to Lucy as it had come to her mother and to Alice. Even when they were alone together, at home, or with the animals, Marnie wondered if Lucy was wishing her mother was someone different, someone better, someone capable of giving her more.

With the dogs, it was easy. There was no need for second-guessing. They loved being with Marnie and they loved to work, and for fleeting moments Marnie could give herself up to instinct and connection and be happy.

It was this happiness that she conveyed to her students and that they wanted to learn. It went far beyond the training of dogs.

Jenna arrived in good time that morning and they ran through the lessons, and after that the clients came. Their talk was all of the bones found at the holiday park and of the girl who had disappeared. Two of the six hadn't even been born when Alice went missing. They didn't know the story and were curious and worried. Marnie listened while they gossiped, and was relieved that she could not join in, that she did not have to declare her own interest, or that she had known Alice. Jenna kept shooting glances towards Marnie, worried about the effect the conversation might be having on her. After a few minutes Jenna put an end to the chat by clapping her hands together and saying it was time they started the class.

Marnie wasn't good with people like she was good with animals, but she could cope with teaching, partly because Jenna was there but mainly because she knew what she was doing. She'd practised the day's lessons already, she'd printed fact sheets. She knew exactly how long each exercise would take, and how difficult her students would find it. She knew who worked well with their dogs, who lacked confidence, who thought they were better than they actually were. She watched the dogs and the dogs told her everything she needed to know, and Jenna watched Marnie and they made a great team.

Marnie set the students up with an exercise and Jenna joined in. While they were working Marnie's mind drifted.

She was kneeling on the banquette in Alice's caravan, and Alice was telling Marnie to hold up her hair so she could fasten the clasp of the necklace at the back of Marnie's neck.

'We should get you a matching necklace with an "M" instead of an "A",' said Alice.

'Then will we look like sisters?' Marnie asked.

'That's exactly what we'll look like!'

They'd gone for a walk, Marnie wearing the necklace, and they'd seen Camille deVillars drifting through the park wearing a kimono that looked as if it had been made of macramé over a patchwork dress. Her fair hair had been tied up in a messy bun, wisps of it loose all over her face. She was a life-size fairy, her smile wide, her teeth gappy. She was out of place amongst the holiday-makers and at the same time entirely at home.

'Look at her!' said Alice. 'Isn't she amazing?'

'Yeah,' said Marnie, who was used to Mrs deVillars' Bohemian ways.

'She doesn't look like the kind of person you'd expect to be running a holiday village like this.'

'She was born here,' Marnie said. And then she repeated a phrase she'd heard Angharad Jones use more than once. 'It's all she's ever known.'

Marnie knew the park's history because her father had a book about it given to him by Mr deVillars, a copy of the same book that Guy later gave to Alice. Denise didn't like the book. She said it was deVillars family propaganda, a poorly written example of self-indulgent vanity publishing. Probably she was cross about it because she believed John was too much at Mr deVillars' beck and call. 'You're like a dog,' she used to say, 'it's embarrassing how you're so eager to please him in return for the slightest bit of attention,' and when she said this John would sigh but keep his mouth shut.

Marnie didn't look at the book when Denise was around but secretly she loved to study the pictures, which dated back to when the park was established in the early 1960s by Camille's parents, Lord Mills and his French-born wife. There were fantastic photographs of happy campers queuing outside the refectory where meals were served three times a day in two sittings, and the pictures of the fun and games that would ensue: beauty parades and knobbly-knee competitions, glamorous grannies, talent shows. Marnie thought it must have been wonderful!

The book also had a chapter dedicated to the Mills family history. Camille was an only child and the holiday park was her destiny. Although she shared her parents' altruism, she didn't have a natural bent for business. When the young Edward deVillars was drafted in to be the park's duty manager, it didn't take him long to fall in love with Camille. Of course it didn't. He'd have been a fool not to! They made the perfect couple. Both committed to the park, she was creative, energetic and sociable, full of ideas and plans, and he understood the economics and the business side of things. They were soon married at Severn Sands church – there was a lovely picture of them on their wedding day. After that, Camille's parents retired to the South of France and Edward and Camille took over Blackwater House.

As often as not, in the old days, when Camille went on her wanderings around Channel View, Edward would be with her. It was blatantly obvious to anyone with eyes in their head, even a child like Marnie, that he adored his wife and would have done anything for her.

23

Will Jones bought himself a late breakfast in the Dolphin café. Although the dolphin on the sign outside was holding a hot-dog, the café was vegan, one of those no-waste places that used up other establishments' leftover vegetables; the kind of café of which Saoirse was particularly fond. Will ate a surprisingly tasty full English served to him by a Lithuanian woman with bright black hair streaked with electric blue and tied with a band that reminded Will of the way Alice used to tie her hair back: like a housewife in a 1940s advertisement. The vibe of the café, the bright colours of the interior and the chirpy radio music, big, plate windows, giving out onto the vast greyness and stillness of the estuary, filled Will with an almost unbearable nostalgia. If only there was a way to turn back time, to transport him back to that summer when the bridge hadn't yet been completed, when the sun shone down and Alice Lang was alive, a happy, tattooed whirlwind in Caravan 49.

In the beginning, those first hours after her disappearance, before anyone realised she was actually missing, he believed what his mother had said, that Alice was staying away because of how he'd behaved and that she would soon be back. He kept expecting her to appear, laughing, her smile fading when she realised how guilt-ridden and worried he'd been.

'Oh, Will,' she would say, holding her hands out to him, 'I'm sorry, I didn't mean to frighten you. I only wanted to teach you a lesson.' And he'd have apologised too, told her a million times how sorry he was, and Alice would have forgiven him.

As time went by and there was still no sign of Alice, an awful fear had taken hold of Will. He truly didn't know how he would go on living if she did not come back.

All he knew was that he and she had argued, and that she had spent the evening with Guy deVillars. It did not occur to him, not at that point, that Guy might have done her any harm. He thought it likely that she'd told Guy about the fight and he had advised her to stay away from Will.

He took to watching Guy even more closely than before, following him in case he was seeing Alice somewhere else. When the police questioned him, he kept tilting the conversation back to Guy and Guy's obsession with Alice. And then the witness came forward to say they'd seen Alice leaving the park and walking down towards the sea on the night she disappeared. Soon after, her dress was found and hope of her return had faded almost to nothing.

Will finished the coffee, put a handful of coins on the table, and left the café. He walked along the seafront, hands in his pockets, gazing out across the estuary, the cold wind in his face. Eventually he reached a spot from where he could see the place he'd gone to kill time while he waited for Alice the night she disappeared. It was an unassuming hollow where he'd taken the bottle of stolen vodka. He'd sat on the grass at the estuary edge and stared at the water, watching the moonlight reflected on its surface, watching the movement of the light, the caretaker's cottage a dark silhouette against the sky to his left.

Alice had told him she would come to meet him there.

'I'll find you,' she'd said, 'and then I'll explain.'

'Why can't I meet you at the caravan?'

'Because I need you to leave me alone tonight, Will. I need you to promise me you'll stay away.'

Her voice had been pleading. It was this that had frightened Will more than anything. She was desperate for him *not* to come to the caravan so he wouldn't see the person she'd invited in. Alice knew how Will felt about Guy. She knew he would rather she was spending time with anyone else in the world, which was how Will knew her date that evening could only be with Guy. It was this that had started the argument that had very quickly turned bitter and that ended with Will throwing a handful of gravel at the caravan as Alice shut the door in his face.

He hadn't meant to hurt her. He hadn't meant anything by it. It was merely an expression of his frustration.

After that, he had gone to the bar stores and taken a bottle of vodka – knowing Angharad would kill him when she found out – and then, holding the bottle by its neck, he had walked towards the park's exit and crossed the road, scrambling down the grassy slope to the estuary. He had sat in the hollow beside the path that led down to the rocky shingle, which was euphemistically known as the beach, although it was submerged that evening beneath a high tide, waves splashing against the shore.

He had waited and waited but Alice hadn't come. Will believed she hadn't come because of Guy. He'd imagined Guy turning up at the caravan with flowers, wine, maybe other gifts: proper jewellery, not the silver trinkets that had been all Will could afford. He had tormented himself imagining the two of them together in the caravan's tiny living area, sitting on two sides of the table, talking, Alice, nervous, tucking her hair behind her ear, fidgeting. And then he imagined a sudden silence, a glance, and Guy leaning forward, taking Alice's hand, and she leaning her mouth towards his, their lips meeting in a kiss. And then? Then she'd stand and take his hand and lead him into the bedroom. He pictured her sitting on the edge of the low bed, her cheeks flushed, her eyes full of promise, and holding up her arms so Guy could pull the scarlet dress off over her head; the warm smell of her skin. He had imagined her letting herself fall back onto the bed, and Guy, seeing how lovely she was, unbuckling his belt, stepping forward to join her. Will had imagined all manner of things and now he hated himself for that, because now it seemed far more likely that Guy had tried to seduce Alice, and she'd rejected him, and that was why she was dead. The thought of her brave fidelity was more painful to him even than the thought of her betrayal.

There was only one tiny problem with this line of thought, one contradiction. If it was Guy who had killed Alice and buried her body, then why sell the land for development at the first opportunity, knowing the bones might be discovered?

Could Guy have considered it a risk worth taking? Or could it be a double bluff? Guy, knowing forensic evidence would have been lost in the years that Alice's remains were underground, deliberately orchestrating a situation in which they would be found to put himself out of the picture?

Will took his phone out of his pocket and scrolled through his contacts, looking for Emily, the journalist who had accompanied him to the publishing party by the river. He called and she answered, cautiously.

'Hey, stranger, this is a surprise.'

'A nice surprise?'

'Don't push it, Will.'

They chatted for a moment or two, catching up on elapsed years before Emily asked: 'Why did you call? Is there something you want from me?'

'I'm looking for information about our mutual acquaintance,

Guy deVillars. I need to know if there's any reason why he might have needed a large sum of money quickly a few months back – a divorce settlement or a court case or something, perhaps?'

'O-K. This is something to do with the holiday park murder, right?'

'It could be. Guy sold the park against the express wishes of his parents and it'd be good to know why.'

Emily promised to look into it. She said she'd let Will know if she came up with anything.

Next Will called Tony Costello at the Avon and Somerset Police. Tony answered in a pissed-off tone of voice that made it clear to Will that he was at work and didn't appreciate being interrupted.

'Just a quick one,' Will promised. 'The holiday park case. Remember the witness who said they saw Alice walking down to the estuary in the early hours on the night she disappeared?'

'Yep.'

'Whoever it was must have been lying.'

'Yeah, we worked that out for ourselves.'

'So this witness – and I'm guessing his name is Guy deVillars – will now be your prime suspect, right? You'll be interviewing him as soon as you can?'

'It wasn't Guy,' Tony said quietly.

'No?'

'No.'

'Oh. Who was it then?'

'You know I can't tell you that.'

'But they, this witness, they positively identified Alice? They told you it was definitely her?'

'Hang on...' The sound became muffled and then Will heard footsteps. He guessed Tony was moving away from his desk. When he next spoke it was in a forced whisper. 'Listen, Will, I know how you felt about the girl but you can't keep calling me like this. I only called you yesterday because we're mates.'

'I know, I won't, but this is important.'

'OK. What I will tell you is that we attempted to re-interview the witness yesterday but we couldn't because she's elderly now and frail. You got that?'

Will inhaled deeply. 'I've got it.'

Camille deVillars then. Not only had she been the one to find Alice's dress, but it was she who had misdirected the investigation in the first place to make everyone believe Alice had drowned.

Why would she have done that if not to protect her son?

24

After the group lessons, Marnie and Jenna had a session with a client whose dog had behavioural issues and then Jenna left and Marnie let the dogs out and watched them revelling in the peace of the winter garden. She tried to keep her worries at bay, but her mind was too full.

Her father was her most pressing concern. What if there were so many complaints about 'Layla' last night that he was kicked out of the sheltered housing complex? He and TT would have to move into the cottage with Marnie and Lucy – there was no other option. All her efforts to keep bad thoughts and negativity away would be pointless if John Morahan moved in with his temper and his black moods, the wariness he'd always had around his daughter, behaving as if he was suspicious of her. How would Marnie manage if he was here permanently, in her own lovely, restful haven? Her father with his smoking and his insistence on having the television on all the time, his untidiness, his swearing, his drinking, his bloody Eric Clapton, his constant *noise*.

Oh God, she wouldn't be able to bear it.

Then there was Will Jones, he of the lies and broken promises.

Over the years, Marnie had followed Will's career, borrowing his books from the library and reading the dedications at the front, hoping against hope to see her own name there, some message; a 'thank you'. But she never found anything. Every one of Will's books was dedicated to Alice Lang.

The books were about unsolved crimes, not so much the crimes themselves, but their impact on the families, colleagues and friends of the victims. It was obvious to Marnie that each was a fruitless attempt by Will to purge the psychological trauma he'd endured after Alice's disappearance. It had also occurred to her that, in writing about the wrongdoings of others, he was disassociating himself from them. Despite Will's sensitivity to the devastating impact of a serious crime on the surrounding community, there were no subliminal messages to Marnie that she could see; no explanations, no apologies, no sense that he realised she'd been hurt too.

But the book about Alice would be different. The child Marnie would have to be in that one, wouldn't she, if Will was to tell the whole story? And if Marnie was a character in the narrative, would Will tell the truth about her, about the role she'd played, about the things he'd asked her to do and the ways he'd let her down?

She didn't think so. Because if Will told the truth about Marnie, then he'd have to tell the truth about himself.

The frost had melted in the side of the garden where the sun had reached, although the fallen leaves blown up against the feet of the hedges were crisp and hemmed in white. The trunks of the old cider apple trees were patterned with lichen like layers of lace, and mistletoe hung from the crooks of leafless branches. Blackbirds searched amongst the debris on the grass for hidden apples on which to feast, tossing leaves aside with their beaks. The robin was guarding the feeder; tits twittered in their family group in the hedge, snowdrops bobbing at its feet. Crocuses were pointing their sharp little leaves through the lawn and the daffodils were coming.

Soon it would be spring. Spring had been Alice's second favourite time of year, next to summer.

Marnie whistled to the dogs. She put Mister back in the stables and took the other two inside; scattered kibble for them to seek out while she warmed herself by the stove. She drank another mug of coffee and prepared toast, butter and honey, an apple cut into slices, the same snack her mother used to enjoy. As a child the taste of honey had disgusted Marnie, but after her mother died, and there was no breakfast cereal left in the larder cupboard, she took to eating honey and soon she began to crave the stuff to the point that she would take the pot up to her bedroom and suck it from her finger. When the jar was empty, she stole a replacement from the park stores. She'd been obsessed with the stuff, and this was what had brought her to Alice.

It was the second week of the school holidays. Ten-year-old Marnie had been riding an imaginary horse around the holiday park, jumping it over ditches, galloping up the long grass verges, bravely staying in the saddle when the horse, which was easily spooked, reared and shied, when she spotted a distinctive jar on the table outside Caravan 49, together with a glass containing the dregs of orange juice, a side plate, an apple core and a knife. Sparrows were on the table pecking at toast crumbs on the plate. Marnie had a sudden feeling that her mother might be inside the caravan, that it was where she'd been hiding for these last months since everybody believed she had died. Her heart began to pound. What if Denise had been here all along? What if she'd left the honey jar on the table as a signal to Marnie?

Marnie tied up her horse and tentatively approached the caravan door which was slightly ajar. She wanted to call for her mother, but she was afraid: afraid that her mother would be inside and be cross that Marnie had bothered her when she was trying to have some peace and quiet, but more afraid that she wouldn't be there. In the end she had knocked on the side of the caravan and, when there was no answer, she'd climbed the step and looked through the crack in the door.

Alice had been sitting on the banquette, one tanned leg up on the table, painting her toenails with a lime-green polish. She was wearing yellow shorts and a white cheesecloth top with orange stripes. Her shoulders were bare and a band was tied around her hair, fastened in a floppy bow on top of her head. She'd turned at the movement and smiled when she saw Marnie at the door. Her teeth were the prettiest, whitest teeth that Marnie had ever seen, with a neat gap in the middle of the top front two.

'Hi,' she said, 'who are you?'

Marnie said nothing.

'I'm Alice,' the young woman said. 'It's nice to meet you, Girl-With-No-Name. Why don't you come in and make yourself at home?'

Marnie looked around the caravan, which smelled musky and sweet – a perfume that forever after she would associate with femininity – and was gloriously, artistically untidy without in any way appearing dirty.

'Is my mummy here?' she asked in a small voice.

Alice shook her head.

'No,' she said. 'Sorry, but she isn't.'

Marnie nodded. She felt like crying. How stupid she was, what an idiot. There were millions of jars of honey in the world – there must be at least ten on the shelves of the park stores – how babyish to think it meant something just because she'd seen a jar where she hadn't expected to see one. She stared at her feet, her big toenail peeping through the hole in the rubber of her left dap, her legs dusty and scabbed from where she'd scratched at insect bites.

She thought of her imaginary horse tied up outside. She felt ridiculous.

The young woman in the caravan was looking at Marnie; not in the way that people normally looked at her, with a varying ratio of sympathy and disgust, but in an interested, friendly way.

'Have you lost your mummy?' she asked.

Marnie nodded and looked at her feet.

'Properly lost her? Has she died?'

Another nod.

The young woman was leaning towards Marnie, her eyes full of kindness. 'What was her name?'

'Denise,' Marnie whispered. She wiped her nose with her wrist.

'Denise Morahan?'

'Yes.'

'Is your name Marnie Morahan?' Alice had asked.

'Yes.'

'Well,' Alice murmured. 'Wow!'

She put the varnish brush back in the bottle and stared at her toes of the foot that was on the table for a moment, separated from one another by blobs of cotton wool. Marnie could see her chest rising and falling as her breath moved in and out. Her cheeks were flushed pink. Marnie stood, silent, waiting to be told what to do.

Eventually Alice pointed across the caravan. 'See the hairdryer, over there, on the shelf beneath the mirror! Fetch it for me, would you, sweetheart? Plug it in. We'll dry my polish and then we'll have a proper chat.'

And that's what they did. Marnie held the dryer to blow warm air at Alice's toes, even though it was already hot in the caravan, and then Alice took a bottle of lemonade out of her fridge and poured them both a glass. She had ice in a mould in the small freezer compartment: she banged the mould on the sink to free the ice and shared it between the two glasses. She had chocolate in the fridge too, a Bounty bar; they had a segment each. Alice said she loved coconut, it was one of her favourite flavours. All the time she asked gentle questions about Marnie and her life and Marnie answered as best she could.

'You must think I'm really nosy,' Alice said – Marnie didn't – 'but I've always dreamed of having a little sister exactly like you! And then you turned up and came into the caravan entirely off your own bat and you found me! Isn't that the most amazing thing? Isn't it?'

Marnie, happier than she'd been in all the weeks since her mother died, agreed, through a mouth sticky with chocolate, that it was.

25

As Will approached, he could see that the road outside the old holiday park was busier than it had been the previous evening. As well as the contractors' and police vehicles, a host of cars and outside broadcast vans had gathered. Journalists were milling in an area set aside for them by the police. A burger van was doing a roaring trade. Will heard laughter, old friends from different news agencies catching up and exchanging gossip. He walked past them, looking through the gaps in the cars and the fencing. He glimpsed what was beyond, seeing the devastation more clearly in daylight. Most of the old caravans had been cleared, their carcasses piled together to one side, ready to be recycled or burned or compacted or whatever happened to park homes when their useful lives were over. Bulldozers were static now but had been moving earth; plots had been marked out with tape. The men in high-vis jackets and boots and safety hats were hanging back, trying to keep out of the sight of the journalists.

Will stayed on the estuary side of the road, where he could observe without drawing attention to himself until he had passed the press crowd, then crossed over, continuing until he was more or less parallel to where the old funfair had been sited. This was where Marnie had climbed over the fence. In daylight it was clear that Mrs deVillars had been wandering towards where the old funfair used to be.

In the old days, that area had been surrounded by fencing decorated with murals of lasso-swinging cowboys, bucking broncos and smiley-faced cacti, with strategic viewing holes giving tantalising glimpses of the gardens and the rides inside. Now the fencing was gone and it looked like a set for a zombie film. The scaffolding that once supported the flume was half collapsed like an old drunk slumped down on one knee. The fun-house was boarded up, the bumper cars huddled together at the far end of their rink, which sloped downwards so that the lower end was submerged beneath dirty water. Broken blocks of concrete and churned-up mud were everywhere. Beyond was the police tape and, mostly hidden beside two strategically placed dumper trucks, the sinister tent that covered the place close to where the old carousel used to stand.

A small group was gathered nearby. Police officers, contractors and a man in a long coat and a hat. The man had his back to Will but Will heard him say: 'It was my mother. She's in the advanced stages of Alzheimer's and has a tendency to wander.'

Will's heart began to race and the old fury flickered: Guy deVillars.

'I must say,' Guy continued, speaking with the trademark confidence of the born-privileged, 'I'm appalled she was able to get so close to the machinery. One would have thought security would have been in place.'

'The guard was patrolling the other side of the site at the time,' said one of the officers.

'If any harm had come to her...'

'I appreciate your concerns, Mr deVillars, but we can't be watching everywhere all the time.'

Guy had a point. It was surprising that someone as frail as Camille deVillars had managed to come so far into the park, but then she had known every inch of it since childhood. If there was somewhere inside Channel View, what was left of it, where she wanted to be, Will didn't doubt that she would find a way in.

He took out his phone and made a video, feeling nostalgia for the funfair as it used to be. It had been open to the general public as well as the campers, and during summer weekends and school holidays it was packed. The air used to smell of fried onions and candy floss; the place was full of sunburned shoulders, kiss-me-quick hats and kids hyped up on coconut ice and fizzy pop.

He pointed the phone towards an old sign that read: 'AMUSE-MENTS', a faded plastic representation of a laughing donkey wearing a straw hat. They certainly used to be big on anthropomorphism in Severn Sands. On a patch of disintegrating rubber matting were coin-operated children's rides: a London bus, a giant crab waving its claws and a Noddy car. The rides were chipped and dirty, bolts rusting, litter about their footings, puddles in the holes in the disintegrating matting. The board beside the shuttered window of the kiosk that used to sell pop, hot dogs and candy floss was still there, weather-worn, its faded wording advertising ice-cream shells and bottled beer. Marnie used to work there sometimes, only for an hour or two here and there, while whichever adult was supposed to be in charge went off for a break. She'd stood in for Will during the Alice afternoons several times. She was a competent, clever little thing and Will could picture her clearly, wearing that band that Alice had given her on her head, looking more kempt than she'd looked since her mother's death because Alice had taken charge of the child's hair and clothing, framed by the square hatch of the kiosk, handing out ice lollies to the punters. She was only ten years old, and she had to stand on an upturned fruit box to see out of the hatch, but she'd managed the calculations; never put a foot wrong.

Ahead, Will could see the park's old service area: the derelict launderette and the small shop that used to be known as the park stores, sinks where campers used to clean their barbecue equipment and a large, wooden pagoda-type construction marked 'Clubhouse'. This was new – or new since Will was last there – larger and grander than its predecessor, where Angharad used to work. Two men in white paper suits and goggles were walking around that area, staring at the ground.

Will put his phone back in his pocket, turned round and walked back the other way.

He had almost reached the old entrance to the park when a police car pulled in, followed by an unmarked saloon. The media pressed forward, buzzing with excitement. Lights were lit, video cameras raised to shoulders, sound booms stretched overhead like fishing rods and a plethora of smartphones were held at the ends of outstretched arms. Will held back and watched. The driver of the car got out and walked round to open the rear passenger door. A man climbed out, and then he went to the other side and helped an elderly woman out. The woman was holding a long-stemmed flower in her gloved hands.

Will caught his breath.

He recognised the two old people: Cynthia and Adrian Lang, Alice's adoptive parents.

26

Marnie filled the pockets of her old coat with dog treats and poo bags, sorted her collection of leads, muzzles and harnesses and took the dogs out for a walk. Her intention was to go to her father's bungalow to make sure he was all right, but when she reached the crossroads she couldn't bear the prospect of having to run the gauntlet of angry retirement complex residents and possibly an upset warden as well as her father, hungover and bullish after the night before.

She wondered how her father felt about the police reopening their enquiry into Alice's disappearance; now her murder. He'd been questioned twenty-four and a half years earlier and a combination of his looks, his arrogance, his refusal to respond in kind when asked a polite question and the fact that he had only recently lost a young and attractive wife, meant he had come across as dodgy, untrustworthy and predatory. Angharad had later told Marnie how the press had turned against John from the start. Angharad had been relieved because it deflected attention from Will, but angry on John's behalf.

For the first days after Alice's disappearance Marnie had been too sick to leave the caretaker's cottage, but she wasn't immune to the hurtful talk. The windows were open because of the heat and she could hear what people were saying outside. The travellers who walked by on their commute between the camp at Catbrain Point and the holiday park knew about Marnie, and kept their voices down, but the holidaymakers and police had no such compunction. Marnie heard the theories. She heard it said, more than once, that it couldn't be a coincidence that John Morahan was connected to two women who were both gone from the same place within months of one another. For a long time after, Marnie heard the same theory repeated in the school playground and even amongst the travellers when they didn't notice she was listening. There was speculation that John must have had something to do with his wife's death, whispers about the way he'd treated her – wasn't it odd that Denise was so rarely seen in the holiday park or the town? Why did she never come to staff parties, or seasonal celebrations? Wasn't it obvious that she wasn't happy, never had been? – and other rumours: that John had had his eye on Alice Lang, that he was a ladies' man, that he'd fathered children he didn't even know he had.

People whispered about Denise's death but they fell silent when Marnie drew close. She learned enough to know that many believed her father had somehow contributed to it but couldn't make sense of what she heard. Her mother had died of a weak heart, everyone knew that. How could that have been anything to do with her father?

Marnie was ten years old and her dad was her dad. He was miserable and ill-tempered but she had never seen him raise a hand in anger, although he used his voice to good effect. He was quite capable of defending himself, so Marnie never felt that she needed to intervene on his behalf. Who would take any notice of her anyway? She kept her head down and kept quiet. People left her alone; they moved away to avoid having to talk to her. Angharad came over to the caretaker's cottage one day and as she tidied, she grumbled that the speculation about John Morahan was all nonsense and Marnie shouldn't take any notice.

'He's a good man, your father,' Angharad said. 'He's loyal and he looks after his own. He never had designs on that girl from Caravan 49, you hear me? Never! Don't you listen to what those ignorant people say. It would have been disgusting. For goodness' sake, she was young enough to be his daughter!'

27

So, Will realised, it wasn't concern for his mother's wellbeing that had brought Guy deVillars to the building site, but the desire to be present when Mr and Mrs Lang turned up to see where their only daughter had lain buried for all these years.

Wasn't that odd behaviour in itself? There was no need for Guy to be there. He didn't own the land any more. There was nothing he could do to mitigate the pain or grief for the Langs. Might it be because he wanted to maintain an element of control? To check what was being said and done, to steer suspicion away, if suspicion veered towards him?

Will kept back from the media pack but watched attentively. Behind the Langs, hanging back, was an overweight, middle-aged man: their adopted son, Jeremy.

The Langs stood side by side by the car while the police officer who had spoken to Guy earlier introduced his superior and some bigwig from the construction company. Cynthia Lang was holding a single white rose, her husband, Adrian, a bunch of flowers, a tasteful arrangement of spring blooms and greenery held together by a black ribbon tied in a floppy bow like the bows Alice used to wear in her hair. For all their clumsiness in loving her, the Langs had cared enough to pay this homage to their daughter. Will had a sudden, unexpected lump in his throat. Saoirse would appreciate this. He reached his hand into his pocket, felt the smooth sides of his phone, thought he'd call her as soon as this was over and then remembered that he'd promised himself he would not.

The Langs were formally dressed, Mr Lang wearing a long woollen coat over his suit and his wife buttoned up in a navy coat with a scarf around her neck. She had faded over the past twenty-four years. She had been a strong presence – once she had thrown Will out of their house after he went to talk to them about Alice – now she looked like a frail old woman, her ankles thin, her legs little more than bone encased in American-tan tights, linking the space between her navy-blue shoes and the hem of the coat. She kept shooting nervous glances towards the media. Mr Lang was aware of her discomfort but clearly didn't know what to do about it, and Jeremy was doing nothing to help his parents.

Guy deVillars assumed control. He stepped forward, took Mrs Lang's hand, and lifted it almost, but not quite to his lips, and then he turned and reached out his hand to Mr Lang and they shook. Both men were wearing gloves. The clicking of cameras was frenzied.

After that, Guy held out an arm, inviting the Langs to step forward. Planks had been laid to form a pathway across the mud.

They didn't go right inside the building site but stopped beside a small holly tree that had somehow survived the onslaught of the bulldozers and stood on a patch of raised ground. Mr and Mrs Lang stepped forward and Mr Lang laid the flowers at the base of the shrub. Mrs Lang put down her single rose and the couple gazed at this tentative shrine to the girl they'd adopted when she was a baby and struggled with from the day she was old enough to fight them until the day she disappeared.

Will didn't doubt Alice's descriptions of her troubled childhood: the parents she perceived as cold and unloving, her distress at their unwillingness to accept her as she was, their determination to make her conform to their idea of what she should be, their fear that she might turn out to be promiscuous, like her teenaged blood mother. When he was younger he'd despised the Langs. Now, having found out more about Alice and her demons, he had some sympathy for them.

They'd done the best they could. They had *tried*. Their ways were old-fashioned, perhaps they would even be considered cruel by today's standards, but it was all they knew. Their approach had worked with Jeremy, who'd turned out exactly how they wanted. How were they to know it wouldn't work with Alice?

Mrs Lang opened the clasp of the handbag hooked over her arm, like the Queen's, and took out a handkerchief. She dabbed at her nose, then she looked up at her husband and they came to some unspoken agreement and turned. Mrs Lang's shoe had sunk into the mud, and she struggled to raise her left leg. For a moment it looked as if she might fall, but her husband caught her elbow, and Guy stepped forward and bent to pull the heel free. The cameras clicked. Then the couple walked back to the car with Jeremy and Guy a few paces behind them. Will's eyes flickered between Guy and Jeremy. While Guy delivered a few words of sympathy to Mr and Mrs Lang, Jeremy stood for a little longer, gazing not at the holly tree but beyond, to the building site, to the police tent that had been erected over the trench where the bones had been found. As Will watched, Jeremy brought one hand to his lips, kissed the fingertips, and then blew the kiss towards Alice's makeshift grave.

28

The sun was high in the sky and the tide was out. Marnie and the dogs walked the estuary path. She watched the birds, delicate waders with narrow, scooped bills feeding in the mudflats and, beyond, small flocks of white gulls that hung in the air then swooped and danced, describing the wind with their movements. Marnie missed the feeling of Alice being with her but there was a kind of relief too. For the first time in more than twenty-four years, she was not afraid of finding Alice's bones washed up on the estuary's stony fringes. The sea assumed a new innocence that day. She felt a new affection for its great expanse and the black ribs of long-sunk vessels that protruded from the mud, the driftwood, the patterns of a billion tiny worm-casts amongst the ancient black rocks.

Marnie stayed on the shore, low down, out of sight of the journalists and police. She didn't want to run the risk of seeing Will again. She didn't doubt he'd be out there, lurking around the holiday park, watching, asking questions to which he already knew the answers so he could incorporate them into his story. It should be *her* story, Alice's. Why should he get to write it, he who had lied, who had made Marnie lie too? He who had shouted at Alice the same day that she disappeared, and called her names, and made accusations? He'd been horrible to Alice, that last day. Mean and jealous and unkind. And it had been partly Marnie's fault because she was the one who'd told Will that Alice was seeing Guy deVillars that evening and that was what had triggered his jealousy.

Feeling disgruntled and annoyed with Will, Marnie walked all the way down to the old caretaker's cottage. Tape had been strung around the perimeter with signs saying: 'Warning Danger Keep Out' – but Marnie didn't care about the tape. She ducked beneath it and walked the overgrown track that led to the gateway to the garden, almost invisible amongst the old, wind-worn bushes. Behind the gate was the short path that led to the squat, pebble-dashed house, the caretaker's cottage where Marnie and her mother and father had lived together.

The cottage, like the park, was condemned. It would soon disappear beneath the bulldozer's tracks, to be replaced by a quartet of executive homes, these ones designated 'luxury residences' because of the sea views. An artist's impression was shown on the board at the side of the road, all black slate tiles and floor-to-ceiling windows, blonde women with long-stemmed glasses of Sauvignon Blanc in their hands standing on balconies overlooking the estuary. Whoever would have thought this would become a desirable place to live? When Marnie was a child, the Severn Sands townspeople had regarded the caretaker's cottage as a slum. Denise used to do her best to make it nice but it was a cold, damp little house, set so close to the water that it was the first building in the town to be engulfed when fog settled on the estuary. The damp was always coming in and leaving behind evidence of itself: dark stains between the covings and the ceilings, a fungal smell emanating from deep inside the walls. Marnie remembered her mother standing on a chair holding a brush and a bottle of bleach, trying to scrub away the stains, wiping her hair from her face with her wrist, muttering, 'It's hopeless.'

One awful day, Denise discovered the damp had got into her books, her beloved collection carefully arranged on the shelves John had built into the alcove at the side of the chimney breast. She had taken the books outside and put them on a tarpaulin spread in the sunshine in the back garden, trying to dry out the pages, and she'd tended to those novels as tenderly as if they were sentient beings. Watching her, kneeling amongst them, pushing back the long hair that kept falling over her face, the child Marnie had felt such love for her mother, and for the care she took of her books.

Marnie used to play out here for hours on her own, riding the bike Mrs deVillars had given her up and down the path, or balancing on the roller skates, also a present from Mrs deVillars, her arms held out wide; Trip barking at the clattering of the wheels as she rolled down the slope and her mother, invisible but inside the cottage, reading; always reading or standing on the landing, looking out of the little window that looked over the road, across to Channel View holiday park.

The caretaker's cottage was the only place where Marnie felt any tiny thread of residual connection to Denise. She could recall moments from her childhood, not specific but flashbacks. As a small girl she'd assumed her mother would always be there, cooking, cleaning, mending, tending to the needs of her daughter and husband. Denise occasionally threatened to leave but Marnie had thought that was part of the maternal role too, nothing to worry about. She saw no reason to panic because her father had been so unconcerned by these threats.

'And where are you going to go, Den?' he'd ask fondly from the other side of the kitchen table where he was dismantling some oily piece of carousel motor. 'How are you going to look after yourself, eh?' And he'd go round the table and put his arms round his wife, she turning her face from him, trying to keep his dirty hands from her clothes. 'You're all right here,' he'd say. 'You live your life, you read your books, you don't have it as bad as you think you do.'

'I don't like it here, John,' Denise said, risking her luck when John was in a good mood. 'There's nothing to do, no future in Severn Sands. Can't we go to the city? I could get a job and—'

'Oh, don't start that again,' John replied. 'We'd end up in some flea-bitten flat and we'd both have to work all hours to afford it. You don't *need* to get a job here. Everything's taken care of. Don't you realise how lucky we are?'

But Camille deVillars had been right when she said Severn Sands wasn't good for Denise. The only times she'd been happy were when she was lost in a book.

'Go and ask your father,' she'd say if Marnie asked her for something while she was reading. 'Go and find him!' and then, in a different voice, 'Oh, but you can't, can you, because he's not here. He's where he always is, trailing round after Edward deVillars like a starstruck teenager!'

Marnie let the dogs off their leads and they followed her round the narrow path at the side of the caretaker's cottage, slippery with sodden leaves, and into the back garden. It was overgrown, reverted to the wild, although Marnie could still make out the shapes of her father's vegetable beds and the swing he'd bought second-hand from the small ads of the local paper and put up for Lucy when she was a little girl. The back door was unlocked. It always was. Nobody bothered with this place. Nobody ever came except Marnie and, occasionally, John. She went inside. The cottage had the lonely, unloved feeling of empty buildings everywhere even though much of the old furniture was still in situ, it being too big to fit into John's new bungalow. It smelled of damp and sea air, of wind and shipping oil and mice.

The electricity supply to the cottage had been disconnected

when John moved out, but the gas cooker was supplied by cylinders, like the ones used in the holiday park. For as long as the cylinders contained some residual propane, they provided Marnie and John with a convenient means of sourcing heat and hot drinks while out walking. She filled the pan left behind in the cottage for this very purpose with water from the tap, lit the gas with a match, spooned coffee granules into one of the two remaining mugs and stood as close as she could to the flames, waiting for it to boil.

It was graveyard cold inside the cottage, ice patterns on the insides of the windowpanes and spider webs occupying the corners. The small flames didn't make much difference. When the drink was made, Marnie took it outside and sat on the back step in the weak sunshine, cupping the mug in her hands. Birds were singing in the overgrown, raggedy trees, the estuary glimmered beyond; Tessy came and settled beside her, Luna stretched out in a patch of sunlight beside the swing and Mister stood, squat, panting and nervous, waiting for trouble.

Memories crowded around Marnie. Going for long walks with her father and Trip alongside the estuary, birdwatching, binoculars on a strap round John's neck and she skipping along happily beside him, mud on her legs, plastic sunglasses with lenses shaped like hearts, an elastic of sherbet sweets looped around her neck. Marnie loved their barefoot expeditions along the beach; John, who did not share Denise's fear of sinking sand, allowing his daughter to run free. She remembered cartwheeling on the grass fringes of the beach, her hair whipping, the sun catching her eyes; climbing onto the rib of one of the wrecks and adopting a yoga pose copied from Camille deVillars, balancing on one bare foot, the other leg bent at the knee, her hands pressed together as if in prayer beneath her chin and her hair blowing behind.

'Look at me, Dad! Look at me!'

She used to hold his hand then, back in the days when they

were a family, before Denise died, when her father used to be open and friendly. She used to help him with the mechanics of the funfair. They were Chief Mechanic and Oily Rag. When they came in, filthy dirty, Denise used to shake her head and say: 'John, this is no way to bring up your daughter!' and John said: 'It's the best way to bring her up!' and then Denise would start asking again if they could move away, live somewhere else and there'd be a half-hearted argument.

Marnie and her father had been thick as thieves. She used to be proud of being her daddy's girl, that big, strong, handsome man who everyone respected. She never thought that maybe her mother felt left out. It wasn't as if she was deliberately excluded. She could have come over to the holiday park any time she liked. She could have had a free ice cream or can of pop and sat on one of the benches in the gardens and enjoyed the fun. She could have made friends. But she never tried. She never made any effort.

It wasn't that she didn't care for John. They were two very different people: Denise, thoughtful, quiet, bookish; John, a practical man who spoke his mind. Denise had once told Marnie that she had fallen in love with John the first time she saw him.

'He was like a film star,' she'd said, 'or a gypsy prince!'... something like that. Marnie had a hazy recollection of Denise explaining how John had come riding into town on his motorbike (which he later swapped for the van) and, thrillingly, carried her off into the sunset. 'He promised to save me,' she'd said. 'He'd promised to be my Happy Ever After.'

Had she actually said those words, or had Marnie added them to the story herself? She couldn't be sure. Thinking back, it seemed unlikely Denise would have been so whimsical. And anyway, the words didn't make any sense. Save her? From what?

29

Will sat in one of the seafront shelters, rested his wrists on his thighs, and turned the phone in his hand.

Another text had come from Saoirse:

Last chance, Will. Call me or I'm leaving.

Will had had texts like this before, from different women. He'd had other last chances and he'd let them go. It was easier than enduring the exhausting process of tortuous reconciliations that inevitably collapsed into bitterness and resentment and blame after a few days, or weeks, or months.

Of course, there was a possibility things would be different now there was no prospect of there being a future for him and Alice. Maybe at some point, he would be able to move on, but he couldn't see it. The confirmation of Alice's death only made her more precious, her memory more fragile, something to be worshipped and treasured because now there never would be any more memories. There was no future, only the past, and Will owed it to Alice not to let her go. What else could he do for her? What else had he ever been able to do? He was to be the writer of her story; the gate-keeper to her memory.

A light wind spilled from the sea. The tide was receding. Will could see the first hints of sandbanks emerging in the shallows in places, their outlines picked out by the burnished metal colours of sunset, their shadows long and dramatic. In other spots, the hidden rocky landscape, like somewhere from a different planet, was emerging. Gulls called overhead, flashes of white drifting against a wide grey sky. In the distance, the closer of the great bridges spanned and rumbled.

Fossil hunters used to come to stay in Channel View holiday park: professional palaeontologists from international museums and universities, who needed cheap, local accommodation while they worked. There was one particular small cliff on this stretch of the coast where numerous bones had been found including species previously unrecorded. That was where Marnie used to have her secret 'cave', in fact just a small cavity left behind in the rock by the scientists.

Marnie was fascinated by the palaeontologists. She collected plastic models of dinosaurs and knew all their names. John Morahan, Will remembered, had taken his daughter to see the film *Jurassic Park* a few weeks before his wife's death. Marnie had returned from the expedition breathless with awe. She had recounted the plot to Will in one long monologue, probably the longest speech that Marnie ever made in her life. She acted out the dramatic parts, being both monstrous creatures and hunted children. 'They're so *big*, Will, and they run so fast! And their breath is like...' *pant, pant, pant,* '... all steaming up the window!'

John had promised to take Marnie to Bristol Museum to see some of the dinosaur fossils found near Severn Sands, which were displayed beside models of the terrible creatures they'd come from: creatures with giant crocodile mouths and teeth like kitchen knives.

But Denise had died and it was obvious that John would never fulfil his promise, and although Will always meant to step in and take Marnie to the museum himself, what with Alice and the police and then university he never quite got round to it.

Will had nothing but fond memories of Marnie until the summer of Alice, when everything was soured. She used to be a mudlark, hunting for treasure at low tide. She found a few bones. She must have known deep down that they were the bones of sheep and seabirds, not T-Rex or Triceratops; still Will went along with the pretence that they were prehistoric, invaluable, priceless. He recalled her running along the shore in her rubber daps, leaving prints that soon filled up with water and were erased, having the whole expanse of mudflats, miles and miles of land exposed by the receding tide, to herself. It was her grey, windswept kingdom, the bones her sea-blasted fortune.

Will missed the days when Marnie was like his kid sister. Theirs had been the least complex relationship he'd ever had. Kind of inevitable that it was fucked up now too. Typical that it was his fault.

The phone vibrated and rang, making him jump.

It was Saoirse.

He wouldn't answer. He'd let it ring out. He'd text her later and say he'd left the phone in the café. He'd call her back when he'd thought of what he wanted to say to her. It would switch to voice-mail any minute now. It would stop ringing. Oh bollocks.

He answered.

'Hi.'

There was a scuffle at the other end of the line.

'Oh! Hi. I thought you weren't going to answer. I was going to hang up!'

The moment Will heard Saoirse's voice, he knew he shouldn't have answered. He should have let her go quietly. His thumb hovered over the button. He could cut her off. He could pretend the signal had died, or the battery. It was, in fairness, a pretty crap signal out here. He could...

'Will? You are there, aren't you?' Her voice still sounded thick with cold. Or perhaps she'd been crying.

'Yeah. I'm here. How are you feeling?'

'Like shit. I've been trying to call you.'

'The signal here is terrible.'

'Oh. That's why Ciara got cut off?'

'Yep.'

'Did you see my text?'

'Yes.' There was a silence. 'Saoirse, I...' Will began but at the exact same moment Saoirse spoke. 'You go,' he said.

'OK. I'm sorry about the text. You know me, I'm not one for ultimatums, but Ciara said I should send it. She said I needed to know where I stood.'

'Where is she now?'

'Outside, talking to Finn...' She trailed off, then said in a quieter voice, 'Severn Sands was on the news this morning. They showed the caravan place. It looks awfully lonely down there.'

'You know me,' he said, echoing her earlier words, 'I like being on my own.'

'... with your ghosts.'

'Saoirse...'

She sighed. Then she coughed and he heard her blowing her nose. He imagined her tossing the crumpled tissue into the bin beside her, imagined her small feet inside the big pair of woolly socks she wore when she was feeling fragile, and he felt a combination of rage and affection that was so contradictory his heart began to race.

'I'm OK,' Saoirse said quietly, although he hadn't asked. There was a long pause. Then she asked: 'Do you *want* me to leave you, Will?'

'I can't think about it now.'

'If you won't ask me to stay, then I'm going to go.'

Silence.

'That was your chance to ask me to stay,' Saoirse said. 'I actually handed it to you on a plate.'

Silence.

'You know,' she said, 'you could have us both. Me and Alice. We're not mutually exclusive. You could write about her and still have me in real life.'

It wouldn't work.

Alice took up too much of Will. She needed so much of him that there wasn't enough left for Saoirse. He couldn't tell her this, so he said nothing.

'You're an arsehole,' Saoirse said.

'You always knew that.'

'Yeah.' Silence. 'I'll see you then.'

'OK,' said Will. 'Saoirse?'

'Yes?'

He breathed in and out. He tried to capture the words he needed to say to her as they darted around him like flashes of light. But he couldn't.

'Nothing,' he said. He ended the call.

30

Angharad had tried to help Marnie after Denise's death. Her helping had taken the form of the provision of food and a superficial cleaning of the cottage. There was a fine line between what John perceived as helpfulness and what he believed to be interference so there was a limit to what she could do. She hadn't known what to say to Marnie. Nobody had. Marnie had been adrift until Alice came along.

Alice had staged a gentle intervention in a way that did not humiliate or criticise. It began one afternoon when Marnie and Alice were sitting on the grass outside Alice's caravan, in the shade of the parasol. Marnie had brought her mother's locket to show Alice, and Alice had opened it and looked at the pictures inside. She'd been absolutely entranced.

'That's me as a baby,' Marnie said, pointing to the picture on the right. She liked the picture. The baby had its eyes tightly closed and its mouth was hidden behind a dummy. There was a spot on its forehead which Denise had told Marnie was due to a speck of dust on the camera lens.

'I was only a few hours old. And that's me when I was two.'

'And your mummy gave this to you?'

Marnie had nodded proudly.

'Wow!' said Alice.

Both pictures must have once been part of larger photographs. Marnie remembered the original of the toddler image. In it, her father had been standing beside her, holding an ice cream, which the two of them were sharing. Her mother had cut Marnie's face from the picture with a pair of nail scissors to make it fit inside the locket. She'd screwed up the rest of the photograph and put it in the bin.

Alice said, 'You were a gorgeous toddler, Marnie. And you're a pretty girl now. But you need to look after yourself.' She had combed Marnie's hair with her fingers, but didn't get far because of the knots. 'I expect your mummy used to do your hair for you, did she?'

Marnie nodded.

'How did she do it? Did she plait it? Did she put it up in a bun?'

Marnie shrugged.

'Go on, tell me!' Alice tickled Marnie in the ribs. 'Tell me about your mummy! What was her hair like?'

Marnie considered this and, to her horror, found that she couldn't remember. It had only been a few months since Denise had died but already she was forgetting her. She couldn't even remember what colour Denise's hair had been, or how it had been styled. Tears had rushed to her eyes; it was as if she was losing Denise, letting go of her. Alice saw that Marnie was upset and she put her arms round her.

'Oh, sweetheart,' she said, 'I'm so sorry. Please don't cry! You've had a horrible time and it's no wonder everything's muddled now. It will get better, I promise! Let's do something together now, something nice. Let's do your hair.'

Alice took Marnie to the shower block and they both stripped to their underwear and went into the shower together. Alice put a blob of shampoo into Marnie's hair and lathered it, then she rinsed it, conditioned it and rinsed again. She showed Marnie how to use bodywash and special cream for the delicate skin on her face. Everything smelled wonderful; like fruit and flowers. The pair of them giggled, throwing suds at one another, skidding on the tiled floor. Once they were rinsed, they wrapped themselves in towels and came back to the caravan. Marnie sat cross-legged on the grass in the sunshine while Alice kneeled behind her, combing her hair straight, teasing out the knots and cutting away sections that had become matted, taking care not to pull.

Marnie picked at the clover in the grass. She had already decided if she found one with four leaves, she'd give it to Alice. She could feel the warmth of Alice's body behind her, Alice's breath on her cheek. Nobody had touched her so gently and tenderly since her mother's death.

'It's important that you wash your hair at least twice every week,' Alice said, 'otherwise you'll end up with hair like wire wool and you don't want that, do you?'

Marnie agreed that she didn't.

'You can borrow my stuff anytime you like,' said Alice. 'And tomorrow I'm going to go into town and buy you your own shampoo and conditioner. OK?'

Marnie gave the smallest nod. She didn't know what she'd done to deserve all this kindness. It was overwhelming and it was lovely.

'Do you have any brothers or sisters?' Alice asked.

Marnie did actually have a half-brother, Justus, but he was from her dad's old life, when John Morahan had been in the army, in Germany. She had never met Justus, only ever seen the small picture of the boy with his mother that John kept folded in his wallet. The picture used to make Denise cross. All this was too complicated to explain so she shook her head.

'Hmm,' said Alice. She snipped at a matted clump of hair with her nail scissors. The noise was crunchy right by Marnie's ear. Alice dropped the clump into the saucer she was using as a bin.

'Have you got any?' Marnie asked.

Snip, snip, snip as Alice cut away the tail ends of the knot.

'I've got one brother,' she said, her voice warm and sweet behind Marnie, 'but we're not actually related. We're adopted. Do you know what that means?'

Marnie had read *Ballet Shoes*.

'Yes.'

Alice fell quiet for a moment or two, combing Marnie's hair with her fingers.

Then she said: 'You know, in a way you're luckier than me. Because even though your mum's dead and that's really tough on you, but... how old are you?'

'Ten.'

'And how old were you when she died?'

'Nine.'

'Well there, see, at least you had nine years with your mum.'

A ladybird landed on Marnie's arm.

'How long did you have with yours?' she asked Alice.

'I don't know. I was too small to remember.'

Now Marnie's skin was so clean, she could see that it was honey-coloured, covered with little blonde hairs. She turned her arm as the ladybird crept over it, over the delicate blue veins on the inside of her wrist. The ladybird extended the covers to its wings, then took off.

'Fly away home,' Marnie said quietly.

Alice sat back on her heels and sighed. 'Your hair looks lovely now. Come and have a look in the mirror.'

She'd stood up and held out her hand for Marnie to take, and Marnie took it. Alice helped her up and they went into the caravan.

There was a mirror on the back of the door. Marnie looked at herself. Alice's face was behind hers.

'Hold on,' said Alice. She disappeared into the bedroom and returned a moment later with a hairband. 'Here,' she said, and she fastened the band around Marnie's head, so that there was a bow at the top and to the left, exactly the same as the band on Alice's hair. 'There,' she said, holding her face so close to Marnie's that their cheeks touched. 'Look at the two of us now!'

* * *

Marnie pushed herself to her feet and took the mug back inside the caretaker's cottage, swilled it beneath the tap and left it upended on the drainer. She stood for a moment in the kitchen, listening to the silence.

She'd been here many times since her father moved out, mainly not venturing beyond the kitchen, although once, caught out by a sudden thunderstorm, she, Lucy and Tessy had sheltered in the living room until the hammering of hail on the window-panes had eased. Marnie had made a fire and it had been cosy, cuddled on the couch, although Marnie had kept her eyes away from the alcove where her mother used to keep her books. After they were damaged by damp, Denise had glued woodchip wall-paper into the alcove. She'd painted it with anti-moisture paint, egg-yolk yellow. It hadn't worked. Black spores bloomed on the wallpaper which had long since peeled from the wet old plaster behind.

When the storm passed, and the time had come to leave, Marnie had been afraid of opening the living-room door; afraid of the darkness gathering and what lay beyond. She knew, rationally, that it was nothing more sinister than a small, damp building, with small, cold memories, but her fear had been visceral. She hadn't gone back into her memories to try to track the fear back to its root. She hadn't wanted to do that.

Now, it being a clear day, Marnie opened the kitchen door and went into the narrow hallway beyond. The dresser was still there, a cheap, pine thing from B&Q, the wood yellowed beneath its old gloss, covered in dust. Marnie put one hand on the newel post and looked up the stairs. She hadn't been up to her old room since her father moved out. Why not? What was stopping her?

Out of sheer bloody-mindedness, a refusal to be cowed by superstition, she began to climb, the sixth step sagging and groaning as ever. Denise had asked John to fix that step right up to her death and he'd always said: 'It's next on my list,' but the step still hadn't been fixed. It had creaked and sagged for almost the whole of Marnie's life.

The landing was tiny, the carpet wrinkled, damp peeling the wall-paper from the walls, cobwebs in the corners. Marnie pushed the door to her old bedroom and it swung open. The furniture was still in situ: the white plywood wardrobe that Marnie had covered with stickers, the single bed with the pink velour padded headboard, frayed and worn now, damp stained. The wardrobe doors were warped; the room smelled of decay. Jesus was gone from the wall. John must have taken Him down at some point; he'd never liked having Him in the house. It was Denise who had insisted He be in Marnie's bedroom, watching over her while she slept, keeping her safe from evil. Jesus had been another point of conflict between John and Denise.

'What's He ever done for you?' John would ask when he caught Denise whispering a prayer. 'How has He ever made you happy?'

Marnie sat on the mattress. She closed her eyes. She tried to feel something, anything. Alice, her mother, some clear, uncomplicated fact about the past. She remembered one winter when she was very small. The carousel had been dismantled for a service and her father had brought a large wooden horse into this bedroom, propped it against the wall. It had been a black horse, a galloper, wild red eyes, a flailing tail, its teeth bared.

But no, that was ridiculous. Her father would never have brought a carousel horse upstairs. He couldn't have. They were too big and heavy and there was no reason on earth why he would have put one in his daughter's bedroom.

Yet Marnie remembered creeping out of bed to go into the bathroom, she remembered the sound of hooves in the night, being terrified of opening her eyes because the horse was there, stamping its feet, blowing through its nostrils, threatening her.

It *couldn't* have been!

It was a dream, she realised. She was remembering a dream!

God, what an idiot she was! What an absolute dipstick! She laughed at herself, dropped her head into her hands and rocked for a moment on the bed. Then, emboldened, she went into the main bedroom, her father's room, previously the room that he used to share with her mother. As in the rest of the house, the large pieces of furniture were still in place but all the pictures, the knick-knacks, the personal items, were gone. She walked across to the chest of drawers, pulled open the top one. This was where her father used to keep his paperwork: manuals for the funfair rides, receipts, cheque books and so on. Some scraps of paper still remained. She flicked through them – nothing of note except for a small, square photograph, face down, at the bottom. She picked it up, turned it over. It was a picture of a young woman standing beside one of the carousel horses, holding onto the pole, leaning out towards the camera, smiling.

Marnie knew who it was, of course, that small, solid little person with her womanly figure, wearing wedged espadrilles, a chalky green cheesecloth halterneck dress, her hair tied back by one of those floppy bows she used to favour. It was Alice, and she was smiling; posing. Flirting.

Marnie studied the picture for a long time, staring at Alice's smiling face, the balletic extension of the arm that wasn't holding onto the pole, the palm of the hand held out towards the photographer as if inviting him to dance. There was something about the pose, something playful; something sexual.

Marnie folded the photograph and put it into the back pocket of her trousers. She stood up and left the room, pulling the door shut behind her.

Oh, Dad, she thought, not you. Not you too.

31

As Will Jones approached the guesthouse that evening, he could see from the window above the door that the only light burning was in the hall. He used the key Mr Bradshaw had given him to open the door and went inside. The house was still and quiet; no radio playing, no TV. He crept towards the living room and rapped lightly with his knuckles. The door swung open and Will saw it was empty. Without the glow of its lamps, it seemed a cold, character-less room. The cheer, if there had ever been any, must have left when Mrs Bradshaw died. Daisy's photograph gazed reproachfully from the walls.

Will looked around and then, feeling like a cartoon thief, crept towards the alcove where the desk stood, its chair neatly aligned in the central gap, with the filing cabinet beside. A small pile of paper-work was on the desk, held down by a clay paperweight in the shape of a crude hedgehog made by a child, one of Daisy's kids, perhaps. The top letter bore the logo of the building company working at the old holiday park, Loxton's. Will peered down to read the first line: 'Ref: Your complaint about heavy vehicles driving through Severn Sands.' Ha! The old bugger would have more to complain about than a few lorries now! Will reached down to pick up the letter, but at that exact moment his phone rang in his pocket. The noise startled him and in his rush to silence it he dropped it and it slid under the fringe at the base of an upholstered armchair. As he scrabbled on his hands and knees to retrieve it, he heard a key in the lock of the front door. He grabbed the phone and muted it as the door swung open. Mr Bradshaw, in the hallway, coughed, sighed, shut the door, and walked past the living room along the hallway passage beside the stairs and into the kitchen. He moved painfully slowly, the floorboards creaking with every step. Will's heart was beating so hard in his chest he was afraid the vibrations might alert the landlord to his presence. A moment later, he heard the sound of a kettle being filled in the kitchen and he crept quietly back into the hallway, and trotted up the stairs. Halfway up, it occurred to him that he should have pretended to have come in through the front door, opened and closed it, but by then his phone was ringing again and the opportunity for any subtler subterfuge had been lost.

He answered the phone as he ran up the second flight of stairs. It was his mother.

* * *

Angharad Jones had emigrated to Majorca to live with her sister when she retired from her role as bar and entertainments manager at Channel View holiday park. Now, most of her contact with Will was via FaceTime, although she came back twice a year to spend weekends in London so, as she used to say with tedious predictability, she could be introduced to Will's latest fling. Age had not made her quieter, nor less flamboyant, and she expected to be taken out to dinner and to the theatre, or treated to some other form of glamorous entertainment. She flirted outrageously with Will's male friends, and tried to befriend the female ones by lavishing them with compliments and gifts. Will was never quite sure if he looked forward to his mother's visits, or dreaded them.

Angharad was always full of news about her sister, Marie, and the sandwich shop that Marie ran specifically for British holiday-makers (white sliced bread, salad cream, Dairylea, tinned ham). Will realised with a sinking heart that he would have to break the news about Alice to his mother. If she didn't hear it from him, she'd read about it in the weekend papers when they eventually made their way to the Balearics and that would be a huge shock to her.

Angharad paused her monologue to ask: 'What are you doing? You sound out of breath.'

'I'm going upstairs.'

'Oh. Are you at home?'

'No.'

'Where are you then?'

Will had reached the door to his room. He tucked the phone under his chin while he unlocked it.

'Where are *you*, Mum?'

'At a bar with your Auntie Marie. We're on the Rioja. Look!'

Will went into the room and looked at his phone. His mother's nut-brown face, bordered by huge earrings, was taking up most of the screen. Her hair, black streaked with grey, was pulled back. She was wearing her trademark red lipstick and her eyes were outlined in eyeliner, with a dramatic wing painted onto each lid. Her décolletage was flat and deep beneath a flouncily trimmed scarlet blouse and she was sporting a good amount of colourful paste jewellery. Behind her, the sun was setting over a sea that bore no similarity at all to the estuary beyond Severn Sands; this was a glamorous harbour where pristine white yachts bobbed.

'Where are you?' his mother asked again, trying to peer around him. Will rotated the phone to show her the room. The floral wallpaper, the single bed, the laptop plugged into the socket to charge.

'Oh!' said Angharad. Then: '*Ohhh!*' and then, in a stage whisper: 'Are you in some woman's boudoir?'

'No!' Will said, and he laughed at the thought that he might be in a relationship with anyone who had a bedroom that could be described as a boudoir. 'I'm in a guesthouse in Severn Sands.'

'Not Bradshaws!'

'Yes.'

'What are you doing there? Have they forgiven you for breaking Daisy's heart yet? I'm surprised they let you over the threshold.'

'Mrs Bradshaw's passed on and... I had to come back, Mum. Something's happened.'

'That sounds ominous.'

'There's something I need to tell you?'

'Oh God, you're not pregnant, are you?'

Cackles of laughter rang out of the phone. Angharad's sister, Marie, appeared on the screen, her head pressed against Angharad's. Marie's hair was bleached blonde, permed. False eyelashes cast spidery shadows on her cheeks. In the background, a mixture of tourists and Spaniards walked along the promenade, past a revolving rack of postcards, a display of wicker tourist tat. Marie waved to Will with her fingers, nails like talons.

'Mum, listen, it's important.'

'OK, sorry, Will. Sorry. What?'

Will sighed. How did you break news like this to someone so far away?

'What's happened?' Angharad asked, her voice tense now, all the jokiness and jollity gone. 'What is it, Will?'

Will looked at her face, looking back at his. She could be a nightmare, but she was his nightmare and he'd never for a second doubted her love for him. He didn't want to hurt her.

'They found some bones buried in the holiday park,' he said. 'Alice Lang's bones.'

Angharad let out a small gasp of distress.

'Are you sure?' she asked. 'I mean, are they sure it's Alice?'

'Yes. It's not official yet, but... yes.'

'Jesus.' There was a brief, anxious silence. Then Angharad asked: 'Why are you there, Will? Why have you gone back to Severn Sands?'

'I had to come, Mum. I'm writing a book about Alice and—'

'But why go back? Why get involved? They'll be asking questions, Will. They'll want to know what you were doing that night and—'

'I'll tell them what I told them last time: that they need to investigate Guy deVillars.'

'You shouldn't do that, Will. You'll end up in trouble.'

'I won't. Did you know that it was Mrs deVillars who came forward to say she'd seen Alice going down to the sea that night?'

'I did know, actually.'

'How?'

'She told me.'

'What? What did she say?'

'She said she couldn't sleep and she decided to take a fresh bottle of lemonade over to the caretaker's cottage for little Marnie Morahan. Little mite was poorly, remember?'

'And you believed her?'

'It was true. She did take the lemonade. John told me.'

'But the seeing Alice bit was a lie, we know that now. And why would she have said that if it wasn't to protect Guy? She's in no state to remember now, but she must have believed he was involved in some way at the time.'

Angharad sighed. 'Will, *you* were the one under suspicion until Mrs deVillars came forward. Don't you remember? I was worried sick. Mrs deVillars was so kind to me. She told me not to worry. She said she'd go back to the police and tell them she'd seen Alice to get *you* off the hook. If it hadn't been for her I don't know what I...' she trailed off. 'Have you spoken to John Morahan?'

'No. I saw Marnie yesterday but... Why should I speak to John?'

'Don't talk to the police until you've spoken to him. Make sure he's clear about what he's going to say if they question him again. You can't change the story now, either of you. You have to tell the police what you said before or else they'll compare notes and see that it's changed and they'll be convinced that you're covering something up...' She was talking faster and faster and then suddenly she stopped and Will heard, instead, laboured breathing.

All he could see on the screen was a section of the awning of the bar where Angharad and Marie were sitting, and a chunk of flesh, perhaps an arm.

'Mum? *Mum?*'

He heard murmurs and then Marie picked up the phone. She held it very close to her face so Will had a distorted view of his aunt's snub nose.

'Your mum's having a bit of a turn, Will, love,' she said. 'We're going to go inside and get a drink of water. She'll call you back when she's feeling better. She says don't do anything until you've talked to John.'

'OK,' said Will, 'tell her I...' but the line had already gone dead.

32

Something had been left on the doorstep outside Marnie's cottage. When she came close, she saw that it was a plant pot containing a slender stalk, about three feet high, with three offshoots, each with several good, fat buds. The plant pot was inside a plastic bag secured at the rim with an elastic band. She hefted it up, took it into the house and put it on the kitchen table. A card was tucked inside the plastic. Inside was written in a neat script:

An apple tree to replace the one we destroyed.
    Your friend, Gabriel Romanescu

* * *

At six o'clock, Lucy and Marnie did what they did every Friday evening. They put on their coats, and walked down to the seafront to pick up three chip suppers from the fish van that parked there for an hour between six and seven, and then they walked round to John Morahan's bungalow, the food steaming inside its paper wrappings.

This time there was no music blaring. Lucy and Marnie found John sober, and in a quiet mood, the drop-leaf table in the corner of the living room extended and laid ready with three settings, the mess that had been on top of it tidied and replaced with sauce bottles, vinegar and the salt and pepper pots. John had given the bungalow a thorough clean since the previous evening. The cans were gone, and the smell of old cigarette smoke was overlaid with the odours of furniture polish and air freshener. A chill in the room pointed to the fact that the windows had been opened to give the place a good airing.

Most of the photographs displayed in John's living room were of Marnie and Lucy, but one large picture hung on the wall over the table: John and Denise were standing beside the static caravan where they used to live before they came to Severn Sands. Marnie was sitting on John's shoulders, her fat little baby legs on either side of his face. He was reaching up, holding her hands in his to make sure she would not fall. Marnie loved this picture, because in it Denise was laughing – really laughing. Her head was tipped back and her lips were stretched wide and she seemed completely happy.

Marnie did not remember her mother being so carefree ever.

The photograph had been taken before the night when Mr deVillars' car broke down on the dark road outside the farm, the night that had become so significant to the Morahans. John used to say that it was fate dealing him a good hand, that car breaking down where it did but Denise hadn't thought so.

* * *

Father, daughter and granddaughter ate their supper at the table on plates John had warmed in the oven, watching the television at the same time. Marnie observed her father throughout the meal, studying his face for signs of tension when the news came on, waiting to see his reactions. The police had confirmed that the remains they'd found were those of Alice Lang. There was a report about Mr and Mrs Lang coming to pay their respects. John was quietly reflective, giving nothing away. When they had finished eating, Marnie took the dishes through to the kitchen to wash up, while John and Lucy cleared the table to play cards.

Marnie had put the photograph she'd found in her father's old bedroom at the back of the safe drawer in her own kitchen dresser, next to the box that contained her mother's locket, and the collection of hairbands and other small gifts that Alice had given her.

She hadn't yet decided what to do about it. She could ask her father about the photograph directly; confront him with it, but the thought made her queasy. Angharad Jones had reassured her that John had never behaved inappropriately towards Alice Lang, but Angharad didn't know about the photograph. And John had gone out the evening Alice disappeared. He'd gone somewhere. And he'd been behaving oddly all day.

Marnie wiped the cutlery, rinsed it, stacked it in the drainer. She gazed into the soap bubbles and thought back. In the afternoon, after Trip killed the guinea pig, Camille deVillars said she'd been looking all over for John and couldn't find him. Marnie had looked too. She'd searched high and low, and he wasn't in any of the usual places. He wasn't in the funfair; only the travelling men had been there, and when she'd asked after her father, they'd told her they hadn't seen him. And later, when she woke up sick in the night, she'd been alone in the caretaker's cottage, she was certain of it.

So where was her father? Where had he been?

When the dishes were finished, Marnie gave the rest of the kitchen a cursory clean, watered the pot plants on the window sill, swept the floor and cleaned TT's bowls. She took her father's musty laundry out of the washing machine and hung it over the airer in the tiny conservatory where the sun, if there was any the next morning, would find it. Then she made coffee and took it into the living room, on a tray. The card game had finished.

'Your girl made mincemeat of me,' John said. Lucy was kneeling on the floor, ordering the cards with a self-satisfied expression on her face. She put the cards back in their box and shuffled onto the rug by the fire to stroke TT. She was a girl so comfortable in her own skin that it made Marnie proud simply to look at her. She avoided her father's eye and went to stand close to Lucy. Lucy reached for the controls and turned up the volume on the television. The BBC local news was showing an 'in-depth' report from the holiday park.

'Alice, who was twenty-three years old, had come to Severn Sands for a holiday,' the reporter said. It was the same woman who'd tried to interview Marnie the day before.

'She'd be forty-seven now, if she'd lived,' said John.

Lucy turned round and looked up at her mother. 'Older than you?'

Yes.

'Really old then!' murmured Lucy. Marnie kicked her gently with the toe of her sock.

The television cut to video of an old report from the time of Alice's disappearance although the same reporter was still talking. Severn Sands looked like a fictional town, one from a period TV drama: the dated cars, the swishy haircuts, every other person in tracksuit bottoms and trainers.

There was the caravan, Caravan 49, with the dent in the outside wall as if someone had punched it. The reporter was saying that questions were being asked about why the police hadn't investigated Alice's disappearance more thoroughly at the time.

'Because everyone thought she'd left of her own accord,' John said.

'The only clue was an empty champagne bottle that had been placed in the bin beneath the sink inside the caravan,' said the reporter. 'The only fingerprints on the bottle were Alice's. Two glasses had been washed and left on the drainer.'

'So whoever she drank the champagne with killed her?' Lucy asked.

'Probably,' said John.

'But they don't know who that was?'

'No.'

'Couldn't they look on the CCTV to see who went in and out?' Lucy asked.

'They didn't have CCTV at the park back then,' said John. 'Anyway, you don't want cameras everywhere watching your every move when you're on holiday, do you? You want to relax.'

'They have them at Channel View now. I mean they used to; before it shut down.'

'That's why everyone's always so stressed all the time. Cameras everywhere. Big brother, watching you, not letting you get on with anything.'

'What happened to the caravan?'

'Caravan 49? They took it away.'

It had gone on the back of a flatbed lorry and was never replaced. Instead, Mr and Mrs deVillars put planters on the concrete base where it used to stand and let the grass grow around it and children used the open space between Caravans 48 and 50 as a playground.

33

Will lay back on the guesthouse bed with his hands behind his head and closed his eyes. He was exhausted: racked.

It was partly the residue of his hangover, partly grief and partly simply having reached the end of a trying and traumatic twenty-four hours where nothing, not one single thing, had gone as he would have wished. Witnessing Camille deVillars' distress the night before had troubled him, the phone call with Saoirse had been difficult, speaking to his mother had been painful and he'd almost been caught sneaking around Mr Bradshaw's front room. But out of everything, it was Marnie's antipathy that played on his mind the most. It hurt. It hurt because he knew she had every right to hate him. He'd behaved like an absolute dick towards her. He could justify his betrayal of Marnie any way he liked: yes, he'd been scared; yes, he'd been distraught; yes, he was little more than a kid himself, but all these applied to Marnie too; more, because she had no choice in what happened to her.

Marnie was the only person on earth who he could talk to about Alice, who would understand because she'd been there, and she'd loved her too. But he couldn't talk to Marnie because he'd fucked her over when she was ten.

Will Jones squeezed his eyes shut and wondered if there were any way to put things right between him and Marnie, or if it was too late; if there was no going back.

The irony was that shutting Marnie out of his life hadn't made the memories go away. They'd haunted him anyway, trailing him, waiting for him to be in one of those rare moments of uncomplicated happiness so they could come creeping up behind him, breathing down his neck and whispering in his ear. He remembered every detail of the aftermath of Alice's disappearance, every microscopic thing, in the way he'd heard people recall the details of the moment before a car crash. Which was ironic, as he could remember next to nothing about the actual night.

He clearly remembered waking the morning after that fateful night when Alice never came to meet him at the seashore. He was wearing a T-shirt and a pair of boxers. He remembered crawling out of bed and discovering a deep pain on the ball of his left foot. When he examined it, he found the sole of the foot was deeply and cleanly cut, as if by glass. He had heard voices and limped into the chalet's main room. John Morahan was there, talking with Angharad. When Will came into the room, they both looked up and fell silent. He realised something was wrong and that they had been talking about him.

'What?' he asked, looking from his mother's face to John's.

John exhaled heavily. Angharad stepped forward so her face was close to Will's. 'God's sake, Will, you've gone too far this time!'

'Why? What have I done?'

'Don't you remember?'

Will remembered being at the estuary, waiting for Alice. He remembered the vodka bottle being half empty and hiding it in the sand. He didn't remember anything beyond that.

'He was too wrecked,' John said. 'He's no idea.'

Angharad's eyes were blazing. A feeling of dread had begun to creep up through Will's bones, cold as the rising tide.

'What?' Will asked again. 'What did I do?'

He saw John's eyes flicker towards Will's hands. He looked at them. He saw that the knuckle joints of his right hand were bloody and bruised. Oh Jesus, he hadn't hit someone, had he?

'You punched Caravan 49,' Angharad said. 'Put a dent in the side. You were threatening all sorts. And I went round just now to make sure the girl was all right, to apologise on your behalf, but she's not there – or if she is there, she's not answering.'

'Not there?' *Is she with Guy? Has she gone back to the Big House with Guy?*

'Wherever she is, I expect she's shaken up,' Angharad continued.

'Why would she be shaken up?'

'Because you were outside her caravan threatening to kill her, buddy,' John said, 'her and Guy deVillars. You were calling him all the names under the sun.'

'You were seen,' said Angharad, 'and heard.'

'One of the travelling women,' said John, 'she'd been waitressing and was on her way home. She came to find me.'

Will looked at his hand; extended the fingers, turned them over. 'Was I that bad?'

Angharad sniffed. 'We'll be lucky if we don't lose our home and our jobs over this.'

'I brought you back here before you could do any real damage,' John said. 'I put you to bed.'

'It was bloody lucky the woman fetched John and didn't call the police,' said Angharad.

Will realised the situation must have been serious for his mother to say something even mildly positive about a traveller.

'Did you see Alice?' Will asked John. 'Did you talk to her? Was anyone with her?'

'I knocked on the door and told her that you wouldn't bother her any more.'

'Which would have been the end of it,' said Angharad, 'if you hadn't bothered her any more.'

Will groaned. He dropped his head into his hands.

'What else did I do?'

'Who knows? Who the hell knows? When I went to bed last night you were on your bed snoring like a trooper and when I got up this morning you were back but there were bloody footprints leading from the chalet door, which was open, by the way – any Tom, Dick or Harry could've come in – and the footprints led to your bedroom. You *did* go out again, Will. You went out in the early hours and God knows if you went back to Caravan 49 and were shouting your mouth off again, and if that girl makes a complaint about you to Mr deVillars and I lose my job and my home then I swear to God I don't know what I'm going to do.'

To Will's utter horror he saw tears stacking in his mother's eyes, tears that escaped and ran down her face.

'I'm sorry,' he mumbled.

'I didn't bring you up to carry on like this, to go making threats to young girls on their own and—'

'I was upset, I was drunk, I...'

A second awful thought crept into Will's mind. If Guy had been inside Caravan 49 when he was outside making his threats, then Guy would certainly tell his parents. Angharad wasn't exaggerating, it would kill her if she was kicked out of the holiday park in shame because of this. She loved the place. She used to say if you cut her in half you'd see the words 'Channel View' running through her.

'I'll tell Mr deVillars that any trouble was all down to me that it was nothing to do with you and that I'm going away anyway. I'll go and see him now. I'll leave straight away. I'll—'

'No!' Angharad looked up, her eyes blazing. 'Don't go confessing to something Mr deVillars might not know about.'

'But if someone complains...'

He meant Guy, but Angharad misunderstood him.

'We don't know that they will. Caravans 48 and 50 were empty last night. The travellers are moving on this weekend and perhaps...' she glanced at John, 'perhaps we could slip them a sweetener to make sure nobody says anything. I'll pop back to the caravan later, have a word with the girl, see how she's feeling about all this carry-on.'

Will nodded, utterly miserable.

'If the worst comes to the worst,' said John, 'we can say it was someone else; some other lad come in off the street.'

'But Alice knows me,' Will said quietly. 'She'd know it was me.'

'Then we'll have to hope she's got a forgiving nature.'

'I'll talk to her. I'll apologise. I'll try to put things right.'

'No!' said Angharad. 'Abso-bloody-lutely not. You need to stay away from her, Will. Don't go near her, or her caravan, until this is sorted. We don't want you being accused of harassment. That's the last thing we need.'

'Your mother's right,' John said. 'Nothing you do now will make things better. We all need to stay calm and wait to see what happens next. If the girl wants to come to you that's one thing. You going to her is quite another.'

'Maybe nothing'll happen,' said Angharad. She sniffed then, took a tissue from a man-size box on the sideboard and blew her nose loudly. Then she asked Will: 'Does anyone else apart from the three of us in this room know about you being sweet on that girl? About you being a jealous little idiot?'

Marnie Morahan knew. And Guy deVillars would have a pretty

good idea if he'd been in the caravan when Will was outside shouting his mouth off.

'No,' said Will.

'Well, let's keep it that way. You stay away from that part of the site, don't say a word to anyone and let's pray that all this soon blows over.'

34

Marnie had been questioned by the police about Alice's disappearance but not until after Alice's dress had been found at the side of the estuary. By then the accepted version of events was that she had either deliberately or accidentally gone into the water and drowned. Marnie's testimony was a loose end that needed to be tied, no more than that. She'd told the lies that Will had asked her to tell and when they asked about her father's whereabouts on the night Alice disappeared she'd confirmed he had found her sleeping beneath the flume and had taken her back home because she was poorly and that she'd gone straight to bed. She was never asked if she'd spent hours searching for her father before then, or if she'd woken up or called for her father during the night. She said, yes, Mrs deVillars had brought a new bottle of lemonade over. No, she hadn't seen her, but it had been there, in the fridge, in the morning.

She'd been pretty much recovered from her fever by the time of the interview, but was still weak and her voice had all but left her. It was assumed that the near muteness was a symptom of her sickness, a temporary aberration. The police had mostly asked questions to which she could respond with a nod or a shake of the head.

Lying had been easy and the questioning hadn't lasted long. It didn't seem to occur to the police that Marnie might have any useful information. She was the kind of child who tended to be overlooked. Also, when people thought of Alice, she glowed so brightly that she dazzled. Anyone standing close, especially someone as small and unobtrusive as Marnie, was at risk of being lost in the glare.

At the time, the lies hadn't bothered Marnie. But now she knew that Alice was dead they were eating into her: not only the lies Will had made her tell, but also her father's lies and all the others, large and small, in between. Wouldn't all this misinformation muddy the water now that it was certain Alice had been murdered? Wouldn't they make it harder for the truth to make itself known?

Marnie tried not to dwell on the events of the day that Alice disappeared, because thinking about them upset her. Sometimes snapshots came to her in dreams, or some small, random thing would trigger a memory. The Rolling Stones' 'Paint It Black' would play on the radio and she was ten years old again, lurching amongst the afternoon crowd in the Channel View funfair with the noise booming around her; bumping into people, disorientated even though she knew every inch of that place like the back of her hand. She was looking for her father, she wanted to tell him about Trip and how she felt hot and sick, and how Mrs deVillars had been upset because of the guinea pig but he wasn't there; he wasn't anywhere.

Oh, for goodness' sake, why was she thinking about it again? It didn't help. It didn't change anything.

She checked the time. It was getting late. She caught Lucy's eye and tapped her wrist. *Time to make a move.*

Lucy moved closer to TT, so that she was lying beside him. The little dog rolled lazily onto his back, his body pressed against hers.

'Aren't we staying for Graham Norton?'

No.

Absent-mindedly, Lucy scratched at the hairy junction between the inside of TT's thigh and his belly. His leg kicked, triggered by some nerve.

'Who do you think killed Alice Lang, Granddad?' Lucy asked.

Marnie exhaled in frustration.

'Do I look like a detective?' John asked.

'Someone must know.'

'Not me.'

John reached for the whisky bottle, the whisky that Edward deVillars had brought the day before. He filled his glass, glug, glug, glug.

'It's scary,' said Lucy. 'Isn't it, TT? Isn't it scary? There's a murderer among us!' She leaned over the little dog and nuzzled her face into his upside-down cheek.

She knew better than that. She knew better than to intrude on the dog's personal space while he was in a vulnerable position. Marnie's father saw the anxiety on her face.

'It's OK, Marnie, he won't hurt the child.'

Marnie licked her lips. She imagined TT snapping, digging his sharp little teeth into Lucy's cheek.

'He won't hurt her,' her father repeated, more forcefully.

Marnie clicked her fingers. The terrier rolled over, jumped up and ran to her. *Good boy, good dog.* Marnie slipped him a treat. TT shook himself, a sign that he *had* been stressed. She'd known it.

'Shake a leg, Lucy, your mother's waiting,' said John, and this time Lucy sighed extravagantly and made a meal of getting up off the carpet. She sidled over to her grandfather and leaned against the padded arm of his chair.

'I'll see you soon, Granddad.'

'Yes,' said John. He reached up, took Lucy's small hand and

squeezed it. His own was hoary and big and square. 'You'll see me soon, my best girl. Don't you worry about that.'

35

Will couldn't sleep. Guilt was keeping him awake. Guilt and frustration.

He got up and switched on the light. Stupid small room, he couldn't even pace properly. He picked up his laptop from where it had been charging on the table and brought it back to the bed. He opened up the Alice file and looked at the official photograph, the famous one that the Langs had given to the police after her disappearance, the one that was in the newspapers until the dress was found.

Have you seen Alice?

The photograph had been taken at a family wedding. Alice must have been told what to wear by Cynthia Lang; she looked nothing like the young woman Will remembered. Her hair was shorter, styled in a conservative bob and completely blonde; she hadn't started to grow out the colour. Either she was wearing pale make-up or she hadn't been outside much, because her skin was lighter than Will remembered. She was wearing a voluminous flowery dress, which came to mid-calf, with a little white Peter Pan collar at the neck, unflattering, fawn-coloured tights and a navy jacket, navy shoes with a small buckle at the toe, a brooch on her lapel. Her make-up was minimal. She was standing between her parents like a prisoner between two guards, smiling at the camera, her trademark, wide gap-toothed grin, but if Will put his finger over her nose and mouth, on the screen, then it was obvious that her eyes were not smiling. There she was, playing the part, little Miss Perfect Daughter, which was what the Langs expected of her.

'As long as I wear what they want, say what they want, do what they want, look like they want me to look, then they like me,' she had told Will. 'When I don't, they withdraw their affection. They don't like the real me. They'd like that part of me to be dead.'

Will tried to understand but it was hard for him because, as a parent, Angharad was the opposite. She adored Will exactly as he was. Almost every day, she would gather him in an embrace and say: 'Don't you ever change, you gorgeous, beautiful boy.' She wasn't soft, wasn't averse to smacking the back of his head if he swore or misbehaved, yet she never tried to make him be something he was not. Even when Mr deVillars planted the possibility of university in his mind and Will decided it was something he'd like to aim for, she never once tried to stop him; never said a word to make him feel guilty or selfish even though he knew she would miss him terribly when he went away.

As it turned out, the leaving had been a blessing.

In the little room at the top of the guesthouse, Will stared at Alice staring out of the wedding picture on the screen until his eyes began to burn.

She had told him about her parents while they lay together on her bed in the caravan, the room hot as an oven, the sheets crumpled and damp beneath them. Alice was on her back, one knee bent, her top half propped up by pillows, unselfconscious in her nakedness. She was smoking. The room smelled of her perfume and of sex and cigarettes. She hadn't looked distressed, she spoke in a matter-of-fact way, but whenever she spoke of Cynthia and Adrian Lang, the energy in the air around her altered and she seemed to shrink a little and be diminished.

Years later, Will had gone to see the Langs, hoping to find out more about Alice and her background. The couple had been reluctant to meet him at all, knowing by then what they hadn't known before: that Will had known Alice during her short time at Severn Sands, that it was his DNA that had been found in her bed, that he had admitted to sharing a spliff with her on that last afternoon. When he told them he intended to write a book, they'd been horrified. They hadn't wanted their adoptive daughter's tragic life sensationalised and Will's promises that he had no intention of dishonouring Alice's memory had fallen on deaf ears. He'd found out very little that he didn't know already, only that Alice had been born in Brighton and handed over for adoption when she was just a few hours old.

In the guesthouse, Will took a swig of vodka from the mouth of the bottle then touched the picture on the laptop screen with the tip of his finger, rippling the pixels. Alice buttoned up in that demure outfit, between her parents, Jeremy hanging slightly back, he the only one in the picture whose body language wasn't indicating extreme stress. You wouldn't know from this picture, nor from the early media reports of the time, climbing over one another to describe what a 'good girl' Alice had been, that she'd been expelled from three different schools, that she'd been seeing a psychiatrist on and off for more than five years, that she was on medication to help control her anxiety, that she'd been treated for a long-term eating disorder, or that she had tried to kill herself twice, firstly by jumping out of the window of the boarding house at the last school, one that specialised in the education of emotionally damaged girls, and more recently via an overdose of sleeping tablets.

Will's eye travelled across the photograph, from Alice's face to the faces of her parents. They too were smiling, each a kind of rictus grin. They weren't comfortable being this close to Alice. They might have loved her in their own, difficult ways, but they didn't understand her. She was the grit in their shell, the cuckoo in their nest.

Mr and Mrs Lang had been to Severn Sands once before, after the scarlet dress Alice had been wearing the evening she disappeared was found washed up on the banks of the estuary. Angharad had told Will to stay well away so he'd watched the report on television. The Langs had come to the place where the dress had been found, an old boarded walkway once used by fishermen to secure their boats when the tide was in. They had stood together on those black, rotting boards and thrown flowers into the dirty grey water. The flowers had spun on the water's surface, and then been carried out to sea. The Langs had watched until the flowers became too small to see, lost amongst the light falling on the water and then they'd turned and, accompanied by a police officer, had carefully walked back along the walkway and across the shore. Mrs Lang had been wearing similar, unsuitable shoes to the ones she'd worn earlier. She had been clutching a similar handbag, in the manner of the Queen.

Will took another drink. The vodka was in his blood, making him feel pleasantly swimmy. His throat was aching with the effort of suppressing pain. This must be how Marnie felt. It was grief that stopped her talking. Grief that had got her tongue.

He didn't want to think about Marnie. He only wanted to think

36

SATURDAY

Marnie was always up early on agility competition days because more often than not there was a long drive to get to wherever it was she was going and course walking usually took place before 8 a.m. That Saturday was no different. She was up and dressed by five thirty and by five forty-five had loaded up the old car with everything she and Tessy needed for the day: bedding, leads, treats, poo bags, blankets and coats for the dog and changes of footwear and clothing for herself. Plus water, coffee, apples, biscuits, chocolate. When this was done, she took Mister and Luna for a stroll around Severn Sands. The sun hadn't risen and the air was bitterly cold, sitting heavy above the surface of the gunmetal-grey water.

Marnie walked quickly and soon her blood was pumping. By the time she returned to the cottage she was wide awake and ready to go. She took Mister back to the feed room, checked his bedding, refilled his water dish and gave him a beef knuckle to chew. Jenna was coming to take him and Luna out later that morning.

She mucked out and fed the donkey and the pony. The radio was playing at low volume in the stable and the blackbird was singing from his perch on top of the telegraph pole. Finches were in and out of the hawthorn, swinging on the feeders. Spring was on its way. The sapling that Gabriel Romanescu had given her was in its pot, waiting to be planted in the orchard.

A cynic like her father would say Gabriel had given the sapling to Marnie to forestall her complaining to head office about the destruction of the old tree. But Marnie didn't think that was the reason. Gabriel was a kind man; she'd sensed it from the start. He had never regarded her muteness as an impediment or as an obstacle to their tentative friendship, just accepted it was part of her. And he'd told her some things about himself, offered her the knowledge as a kind of gift. He had grown up in a small, rural town in Romania, and met his wife, Elena, at university. Elena was a nurse who had died of cancer. The couple had no children. While he was working in Severn Sands, Gabriel was lodging in a shared house in Avonmouth, with six other men. He had his own room, but it was cramped and he had no privacy. Sometimes he slept in his office, on the building site. He was fond of reading, like Marnie's mother, and of bird-watching, like her father.

Marnie thought she should do something nice for him. She could invite him round to the cottage for a meal but perhaps that would be too much. Marnie never invited anyone round and she wasn't sure if it would be appropriate. She couldn't decide how Gabriel would feel if she were to invite him. Politeness would make him accept even if he didn't want to come. And if he came, it would be Marnie's job, as hostess, to make him feel comfortable and relaxed. She wasn't sure she'd be up to it.

Marnie could picture the three of them, herself, Lucy and Gabriel, sitting round the kitchen table eating her best vegetarian pasta with a green salad and fresh bread, a bottle of cider open and the lamps on and they could play some music. It was a cosy picture. But if Gabriel had only come out of kindness then the picture took on a different hue. What if, although he was smiling, complimenting the food, he was itching to get away? What if the whole evening was a nightmare for him? What if, afterwards, he did all he could to avoid Marnie, so he never had to be in that situation again? What if, by trying to strengthen their friendship, Marnie ended up destroying it?

* * *

Before she set off for the agility show, Marnie went upstairs, crept across the landing and pushed open the door to Lucy's room. The door stalled against the clothes spread on the carpet. Marnie stepped over them. She manoeuvred round Lucy's school bag, her riding hat, Scrumpy's saddle that Lucy had been cleaning on the floor, a tin of saddle soap and an oily cloth, a copy of *Jill Has Two Ponies*. The walls were covered with posters of horses, and pictures torn from magazines of show-jumpers and cross-country competitors. The air inside the room was warm and smelled sweet.

'Mum?'

The bundle of duvet and blankets on the bed shifted slightly. A web of dark hair silken on the pillow, a small hand, fingernails with chipped varnish the colour of lichen.

'Are you off now?'

Yes.

'I know what to do. If I need you, I'll text, but I won't, I'll be fine. I won't let any strangers in. Go away. Have a nice time.'

Marnie paused, her hand on the door frame. She half-wanted to step over the detritus on the floor and climb into the bed beside her daughter, hold her in her arms as if she was a small child again, feel her heartbeat, wrap her up and keep her safe.

'What?' Lucy asked. 'What are you waiting for?' She groaned

and pulled the covers up over her head. 'I'm not going to get murdered. Go away, Mum, win all the classes!'

* * *

Marnie didn't enjoy driving in the dark, and now rain was falling too. The satnav directed her across the Somerset Levels, and the road undulated and bumped beneath the car, jolting the sleeping dog, the peat beneath the tarmac sinking and floating, moving in its ancient ways regardless of what was above it. Every now and then the road elbowed sharply over some tiny, fierce bridge that almost bottomed the car. Glastonbury Tor loomed in the distance, its tower pointing into a paling sky.

Marnie gripped the wheel tightly with both hands and stared straight ahead. There were deep rhynes and ditches on either side of the roads and the fields were flooded so sky and countryside reflected one another, the same colour, the same texture of water. The clouds loomed low and grey, the rain fell and Marnie relished her freedom. She was glad to be away from Severn Sands for a while, going somewhere where there'd be no talk of bones or lost girls or murder.

When she eventually reached the remote part of the Levels that was her destination, she could see the showground, six arenas set up in a large field on the other side of a wide rhyne lined by stunted blackthorn and dipping willows woven with ivy. Already cars and vans were lined up on the outskirts of the field. People huddled in macs and cagoules were exercising dogs, mainly collies. Others were queuing up outside the food kiosks. Marnie was directed to park next to a van containing a number of excitable dogs, yapping at ear-splitting volume.

Tessy growled disparagingly at her neighbours, then, with an expression that was the canine version of eye-rolling, turned round and settled amongst the blankets and cushions that Marnie had arranged in the boot of the car with a deep, unforgiving sigh.

Marnie turned to stroke her. She thought of the hours that were to come, hours when she would think of nothing but herself and the dog and the competition, and she was happy.

37

Will made it down for breakfast on Saturday morning, not because he relished the prospect of Mr Bradshaw's company, but because he hadn't had much to eat at all the previous day, had drunk several inches of vodka during the early hours, and was desperate for the comfort of food in his belly and sugar in his bloodstream.

Mr Bradshaw stood beside Will's table in tartan slippers, a buttoned-up cardigan and tie, with a small notepad and pencil clutched at chest height ready to take Will's order. Will asked for a full English, coffee and toast. He hadn't had a proper, non-vegan cooked breakfast since Saoirse moved in and he'd found himself, mostly, going over to her way of thinking. But that morning, he needed to clear his head, he needed to draw up a plan for the new book; he needed to think of the best way to make sure Guy deVillars was brought to justice. He wouldn't be able to do that unless he was adequately nourished and right now his body was craving protein.

Over the course of serving a plate of thick-cut bacon, sausages and two fried eggs, frazzled around the edges and satisfyingly sitting in a pool of cooking fat, Mr Bradshaw mentioned that he had an appointment at the optician's that afternoon. However, it was obvious from the slow way the landlord dealt with breakfast, screwing the lid back onto the marmalade pot with the deliberation of a man who was not in a rush, that he was set for a morning at home, which was annoying because Will would have liked to have gone back to bed. He didn't feel he could do that with his landlord hovering around.

After breakfast, Will went back upstairs to his room and called his mother, who had calmed down now she'd had a chance to process the news about Alice. She told Will not to speak to the police without a responsible adult present 'by which I mean a solicitor, and you let *them* do the talking, all right?' and then he spent a short while searching the internet for stories about Alice Lang and Guy deVillars in case any investigative journalist had come up with anything he had missed. It didn't seem that they had. Most of the articles were, however, focusing on police efforts to identity whoever it was that Alice had shared the champagne with on the night she disappeared. One detective was quoted as saying: 'All previous persons of interest will be interviewed again.' So far, no publication or media outlet had named those 'persons of interest' – although it was only a matter of time. Will couldn't bring himself to search for his own name on social media although he was certain Twitter would have outed him by now. His connection to Alice Lang was no secret.

The piece that interested him most was on the *Guardian* Online, an article that focused on Alice's life, rather than her death, and which reported that, at the beginning of her life, Alice had been:

> given up into the care of a Brighton-based adoption agency that found homes for the illegitimate offspring of young Christian girls

and placing them with families where they'd be assured a
respectable, religious upbringing.

This wasn't news to Will. Thanks to the little information he'd
gleaned from his visit to the Langs, he'd managed to identify the
adoption agency in question, but he was too late. It had folded years
earlier, when new legislation made it illegal to discriminate on the
grounds of religious beliefs. Its records had been archived with a
firm of solicitors. Will had visited their office and spent hours
searching through boxes of paper until he found the documents
pertaining to the child who had been registered as Alice Catharine
Lang. The signatory on the adoption papers was one Sylvia Riley,
from Hastings in East Sussex. Further investigation revealed that
Mrs Riley worked for the adoption agency as an administrator and
regularly acted as signatory when one was required for the purpose
of formalising some legal process *in loco parentis*. The fact that
Alice's mother hadn't signed the adoption papers herself meant she
was either physically or mentally incapable of doing so, or under-
age. It also implied that Alice's mother's parents hadn't wanted their
names associated with the baby; they'd distanced themselves from
the matter entirely. Will had tracked Mrs Riley to her last registered
address, a neat, modern house on an estate on the outskirts of Hastings, but discovered that she had died. She was survived by a
husband and two daughters, but they were unable to shed any light
on Alice's story.

Somewhere about that time, although he had no proof whatso-
ever, Will had an inkling of an idea about who Alice's birth mother
might have been, someone who would have been a young teenager
at the time of Alice's birth and a devout Christian, but he dismissed
it. It seemed too great a coincidence; it could not be true.

Will heard a rattling from downstairs, and then the sound of a
vacuum cleaner starting up. Mr Bradshaw was cleaning the hallway,

banging the machine against the skirting so deliberately that Will was certain his landlord was trying to annoy him into going out.

Fuck him.

He closed the laptop and heard the 'ping' of an incoming message on his phone. It was a text from Emily, the journalist. Will opened the message and skim-read it.

Good news! I've found something about Guy deV!!!

The nub of it was that five years previously, Guy had put almost every penny he owned into a high-risk investment fund that had been delivering huge returns. He had also invested a sum of money belonging to his father-in-law. The fund had tanked. Guy had been at risk of losing everything, and his wife's father had too. The holiday park falling into Guy's hands when it did must have seemed an absolute godsend. No wonder he'd been so keen to maximise the value of the land and then sell it at the first opportunity. No wonder he had been willing to risk the past being uncovered; it was a gamble worth taking because the stakes were so high.

This changed everything.

Will forgot the agonising over Alice's mother. Instead his heart began to pound with the thrill of the chase. He had Guy cornered at last!

He replied to the message:

Thank you, Em, that's exactly what I needed.

He thought for a moment, then added:

Here's a tip for you: keep investigating Guy deV. He was obsessed with Alice Lang. There's a photo of them together in his parents' house. He was the phantom champagne drinker. The story's your exclusive if you can make it stand up.

Two minutes later another text came back:

You sure about the champagne?

100 per cent.

Can you get hold of that photo for me?

I'll try.

38

Marnie signalled *Sit!* Tessy, quivering with anticipation from her whiskers to the end of her tail, lowered herself slowly until her bottom made contact with the wet grass. She stared intensely at Marnie with her clever, brown eyes. *Good girl!* Marnie used her thumbnail to prise a tiny piece of meat from one of the cocktail sausages in her pocket – a treat reserved for agility competitions – and offered it to the dog, who licked it from the end of her finger.

A cold rain was falling. Marnie's head was wet and the water that puddled amongst the grass on the competition field was beginning to soak into her trainers. Dawn had never quite broken and the sky was bruise coloured and sullen. The cold was haunting Marnie. Alice was haunting her. Alice with Will's necklace fastened around her neck, the silver shining brightly against the soft tan of her skin; the little hairs on Alice's arms, the red, sequined dress sparkling in the early evening sunlight. Marnie, going back to the caravan to tell Alice that she couldn't bring the tin because the tide had come in, hearing Alice shouting inside: 'No! *No!* You're not listening to me!' Will shouting back: 'Well, tell me the truth then!'

And later, days later, Will coming to Marnie's bedroom, telling her that she mustn't tell anyone about him and Alice because if she did Alice would be in trouble.

Marnie pictured Alice's small bones laid out on a table somewhere, her skeleton roughly recreated and people in white coats picking up those bones, looking at them, measuring them, searching for the nicks and dents that might determine how the young woman had died. She tipped back her head and let the raindrops fall on her face to chase away the grief.

* * *

The atmosphere among those in the queue for the agility arena was tense. Most people were anxious until they had the first run of the day over and done with, and agility was the most demanding of the competitive disciplines.

Marnie should have been strategising, mentally going over the course one more time, making certain that she knew her way round and that she was confident of the signals she would give to Tessy when they ran, but her mind kept drifting. She tried to pin down memories but it was like trying to find her way back to a place she'd visited as a child without a map or signposts.

A detail came into her mind: something she'd forgotten before.

'Something amazing is going to happen tonight,' Alice had said, that last day, and she'd been smiling and her eyes were bright. It was just after she'd said: 'See you later,' to Guy. They were outside the launderette. Guy had walked away and Alice had watched him go and Marnie had sensed that whatever it was that Alice was looking forward to was somehow connected to Guy. Alice's mood had been like Tessy's was now: excited but also apprehensive, as if she was about to take a risk. But she'd definitely been happy. The sun behind her was shining brightly, making a halo, catching the frayed edges of the ribbon that was holding back her hair.

That day had been blisteringly hot, like the one before it and the one after. The holiday park was packed. Marnie's head was throbbing with the funfair noises, the music that blared out from the dodgems, the chiming and piping of the carousel organ. Alice was leaning against the wall outside the laundry room, and the flowers behind her were bright spots of colour that dazzled Marnie's eyes. The paving was spotted – somebody had been by to water the hanging baskets and containers: Will or Marnie's father, or perhaps even Mr deVillars himself.

'What amazing thing is going to happen?' Marnie had asked.

'I'll tell you about it after.'

'Tell me now!'

'I can't, Marnie.'

Marnie must have looked dejected.

'It's to do with the Big House,' Alice said. 'That's all I'm going to tell you. Tomorrow you'll find out.'

And it was then that her expression had softened. 'You don't look very well. You need to get out of the sun.'

Alice had left and Marnie had gone into the laundry room. She'd checked the timer on Alice's drier. It still had almost an hour to run. She sat on the wooden bench. She took off Mrs deVillars' hat, put it down beside her and sat there, shoulders slumped, wrists between her knees, eyes closed, listening to the sound of the clothes rotating in the drums of the driers. The skin of her thighs, damp with sweat, was sticking to the slats of the bench. It would hurt when she stood up but she couldn't be bothered to find something to sit on. The straw in the hat was beginning to smell. Mrs deVillars had told her: 'You must stay hydrated. You must keep drinking,' but there was nothing in the laundry room to drink and anyway it hurt too much to swallow.

The laundry room was full of the perfume in the white washing powder spilled on the floor, gritty as sand, and the hot stink of the rubber insides of the machines. It was untidy with the paper cups used to dispense the powder and dropped socks and sticky ice-lolly wrappers that attracted the flies. Marnie knew she ought to tidy up – that it was expected of her – but she felt weak. She'd face a telling-off from Angharad or her father if either of them came in and saw her sitting there amongst the mess but she was too sick to care. The washing machines gurgled and churned, emptying and filling with water and sometimes vibrating madly, jumping around. The flies buzzed around her and every now and then a cross-faced woman in orange shorts came in, with a fat, fractious baby on her hip, to see if her machine's cycle was finished.

When the middle drier stopped, Marnie heaved herself to her feet, and opened the door, ducking to avoid the gush of heat. She pulled Alice's clothes into a plastic basket. They were lovely clothes, colourful and flimsy. The scarlet dress was tangled with Alice's bikini top; her underwear, little strips of shiny, lacy fabric. The sequins gave off a chemical smell and were scalding hot. Marnie took care to smooth them flat against the fabric as she folded the dress on top of the other clothes in the basket. It was such a pretty thing.

Think of what it must have looked like when it washed up on the shore after days in the estuary.

No! Don't think of it.

Marnie carried the laundry back to Alice's caravan, the handles of the basket cutting into the soft undersides of her fingers. The park was busy, full of holidaymakers. It was the last full weekend of the season. Barefoot children in their bright summer clothes were playing cricket between the caravans, smoke was puffing from barbecues, music was singing out from the open doors, babies toddled in their nappies and sunhats. Laughter, screams and splashing rang from the direction of the swimming pool.

Alice didn't come to meet Marnie. She had remembered that

part wrong. The door to Caravan 49 was ajar but there was no sign of Alice. Marnie had gone to the door, opened it wide and rested the laundry basket on the step. She'd knocked and Alice had come out of the bedroom at the back of the caravan, hopping as she pulled up her towelling shorts.

She'd come over to Alice.

She was wearing the necklace that Will had bought for her.

'Hey, Marnie,' she'd said, 'thank you so much, you little angel!'

Her hair was messy and her cheeks were flushed and she wasn't wearing a hairband. She leaned down to pick up the basket and the vest-top she was wearing gaped and Marnie saw the swing of the necklace.

Alice put the laundry basket on the table. She picked up the scarlet dress and held it against her body by the straps. She did a little dance, as if she was already wearing the dress, and then she laid it over the back of a chair. 'Fantastic! I need everything to be perfect for tonight,' she said, glancing towards the bedroom door. Will Jones's boots were under the table. The glints of red from the sequins fell on the rough black leather, and the dress Alice had been wearing earlier was there on the floor next to the boots too.

Alice opened the fridge door and then she opened the smaller door to the freezer compartment and took out an ice-pop. She offered it to Marnie and Marnie took it and held it against the side of her neck. Alice smiled.

'That hot, eh?'

She tore at the plastic at the top of her own ice-pop with her teeth, squeezed out an inch of coloured ice, and sucked at it.

'Marnie, will you do one more thing for me today?'

Marnie didn't want to do any more errands for anyone. All she wanted to do was take an aspirin and lie down in the cool grass in the shade of the apple tree and close her eyes and wait for her throat to stop being so sore. Still, she nodded because, of course, she would never refuse Alice anything.

Alice leaned her head a little closer to Marnie's. She spoke quietly.

'You know that tin, the one we put in the cave? I need you to fetch it and bring it to me so I have it for my special date tonight.'

'Why?' Marnie asked.

Something in a different part of the caravan moved. Marnie felt it, a vibration. Alice glanced back towards the bedroom door. She held a finger to her lips. 'I'll tell you tomorrow,' she whispered. 'It's our secret. Remember?'

* * *

Marnie was brought back to the present by a tap on her arm. It was a woman whose dog she used to train, a nice woman, fair hair pulled back in a messy bun, a sun-worn face, small, hairy terrier in her arms. Smiles, chit-chat. 'We'll all be like drowned rats by lunchtime.' The woman laughed and nuzzled her face into the dog's neck.

Then she went away and Marnie was stricken with the uncomfortable feeling she always had when she remembered one particular aspect of the day that Alice disappeared. It was the Quality Street tin. Marnie had promised Alice she'd fetch it from the cave and bring it to the caravan. She'd headed off towards the beach but before she'd even reached the exit to the holiday park, Mrs deVillars had accosted her in a panic.

'Marnie! Where's your father?'

Marnie had shrugged. 'I don't know.'

'That dog of his has got into Pets' Corner and killed a guinea pig.'

'Trip Hazard?'

'Yes!'

'He killed a guinea pig?'

'*Yes!* The little black one. Ragged it, then ran off with it.'

Tears were spilling from Mrs deVillars' eyes. Marnie was horrified. She didn't know what she should do.

'Where's Trip now?' she asked.

'Out in the fields. Will you go and look for your dad, Marnie? Find him for me. That dog needs to be kept under control. I can't have it running around like this. Imagine if one of the children had seen! Imagine!'

So Marnie had gone to try to find her father in the funfair. The Rolling Stones had been booming out of the loudspeakers but her father wasn't there, and then she'd gone over to the caretaker's cottage, but he wasn't there either. Then, because she was worried about what would happen if she didn't catch Trip and put him somewhere safe, she'd gone traipsing over the fields to find the little dog herself.

It had taken her ages to catch Trip, who could be a stubborn little sod and generally didn't take any notice of anyone who wasn't John Morahan. Marnie hadn't had the energy or stamina to play her usual games with him, so resorted to sitting still and trying to tempt him to her with cheese she'd cadged from the travelling woman who made the sandwiches in the clubhouse. Eventually he'd come close enough for her to grab his collar. Then, in the searing heat, she'd carried the furiously wriggling terrier round the holiday park perimeter, along the road and back into the caretaker's cottage, where she'd filled his bowl with water that he'd emptied in one furious, thirsty drinking session, splashing drops all over the floor. Only after all that, after at least two hours had elapsed, had Marnie forced herself out again, to go down to the shoreline to fetch Alice's tin from its hiding place in her secret cave.

Only she couldn't. She had left it too late. The tide had come in. The cave was cut off.

* * *

At the edge of the agility field, in the rain, surrounded by dogs and people, Marnie watched Tessy, who was gazing off into the distance where three ducks were flying in formation across the Levels.

It wasn't my fault, she told herself, but what she meant was: it was.

Nobody had ever blamed Marnie for Alice's disappearance but nobody knew she had been supposed to fetch Alice's tin and take it back to the caravan, or that she had promised that she would.

Marnie had always worried about breaking that promise and now that she knew that Alice had been murdered the oversight was more significant. If Marnie had delivered the tin to Alice, if Alice had received whatever it contained that was so important, then maybe she wouldn't have been killed. Maybe whatever-it-was would have protected her.

It was too late now. No harm could come from opening the tin, no good either.

Marnie decided that, when the opportunity arose, she would return to the cave and fetch the tin and find out what was inside.

39

'Will?'

Will felt a hand on his shoulder and jumped. He turned to see a thin, swarthy face framed by short dark hair. It was Finn Jackson, art-photographer-cum-paparazzo; Ciara's partner.

'Hi,' said Finn in a manner so consciously relaxed that Will immediately smelled a rat.

'What are you doing here?' Will asked.

'Came to see what was going on.'

'Yeah? Did Ciara send you?'

'I was thinking of coming down anyway. Saw the reports on the news and thought this looked an interesting place.'

Finn didn't believe that.

'So Ciara sent you to spy on me?'

'Not Ciara,' said Finn, 'Saoirse.'

Will laughed disbelievingly.

'Why? What does she think I'm doing?'

'It's not like that. It's not a trust thing. She's worried about you. She thought you might need a friend and she wasn't up to making the journey herself so...'

'No,' said Will. 'No, I don't need a friend. I need to be left alone and—'

Finn held up his hands in submission. 'Look, buddy, I'm not here to cause any trouble. I came because she asked me. I'm going to have a look round and then I'll go. I'll tell her I saw you and that you're doing fine. I'll tell her whatever you want me to tell her. It's all good.'

He patted Will's shoulder. 'Make the most of me being here. Use me. I could take some pictures for your book. There must be something you need.'

They walked on together, Finn dressed in an old combat jacket and canvas trousers with a camera attached to an enormous lens slung over his shoulder. Will couldn't put his finger on what it was, exactly, but everything about Finn wound him up the wrong way.

After a while Finn started to whistle. To shut him up, Will nodded towards Finn's camera and asked: 'That's a zoom lens, right?'

'Telephoto, yes.'

'So, it could take a picture, for example, through a window?'

'What are you thinking?'

'There's a photograph I need to copy. It's in a private house. I can't exactly go and knock on the door and ask for it.'

'Well, we could try,' said Finn, 'if we can get close to the window and we're not trespassing on private property and if the sun's right and the photograph is facing the window and there's no glare on the frame and nothing in front of it.'

Will didn't think any of those things was possible.

'Or, you could just think of a reason to go into said house and take a photo of the photo with your phone.'

Shit! Will could have done that himself on Thursday evening!

Finn hitched his camera strap higher.

'Saoirse said you knew the girl who was murdered,' he said, after a while.

Will didn't answer.

'Then all this,' Finn indicated broadly the media pack, the police cars, the tent, 'this must be tough on you.'

In one heartbeat Will was irritated that Finn Jackson was even talking about Alice Lang, a girl about whom he knew next to nothing and whose life and death were none of his business; doubly irritated because he knew Finn was fishing for information to take back to the sisters. In the next he was overwhelmed by a compulsion to tell Finn everything. It took a huge effort to hold back the flood of memories that rose, like nausea, in his throat.

He couldn't hold it back.

He turned suddenly, leaned one hand against a lamppost and threw up Mr Bradshaw's breakfast. He let out a great sob. What he wanted to do was fall to the ground and weep for Alice. He wanted her back. He wanted to be kind to her, to be gentle, to tell her he was sorry. He didn't want it to be left, between them, how it had been left. He wanted to put it right; to tell her that he loved her. That he always would.

That he was sorry from the bottom of his heart that he had shouted at her and made threats and thrown the gravel at the caravan.

That he would do anything, *anything,* for the opportunity to change things.

He stood beside the lamppost until he managed to get his emotions back under some kind of control. He wiped his mouth with the back of his hand and returned to the path. Finn was tactfully staring into the screen on the back of his camera. He produced a bottle of water from his jacket pocket and passed it to Will, who drank gratefully.

They walked on, their footsteps falling into sync. Finn kept gazing about him, occasionally lifting the camera to his eye to take a photograph or blowing out air between his lips as if this was the most impressive place he'd ever visited and not some shoddy, long-past-its-best little seaside town.

Will returned to Alice. He remembered how he once held her small hand on his lap while he tweezed a splinter from the base of her thumb, feeling a tenderness in his heart that he'd never felt before or since. He remembered his skin turning deep brown in the sun, walking twice as far as he needed to walk so he could divert along the service alleyway and go past Caravan 49 to catch a glimpse of Alice sunbathing, or eating her lunch beneath the shade of the parasol with a book propped open in front of her. When she went to the pool Will would find a nearby patch of garden that needed weeding, or a path that he could sweep while he watched her sleek head bobbing amongst the other heads, the Lilos and the inflatable balls. In the evenings, she showered in the communal block, and then she came back to her caravan to cook her supper, always leaving the door open, and Will used to smell onions frying, sometimes the sweet, spicy smell of curry. His gentle love, with the pale straps on her skin where the sun hadn't reached; that kind-hearted young woman who tolerated Marnie Morahan trailing after her like a shadow. He remembered lying beside her for the first time, on the rumpled sheets on her bed, his heart thumping and he knowing, somehow, that this was the best moment of his life, that it would never be surpassed, and he had been right.

He could never, *would* never, say any of this to Finn, or anyone. These memories belonged to him alone. He would not put them in the book. He did not know how he would write the book. How could he write dispassionately about someone he had loved with such passion? Someone he still loved? Someone whose memory would never let him go?

How could he tell Alice's story without disclosing how he had felt about her?

He would have to deny her again. He couldn't do that.

'She was in a bad way,' said Finn.

'Sorry?'

'Saoirse. When I saw her last night. She looked pretty sick.' He hesitated and then said: 'She said she was moving out of your flat. I told her she shouldn't be even thinking about it while she was so rough but she said she wanted to be gone before you were back.'

Will was silent.

'Maybe you could call her,' said Finn. 'Let her know that she should stay until she's better. Or tell her to wait until you're back so you can sort it out, whatever it is, that's gone wrong. I don't want to see you guys split up. You're good together.'

Will let the words wash over him. He didn't have room in his heart to worry about Saoirse.

They were close to the holiday park entrance. Beyond, Will saw that Mr and Mrs deVillars were standing together by the little holly bush shrine, both wrapped up well against the weather. The nurse was standing to one side. Mr deVillars was holding his wife's arm, and encouraging her to lay the flowers she was holding down beside the flowers that had been placed there the day before. Will couldn't hear what the old man was saying, but he felt a pang of sympathy when he saw how tenderly he guided his wife's arm, how patiently and gently he helped her.

'Who's that?' Finn asked quietly.

'The couple who owned the holiday park.'

'Excellent.' Finn raised the huge camera to his face and directed the lens towards the old couple. There followed a burst of loud clicks.

'Can't you do that more quietly?' Will muttered.

'Nope,' said Finn. He clicked again and a moment later Guy deVillars appeared. He pushed the camera lens roughly to one side.

'What are you doing? This isn't a press call, this is private.'

'Sorry, no offence intended,' said Finn.

Will stared at Guy. Superficially, Guy was in the right, but emotionally that counted for nothing. His rage surged.

'For goodness' sake,' Guy continued, his voice so upper class, so condescending, 'these are two elderly people trying to pay their respects with dignity in private. Could you at least have the decency to—'

Anger overtook Will. He stepped in front of Finn and pushed Guy violently backwards. Guy lost his balance and sat down heavily in the mud.

That was his fine wool coat ruined.

'Jesus, Will!' cried Finn.

'I know what you did!' Will said, leaning over Guy. 'I know what you did to Alice and I'm going to prove it!'

'Hey, Will, come on,' Finn tugged at Will's sleeve, 'there's no need to—'

'You think you've got away with it, don't you? But I know about your financial problems, Guy. I know about the mess you were in and I'm going to make sure the whole world knows about that, and how you stitched up your parents, and how you killed Alice!'

Guy tried to push himself up but his hands found no purchase in the mud. Other people were approaching, drawn to the raised voices. Finn's efforts to pull Will away became more urgent.

'Please, buddy, calm down!'

'I'm going to expose you, Guy deVillars!' Will cried, jabbing his finger in the direction of the other man's chest. 'I'm going to let the whole world know what kind of slime-ball you really are. You're going to pay for what you did!'

'Will! That's enough!' cried Finn. Guy pushed himself to his feet. The sleeves of his coat were soaked to the elbows.

Mr and Mrs deVillars had become aware of the ruckus, and were straining to see what was going on. Conscience was the only thing that held Will back from doing or saying anything more. He wanted to kill Guy, but he didn't want to distress his fragile mother when she was clearly so upset already.

40

After her agility run, Marnie sat in the car for some respite from the weather. Through the bare branches of the winter trees she could see the grey stone of a squat church tower, similar to the one in Severn Sands.

Marnie's mother had been buried in the churchyard there. Mr and Mrs deVillars had pulled strings to make this happen because plots close to the church were limited and there had been some resistance from John Morahan, for whom Denise's strong faith had always been a sore point. Eventually he'd agreed to a religious burial, but under sufferance. Marnie, with little knowledge of what any of this meant, had done her best to explain it to Alice.

They had been to the park stores to buy lemons and sugar. Alice was going to teach Marnie how to make lemonade. Alice listened carefully to everything that Marnie told her about Denise. It had only been a few months earlier, but the circumstances of her mother's death and the funeral were already blurred in Marnie's mind. Alice said that was normal. She said it was the way most people processed trauma. Marnie didn't understand what that meant, but she liked the sound of it.

'Have you been back to the grave to put flowers on it?' Alice had asked.

Marnie, who had not known such a thing was expected of her, had shaken her head.

'Then we'll go together,' Alice said.

This was typical Alice. She was the only person ever to encourage Marnie to talk about her mother. Everyone else tried not to talk about her, but for Alice, Denise wasn't a difficult or painful subject. She teased little anecdotes from Marnie, stories from her early childhood that Marnie had forgotten. Between them, they gave new life to memories; they kept Denise alive. This was a huge relief for Marnie, who had been so afraid of forgetting.

Alice gave Marnie a notebook and encouraged her to write and draw in it. She taught her how to press flowers. They worked together on the book, which was dedicated entirely to Denise. Soon it was full of little poems and pictures and wafer-thin buttercups; a small white feather, a list of the books that Denise had read to Marnie.

Alice and Marnie went together to the churchyard and found the grave. It wasn't hard; it was one of the newer ones. The earth on top of it was still mounded.

Last time she was there, at Denise's funeral, Marnie hadn't dared look into the hole. She had hung back, behind the bodies of the adults, dressed in black; horrified that this was really where they were going to put her mother. It had seemed ridiculous and obscene.

Going back, with Alice holding her hand, it hadn't felt frightening at all.

Denise's grave was quiet and green, covered over with new grass, buttercups, clover and daisies. Butterflies and bees buzzed around. A book was propped against the wooden marker at its head; a compilation of poems.

'Who put the book there?' Alice asked.

'I don't know.'

'Why would they do that?'

'Mummy liked that book.'

'She liked poetry?'

'Yes.'

'That's OK then. That's a nice gesture. It must have been someone who knew her well.'

It was sunny in the churchyard. In the far corner, an old man in overalls was filling a watering can from a tap. A robin perched on a gravestone and scratched its head with its foot. Marnie had expected to feel sad or scared but she didn't. She was calm.

Alice had brought some lilies. She stood for a long time looking down at the grave with the flowers in her hands. She was wearing her yellow sundress and a matching headband. Marnie had made an effort too. Alice had done her hair, and Marnie was wearing one of Alice's shirts over her shorts, and her mother's locket.

After a while, Alice said: 'Wait here.'

She disappeared across the churchyard, spoke for a moment or two to the old man and returned with a glass pickle jar filled with water. She put the lilies in the jar then tried to stand it on the grave but the stalks were too long and it kept tipping over so in the end she had to prop it against the wooden marker.

After that, Marnie and Alice sat together on the grass beside the grave. It was hot and quiet. The robin watched them pick daisies, and when they had a little pile, Alice chose one and made a split in its stalk with the side of her thumbnail, and Marnie passed her another. Together they made a chain, which they looped over the marker.

'Would your mummy have liked that?' Alice asked.

'She loved flowers. Some flowers. Not flowers in Cellophane.'

'What does that mean? What are flowers in Cellophane?'

'Big flowers,' Marnie said, describing the size of a shop bouquet with her arms. She did not know how else to explain them. 'She would like those,' she added, pointing to the lilies.

'Then we'll come another day and bring some more.'

When the shadow of the church fell over them, they stood up and dusted themselves down. They walked alongside the estuary together, back towards the holiday park, holding hands.

When they reached the cliffs where the fossil hunters used to come with their hammers and sieves, Marnie asked Alice: 'Would you like to see my secret cave?'

'I'd love to.'

So they'd gone to look and Alice had climbed up to see inside and had been impressed and observed that it was the perfect place for hiding precious objects.

Later, when Marnie was back at the caretaker's cottage, eating baked beans on toast off a plate on her lap in front of the TV with her father, she realised she didn't feel so lonely about Denise's dying any more. How could she, now that she had somebody with whom to share it?

41

'Fuck's sake. Will,' said Finn, 'you really lost it.'

'It was him,' Will said. 'Guy deVillars. He killed Alice.'

'You know that?'

'Yes.'

'For certain?'

'Yes!'

'How can you be so sure?'

'Because he was obsessed with her. He was literally crazy about her. He kept trying to find ways to be with her. And she had arranged to meet him the night she disappeared.'

'But I thought she was going out with you?'

'She was. I don't know why she agreed to see him. Probably to get him off her back. He was always pestering her.'

Finn whistled between his teeth.

'So, you saw them together that night?' he asked.

'I didn't actually see them. Alice told me to stay away from the caravan.'

'Oh.'

'She didn't want me to see Guy.'

'Maybe she just wanted a bit of time to herself.'

'I heard her saying she had a special date that night. And Marnie told me it was Guy.'

'Marnie?'

'This little kid who used to hang round Alice.'

'How did she know?'

'Alice told her. She told her everything.'

* * *

Finn and Will walked round the holiday park, and back up the side of the estuary, Finn taking photographs of the light and the water. They ate together in the Dolphin café and then Finn got back in his car and drove away. They hadn't spoken about Saoirse again. Will didn't know what Finn would tell her. He didn't care. He lingered on the seafront, waiting for something; he didn't know what. Clouds were blowing up the estuary. Sheets of grey rain curtained the sky, obscuring the Welsh coast, and the wind whipped across the water's surface making wide grey waves that rolled up towards the bridge. It wasn't like London, where there was always a warm shop or a museum or café where a person could take refuge. It was a different world.

The last time they were properly together, Will and Alice, he'd noticed that she wasn't wearing his necklace and she said she'd taken it off because she'd been swimming and she hadn't wanted to lose it in the pool.

'Put it on for me,' she'd said, and she'd kneeled on the caravan banquette with her back to him, holding up her hair so that he could fasten the clasp. He'd looked down at the back of her head, the frizz of tiny hairs at the base of her skull, the soft curves of her shoulders. He'd pressed his lips into her warm skin, then taken hold of the little metal tag at the top of the zip that held together the dress she was wearing between his thumb and forefinger and pulled it down so that the two sides of the dress opened and Alice's back was set free. He'd kissed her, the knobbles of her spine pressing against his lips and then he'd put his arms round her and held her breasts in his hands.

She'd turned and smiled at him over her shoulder and then she'd stood up and the dress had slithered down to the floor. 'Come on,' she'd said, and he'd kicked off his boots and she'd led him into the bedroom.

She'd lain on the bed, her legs slightly open and he'd been so aroused, so desperate that he'd almost fallen on top of her, his shorts tangled about his ankles as he found her, pressed into her; came almost at once.

After, they'd lain together and it had been so nice, so peaceful until Marnie had come to the door with Alice's laundry and Alice had pulled on some clothes and gone out to talk to her. Will had stayed on the bed, sleepy and satisfied, looking around the small bedroom in Caravan 49, Alice's things scattered about, and he'd never felt happier.

Until he heard her talking to Marnie.

Until he heard her lower her voice, and then he'd listened harder, wondering what she was trying to keep from him, and he'd heard the words 'special date' and then her shushing Marnie, telling her it was a secret.

All his happiness had come crashing down then. Before that moment he wouldn't have believed it possible for his emotions to flip so quickly from a state of near ecstasy to one of terror. Alice had just made love to him, and already she was making plans for seeing someone else, someone *special*, later that night!

He had known it was Guy straight away. When he'd challenged

Alice, she hadn't denied it *per se* and later he'd asked Marnie. At first Marnie said she didn't know who the date was, but when Will had lost his temper big-time she'd looked evasive and then said quietly: 'All I know is it's someone from the Big House.'

'Guy?' Will had demanded.

Marnie had squirmed.

'Marnie, is it Guy deVillars?'

'*I don't know!*'

'Well, who else could it be?'

Marnie muttered something.

'What?'

'They were talking earlier. Alice and him. She said she was going to see him later.'

'You're sure that's what she said?'

'Yes.'

'I knew it!' Will shouted. '*I knew it!*'

And so Will's worst suspicions had been confirmed, and although he'd wanted to know to the point of bullying Marnie into telling him, it had killed him to find out the truth. It was still killing him now.

If Guy was a 'special date', what had Will really been to Alice?

Had he been deluding himself that she cared for him, as he did for her?

The toxic mix of love, jealousy and regret raged in Will's heart. He'd been here a thousand times before. The paradox seemed irresolvable.

Alice had never said the words 'I love you' to Will, but in her smile and her eyes and her actions she had told him that she did. And she knew how he felt about Guy. She'd promised him a dozen times that there was nothing between them, nothing 'like that', yet still she had arranged to meet Guy that evening.

She shouldn't have lied.

Look how her deception had turned out.

Will stood up, and began to walk back along the seafront.

He remembered the feeling of Alice's hair tangled in his fingers, the soft down on her jawline, the gold studs she wore in the rim of her left ear, the sweet, musty taste of her breath. He wondered what she would be like now, if she had not disappeared, if she was here, with him. If they had stayed together, married, had kids – Alice had told him she wanted dozens of children – become settled, middle-aged. Would she still laugh like she used to laugh, still skip around, her arm linked through his? Would she have put on weight, run marathons, baked cakes, become an environmental activist?

Whatever she had become, he would have loved her.

The sea was lively, almost violent. Grey rainclouds scudded closer. There'd be a downpour when they reached this side of the water. Will's eyes tracked back towards the path and he saw two people coming towards him: a girl riding a pony and an older man with a terrier at his heels.

For a moment Will was confused. The girl looked exactly like Marnie and the man beside her was her father, John Morahan, with Trip the dog, only the man looked too old to be John. He was in pain, hunched over his stick, tapping his way along the seafront, and Trip must be long gone. It was John. The girl, Will realised, must be Marnie's daughter and the dog was the same dog that had been with Marnie the other night. It spotted Will and began to yap so vehemently that its front paws lifted off the concrete with every bark.

Will didn't want to have to talk to John, especially not after Marnie had told him that John believed Will was responsible for Alice's murder. He turned at once so that they could not see his face, climbed down the sea wall and walked along the grass, the rain soaking his trouser legs. From this lower level he could only see the top half of the young girl. She had Marnie's shoulders, Marnie's upright stance, her hair hanging straight down her back. She was sitting loose-limbed and long-legged on the fat little pony, holding the reins in one hand. The pony's hoofs clip-clopped on the paving slabs. The girl was chatting to her grandfather, telling him some convoluted story and he was nodding occasionally as if he was paying attention, but Will could tell that he was not. The dog still yapped.

'Shut up, TT,' John Morahan said. 'Be quiet.'

When the two of them were almost level with Will, they stopped. The girl, who was closer to Will, and almost above him, turned to look out over the estuary, one hand resting lightly on the pony's back. She was so close that Will, pressed up against the wall, could hear every word when she spoke.

'Look, Granddad, the rain's coming.'

'We'd best get back then.'

John's face was in profile, the same face it had always been. Handsome, large featured; the hair receding but still thick, stubble glistening around the jaw. Only now, there was something resigned in the slouch of John's shoulders, the way his head was inclined forwards on his neck.

They stood for a moment, looking out, and then the girl said: 'My hands are cold.'

John said, 'Put these on, Lucy,' and held up his gloves, and the girl replied: 'I don't want them,' and swatted his hand away. A brief argument followed, the two of them bickering in a friendly, half-hearted way; an easy way that John had never had with Marnie.

The pony stretched one leg forward and leaned its head down to scratch its knee. The girl looked down and saw Will lurking beneath the wall. She stared at him for a moment as if trying to place him, and then grinned. It was a smile Will hadn't seen in

42

The rain had blown in by the time Marnie returned to Severn Sands, great grey curtains sweeping across the estuary, and the tide was in too. She wouldn't be able to go to the cave that evening. The sun was washed out, sliding down a glowering sky.

Marnie noticed the curl of wood-smoke emerging from the chimney pot as she pulled the car up on the drive outside her cottage. That meant that her father was there.

Rather than face him straight away, she pulled up her hood and hurried round to the stable where she found Lucy brushing Scrumpy, who was eating hay from a net. He whinnied a greeting to Marnie and she scratched his whiskery chin. Seashell watched from her stall, one back hoof tilted in a relaxed posture. Lucy had put the heater on and it was cosy in the stable; the smell of hay and horses, the rain pattering on the roof and windows. Tessy sighed, turned round three times, and settled on the rug in front of the heater.

'How did you get on?' Lucy asked as Marnie shook raindrops from her coat.

Marnie held up two blue rosettes, two second places, and then added them to the stash of ribbons pinned to the corkboard at the back of the stable, won by mother and daughter at dog and pony shows.

Lucy paused, brush in hand. 'Well done, Tessy! Clever Mum!'

Marnie kissed her daughter's cheek, then picked up a blanket and began to fold it, tiny shards of hay floating in the air.

'Granddad's here,' said Lucy. 'We went for a walk. Well, I rode. It was nice.' A pause. 'We saw some man you used to know. When he saw us he jumped down off the sea wall and walked along the beach, trying to avoid us. Granddad said he was an arsehole but he used to be your friend.'

Will. So he was still here.

Marnie was tired suddenly. She longed for a bath and bed. She made a fuss of Mister and let him out into the paddock.

The gulls called and she remembered how the birds used to stand on the caravans at Channel View, using them as lookouts. From inside, their big, webbed feet made it sound as if an army was trampling on the roof. There was one particular gull that always stood on Alice's caravan, extending its throat, its long, sharp head, the beak open, screaming: Ach! Ach! Ach! The cry of the gulls had been part of the soundtrack to those burning hot days, one after the other; so hot that the air shimmered queasily and nothing was in focus and you could never be quite sure if you'd seen something or not. She recalled children from the holiday club running through the site on a treasure hunt, wearing their Severn Boar T-shirts, bright blue peaked caps keeping the sun off their faces, their voices high and screeching. Mr deVillars distributing raffle tickets amongst the holidaymakers for free entry into the Saturday evening draw at the clubhouse, first prize a family meal for four, drinks not included. Angharad with a tray of glasses in her arms and Marnie carrying the laundry basket, sequins on the scarlet dress folded on top reflecting pinpricks of red light.

Something else, in the haze: her father in his overalls, changing the gas tanks outside Caravan 79, which was the caravan in the same alignment, but the next row down to Alice's. His outline coming into focus. Not changing the gas tanks after all; not doing anything, but standing there in his overalls, the top half down, the sleeves tied around his waist, and an old T-shirt, once white but now grey and torn, oil-spattered and dark with sweat under the arms. What was he doing?

It wasn't the same day. Not the laundry day, not the day Alice went missing, but a different day that Marnie was remembering. She'd come to find Alice and her route was blocked by her father standing in the shade of Caravan 79, hidden from Alice's view. Alice was outside her caravan, sitting at the table in the shade of the parasol, writing. The Quality Street tin was beside her, and the book about the history of the caravan park. She was oblivious to the man standing so still and quiet in the shade, watching her.

There had been something about her father's stance that day, something about the intensity of the way that he gazed at Alice that had scared Marnie. She had turned and scuttled away without him ever realising she was there.

* * *

When Lucy was finished in the stables, she and Marnie returned to the cottage together. Lucy went upstairs to run a bath and Marnie went into the kitchen. She deduced from the debris that her daughter and her father had made cheesy beans on toast for lunch. Tiny yellow curls of grated cheese were on the counter top and in the well of the hob. Three empty beer cans were lined up beside the sink.

She tidied up, filled the kettle and went to the living-room door. Her father was sitting in the easy chair watching a quiz show on television with the volume turned up painfully high. TT was curled in the corner of the settee. He pricked an ear, opened an eye to look at Marnie and his tail thumped against the cushion but otherwise he didn't move.

'David Moyes!' Marnie's father yelled at the TV, leaning forward in his chair, beer can in hand. 'The answer's *David Moyes!*'

'Who's David Moyes?' Lucy called from the landing, laughing.

Marnie pushed the door shut and leaned against it. The noise! She closed her eyes for a moment, and returned to the kitchen. The kettle boiled and switched itself off. Marnie opened the fridge, took out a can of Thatchers Gold and popped the tab. She took a drink and then opened the drawer where she kept her special things. She reached her hand into the drawer for the photograph of Alice on the carousel but at that instant she heard Lucy say: 'Mum?' behind her.

Marnie turned and pushed the drawer shut with her hip.

43

The first raindrops fell hard, slicing from a glowering sky, bouncing on the pavement. In his attempts to avoid John Morahan, Will had gone further than he'd meant to. He was a long way from the town. He quickened his pace, keeping his head down, his hands in his pockets. As he ploughed through the downpour a large, pale-coloured car pulled up alongside, and the window was automatically lowered from inside. The driver leaned across, towards him.

It was Edward deVillars. Will expected a rebuke, but the old man spoke in a friendly voice.

'Will? Where are you going?'

'Er... Bradshaw's. Mr Bradshaw's guesthouse.'

'I'll give you a lift. We're both heading in the same direction and you're getting soaked. Hop in.'

Will hesitated. He didn't feel comfortable at the prospect of spending time with Mr deVillars, but good manners and a lifetime of deferring to the man made it difficult to refuse.

'Hurry up, old chap, or the rain will mark the leather.'

Will opened the door and climbed in.

Inside the car was warm and dry. Mr deVillars was dapper in

fawn trousers, a navy-blue blazer and a cravat. His white hair was oiled, his nails clipped. His skin, always slightly inclined towards rosacea, was pink against the white of his hair. He smelled of citrus and sandalwood and looked like an old-fashioned movie star. He was exactly as he'd always been.

The old man pressed a button that locked the doors and then pulled the car away, the wipers swishing smooth as a heartbeat; the engine purring. There was hardly any sense of movement as they headed, slowly, along the road.

Will thought he'd better take the initiative. 'Sorry,' he said, 'about earlier. I didn't mean to upset you or Mrs deVillars.'

'We're all a bit out of sorts,' said Mr deVillars. 'These are unprecedented times.'

'Yes.'

Will stared ahead, through the windscreen. He could not think of a single thing to say that wouldn't be weighted; not a single question he could ask.

The wipers smeared the raindrops across the glass. Will glanced at Mr deVillars. The old man was looking at the road. There was something of steel in his expression.

'Actually, I've changed my mind,' Will said, 'it's really kind of you, but if you don't mind, I'd rather walk after all. I could do with the air.'

Either Mr deVillars didn't hear, or he chose to ignore this.

'This situation is difficult for all of us,' he said. 'Especially my poor Camille. She doesn't understand what's going on, but she senses the tension. It's not good for her.'

'I'm sure it's not. Would you stop the car, Mr deVillars?'

'Funny thing happened this morning, Will. A journalist called. She was asking questions about Guy. Accusations have been made, apparently. She wouldn't reveal her source, but Guy says you and she were once a couple. Is that right?'

'Er... if you're talking about Emily Richards then, yes.' Will's fingers slid towards the door handle.

'It's centrally locked,' Mr deVillars said without taking his eyes off the road. 'Did you put Ms Richards onto Guy? Was it you?'

There seemed little point lying.

'I told Emily that Alice had arranged to meet Guy in her caravan on the evening she died,' he said. 'Yes.'

'So, you believe Guy was responsible for what happened to that unfortunate young woman?'

'Logic would suggest...'

'Guy is a gentleman.'

'With respect, you would say that, wouldn't you? You're his father.'

'And I know my son. Guy is incapable of that kind of violence... the kind of violence necessary to... Well. You know.'

'It's your job to think the best of him.'

'I *know* him. I know he didn't lay a finger on the girl.'

They had reached the far edge of the holiday park. As they passed, a bulldozer raised its bucket high and brought it down on the roof of one of the few remaining caravans, breaking the structure's back. Will heard a dreadful creaking and snapping, like the breaking of old bones. He felt the pain inside his body, as if some part of him was being damaged too.

'I had a long chat with Ms Richards,' said Mr deVillars. 'I told her there were some alternative theories about who might be responsible for Alice Lang's death. I asked if you'd been open with her about your movements that night.'

'I was with my mother.'

'Were you? All night?'

'Yes.'

'Strange then, how you were seen behaving aggressively outside Caravan 49.'

Will was shocked into silence.

'For your information, Will,' said Mr deVillars slowly, 'my son wasn't in Severn Sands on the evening the girl disappeared. He'd gone to the music festival in Weston-super-Mare. Afterwards, he and his friends drove up into the Mendips and camped out near Cheddar Gorge. The following day they were at the festival again. Guy didn't get back here until lunchtime on the Sunday.'

The wipers moved backwards and forwards. A small leaf was caught under the rubber flap of the left one. It made a smear on the screen with each pass.

'Guy's alibi was checked by the police and corroborated. He shared a tent with two friends. It would have been impossible for him to get back to Channel View, do away with the girl, and get back to the campsite before morning. Absolutely impossible. So, whatever happened to her, it was nothing to do with him.'

He paused for a moment, then continued: 'I told your journalist friend that any more of this sort of nonsense and I'll be having a word with our solicitor and her editors. And if I were you, Will, I'd tread very carefully.'

Will watched the leaf on the windscreen. It couldn't be true. Guy must have gone to the festival after he killed Alice. He must have manipulated the truth somehow, changed the timeline...

When Mr deVillars next spoke, the tone of his voice had changed.

'I knew this news would affect you profoundly, William. You never could hide your feelings. Heart-on-your-sleeve kind of fellow, aren't you? I know that at the time you tried to keep it quiet, you and your mother, but everyone knew you were mad about that girl. Everyone knew how possessive you could be. Everyone saw you mooning after her, like a dog.'

Will felt as if he was being circled. He had no idea where this was going.

The old man was quiet for a moment, then he seemed to change tack once again. 'Camille and I have followed your career, you know. We've bought all your books. How many is it now? Ten? Eleven?'

'The twelfth was out in November.'

'You've done well for yourself. Made your mother proud. We're pleased for you.'

He turned the car into the Aust Road, one wheel splashing through a puddle, spraying the pavement and pulled up outside the guesthouse. He turned off the engine and they sat for a moment, condensation forming on the inside of the windows. The doors were still locked.

'Listen to me, Will,' Mr deVillars said slowly, 'you need to be careful. You're standing on very shaky ground. Guy has a watertight alibi for the evening the girl was murdered, whereas you...' He let the words hang for a moment and then said: 'I know that John Morahan found you making threats outside Caravan 49 that evening. I know he took you back to your chalet. I know that you, your mother, John, all lied to the police about this. That's an offence in itself. All three of you would be in trouble if *that* came to light.'

Will said nothing. His mouth was dry.

'I also know that you went out again, Will, in the early hours. You were seen staggering around the funfair, out of your head.'

'How...? Who?'

'That doesn't matter. What matters is *you* were in the park at the time the girl disappeared. You were so drunk you didn't know what you were doing, you were raging incoherently...'

'I didn't hurt Alice.'

'Or you don't remember hurting her?'

Will suppressed a groan. He couldn't have hurt Alice. He couldn't have. He loved her. Even drunk as he was, he wouldn't have hurt her. No.

'You see the problem,' said Mr deVillars, 'if people go about making accusations about other people?'

The old man pressed a switch and unlocked the car doors. Will was in such a hurry to get out that he fell onto his hands and knees on the pavement.

44

As Marnie walked the dogs that afternoon she was relieved to see that most of the media pack had gone away. There was nothing left for them to see. It had been a brief invasion.

She walked towards the Big House. Mrs deVillars was standing at the top window, beneath the gable, gazing over the old holiday park.

The last parts of the flume were being demolished and the remains of its carcass stacked ready to be taken away. Posts and tapes marked out the spaces for new houses.

Marnie paused to let the dogs sniff at the verge when she heard footsteps behind her. It was Gabriel. She gave a tentative smile.

'We've been waiting for the police to finish,' Gabriel said. 'They've done what they need to do. We can't go near where we... where they... you know. But apart from that we can get back to work. Head office will be happy.' He leaned down to make a fuss of Tessy. The shoulders of his bulky yellow coat were slick with rain drops.

'Did you find the tree I left for you?' he asked. 'I hope it helps make up for the old one. It's not the same, I know, but it was the least I could do.'

He took off his hard hat and scratched his head. His hair, brown and curly, had been flattened by the rim. 'I thought you'd like it,' he said. 'You're like Elena. You like the same things she used to like.'

They stood there in silence, side by side. It wasn't awkward for Marnie to be silent with Gabriel as it sometimes was with other people.

'You know, if you ever need anything,' Gabriel said, 'you can call me. Or text. Whatever.'

Marnie pulled her coat tighter around her. She looked at the ground.

'If you give me your phone,' said Gabriel, 'I'll put my number in it for you.'

She gave him her phone and he took a pair of glasses out of a case in his pocket and put them on. He added his name and number to her contacts, then gave the phone back to her.

'Would you like a lift home?' Gabriel asked. 'The dogs could go in the back of the van.'

She shook her head, but smiled to show that she was grateful anyway. She pointed to the dogs. Their paws were filthy. Gabriel looked as if he was about to say he didn't mind, but held himself back. She could tell he didn't want to push her.

They parted and Marnie walked away, back towards the town. She had a small, private smile on her lips and as she walked Alice came back to her, and walked beside her.

Marnie would have liked to tell Alice about Gabriel just as she would like, one day, to tell Gabriel about Alice. Only now wasn't the time.

* * *

The last morning of Alice's life hadn't started differently from any other. It was hot, indistinguishable from the days in the weeks before. Sunlight streamed through the gap between Marnie's bedroom curtains. She'd woken with the same disconnect she'd felt every day since her mother's death. She opened her eyes and for a moment it seemed as if everything was normal, as it should be, and then she remembered that Denise wasn't there.

Marnie's sheets were greasy and crumpled. The beds in the caretaker's cottage hadn't been changed in ages. Marnie knew sheets and pillowcases were supposed to be laundered once a week, she knew the clean laundry should be dried on the line, then ironed and folded onto the top shelf of the airing cupboard at the top of the stairs. She knew how the washing machine worked, but there was no detergent in the box that sat at the side of the machine. It was an industrial-sized box, one of those her father ordered to stock the dispensers in the laundry room at the holiday park. It was the same box that had been in use when Denise died and it was still there, with its plastic scoop for measuring the detergent at its base, but there was no washing powder left. There hadn't been any for weeks and Marnie couldn't bring herself to mention this to John because no matter how she framed the sentence in her mind it sounded like a criticism. They had never run out of soap powder before, and if she raised the subject it would be like saying: 'Mummy isn't here and nothing is as it should be.' So she said nothing, and she slept on sheets that smelled musty. She was used to them now.

That morning, when Marnie went downstairs, her father wasn't there but Trip was lying on the kitchen floor panting. His water bowl was empty. Marnie filled it for him and then she looked for something to eat, but there was nothing she wanted and the freezer door was frozen shut because nobody had defrosted it so she couldn't check to see if there were any ice cubes for her throat. She drank some tap water from a cup and picked a bottle of aspirin from the kitchen window ledge, opened it, shook out its contents. Only two tablets were left. She put them in her mouth and sucked them, letting them dissolve on her tongue. Then she went upstairs, changed into her shorts and T-shirt and put on her daps.

Taking Trip with her, she crossed the road, went into Channel View holiday park. It was busy. The heat drew more people in during the summer, especially to the funfair. Probably they thought the rides might cool them down. Even at 10 a.m. it was boiling hot and booming with noise, people everywhere, more than normal. Marnie drifted round the park. She sat in the kiosk for an hour, taking money, to give one of the travelling men a break. Or perhaps it was Will who had asked her to cover for him. She couldn't remember. Her father materialised, he didn't say where he'd been. He told Marnie she looked poorly.

'Go home,' he'd said, 'get out of the sun.' He whistled to Trip. 'You stay with me, TH.'

Marnie went back across the road, to the caretaker's cottage. She drank some more water. She went into the bathroom, opened her mouth wide and tried to look down her throat in the mirror, to see if it was bleeding or covered in scars, but it was impossible to see; the mirror was dirty, speckled with toothpaste and crusted dots of shaving foam. She pressed her fingertips into the soft skin beneath her jawbone. She tried to think what Denise would tell her to do and she missed her mother so badly that she wanted to cry, only her throat was too sore for that.

Marnie needed help. She crossed the road to the Big House in search of Mrs deVillars, who was always good for a kind word.

She found her in the garden of the Big House, sitting beneath the shade of one of the huge old beech trees, her long legs sliding out from beneath the fringe of a cheesecloth kaftan, a sketch pad on her lap and coloured pencils scattered around her. She was drinking something pink. The drink was long and cool and fruity in a tall glass full of ice. Marnie stared at the ice, coveting it. The grass that used to be the lawn was dried up and dead, yellow like straw. The bushes and shrubs were wilting. All the water collected over-winter was being used to keep the flowerbeds in the holiday park spritely; there was nothing left for the Big House garden.

'Hello, sweetie,' said Mrs deVillars. 'Is everything all right?'

'I'm hot.'

'Aren't we all!' Mrs deVillars laughed and then she held the cool back of her hand against Marnie's forehead. 'Um,' she said. 'You *are* hot. It might be heatstroke.' She took another drink then offered the glass to Marnie. 'Hold this against your face.'

Marnie did as she suggested. The glass was blissfully cool. She rolled it along her forehead.

Camille deVillars laughed. 'Is that better?'

'Yes.'

'Heatstroke then.'

Mrs deVillars took Marnie into the Big House, airless and gloomy. Canvas bags and a rucksack were piled in the hall: supplies for a camping trip.

In the cool of the boot room Camille deVillars squeezed sunscreen onto the palm of her hand then patted it onto Marnie's exposed skin. She found a moth-eaten straw hat for her to wear.

'That'll keep the sun off your face,' she said. 'You need to keep drinking plenty and stay out of the sun, OK?'

She gave her a carton of apple juice, which she said was good for rehydration. Marnie obediently drank the juice and, definitely feeling a bit better, went back to the holiday park. As she was walking past the service area, she met Alice Lang, who was leaning against the wall outside the launderette, one foot pressed against it, flowers tumbling from the planters behind her, talking to Guy. Alice asked Marnie if Marnie would wait for her laundry that was in the tumble drier in the launderette. And that's what Marnie had done. While she was in the laundry room, it occurred to her that she could steal some detergent to take back home to the caretaker's cottage to wash the bedding. So she swiped a box of Daz that one of the holidaymakers had left on top of a machine and hid it amongst the flowers in the bed outside. She never went back to collect it.

45

Will let himself into the guesthouse. He stood on the coir *Welcome* mat by the front door, Mr deVillars' words ringing in his ears.

What if there was some truth in what the old man had said? What if Will had hurt Alice but had been too drunk to remember? What if *he* was the one responsible for her death?

No. *No!* He must not go down that rabbit hole. He mustn't.

Everything was so quiet in the guesthouse that the tick-tocking of the clock in the hall seemed obscenely loud. Will stood perfectly still, giving Mr deVillars time to drive away. When enough minutes had elapsed, he peered through the small hall window. The car was gone.

Will turned back into the house.

'Hello!' he called. There was no response. 'Hello! Mr Bradshaw! Hello!'

He listened hard. He heard nothing. Not the creak of a floorboard above him. No movement. Nothing.

For good measure, he picked up the guest hand-bell on the radiator shelf and rang it as hard as he could. Chimes echoed up the stairwell and bounced from the walls, but nobody came. Will had the house to himself. Thank the actual fuck.

He had been so shaken by the encounter with Mr deVillars that the first thing he did was slip into Mr Bradshaw's living room and help himself to a large swig from one of the two decanters on the silver tray on the cabinet. Its contents were sweet and syrupy – sherry, probably – but the alcohol hit Will's bloodstream instantaneously, for which he was grateful, and soon his heartrate began to calm. He took another swig and then wiped the rim with his sleeve, replaced the stopper and put the decanter back where he'd found it. He breathed deeply, trying to process what he'd been told.

Mr deVillars knew that John Morahan had found him outside Caravan 49 the night Alice disappeared and taken him back to his mother's chalet.

Someone had heard his drunken threats.

Someone knew he'd gone out for a second time in the early hours.

Who could it have been? One of the travellers? A holidaymaker? Who?

Will was sorely tempted to go into Mr Bradshaw's kitchen and check if there was any beer in the fridge, but he resisted the temptation and went back up to his room. He locked the door, turned on the TV for company and lay down on the bed, on his side, like a child. He'd done everything he could to bring back the hours he couldn't remember from the night Alice disappeared – he'd even undergone hypnotherapy. But he'd drunk so much that evening that he'd blacked out, and alcohol blackouts, he'd been told, inhibit the formation of memories. He couldn't remember because there were no memories. Those hours were gone from Will's mind for ever. Nothing would ever bring them back.

He remembered the 'before' clearly enough. He remembered it

with crystal clarity: the aftermath of his lovemaking with Alice, the bed, the rumpled sheets, his fingers playing with Alice's hair, Marnie's small voice at the door.

'A special date,' Alice had said to Marnie. Or maybe: 'A very special date,' or 'I'm seeing somebody special,' whatever... she needed the scarlet dress because she wanted to look her best for whoever it was who was coming. And 'Shh!' she'd whispered to Marnie. 'It's a secret!' Meaning she didn't want Will to know about it because it wasn't as if anyone else was likely to overhear! Lying in the bed behind the flimsy partition wall, a few yards away, Will's blood had run cold.

Only a few minutes earlier he and Alice had been lazily planning how they would go travelling. Will hadn't been quite sure if Alice was being serious but he'd gone along with everything she suggested, deliberately avoiding mentioning obstacles such as his university place. 'You'll need a passport,' Alice had told Will and he'd promised he'd go to the post office in Severn Sands in the morning to pick up an application form. They'd been talking about Thailand and India; about sunsets and elephants; about street food and exotic flowers and sleeping on beaches; full moon parties, hiring mopeds and disappearing down dirt tracks. Will didn't know how they were going to afford the plane tickets, but Alice had told him not to worry.

'Fate will see us right!' she'd said.

Then Marnie had come with the laundry and everything had changed.

Afterwards, after Marnie had left, Alice came back into the bedroom. She was holding a glass of water, which she offered to Will, who shook his head.

'Marnie is such a little sweetheart,' she said.

She slipped back onto the bed, put her small hand on Will's

stomach, the fingers tangling in the damp hair beneath his navel, and although he couldn't help but respond, he didn't want to. He moved away from her. The room was so small that there wasn't space to stand up on his side of the bed. Instead he shuffled to the end and reached down for his boxers.

'Oh!' Alice said. 'Do you have to go?'

He nodded. He couldn't bring himself to speak to her.

'Is something wrong?' she asked, and he saw a flicker of panic cross her face that she immediately disguised, turned into an expression of concern. But it was enough for him to know that she was wondering if he'd overheard what she'd said to Marnie. The fact that she didn't immediately explain, or laugh it off, was, to him, absolute proof that she was hiding something from him. Not that he needed any more proof.

'Where are you going?' Alice asked, sitting up on the bed, one leg on the floor, the other on the bed, bent at the knee, so that he could see between the legs of the towelling shorts. Her hair was all tousled. She had never looked sexier.

'I have to work,' he said, and then he added, as a test, 'I'll come back later. We can do something this evening.'

'No,' she said. 'No, not this evening. I'm busy.'

'Doing what?'

'Nothing,' she said, tucking her hair behind her ear. She picked absent-mindedly at a fingernail.

'Busy doing nothing?' he asked coldly, and Alice shrugged.

He'd left her and gone back to work in the funfair gardens; he'd been deadheading flowers, cutting back plants that had grown leggy or twiggy or gone to seed and with every snip of the secateurs he'd grown angrier and more afraid until in the end he couldn't hold his emotions in and he'd gone back to Caravan 49.

He couldn't be sure what time it was. Evening was coming in, the dew was settling on the grass in the way that it does on late summer evenings, previewing the approaching autumn, and the air was midgy. Families, fresh from the shower, the children's hair combed while it was wet, were making their way across the site from the caravans to the bar and the holiday club because there was a family fun show every Friday evening and it was always popular. The site was unusually quiet because so many people had caught the coach to Weston-super-Mare for the beach festival. Will had gone in the opposite direction, away from the bar and towards Caravan 49. He'd seen that the lights were on inside but the curtains were drawn and the door was closed. He'd strode up to the door and hammered on it with his fist.

'Alice, it's me! Open the door.'

She opened it. Nobody else was in the caravan, not yet, but she'd tidied up and candles were burning in little glass jars on the ledges, and there were flowers in a jar on the table – flowers she'd obviously picked from the gardens in the funfair – and she'd covered the lamp with a pink and green shawl with spangles sewn around the edges so it gave off a soft, romantic light. Two glasses were on a tray on the kitchen counter, and worst of all, Will could see the top of a champagne bottle poking out of the sink. Although he couldn't see, he just knew that Alice had filled the washing up bowl with ice, that she was cooling the bottle ready to serve the champagne to whoever it was who was coming.

She'd never bought champagne for him.

She'd never picked flowers.

He stood on the step and took all this in before he even looked at Alice. She was barefoot and her toenails had been painted blood red, to match the sequins on her scarlet dress, and there was a line of crimson eye shadow above her green eyes, and a velvet ribbon in her hair. She'd done something to her face, made it up so that she looked older and more sophisticated. Her lips were fuller, her cheeks were flushed, she was breathing quickly with nervous agitation. She was wearing the necklace Will had given her.

'Will, you can't come in. I told you I was busy,' she said at once, pre-empting his questions.

'Who is he?' Will asked. 'Who are you seeing?'

'It's none of your business.'

'But it is my business, of course it's my business! Alice, you're mine! You're my girl!'

'I'm nobody's girl!' Alice retorted angrily. 'I'm nobody's business. Go away, Will. Leave me alone. I don't have time for this now.'

'You're sending me away?'

'Yes!' She moved to shut the caravan door and he held out his hand to stop her. 'Will!' she cried. 'Stop this! Stop being so childish! Tonight's important to me!'

'And you don't think this afternoon... what we did, the things we talked about, you don't think *that* was important?'

'That was then and this is now. I can't talk about us now. Please go away.'

'I won't!'

'Look,' her tone softened, became conciliatory, desperate, 'I'll meet you after. Tell me where to meet you.'

'Down by the estuary.'

'OK. Later, I'll walk down to the estuary,' she said. 'I'll find you and then I'll explain.'

'Explain about you drinking champagne with your special date? Explain about you fucking him?'

'For God's sake, Will, you're behaving like a brat!'

'If you send me away now, then we're over!'

'Good! Because I didn't realise you were still such a child. Get your hand off the door.'

'Not until you tell me what's going on.'

'Nothing's going on. And even if there was, it's my life, it's nothing to do with you!'

'You're mine!' Will cried, desperate. 'You *love* me!'

'Will, *stop it!*'

She stared at him coldly, her eyes furious, cheeks flushed. Will had never seen her like that before. 'Go away,' she said. 'Go away now or else this really is the end of us. *I mean it!*'

Will moved his hand from the door frame. He was panting. His heart was racing. He wanted to fall down on his hands and knees and beg her; to convince her of how desperate he was not to lose her. He was so distraught he'd have done anything at that moment for a kind word from her, a word of reassurance, a signal that things were going to be all right between them. He would have driven a knife between his own ribs, but some small, rational part of him knew that he needed to stay calm.

'You'll come to the estuary?' he asked in a quieter voice.

'Yes. I said I would.' Her voice was calmer too.

'I'll sit by the path and wait for you.'

She'd given a small nod. Will couldn't be sure, now, if it was acquiescence or merely the desire to be rid of him. At the time he'd held onto it as a signal that she would come; that they would end the day as a couple, close again, happy, or at least that there was a chance that was what might happen.

'Alice,' he'd said, 'Alice, listen, this man... whoever it is, you won't...'

She'd shut the door. Shut it in his face. Even now, two and a half decades later, Will remembered the impotence he felt at that point, the frustration, the humiliation. He'd reached down and picked up a handful of gravel and thrown it as hard as he could at the door. Childish and petulant, stupid, but he couldn't help himself. He knew the clattering of the little stones would be loud inside the caravan.

'Alice, listen to me!' he'd shouted. '*Listen to me...*'

He'd felt a tug at his sleeve. He looked down. It was Marnie. She'd held a finger to her lips.

'You mustn't,' she'd said.

Then she'd taken his hand and led him away.

46

Marnie was almost within touching distance of home when she saw the police car turn into the road that led to the retirement estate.

She took a short cut through the ginnel and arrived in time to see the car pull up outside her father's bungalow. Eric Clapton was playing again, 'Lay Down Sally' not at as great a volume as 'Layla', but still loud enough for the words to be distinguishable from thirty yards away. Marnie hurried down the road as two officers got out of the patrol car and headed towards her father's front door. She reached the end of the path just as the officers rang the doorbell. Inside the bungalow TT yapped an enthusiastic response.

A moment later, John opened the door, the volume of the music rising several decibels as he did so. He showed no surprise at the sight of the two officers, nor Marnie standing just behind them.

'Come in,' he said. 'I've been expecting you.' He nodded towards Marnie. 'This is my daughter. Is it OK if she comes in too?'

'Certainly,' one of the officers replied.

'Join the party,' said John. 'Why not?'

The police stepped inside and Marnie followed. She put Mister into the bedroom on his own and her other two dogs in the kitchen, then went into the living room where the officers were waiting with John standing hunched in front of his chair, TT in his arms. The television, as always, was tuned to a sports channel, the commentary fighting against Clapton's vocals. Marnie picked up the controller and turned the TV off, and then she lifted the arm from the record player. The silence that followed was so intense she heard the blood pumping in her ears.

'Why don't we all sit down?' said the male officer. 'This is an informal chat, nothing to worry about.'

John, obediently, sat on his recliner. The officers perched side by side on the small sofa.

Marnie hovered behind her father's chair, looking down on his head, at the black, curly hair that surrounded his tonsure, the skin tanned tobacco brown, the ears jutting out. He was clutching TT with one big hand, smoothing the dog's head and neck with the other, flattening his ears. Marnie could tell from the rhythm that John was stressed.

'We need your help with something, Mr Morahan,' the male officer continued. 'We're trying to establish the layout of the Channel View funfair so we can work out where exactly the bones were buried in relation to the rides. We hope that'll give us a clearer idea of what might have happened.' He took out a folded piece of paper and looked about him for somewhere to display it. Marnie stepped forward to clear an ashtray and several mugs from the small table. The officer opened up the paper and put it on the table. It was a crude, hand-drawn map.

'Here's the road and here's what's left of the boundary fence,' he indicated lines on the paper, 'and the foundations for the carousel are here... This is where the human remains were found.' He indicated an area. John's head was lowered, concentrating on the little dog.

'Mr Morahan?'

'That there was part of the gardens,' said John Morahan, apparently without even looking at the paper. 'A flowerbed.'

'And can you remember what was planted there at the time Alice Lang went missing?'

'Roses, delphiniums, sweet william.'

'And who looked after the gardens?'

'I did,' said John gruffly, speaking into his lap.

'By yourself?'

'I had help.'

'Can you tell us who?'

'Will Jones. He helped when he wasn't studying. You'd have to ask Mr deVillars who else. He'll have all the records of who was employed and when.'

'So... in late August, at the time of Alice's disappearance, what would have been happening in this flowerbed?'

'The Michaelmas daisies were getting ready to bloom. The lilies were good. Roses were still going. Zinnias.'

Dahlias, thought Marnie.

'Dahlias,' said her father. 'It was a good year for dahlias; a dry summer. We had to keep watering.'

'So you'd have noticed if anyone had disturbed the flowerbeds?'

'I'd have noticed.'

'But would anyone have noticed if *you* had changed things around?'

'Of course they bloody would have! You can't go digging up established plants in the middle of summer. For one thing the ground was solid, parched. It was like rock. And...' he trailed off, remembering something. 'The willow. We took out the willow that summer.' He sat up straighter, tapped his fingertips on his knee. 'There was an old willow hanging over the pond. It had died; couple of dry summers had finished it off and we took it out.'

Marnie remembered now. There had been a digger...

'We hired in a mini-digger,' John said, 'for a couple of days to dig out the roots. They were invasive, damaging the path on the other side of the fence.'

'So, there was a hole already dug?'

'A bloody huge hole. We'd started filling it in. We'd covered the base with rubble and then ordered in some topsoil for over. We'd bought an ornamental cherry to replace the willow...'

'So someone could have used the digger to clear the rubble and hide a body beneath it and then push the rubble back?'

John nodded.

'Was the hole obvious?'

'Only if you knew it was there. It was at the back, behind the flowers. If you didn't know the willow used to be there, you wouldn't have known about the hole.'

'So the holidaymakers, for example, wouldn't have been aware of it?'

'No.'

'But staff at the holiday park would have?'

'Yes.'

'And this area, was it far enough away from the caravans for activity to have taken place at night without disturbing the campers?'

'Yes. That was the point. We had to work when the funfair was shut. You couldn't have machinery like that operating with kids running around. So we'd wait until the funfair was closed, then use the digger.'

'Do you have any photographs, by any chance?' the male officer asked. 'Of this particular spot as it used to be?'

'The brochures,' John said with a nod to Marnie. 'They're under my bed.'

Marnie went into the bedroom. Mister was in the exact same spot where she'd left him.

She kneeled down and reached under her father's bed. She pulled out a battered old suitcase, a cardboard box full of knick-knacks brought from the caretaker's cottage and never unpacked, a fishing box and several old carrier bags full of junk. Right in the centre was a pile of brochures, tied with string, for Channel View holiday camp, one for each year from when John became caretaker, until the brochures went digital. Marnie had fond memories of these publications. She used to turn their pages compulsively, trying to find her mother in the old photographs because she was there, in a couple of them, standing like a little ghost amongst the holidaymakers, a small, pretty woman with her hair tied back.

Now Marnie sat back on her heels and extracted the brochure for the year Alice went missing. She turned the pages until she found the pictures of the funfair, and there was the flowerbed in question, gloriously full of blooms, the bright colours enhancing the jewelled paintwork of the Bordelaise carousel. The photograph had been taken the summer before, and the willow tree was obviously dying then, its leaves sparse and yellow, its fronds thinning like the hair of an old man.

She took the brochure back into the living room and passed it to the female officer, who showed the picture to her colleague.

'That's great,' she said, 'really helpful. Thank you. We'll need to take this, Mr Morahan, if that's OK with you.'

Marnie's father shrugged his assent.

Then she said: 'When you spoke to our colleagues twenty-four years ago, you said you were at home in the caretaker's cottage for the whole evening on the date that Miss Lang disappeared.'

'That's right.' John nodded to Marnie. 'She was sick; tonsillitis. She fell asleep under the flume, late afternoon.'

'I remember the flume,' said the female officer. She smiled. 'It was a great ride. Everyone got wet.'

'It was built on scaffolding,' John explained. 'There was a

hollow space underneath where Marnie used to hide. When she... when we couldn't find her, I guessed she'd be there. I carried her back to the caretaker's cottage and put her to bed.'

Marnie had vague memories of being moved, of the jolting of her body in her father's arms; whispers, voices around the two of them as the day faded.

'What time was this?'

'Eight-ish. Nine, maybe. I'd have had a better idea when I was first questioned.'

TT jumped off John's lap and lay down on the rug by the radiator. Marnie's father's hands were clasped. The tip of one index finger was tapping against the knuckle of the other. Otherwise he was composed. She could hear a faint whining from Mister in the bedroom.

'And you stayed with your daughter all night?'

'Yep,' said John Morahan. 'That's right. I did.'

Across the room, Marnie signed to her father.

I woke up that night. You weren't in the cottage.

He looked at her long and hard as if he was weighing up whether or not to tell her something.

They stared at one another. He was stronger. She turned away first.

* * *

While Marnie's father was showing the police out, she went back to the bedroom to tidy up, pushing the clutter back under his bed. One of the old carrier bags had split and its contents spilled out: documents and cards.

She collected them up. They were condolence cards sent to her father after her mother's death. Marnie remembered the envelopes arriving on the doormat in the caretaker's cottage, dozens of them.

John had opened them, but hadn't put the cards up. Marnie had never had a chance to look at them before; now she took a few moments to read the sentiments inside. It was soothing to read what people had written; kind words about her mother; sympathy and good wishes.

Inside one of the cards, along with the thoughts and prayers, was a newspaper cutting. Marnie unfolded it, turned it over so she could read the headline.

Beloved mum in overdose tragedy.

Marnie's heartbeat slowed almost to a standstill.

No.

She read the headline several times in case she'd somehow misunderstood, but it was quite clear.

Her mind grappled for explanations. It might be a cutting about someone else's mother – but the date matched Denise's death.

Marnie narrowed her eyes and glanced at the photograph, literally glanced, so her brain barely had time to register what it was seeing. It was a poor reproduction of a picture of a woman who looked like Denise.

But it couldn't be true! Denise had died of a weak heart. It had been a tragedy, certainly, but 'overdose' didn't come into it.

The cutting had to be a coincidence, some woman who bore a passing resemblance to Denise Morahan had taken an overdose at about the same time as Denise's weak heart had given up and some idiot from the cricket club had seen fit to include the cutting in the card he sent to John.

Marnie couldn't bring herself to read the article. But she was remembering that something about her mother's death had always bothered her.

On the day Denise had died, she'd put her locket under

Marnie's pillow. How had she known to put it there on that particular day? Marnie once asked Mrs deVillars this very question, during one of their sign language lessons, and Mrs deVillars, looking very sad, had replied: 'Maybe she could feel that her heart was growing weaker.'

Marnie must have looked doubtful. 'It happens a lot,' Mrs deVillars assured her. 'Sensitive people often know when their time is up.'

Mrs deVillars had been spending a good deal of time with Angharad Jones.

Marnie leaned back against the wall in her father's bedroom. Mister stood beside her, drooling and looking concerned.

A little voice inside Marnie's head said: 'All you have to do is read the article.'

But Marnie wouldn't. It was ridiculous even to consider that Denise might have taken an overdose; crazy. Why would she have done such a thing?

No, she had hidden the locket beneath Marnie's pillow and then gone to the main bedroom alone for a little lie-down. Denise often took an afternoon nap. The only thing that was different this time was that her heart had stopped beating while she was sleeping.

Marnie closed her eyes, pressed the palms of her hands over her face.

She remembered her father's face when he was fetched from work that afternoon, he still in his overalls, grease on his hands; his expression frozen in shock. Angharad had come bustling over from the holiday park. She'd put her arms round Marnie – 'Come on now, sweetheart, you come with me.' Mr deVillars stood at the side of the road watching as the paramedics loaded the trolley into the ambulance. A child was screaming. It was her, Marnie. She'd been screaming: 'Mummy Mummy Mummy Mummy Mummy!' Angharad held her tight.

'She's going to be fine, darlin', shush now, she's going to be fine.'

Marnie felt dizzy. She blinked and saw her mother's face in her mind's eye as clearly as if Denise was in the room with her. It was the day before her death. She was sitting at the table in the kitchen of the caretaker's cottage, staring at the pictures in the locket that she would, the next morning, hide under Marnie's pillow.

Marnie had come in from outside. She remembered that she was cold and that Denise had been so lost in thought that she'd seemed surprised to see her.

'Hello,' Marnie said, putting down the plastic carrier bag she was carrying, going to her mother, putting her arms round her waist.

'Hi.' Denise kissed the top of Marnie's head. 'What've you got there?'

'A present.'

'For me?'

'Yep.'

Marnie had heaved the bag onto the table. It sagged as it lay down.

Denise peered into the bag, then she started back in disgust. 'Oh God! What is it?'

'It's a fish,' said Marnie. 'Mr deVillars caught it for you.'

'I don't want it,' Denise said.

'But—'

'I don't want it! What are you doing bringing disgusting things like that into the cottage?'

Denise had stood up angrily, pushing back her chair. She'd picked up the bag and taken it outside. Marnie stood at the back door and watched as her mother walked in her slippers down the incline to the bottom of the garden, swung the bag back by its handles and then threw it. It flew into the air and fell into the mass of undergrowth that lay between the end of the cottage garden and the start of the estuary.

'There,' she said. 'Let the magpies have it.'

She'd turned and marched back into the cottage. She'd washed her hands under the cold tap and dried them on the tea-towel, then she'd sat back down on the chair, and she'd started to cry. There was no reason for her tears that Marnie could see, but it was frightening to see her mother crying like that, as if her heart was breaking.

'It's never going to stop,' she'd sobbed. 'It'll never be over.'

Marnie had gone to Denise and stood beside her, patting her back, trying to comfort her.

'I'm sorry, Mummy!'

'It's all right, Marnie. It's not your fault.'

'Please don't cry.'

'I'll be fine in a moment. Don't worry. It's nothing. I'm being silly.'

* * *

The handle of the door to John Morahan's bedroom turned and the door opened a crack. Mister stood to attention. Marnie slid the cutting back into the card, snapped it shut.

'Marnie? You OK in there, love?'

She shoved the card back into the pile of her father's discarded stuff. And from somewhere managed to fake a smile of reassurance as the old man's anxious face peered round the door.

47

After Marnie had taken his hand and led him away from Alice's caravan on the evening she disappeared, Will had stolen a bottle of vodka and taken it down to the beach. He'd drunk almost half its contents and then he'd left the bottle in the sand and staggered back into the holiday park. John Morahan, alerted by the traveller woman, had found him outside Caravan 49, taken him back to the chalet, and put him to bed. Will had vague memories of John telling him he was a prat, but that was the last thing he remembered. Later still, he'd got up and gone out again; the only evidence for this was his cut foot. It was possible – *probable* given what had happened before – that he'd returned to Caravan 49.

The not remembering was killing Will. Those lost hours. What had he done? Who had seen him?

His memory of the following morning was clear, although the remembering was shameful. Horribly hungover, weak, nauseous and sore, he'd promised his mother that he'd leave Alice alone even though he was desperate to see her.

He'd splashed cold water on his face, brushed his teeth until his gums bled, and showered, scrubbing himself raw. He'd put anti-septic cream and plasters over the cuts on the sole of his foot. Then he'd picked at the breakfast that Angharad had made for him, she insisting it would do him good, he thinking it would be impossible to feel any more wretched.

The day was already hot; a heat haze on the horizon; the sky a colour that was neither blue nor grey. The trees gave little shade. They were thirsty, their leaves losing their green. Some of the trees would never recover from the drought. Everything was changing, the season turning. In two weeks the children would be back at school and there'd be the taste of autumn in the air, and the T-shirts and daps they were wearing now would be replaced by woollen socks and jumpers. Fires would be lit and fallen leaves raked into piles.

For now, though, it was still summer. Will told himself it wasn't too late. He told himself there was still time to make things right with Alice. He needed to be calm. He needed to show that he could be an adult.

He attended to his responsibilities. He limped to the swimming pool, unlocked the metal safety gate, switched on the pump and the crystal-blue water at the base of the pool shimmied, sending patterns of light into the arms of the trees. Will picked up the long-handled net and scooped out the insects and leaves that had fallen into the pool during the night. The net was heavy, and you couldn't rush the job. He tipped the rubbish out onto the grass away from the sun loungers and the poolside showers.

After that, he swept the poolside, cleared away the glasses into a large plastic tray and straightened the sunbeds ready for the day ahead.

It was early. Few of the holidaymakers were up but the young father from Caravan 112, was walking lengths of the path, jiggling his baby in his arms, and some of the families who were leaving that morning, those who had a long way to drive, were unloading buckets and spades and bags of groceries onto the lawns outside their caravans. A queue was forming outside the park stores, people wanting to buy milk and bread, and the village women who came in on changeover days to clean the caravans and replace the linen were hovering in the service alleyways, the smoke from their cigarettes curling up into the blue sky.

Will's next job was to empty the bins that had been put out ready for the changeover. He had a trailer that he pulled round after him and he put the full bin bags into the trailer and then stored them in the waste compound, ready to be collected and taken away. Because of the heat, the plastic bags were swollen, flabby with gases. Will was wearing his gauntlets, sweating alcohol, listening to the sounds of the caravan park waking, when Mrs deVillars hurried past. She didn't notice him but he noticed her, partly because it was unusual to see her in the park so early but mainly because of her expression. She looked furtive and worried. Will put down the handles of the trailer and, keeping his distance, followed Mrs deVillars across the park to Caravan 49.

Once there, she stopped and gazed in dismay at the dent Will had made when he punched the caravan the night before, and then she'd knocked on the door.

'Hello!' Mrs deVillars called, keeping her voice low. 'Hello, Alice, are you there? Is everything all right?'

A wood pigeon flew overhead, its wings beating like a heart, and the wind chimes sang out from the branch of the old apple tree. Someone switched a radio on and a little girl turned a rope to skip. Will watched Mrs deVillars reach out for the handle, pull it down and open the door to Caravan 49. She put her head inside and called again, 'Hello! Alice!'

48

SUNDAY

A storm was brewing outside, rattling the cottage windows and guttering, the wind powering up to batter the flatlands and strain the sinews of the branches of the big old trees in the fields. Marnie lay wide awake, turning from one side to the other but unable to find a comfortable position. Her legs were tangled in the sheets and Tessy was stretched out on the bed beside her. In the end, she propped herself up as best she could because the mattress was old and soft, and she reached over Tessy to switch on the bedside lamp. The clock on her phone told her it was gone 2 a.m.

Please don't let it thunder, she prayed. Like Denise, she'd always hated thunder.

The storm wasn't helping, but it wasn't the main reason why Marnie could not sleep.

It was the headline on the cutting she'd seen earlier that was troubling her most, but she didn't want to think about that so she searched for another reason for her unease. She didn't have to look far. She had a book beside the bed. It had been recommended by the woman in the library. It was a literary novel, but it was about a murder and Marnie was not enjoying it. The dead character was

female and had been buried in a shallow grave. The mystery of the
book was not who had committed the murder, nor even so much
why, but the identity of the exhumed body. It was a disturbing
story; deeply unsettling and as soon as she spotted it on the bedside
table Marnie thought: That's it! That's what's keeping me awake!

She shouldn't have this book in her cottage.

She slid out of bed, pulled a big old jumper over her head and
went to the window. Outside, the trees were flailing their branches;
the cottage groaned and sighed in response. The wind whistled
under the roof tiles. Marnie hoped the sparrows who sheltered
there were safe.

She needed to get rid of the book, but as it was a library book
she couldn't consign it to the flames inside the stove. She'd have to
put it outside, as far away as possible from the cottage itself.

She left the bedroom, turned on the landing light and went
downstairs. She wrapped the book in a plastic bag, unlocked and
opened the door. The wind snatched at the door, grabbed it from
her and slammed it back against the wall. Tessy trotted out. Luna
scratched at the dining-room door.

Marnie put on her coat and boots and went outside. The wind
buffeted her and almost knocked her over. She walked round the
side of the cottage to where the car was parked, rocking in the wind.
She placed the bag with the book under the car. In the storm, with
all the movement around, it was easy to imagine cold eyes watching
from the shadows; strangers lurking with malicious intent.

But she was being ridiculous. What murderer in their right
mind would come out in weather like this?

Her phone was upstairs at the side of the bed. Gabriel had told
her she could contact him whenever she wanted. But he didn't
mean now, in the middle of the night. She couldn't text him to leave
his warm bed and drive all the way from Avonmouth because her

imagination was working in overdrive; because she was afraid of shadows.

There was a flash of light in the distance, a growl of thunder miles away. Marnie shivered. She recalled her mother's face, pinched with fear. 'It's nothing to worry about, Marnie. It can't hurt you,' she used to say, but the child heard the terror in her voice. Denise used to show her the locket when the thunder came. 'Hold this,' she'd say. 'This will keep you safe.'

Marnie was worried about her animals. She ploughed through the wind across the orchard to the stable block and looked in through the feed-room window. In the dim glow of the nightlight she could see that Mister was asleep, with his back to the window. She could see the up-and-down of his barrel chest as he breathed peacefully, unbothered by the storm. She checked on Scrumpy and Seashell, unsettled but not panicked, and made sure the stable doors and windows were secure. As she headed back towards the cottage the rain began to fall, great sweeping sheets of it. There was a violent lightning flash and a clap of thunder so loud Marnie dropped her torch. She scrabbled for it, pushed herself up and headed back to the cottage. She was almost at the door when she heard a cry.

Lucy was at the threshold, jumping up and down in agitation. 'Luna's gone, Mum! The thunder scared her and she ran! I couldn't stop her! She's gone!'

49

It wasn't the storm that woke Will but the sound of someone moving around in the room below his. After that, he became aware of the wind and the pattering of raindrops, the distant thunder. From that moment, sleep eluded him. Alice was everywhere. He heard her laughter in the soughing of the telephone lines, caught glimpses of her in the flickering shadows on the flowers in the pattern of the paper on the walls. And even more present was his own sense of guilt; his fear. Mr deVillars had put the possibility into his mind that he himself might have done something to Alice and he couldn't refute that because he could not remember.

What if it was true?

What if he *had* done something?

He could face punishment, prison, whatever – that didn't scare him. Worse was the prospect of having to live with himself if it turned out he had hurt the person he loved most in the world. If it was true, then his life might as well be over now.

He'd interviewed a man once who, as a child, had accidentally killed his younger brother. The man had grown up to become desperately religious. He spent his whole life caring for others, doing good works, trying to make up for tipping his brother out of a wheelbarrow when he was five years old. No matter how much the man sacrificed himself, no matter how he tried, he couldn't lessen his own pain. You could see it in his eyes. Everyone else had forgiven him – although there was nothing really to forgive – but he couldn't forgive himself. Will had felt deep pity for the man at the time; he'd never forgotten him. Now he wondered if he would be the same. No, not the same: worse. If Will had hurt Alice and then hidden her body, that would have been a deliberate act. There could be no redemption.

Perhaps if people had started looking for Alice sooner things would have turned out differently, but it had taken a while for anyone to realise she was missing. When she wasn't back in her caravan by Saturday evening, there was some small consternation. Will overheard a conversation between his mother and Mrs deVillars, Angharad reassuring Camille that Alice had more than likely gone to the festival in Weston. She was in her twenties, on holiday, she was at liberty to go out and do whatever she wanted. Camille had been flustered.

'I feel a responsibility towards the girl,' she said.

'But you can't go worrying about every young person who tips up at Channel View,' Angharad had replied. 'You can't control their movements. They're here to have fun. She'll be fine, you'll see.'

After Camille had gone, Will asked Angharad if she meant it when she said Alice would be fine and Angharad told Will that she was sure she would be. She said his behaviour had probably upset Alice to the point where she felt she had to get out of Channel View, 'and who could blame her?' She'd be letting her hair down at the festival, having a whale of a time, mixing with people 'more her own age', a barb intended to make Will feel childish. None the less, it seemed a reasonable explanation and Angharad genuinely did not appear worried.

By Sunday night, people were arriving back from the festival and only when Caravan 49 was still empty on Monday morning had Mrs deVillars called the police.

On Monday afternoon, a search was organised. Alice might have gone walking across the fields, or by the estuary, and slipped and fallen. She might be lying injured somewhere. Will was feeling increasingly anxious. He couldn't eat or sleep or concentrate on anything. Angharad and John told Will not to join the search party, but to stay away; to stay in the chalet. He realised, now, that they too must have wondered if he had done something to Alice. Perhaps that was what they still believed, which explained why Angharad had been so adamant Will have a solicitor with him when he spoke to the police.

On the day of the search, Will waited around the holiday park, as he'd been told to wait. He heard voices in the distance calling Alice's name. He heard sirens. He felt sick to the core.

He was afraid of the police; afraid of being accused of hurting Alice when all he'd ever wanted to do was love her. And he was worried about the one person who knew more than anyone else, the person who could get him in the most trouble: Marnie.

Everyone, including John Morahan, was out in the fields looking for Alice. Will slipped out of the chalet, trotted across the road and let himself into the caretaker's cottage. He called, 'It's me, Marnie! Will!' and went up the narrow stairs, two at a time. He stopped at the top. Through the small square of the landing window, he saw a police car draw up and turn into the park. His heart pounded. The travellers were gone now; Marnie was the only witness to the fight between Will and Alice. He opened the door to the child's room and stepped inside.

The curtains were half drawn but it was stiflingly hot. The slice of space where the light came in was blindingly bright, everywhere else was gloomy. Will could see a section of the bed, the crumpled sheets, one skinny, brown, bare leg on top, a line of midge bites climbing the calf, a scab at the knee, a small, dirty foot.

There was darkness at the head end of the bed. Will's eyes, dazzled by the sunlight, couldn't make out Marnie's face at all.

He heard a small sniff.

'Hey, scruffbag, I brought you these.' He held out a bag of jelly babies he'd bought at the stores. 'Do you want one?'

A tiny voice: 'No.'

'Well, they're for you. You can have them when you feel a bit better.'

Will sat on the edge of the bed and waited until his eyes adjusted and he could see her.

She was propped on the pillows, breathing staccato through her mouth, her fringe stuck to her forehead and beads of sweat glistening on her skin. Her lips were a blueish colour, her cheeks sunken like an old person's. She was wearing a short cotton nightdress and pants. She smelled odd: sweet, like something decomposing in the wetlands in winter.

Marnie lay there watching Will trustingly, her eyes shiny and dark in the dim light, waiting to be told what it was that he wanted.

'Listen, Marnie,' Will said, 'I need you to do something for Alice, OK?'

Marnie nodded.

'If anyone asks you questions about her,' he paused to moisten his mouth, 'even someone like the police, then it's fine to talk about you and her, and the things you did together, but you mustn't tell them anything about me and her. OK?'

'Why not?'

'Because if you do, Alice will be in trouble. She's not allowed to have a boyfriend.'

Marnie's face had remained blank. She was an unworldly little girl. She didn't think to question this explanation.

Will leaned a little closer, so that his face was so close to hers that he could smell her exhaled breath, her unbrushed teeth.

'So, just to be clear, that means not telling people that Alice and me liked one another, not telling them about the necklace I gave her, and the absolute most important thing is that you never tell anyone that you saw me at Alice's caravan the other day, when we were fighting.'

Marnie nodded.

'Do you understand, Marnie? You never saw us fighting. You never saw me throw the stones at the caravan...'

'I understand.'

'The best thing, if anyone asks, is to say that you never saw me and Alice together at all. That way you won't have to answer any extra questions.'

'OK.'

'Promise me, Marnie? Promise you won't get Alice into trouble? Promise you won't say anything to anyone?'

She promised.

He'd stayed a while longer, selling her dreams about a future he knew full well wouldn't happen, gabbling promises he would not keep about the two of them getting a flat together and so on. Marnie loved to hear about the fun they were going to have; the things they were going to do; the places they were going to go. She hung on to his every word while he told all those lies and all the time Jesus-on-the-wall was watching; Jesus with his blond hair and blue eyes. Hadn't Denise put Him there to stop people like Will coming into the bedroom and corrupting her little daughter? Didn't that make what Will had done even worse?

Jesus. Jesus-on-the-wall watching over Marnie. Jesus put there by Marnie's religious mother, a woman who had been thirty-seven years old when she died.

Fourteen years older than Alice.

Will switched on the light and got out of bed. He unscrewed the lid on top of the vodka bottle and poured a good measure into his glass. He took a sip of it neat.

He'd dismissed the idea that Denise might have been Alice's birth mother before, but now he came back to it again. Denise spoke with a south coast accent. She had a deep faith. She was in the right age bracket to have been Alice's teenage mother.

But if Denise was Alice's mother, then Alice must have known. It could not have been coincidence that she'd come, out of the blue, to the same small town where Denise had lived; to the same small town where she had died. And if she had known Denise was her mother, she must also have known that she'd missed her, that Denise was already dead.

Will had reasoned before that Alice would not have come all the way to Severn Sands knowing that her birth mother was already gone. But perhaps he'd been too quick to reject the possibility.

Even without Denise, there were still reasons for Alice to come.

For one, there was Denise's grave.

And for another, there was her half-sister, Marnie.

50

Marnie stood at the entrance to the school playing fields, the wind whipping her hair about her face, and her coat flapping, rain bulleting into her skin, searching the night for the missing dog.

She kept imagining that she'd spotted Luna, but it was only the wind thrashing the shrubs and branches, making wild shadows as the clouds raced past the moon.

A section of the wall that surrounded the cottage garden had been brought down by a fallen branch; Luna had jumped over it and escaped. She would be terrified by the thunder, desperate to find somewhere she felt safe. Even as she searched the town Marnie thought it was most likely that the dog would be heading for the old concrete army shelter on Catbrain Point where she'd originally been found, the place she had, for a while, regarded as home.

The winter trees waved their bony arms, the wind howled. Marnie left the playing fields and went into the street.

Luna, please, she begged, *come to me. I'm here!*

But Luna didn't come and Marnie had almost reached the church, wondering if she should go back for the car and drive to Catbrain Point, when she saw a figure lurching towards her through the night. She stepped back into the shadows. The figure was walking erratically, hunched over and it was only as it stepped out of the church gate and into the light of a streetlamp and she saw the smaller shape of its companion that she recognised who it was. Her heart began to pound. It was her father. He'd been in the churchyard.

It never crossed her mind to go to him. Instead, she crept further backwards, a mixture of fear and pity in her veins, because the man approaching her was drenched, he was old and his demeanour was desperately sad. He was bent over a stick, his face, when it was illuminated, briefly, by the glare of a lightning flash, was scored with lines of grief and loneliness.

TT must have caught Marnie's scent because he raised his head as they passed the point closest to her and looked directly towards her, but he was on the lead and John pulled him away and the two of them continued on their lonely way.

He must have been to Denise's grave.

Denise had always been terrified of thunder and Marnie's father had gone to her grave in the midst of the storm to keep her company; to make sure that she was all right.

51

Will was relieved when the sky beyond the flowery curtains at last began to glow pale. The night had spread itself out between nightmares and thunderclaps, the pipes in the bedroom groaning whenever the person downstairs turned on their taps.

He hadn't been able to sleep, desperate to overlay his fears about the role he might have played in Alice's death with the less pressing mystery of why she'd come to Severn Sands in the first place.

Why had he never asked her at the time?

Why hadn't it occurred to him that it was odd for a young woman to come all the way from Lincolnshire to a little-known holiday resort in the South-West when she had the beauty of the North-Eastern coastline right on her doorstep?

It hadn't occurred to him because he'd been so wrapped up in their love affair that he couldn't see any further than that.

Will sat on the side of the bed, scratching his scalp. If he went to the police and told them everything, would that make him feel better?

But tell them what?

That he might have done something to hurt Alice Lang twenty-four and a half years earlier, but he wasn't sure?

That he couldn't remember?

Was it really fair to get John Morahan and his own mother, possibly Marnie too, into deep trouble in a possibly futile attempt to salve his own conscience?

The smells of bacon and coffee insinuated themselves beneath the door. Despite his anguish, Will felt a pang of hunger. He went into the little bathroom, noticed, as he peed, the new damp stain on the ceiling that indicated a tile was loose on Mr Bradshaw's roof, resolved not to mention it because why should he bother, pulled on a pair of jeans and a sweater.

He went downstairs and into the dining room. A broad-shouldered woman was already sitting at one of the tables, with her back to him. As he entered she turned and looked at him over her shoulder. She smiled, lipstick seeping into the tiny lines around her mouth.

'Hi, Will,' she said.

He didn't recognise her at first. God knew he had enough on his mind without playing silly games that morning, but she pushed her chair back and stood up, and at the same moment Mr Bradshaw came into the room carrying a rack of toast. The smell of the charred bread and the sight of the woman assailed Will at exactly the same moment and he realised: she was Daisy.

'Dad told me you were here,' she said, 'and that you were on your own and I thought it'd be fun to surprise you.' She touched her hair and smiled. 'Why don't you join me?' She pointed to the chair opposite hers.

'No, it's fine, I'll...'

'Please,' she said, 'it'll give us chance to talk.'

Will could hardly refuse. He walked round the table and sat down as Mr Bradshaw placed the toast in the centre of the table.

'Black coffee?' he asked Will, and Will said, 'Please.' Daisy smiled with the fondness of a parent tested by a rebellious child, as if black coffee was a hard drug.

She took a triangle of toast and laid it on her side plate. Her fingers were short and square, the nails trimmed, strawberry-blonde hair cut like her mother's in the picture in the hallway, eyebrows that were beginning to bush. She had a dab of yoghurt to one side of her mouth and she smelled strongly of sweat and perfume.

'So, how's life treating you?' she asked brightly.

'OK, thanks. Yeah, good. Fine.'

'It sounds like more than "OK" to me!' Daisy said coyly. 'I've bought all your books and I follow you on Twitter. I'm always looking at the photographs you post and retweeting them. Sometimes you like my comments. Did you realise it was me?'

Will made a noncommittal 'Mmm,' sound. He hadn't, of course. He needed to start paying more attention on social media. Saoirse was always telling him he should.

Daisy had always been statuesque. As a girl she had been handsomely attractive; now her figure was shapeless, her appearance dull. She had a line of dark fuzz on her upper lip. She dipped her knife in the butter pot and began to spread the fat on the toast. He could smell the warmth from her body, see the engineering of her bra beneath a tight, salmon-pink jumper with a glittery mermaid embossed on the front.

Will couldn't think of a single thing to say to her.

'So, what's it been like coming back to Severn Sands?' she asked. 'Has it been fun?'

'Not really,' he replied truthfully.

'Dad said you're writing a book about Alice Lang.'

She said the two words of Alice's name with deliberate casualness.

'Yes,' said Will. He cleared his throat. 'Yes, I am.'

'At least you know now how the story ends.'

Mr Bradshaw was back with the drinks. 'Breakfasts are coming,' he said.

'Lovely, thanks, Daddy,' said Daisy.

Daddy! She must be forty years old!

Daisy took a bite of toast and chewed loudly. 'So, are you married, Will? Do you have any children?'

'No and no.'

'Dad said you were on your own. He said...' she lowered her voice and leaned across the table towards Will, '... he said you seemed lonely.'

'I'm not lonely.'

'I have two girls,' Daisy said, although Will hadn't asked. 'I'm the opposite of lonely. I crave time on my own. Jennifer is my good daughter – she's seventeen now, just about to sit her A levels – and Erin is thirteen and was put on this earth to test me. The child is a nightmare. I married Dale Parker. Do you remember Dale from school? Quiet boy. Well-built. He used to be mad about *Star Wars*. We're divorced now. We were never really suited. We both did our best for the sake of the girls but...' she trailed off and looked at Will with an expression of tortured sincerity. Will thought, Oh God! Was she was trying to convey that she had never got over him?

Before he had the chance to process this information, the local news came on the radio. The first item was about a crash on the M5. Traffic was in chaos.

This was followed by a solemn announcement that the police had issued a new appeal for witnesses who might remember anything about twenty-three-year-old Alice Lang, who had gone missing from Channel View holiday park twenty-four years earlier. They were especially interested in anyone who'd been at the park on the day she disappeared. They said any information, no matter how trivial it seemed, might be important.

Will had been expecting this but still it was a shock. He could not sit there, opposite Daisy, with her scrutinising him. He could not look into her eyes, knowing that he'd see some tiny glint of satisfaction now that it had been confirmed, once and for all, that Alice was out of the picture. He could not sit there knowing that he, himself, might be the man responsible.

He pushed back his chair. 'I'm sorry, Daisy,' he said, 'but I have to go.'

'Where do you—'

'I've things I have to do.'

'Well, perhaps we could have a cup of tea later and—'

'No,' said Will, 'sorry, but no.'

He left his coffee and he ran up the two flights of stairs back to his small room in the eaves of the house. He turned on the TV and stood, watching the news, blindsided by emotion. He didn't hear the knock on the door, hardly noticed when it opened and Mr Bradshaw came in.

Will paid him no attention, he was fixed on the television but Mr Bradshaw came right up to him and said something loudly, right into Will's ear.

'Excuse me, Mr Bradshaw, I can't hear the television.'

'Daisy's come all this way to see you and you can't even pay her the courtesy of—'

'I need to listen to this.'

'The TV is more important than my daughter?'

'Please, Mr Bradshaw, could you move out of the way?'

'I will not move out of your way. You were a rude, inconsiderate boy and you've grown into a rude, inconsiderate man.'

'Sorry?'

'You heard me! And what's more, you've been sneaking about my house, stealing my alcohol.'

'What?'

'Oh, don't try to deny it! I've got motion-sensitive CCTV in all the private rooms. You waited until I was out and then you sneaked into the living room and drank my Bristol Cream. You didn't even have the decency to pour it into a receptacle. Drank it straight from the mouth of the decanter; disgusting. I've had to tip the rest down the drain.'

The facts were inarguable and Will, at a definite moral disadvantage, could think of nothing to say in his defence.

'I'll replace the sherry,' he muttered.

'It's too late for that. I want you out of here,' said Mr Bradshaw. 'Now!'

'OK, OK. I'll be down in a tick.'

'I'm standing here until you're done.'

Will opened his mouth to say: 'Seriously?' but thought better of it.

The sooner he was out of this place, the better.

Under the gimlet eye of his landlord, Will gathered his possessions together, stuffed them into his rucksack and hefted it over his shoulder. He settled his bill and was off the premises within a few minutes. Daisy was watching from the bay window in the living room, sipping from her teacup and he didn't imagine the self-satisfied smile on her face.

Fair enough, thought Will. She'd earned that small victory.

52

Marnie never made it back to bed. As dawn broke, blood-red streaks across a bruised sky, the wind still beating across the land, she took a cup of tea up to Lucy, signed that she was going out again to look for Luna. Lucy nodded, yawned sleepily, and snuggled down.

Marnie put Tessy and Mister into her car and then drove the sea road as far as the junction with the lane that led down to the point. It was an unassuming track, for many years closed off to the public by the military, who had owned the land, but now the tall fences were broken and the wire had been cut and torn down in places. The sign with the skull and crossbones, which said, 'Danger! Keep Out!' was still there, battered, banging in the wind, but the gates had been taken, sold for scrap.

Marnie had never driven on to the point although she'd seen the pillbox from the beach. The track went on for longer than she expected, winding between sparse shrub-land and waterlogged grass, a lonely place where people had dumped mattresses and torched cars. The post-storm sun was shining so brightly on the estuary that the glare hurt her eyes. The tide was out and the mudflats rippled in the light. A flock of white seabirds described spirals above the water, and the islands of Flat Holm and Steep Holm were distant silhouettes. A rabbit scuttered in front of the car, its white tail bobbing. Marnie pulled down the sunshade and scanned the area for any sign of Luna.

At its end, the track opened into a wide, potholed area, where the travellers parked their vans and lorries when they came. Marnie parked the car and let out the dogs. Tessy ran free, but Marnie kept Mister on the long lead. He stood beside her, squat, the wind lifting his damaged ears, staring about him, sniffing the air.

Marnie could see for miles from here. She scanned the area but there was no sign of Luna.

She walked towards the pillbox at the far end of the point crossing stony, puddled ground: worm-casts, and the first signs of greening in the squat little blackthorn bushes; a family of great tits calling and fluttering.

Everything about the pillbox, from its ugly concrete exterior to the slits that served as windows, was grim.

Marnie shortened Mister's lead and ducked to enter beneath the door jamb. The interior was pitch black and smelled of smoke and ammonia. Marnie waited for her eyes to adjust and then she saw there were no new paw prints, no new excrement, nothing to indicate Luna had been back.

She came out again, into the clean daylight, the sky washed blue, and gazed across the estuary. It was a beautiful morning and she could look along the coast line, back towards the caretaker's cottage. Her phone pinged. It was a message from Gabriel.

I saw you drive past. Is everything OK?

53

Will was walking aimlessly when a car pulled up alongside him. Marnie Morahan wound down the window.

'Hi,' said Will: 'Are you OK?'

She showed him her phone.

Searching for lost dog.

'Right.' He indicated his rucksack. 'I've checked out of the guest-house. Actually, I was chucked out of the guesthouse. Do you know if there's anywhere else I can stay?'

Marnie considered for a moment. Then she switched off the car engine, got out of the car and began to walk down the road. In the absence of any other instructions, Will followed. It soon became obvious that they were heading towards the old caretaker's cottage.

When they reached the gate, Marnie pushed it open and Will followed her down the path, treading the broken slabs that took them to the door beneath a small porch. The inverted horseshoe for good luck was still nailed in the apex of the gable, the same old wind-chimes still hung from the hook inside. Marnie opened the door, and he followed her over the threshold.

Will knew the cottage well. Back in the day, John would often send him across the road to fetch some tool or to give a message to Denise, or to pick up his sandwiches, wrapped ready in the fridge. Being here was like rereading an old book and recalling how a forgotten story had panned out. Will felt a tingle in his fingers. Here he was, in the place where Denise used to live, where Jesus looked down from the walls. If he was going to find confirmation that his theory about Denise and Alice was correct, it would be here.

He looked about him. The walls in the hall were painted a burned orange colour evocative of South American cantinas, which had been popular during the early nineties, brighter oblongs marking the places where Marnie's school photographs used to hang; a picture for every year at primary school, her face gradually growing longer, gaps appearing in her teeth. If he narrowed his eyes, Will could still see the haze of cigarette smoke that used to hang just below the ceiling level, the coats on the hooks by the front door, and the folded newspaper on which John used to place his boots. He remembered the dustbin by the gate, a bouquet of flowers upended, stalks and Cellophane and a pink ribbon sticking from its mouth. And when he'd asked Denise she'd said they'd been delivered to the cottage by mistake.

'Take them, if you like them,' she'd said. 'Give them to your mother.'

So he had.

Will followed Marnie into the kitchen where she lit the stove and leaned over its flickering flames, trying to warm her hands. Will watched her. The dog's bed used to be there, next to the table, where everyone used to trip over him, hence his name.

'Marnie, just so we're clear, are you saying I can stay here?' Will asked.

Without turning, she nodded.

'That's great,' he said. 'Thank you.'

He wondered if he should attempt to apologise. He wondered if there was any way of making up to Marnie for the way he'd behaved, for all the ways he'd let her down; all those envelopes with their childish handwriting on the front that he'd never opened, but couldn't quite bring himself to throw away. He'd left them on his desk in his room in the university halls where they gradually became buried and eventually they'd been lost or someone had torn a strip from the edge to make a spill to light a joint. Sooner or later the letters had been destroyed or discarded, and Will had been able to pretend they had never existed.

Marnie filled a small pan with water and placed it on the cooker. She took a mug and spoon from the drainer, and a jar of coffee granules from the cupboard beneath the sink. When the water boiled, Marnie made the coffee and passed the mug to Will.

It smelled better than the coffee in the guesthouse.

Marnie stood with her back to the kitchen window watching Will sip his drink. She was wearing the knitted hat, pulled down over her head. Her eyebrows were dark and fine, her features sharp and neat. Was there some small resemblance to Alice, or was that only Will trying to make the pieces of the jigsaw fit?

'It reminds me of your mother, being here, in the cottage,' he said, feeling his way forward.

Marnie looked away.

'You must still think of her a lot.'

She winced.

'Sorry,' Will said.

Marnie squeezed past him, heading for the front door. He reached for her arm, 'No, wait, Marnie, don't go rushing off. I want to talk to you, I want to explain. I didn't mean to upset you. I'm sorry, Marnie! Please, can't we talk?'

She shook off his hand, opened the door.

'Wait! If I see the lost dog, what should I do?' Will asked.

She hesitated, then put a hand in her pocket and gave him a lead.

'You'd better give me your number too.'

With bad grace, Marnie took Will's phone and tapped her number in. She passed it back to him and went out of the door.

He watched her walk away.

54

Marnie greeted the dogs and sat for a moment or two in the driver's seat staring out of the window.

She'd put Alice's precious Quality Street tin to the back of her mind in the chaos of losing Luna, but now she remembered. The tide was going out and she could be at the cave in five minutes. If she was going to get the tin, now would be as good a time as any.

When she reached the place, she found it deserted. She let the dogs out and Tessy ran wild on the rocky foreshore. As always, Mister stayed close to Marnie.

Marnie hurried along the path, walking into the wind, the air storm-fresh. She scanned the shore for any sign of Luna. There was none.

She came here, to this part of the estuary, sometimes in her dreams, but rarely in real life, and it wasn't as she remembered. Perhaps the tide had shifted the mudbanks and altered its geography, or perhaps her memory wasn't reliable. The weather was changing again. Bullying clouds were amassing in the west, shreds of grey tearing off and racing through the sky. She came to a small beach around the place where a stream fed into the estuary, the water fanning out into the shape of an opening flower, carving small, pebbled channels. It only existed at low tide, this beach. When the sea came in, it was completely subsumed.

Marnie walked a little way beside the stream. She looked up and saw the anomaly in the rock above her: the cave that had been hollowed out by the fossil hunters; the cave that she'd regarded, as a child, as her secret territory.

Marnie tied Mister's lead to a jutting root, and scrambled up the shingle at the foot of the cliff – there must have been a collapse since she last did this, as the cave was higher up, more out of reach than it used to be. It took three attempts before she was high enough to grab hold of a rock and haul herself into the brambles. She screwed up her face to protect her eyes and struggled to gain the footholds so she could squeeze through the overgrowth and into the cave itself.

The interior was the size of Marnie's under-stairs cupboard, but its roof was lower and she was bigger than she'd been the last time she was there. She could only get inside by crawling.

She used her phone as a torch. There, at the very back, standing in a line on a small ledge of rock was a plastic family of trolls that Marnie had put there as a child. She'd forgotten about them.

There were a few other treasures: a rusting key – she couldn't remember where that came from – a cup that had once belonged to Denise and her stash of old cigarette lighters. And there, behind everything else, was the tin. Alice's tin, exactly where it had been left all those years before. Marnie gave a small sigh of relief, reached out and pulled it towards her.

55

A text came from Saoirse.

I'm out of the flat/your life. Posted key back through letterbox. Good luck. Goodbye.

Will looked at the text for a long time. Then he deleted it and paced around the caretaker's cottage fighting the urge to call her. It would be a mistake. He'd say something he didn't really mean, and would later have to retract, simply to make things feel a little better than they did now, trying to make it so they didn't end on a bad note. It was, in his experience, impossible to end a relationship on a good one.

The truth of it was he wanted to hear a kind voice. He yearned to talk to somebody who would tell him he wasn't as bad a person as he believed himself to be.

But if he'd killed Alice, he didn't deserve compassion. If he'd done that, then he'd rather die in prison than have to face Marnie or his mother or Saoirse or anyone he'd ever cared for again.

He distracted himself by searching the caretaker's cottage. He didn't know what he was looking for. Some letter from the adoption agency, or Denise's old teenage diary, something that would confirm she'd delivered a baby girl and subsequently given up the child would have been ideal, but he found nothing of the sort. There were a few random bills and receipts, lists made by John, instruction leaflets, one of Marnie's old school reports. Nothing more.

Frustrated, he went outside and had a poke around the garden. It was untidy and overgrown. There was still coal in the bunker and logs in the woodshed so he collected enough to keep him warm for the rest of the day, took his haul into the front room, and stacked it by the hearth. He made a small fire in the grate, lit it with the matches he found on the mantelpiece, and sat on the settee with the laptop on his knees. The crackle of the flames was cosy. He stared at the research notes he'd already made, the notes referring to Alice's birth mother and his impressions of the town and how it had changed. No matter how he looked at the words, nothing became any clearer.

When loneliness overwhelmed him, he called his mother in Majorca.

'What is it?' Angharad asked. 'What's happened? Have the police been in touch with you? Are you all right?'

'Nothing's happened,' Will said. 'No, the police haven't been in touch, and yes, I'm fine. I just...'

'What?'

'I don't know.'

'Oh, Will.'

They were both silent for a few moments.

'It'll be OK, you know,' said Angharad. 'It always is.'

'I don't think it can ever be OK.'

'You'll see.'

Will sighed.

Then he said: 'Mum, do you remember that evening, Alice's last evening when I got drunk and John brought me back to the chalet?'

'Yes.'

'What if I did something to Alice?'

'Did something?'

'Hurt her.'

'Oh, no, Will, you wouldn't have.'

'I threatened her.'

'That's what you used to be like: all mouth and no trousers. You said all sorts but you never *did* anything.'

'I went out a second time, while you were sleeping. I cut my foot. What if I met Alice somewhere in the caravan park? What if I took her to the funfair and killed her? What if—'

'No,' Angharad said. 'No, Will, you didn't do anything to that girl. You wouldn't have. I knew it and John, in his heart, knew it. Mrs deVillars knew it, too. But we knew you'd been in the caravan and things might have looked bad for you if that travelling woman had come forward or... Well, anyway. That's why Mrs deVillars...' She trailed off.

'Why she what?'

Angharad sighed. 'Why she said she'd seen Alice walking down to the estuary.'

'I don't understand.'

Angharad sighed again dramatically.

'She told the police she'd seen Alice leaving the caravan park of her own accord to protect you, Will. Because she knew you were incapable of hurting Alice.'

'She did it to protect me?'

'Yes.'

'Jesus.'

They were silent for a moment.

When Angharad next spoke, she said, 'We were all trying to do the best for one another, Will. Me and John and Mrs deVillars. But maybe we shouldn't have interfered. Maybe we should have let the investigation run its course. I don't know. Who knows how things would have turned out if Mrs deVillars hadn't said what she said?'

'I still can't believe that she'd do that for me.'

'For us. For all of us, Will. We were like one big family, remember?'

He remembered.

'Thing is, you weren't really protected, were you, Will? The damage was done. You never got over what happened that summer, did you? You're not over it now.'

'How can you be sure I didn't hurt Alice? How can I be?'

'Prove it,' Angharad said. 'Find out who did kill Alice Lang. Make this be over and done with once and for all.'

They finished the call. Will paced the caretaker's cottage, wiping tears from his cheeks with the back of his hand. Then he put another log on the fire. His mother was right. The only way to get through this was to end it.

He pulled himself together and called Emily.

'I'm not talking to you,' was the first thing she said to him. 'Do you have any idea how much trouble I've been in over the whole Guy deVillars mess?'

'I can imagine.'

'No, I don't think you can, Will. I've lost face, I've lost credibility, I've lost the trust of my favourite editor. I'll never get another commission again.'

'It can't be that bad.'

'It is.'

'I'm sorry.'

'Not good enough.'

'I'm really, truly sorry, Em, and I will find a way to make it up to you, but first can I ask you one more tiny favour?'

'Oh my God, you've got some neck.'

'Please! I don't know who else to ask.'

She was silent for a moment. He imagined her weighing up her options.

'What is it?' she asked at last.

'Could you look something up for me?'

'Why don't you do it yourself?'

'I don't have any internet here. It's nothing complicated. I just need the details from a wedding certificate. You can get those on family history websites, right?'

'Right.'

'So it wouldn't take very long. And I'll reimburse you whatever it costs.'

'Is this still to do with the holiday park murder?'

'Yes.'

'It'll be another favour you owe me.'

'Put it on the tab,' Will said.

He gave her the names, Denise and John Morahan, and their approximate ages. He didn't know where or when they'd married. It wasn't a huge amount to go on but Emily said she'd give it her best shot and promised to get back to him as soon as she had some news.

When the call ended, Will was lonely again.

The fire was dying and so was the battery in his computer so he shut it down to preserve what was left.

He felt wretched.

He needed some air. He needed the space to think, to put his ducks in order and come up with a strategy.

He went out, leaving via the back of the cottage, treading the overgrown path down to the mud-lands exposed by the receding tide. The air was fresh, the smell distinctive: diesel, ozone and sea. The wind ruffled his hair. Gulls called like banshees high above. He had thought he was coming closer to Alice by returning to Severn Sands but all the time she had been moving away.

Will remembered the boy he used to be, and all the years between then and now, years that had passed quickly like dates torn from a paper calendar, and not one of them had given him a memory that came close to the memories he had of the summer of Alice.

And now it was over. No more memories. Alice had been lost and found and lost again; this time for ever.

Eventually, he reached the place where Alice's dress had been found: the ancient slipway into the water, the planks water-logged and black, and the jagged post on which the scarlet fabric had been caught. It was the dress that seemed to prove the theory that Alice had ended up in the Severn, drowned, but it had been a carefully planned red herring.

The mud exposed by the retreating tide was drying in the faint warmth of the late winter sun, a thin crust forming. Signs warned of the dangers of sinking sand, the water now so shallow that it hardly lapped at the estuary's stony shelves. The tide was at its nadir, exposing acres of sand further out into the estuary and rocky outcrops, great fields of silt and mud miles long.

Will strode out, past Catbrain Point with the military lookout squat at its edge. Further on, the wind turbines and industrial chimneys and giant cranes of Bristol docks were growing clearer. The wind grew a little bolder, pushed at him. He walked on until he noticed that the tide had turned, creeping so discreetly that the only evidence was the shrinking silhouette of the exposed sand-hills in the centre of the estuary.

A message came in on his phone from Emily.

'John Morahan, handyman, married Denise Scott, librarian, Bristol Register Office. Her father was Geoffrey, bookshop owner of Church Street, Brighton. Hope this helps.'

Oh, yes. That helped massively.

Will's hunch had to be right. The pieces of the puzzle fitted. He was certain as he could be now that Denise had been Alice's mother.

He'd walked further than he'd intended. He turned and followed the tide upstream, heading back towards Severn Sands. The water was deceptive; it travelled fast; faster than a person could run, or even than a horse could gallop for any length of time. It rushed back in over the mudflats, a plastic bottle on its surface spinning forwards, racing ahead of Will. The sea swallowed back the exposed sandbanks and, as it did so, clouds gathered over the water and eventually the Welsh coastline faded into a blur of mizzle. Will's clothes were damp, his head was cold. Now he was walking into the wind, it was hard work. He didn't mind the discomfort. He was enthused by what he now knew, energised by the story of Alice's birth that he now had clear in his head.

By the time he came close enough to his starting point to make out the chimney pots on the roof of the caretaker's cottage, rain was falling hard. He decided to shortcut across a depressed area of mud around a gulley rather than following the path over the slipway where the dress had been found. He jumped down into the gritty mud and tramped across it. As it sloped towards the gulley, Will stumbled over something that looked like a filthy lump of clothing. If he hadn't tripped, he wouldn't have noticed it, certainly wouldn't have realised it was a living thing. Reluctantly, half-dreading what it might be, he turned to take a closer look.

56

Marnie spent the rest of the day searching for Luna, finding no sign of her.

In the end, she went home, hoping the dog might have returned to the cottage in her absence and that Lucy might simply have forgotten to phone. She found Lucy with Maya, the nurse's daughter, out in the orchard. Maya was sitting on Scrumpy and Lucy was trying to teach her to ride. Luna wasn't there.

Marnie took Tessy and Mister into the house. She put Alice's tin on the kitchen table then, feeling as bad as she'd ever felt in her life, she messaged Jenna to let her know that Luna was missing. Jenna replied at once; said she'd put the word out on social media. She tried to reassure Marnie, but Marnie was beyond reassurance. She paced the bungalow, feeling as if she'd let Jenna down and, at the same time, terribly worried about Luna, who was out there somewhere on her own, certainly hungry, cold and frightened, possibly in grave danger.

The thought of the little dog cowering alone in some lonely place was unbearable.

Marnie considered going out again, but where else could she search? She'd looked everywhere.

She tried to console herself with the thought that some kind person without access to a phone had found Luna and was looking after her, although she didn't really believe it, and that led her to the terrible possibility of Luna having been picked up by awful people, like the ones who used to own Mister; and from there to the chance that she too might be used as a bait dog.

Marnie knew she had to stop this catastrophising. It wasn't constructive and she would drive herself mad. She needed to calm down and think logically about what to do next.

She messaged Jenna again.

I'll make Lucy some tea & then go out looking again.

The message came back straight away.

It's ok lovey, it's all in hand. We'll find her. Rest tonight and if she's not back by morning we'll go out together.

Marnie was still not reassured. But she did remember a few months earlier when their roles had been reversed. Jenna had lost a rescue dog and Marnie had been the one trying to keep her calm and persuading her to behave rationally. Poor Jenna had been in such a state and it was Marnie who'd had to convince her there was no point wandering randomly around in the dark, searching for a dog that could be anywhere; who might well come back of her own accord when she was ready. Marnie had been right. The dog found her own way home. Perhaps Luna would do the same.

To take her mind off things, Marnie busied herself preparing a meal for the two girls.

She set the table and went out to help put Scrumpy and

Seashell away, and then the girls came back into the cottage to eat and Marnie took Alice's tin into the living room.

It had been in the cave for twenty-four years. A line of rust had formed at the seams and the rim of the lid, but the paintwork was intact.

Marnie picked it up – it wasn't heavy – and tried to prise the lid open with her fingers, but it was rusted shut. Next she tried the tin opener, but the tin was too large and the teeth of the opener could not gain purchase.

What Marnie needed was the help of someone who had access to some sort of cutting tool.

She picked up her phone.

She messaged Gabriel.

57

Will turned his back to the rain and crouched down over the thing he'd tripped over. He reached out and his fingers touched fur but it was so matted it had taken on a new texture. The light was fading, but he could see the thing was a dog, and it was stuck, half buried. Its ears were flat back to its head, its eyes clagged with dirt. As Will leaned towards it, it tried to move away but couldn't. It was half-dead, exhausted, freezing cold. It must have been there when he walked down the other way but he hadn't seen it because it was so melded with the estuary mud. It was pitiful, but also disgusting. Will was torn between compassion and revulsion. As he watched, the dog made a feeble attempt to free itself, extending its neck, grunting, but it was too weak. It laid its chin down again, closed its eyes. It had the air of something resigned to death.

It must be the dog that Marnie had lost.

Shit.

Will looked about him, looking for someone who might help, but it was February, it was a cold afternoon and night was falling. Nobody was around.

There'd be people at the holiday park, competent people, police and builders who'd have rope and spades and other tools that might be useful in this situation, but the park was too far away. Behind him, the sea was coming in, racing up the shallow banks. It would certainly reach the dog before Will reached the caravan park. If he went for help, the dog would drown.

Will took his phone out of his pocket to text Marnie, thinking she'd know what to do. But the phone's face was black. Its battery was dead.

Shit shit shit shit shit.

He was on his own. What should he do? What if the dog was terminally injured? It was already half dead. What if it couldn't walk? And what would Will do with it if he did manage to free it?

What if moving it would only hurt it more, prolong its evident suffering?

What the fuck was he supposed to do?

He had two options. Either he at least tried to dig the dog out with his bare hands or he walked away and left it to drown in the incoming tide.

He'd never be able to dig it out. It would be best if he walked away. Nobody knew that he'd seen the dog. Nobody would ever know that he'd left it to drown. It would be the easiest thing to do. Far easier than stay and deal with the consequences of trying to save the poor creature.

'I'm sorry,' Will said. 'I'm sorry but I can't help you, OK. I'm going to go now.' The words sounded weak and pathetic as they left his lips. 'There's nothing I can do!' he said to the dog. 'I can't help you. How can I help you? The fucking tide's coming in! My phone's dead! What can I do?'

The dog looked at him through mud-heavy lashes.

Oh Jesus.

What if he saved the dog? What if he brought it back to Marnie?

Would that make up for what he'd done to her before? For his abandonment of her?

Would the saving of one life in some way compensate for the taking of another?

Will vacillated. The water had come closer in the moments he'd wasted. He didn't know if saving the dog would even be possible. He looked around again. Driftwood lay stranded on the mud, but nothing substantial enough to serve as a spade. He knelt beside the dog. He felt the chill through the fabric of his trousers, and began to scoop at the mud with his bare hands. It was thick and gritty, dark grey like ash, heavy and cold. It scratched his palms, tore at his fingernails. The body of the dog, as he dug away, felt no warmer than the sludge that enclosed it. The fur was disgusting against his skin, slimy, like the hair on a dead body must feel. He talked to the dog as he worked, trying to keep the tone reassuring.

'You stupid animal. What did you have to go and get stuck here for? I'm doing this for Marnie, you know, not for you.'

The dog shivered. Every now and then it struggled. It seemed to Will that the harder he worked to free it, the less he achieved. As the tide came closer, so the stuff in which it was mired was becoming waterlogged. What if it turned to sinking sand? The only difference between sand and sinking sand was the proportion of water. What if Will became trapped as well? He saw himself as he might be, stuck with the dog as the tide came in, lapping, licking, that thick brown water, and he imagined how terrified he would be. In the next moment shame engulfed him; shame that he had considered, even for a moment, consigning the dog to a fate that now frightened him so much.

Then another thought came to Will, this one even worse. What if he couldn't get the dog out in time? Would he have to stand there and watch the poor creature drown?

The water rose sneakily. It was creeping higher, trying to claim the dog by stealth. Will could feel the change in the temperature of the air at this level, feel the encroaching wetness. Each scoop of wet sludge he pulled away was immediately replaced. Desperate, he half-lay on the ground and reached one hand as far as he could beneath the dog, and with the other he grabbed the loose fur around its neck and he pushed upwards with one hand and pulled with the other. He could feel the dog's heart beating in its body, banging like a drum against its ribs.

'I'm sorry,' he said, 'but this is the only way!' and he pulled, and the mud pulled back, sucking at the fur and bone, sucking at the dog's life. Will shouted at the sea: 'Fuck off! You're not having it!' He pulled and pushed, gripping the dog's pelt so tightly he was afraid it might tear, and at last there was a giving in the silt beneath his lower hand, a release and a kind of sigh as the sucking mud fell away and the dog came loose.

Will stumbled. His feet sank; he'd lost a boot. He tried to put the dog down, but its legs buckled and he was afraid of it becoming trapped again, so he picked it up, his arms under its body, like the spokes of a forklift and turned to carry it higher up the bank, away from the incoming tide. He pulled the bootless foot out of the sludge, and reached as far forward as he could, and then he pulled the other foot forward, the stuff sucking and straining to hold him back. The dog was a dead weight in his arms, as much silt as animal. He lurched forward one step at a time and kept going until he reached the place where the grass was growing, where seaweed and plastic rope and drinks bottles thrown overboard by the sailors on the cargo ships were tangled amongst the tough old weeds. He collapsed on the grass, with the dog, cold and heavy, and lay back, gazing up into the darkening sky.

58

Marnie sent another message to Jenna.

I'm going out for a bit, Lucy's here, pls let me know if any news.

She left Tessy with the girls but didn't trust Mister so she put him back in the car and set off again with the tin on the seat beside her.

Gabriel was waiting at the entrance to the building site. He lifted the barrier so she could drive in, showed her where to park and opened the car door. Marnie, who wasn't used to people doing things for her, was not sure if she liked the sensation.

'You found the dog then?' Gabriel asked when he saw Mister.

Marnie shook her head.

'This wasn't the one you'd lost?'

No.

'I'll keep my eyes open. You can wait in the office. Bring the dog with you – it's fine.'

She followed him across the site, covered in puddles in the wake of the storm, to a Portakabin. Gabriel unlocked the door and held it open for Marnie. She wiped her feet on the mat and led Mister over the threshold.

Inside was a tidy space, plans stuck on the walls, papers and schedules on the table. There was a computer, a printer, a video screen showing CCTV footage. A tray, a kettle, mugs, a packet of chocolate digestives, the wrapping twisted tight.

Marnie wondered where Gabriel slept when he stayed here. Did he settle in the chair, or was there a camp-bed somewhere?

'Have a seat,' said Gabriel. 'Make yourself at home. If you give me the tin, I'll go and get it open. I won't be long.'

She gave him the tin and he left. Marnie looked around. The room was warm; there was a small electric heater in the corner. Beside it, a waterproof coat hung from a peg by its hood and beneath that was a pair of lace-up leather boots. She'd never seen Gabriel out of his work clothes. There was a towel and some bottles on the shelf. She unscrewed the lid to the body wash, sniffed, and replaced the lid. On the desk was a photograph of Gabriel, in sunglasses and a T-shirt, with his arm looped round the shoulders of a woman with a small, neat face and laughing eyes. She looked friendly. The kind of person with whom you could be easy.

Marnie took off her hat and jacket and her fingerless gloves and sat down on Gabriel's chair, swinging herself to the right and then to the left, feeding Mister small treats while she waited.

Gabriel returned soon enough with the tin now in two pieces. He had sliced the top completely off. He passed it back to her. Her heart quickened.

'Mind your fingers, the edges are sharp. Listen, I, er, I was about to make a drink. Will you join me?'

Marnie nodded.

'Coffee OK?'

She smiled.

As Gabriel busied himself at the sink, Marnie lifted the lid from the tin. For the first time in almost a quarter of a century, daylight fell onto what was inside.

59

Will's back was aching and he hardly had any strength left in his legs by the time he reached the caretaker's cottage. He staggered inside and laid the dog gently on the settee in the living room. It remained in the same position, curled with its legs beneath it, barely having the strength to keep its eyes open. Will crouched beside it, stroked the top of its head with his fingertips. He could feel the shape of the skull beneath the fur. The very bones were cold. It worried him that the dog was no longer shivering. He'd read somewhere that in cases of hypothermia, not shivering was a bad sign.

The ashes in the grate still held some residual warmth. He screwed up some of the free newspapers and sales leaflets that had been shoved through the letter box and lit a new fire on the remains of the old one. He tipped everything out of his rucksack and used the T-shirt he slept in and his pyjama bottoms to wipe as much dirt as he could from the dog and then he wrapped his fleece around it. The fire burned brightly but it wasn't giving off enough heat to make a significant difference to the temperature of the room. Will sat beside the dog, sharing his own body heat.

'Don't give up, buddy,' he said. 'Hang on in there.'

The poor animal was exhausted. Will was cold and tired too. His clothes were filthy and wet. The flames in the fireplace flickered.

Beside it, the shelves that used to be full of books were empty.

Will remembered how Denise used to sit here, on this same sofa, her feet tucked beneath her, her face resting on the palm of her hand as she read, and how she would look up at Will when he barged into the cottage, clumsy in his apologies. 'Sorry, it's only me. John sent me back for his wrench.'

Why did John Morahan never fetch his own tools? Why did he always send Will?

From nowhere, a deep well of sadness rose inside Will and in the next instant a thought occurred to him.

He believed now that Denise Morahan was Alice's mother, everything pointed to it.

What if John Morahan had been her father?

It was possible! John and Denise could have been young lovers and when she became pregnant perhaps their parents kept them apart but they stayed in touch and reconnected later.

Would Alice have known? Could she have known?

What if the special date that night hadn't been a romantic date after all? What if Alice had arranged to meet John Morahan? The man was renowned for his temper. Something Alice said could have triggered a violent reaction from him. Of everyone, he was the best placed to hide the body in the funfair.

He'd said a travelling woman had fetched him when Will was outside the caravan, drunk. But Will didn't remember a woman. What if John had been in the caravan all the time? What if John, who had originally helped give Will an alibi, was now telling people Will had hurt Alice to make sure suspicion didn't turn towards him?

He was distracted by the dog which made a strange, gasping sound. It was barely breathing. Will tried to soothe the animal. It had a delicate, slender face, the shape of an arrowhead. The eyes were dark and tapered, like raindrops. It struggled for a moment, exhaled and collapsed, like a balloon deflating. This time Will couldn't rouse it.

He had to do something. If he didn't get help soon, the dog would die.

He searched through his stuff but couldn't find the phone charger. In his haste to leave the guesthouse he must have forgotten to unplug it from the wall socket – besides there was no electricity here. He couldn't call for help. What now?

The closest telephone would be at the Big House, over the road. There was nothing for it but to go and knock on the door and ask if he could use it.

60

Gabriel put a coffee mug on the table in front of Marnie, pulled up a chair and sat opposite. Mister lay on the floor beside the heater with his chin on his paws, watching. Marnie had taken off his muzzle. Mister had never bitten a human being, so far as she knew. She wouldn't trust him with two teenage girls, but here in this quiet room with her and Gabriel she was sure he'd be all right.

'Go on then,' Gabriel said. 'Look in the tin. The suspense is killing me.'

Marnie glanced at him. He looked back at her, registered her unease.

'Shall I do it for you?'

She pushed the tin two inches towards him. He sat up and reached inside. He took out a book. 'A Souvenir History of the Channel View Holiday Park,' he read. He turned the cover to Marnie, who recognised it. It was the book Guy deVillars had given to Alice with the old photographs inside; the same book as the one her father used to have. How strange that Alice should have thought it important enough to put in her tin.

Gabriel laid the book on the surface of the desk. Next he picked up an unsealed envelope.

'Shall I open it?'

She nodded.

He lifted the flap, took out a photograph and passed it to Marnie.

It was an old photograph, in colour, but with a white frame around the edge. Marnie had never seen it before, although part of it was familiar. Why did Alice have it? Why was it in the tin?

The photograph showed Marnie's mother, Denise, as a teenager, little older than Lucy was now. She was wearing a black polo-neck jumper and a kilt. Socks. Lace-up shoes. Her face was wan. In her arms was a baby. Marnie recognised the baby. It had its eyes closed, scrunched shut, its fists clenched on either side of its head, the tip of one little thumb sticking out between its third and fourth finger. It was sucking a pink dummy. There was a spot on its forehead where there must have been a mark on the camera lens.

Marnie made a frame for the baby's face with her two forefingers. It was the same baby whose picture was in her locket: a print of the same photograph, the same spot on the forehead.

Which meant that the baby in the locket couldn't be Marnie after all. Denise had been in her late twenties when Marnie was born. In this picture she was barely more than a child.

Marnie reached for the envelope that had contained the picture. Written on the front, in pencil, in Denise's handwriting were the words: 'To baby Alice. From your Mummy xxx.'

Marnie's life ran before her eyes, everything played the same way, but interpreted differently: every word; every kiss; every touch from her mother; every kindness from Alice; the photograph she'd found in her father's chest of drawers of the girl on the carousel. The girl's hair was fair, which was why she'd assumed it was Alice, but when John Morahan first met Denise Scott, she used to dye her hair too.

'Marnie?' Gabriel asked. 'Are you all right?'

She passed the photograph back to him.

'Who is she?'

Denise had been quiet all her life. She had kept her secrets. Marnie hadn't uttered a word in decades. Now it was time to speak up. The Morahan women had been quiet for long enough.

'She's my mother.'

The words were misshapen; a jumble of sounds. Marnie clasped her hands in frustration. Gabriel said gently: 'Try again.'

She took her time.

'Mother,' she said.

'That girl is your mother?'

'Yes!'

Gabriel picked up the envelope and read the words. 'She was Alice's mother too? Alice Lang's mother? The girl we found?'

He held Marnie's eyes. She felt empty; shaken. As if she'd been turned upside down and her history emptied from her. As if she'd been erased and would have to start again.

'You didn't know?' Gabriel asked.

'No.'

'Then no wonder it's such a shock!'

He came round the desk to stand beside Marnie. He turned the chair towards him.

'Is it OK if I...'

She gave a small, awkward nod.

He put his arms around her. She, who was so rarely touched by anyone other than Lucy, stiffened at first, but then relaxed into his embrace. He held her and she was glad to be held; she needed to be anchored; she needed his touch. Without him, she felt as if she might drift away. The foundations on which her life had been built had turned to dust.

It was a shock, yes, but everything was becoming clear to her now. At last there was a reason for Denise's sadness: her baby had been taken from her. And the things that Alice had told her, the things Alice had known about her, now, at last, Marnie understood.

'You're shaking,' said Gabriel.

He pulled back a little and crouched so that his eyes were level with hers, ran one hand gently down the side of her face. He stroked her cheek with his thumb. She looked into his eyes, clear and honest eyes, concerned eyes, and she was grateful that he was there and that he was her friend.

She tried to speak but all she managed to make was a jumble of sounds and the effort was exhausting.

'What is it?' Gabriel asked, gentle as if he was tending something infinitely precious and fragile.

Marnie pointed to the baby in the photograph.

'Alice was my sister!'

She covered her mouth with her hands to contain the sobs.

'Hey,' said Gabriel, 'it's OK.'

Denise must have hoped that one day the two of them would find one another and put the two pictures together – the one given to Alice, the other in Marnie's locket – and that they would understand the truth. The timing had been so awful! If Alice had only come a few weeks earlier then everything could have been so different!

Marnie shook with distress. Mister waddled over and put his head on her lap.

'I'll get you a glass of water,' Gabriel said.

He stood up and moved to the sink, glancing into the tin.

'There's another photograph.'

He passed it to Marnie. This picture was of a school cricket team, a line of young men seated outside a grand pavilion. Swathes of green countryside disappeared beyond, and in the distance was the sea. There was something familiar about this photograph too. Marnie thought she might have seen it before, somewhere else.

'That's the South Downs,' Gabriel said, 'outside Brighton.'

'You know it?' Marnie asked. Her speech muscles were out of practice and the sounds were barely more than a whisper, but it was enough for Gabriel to work out what she was attempting to say.

'We had a job there a few years back. I used to go walking along the Downs. There's a school there, a great boarding school, all towers and turrets. St Aubin's. You see the pupils walking round the city in their uniforms. That picture was taken at the school.'

Marnie didn't know what it meant. Gabriel filled a glass with water, passed it to Marnie.

On the table, face-up, her phone pinged.

'Shall I look?' Gabriel asked. Marnie nodded and he picked it up.

'It's a message from Zoe,' he said. 'It says: "Will you come to the Big House now, right away? It's urgent."'

61

Will was in the hall, struggling into his filthy jacket when he saw, through the glass in the top of the door, a light approaching down-hill towards the cottage. He opened the door, assuming it was Marnie, and found himself face to face with John Morahan. John was holding a torch and brandishing a large stick.

John pushed the door wide with such force that it banged against the wall. Will stepped backwards, holding up his hands. 'It's me, John,' he said, 'Will Jones.'

John stood there, stooped and ferocious with bags beneath his eyes and lines on his face. Like the cottage, he seemed smaller than he used to be, although the threat of violence was large. The little terrier dog stood beside him, showing its teeth, hackles high on its back. The old man was so fired up that it took a moment for him to register that he was looking at Will. When he did, he slowly lowered the hand holding the stick.

'Will Jones? What the bloody hell are you doing here?'

'I got kicked out of my lodgings. There was nowhere else to go.'

'This is private property.'

'Marnie said it would be OK.'

'It's not up to her.'

'Then I'll get out.'

'Too right you will!'

Will's heart was pounding but he stood his ground. 'But first, John, will you help me. I found a dog by the estuary... it's in there. It's in a bad way.'

He indicated the living-room door and stepped back so John could go in. Will followed. John whistled between his teeth when he saw the animal.

'Bloody Nora. The state of it!'

'I pulled it out of the mud but it must have been stuck for a while. It's very cold. I think it's Marnie's. She was looking for it earlier. My phone's dead so I can't call her.'

John crouched beside the dog.

'I didn't know what to do,' said Will. 'I didn't know where to take it. I don't have a car or anything. I was trying to warm it up.'

John lifted the dog's lip with his thumb, then its eyelid.

'It's dying.'

'No!' Will said. 'No, it's not going to die. How do we warm it up? Can we heat enough water for a bath here, or—'

'Will, it's beyond help.'

'I'm not going to let it die.'

John looked up at Will.

'I mean it,' Will said. 'I don't care what it takes or how much it costs. What can we do to help it? How do we keep it alive? Can we get it to a vet?'

'It won't last that long.'

'What then?'

'I don't hold out much hope but—'

'What do we do?'

'We'll take it over the road,' said John, in his slow, West Country way. 'We'll take it to the Big House and put it in warm water. We'll try and warm some life back into it.'

'Mr deVillars doesn't like me. I don't know if he'll let me in.'

A question flickered across John's face but he suppressed it.

'Don't you worry about him. I'll make it right.'

Will really didn't want to have to face Mr deVillars again, but his determination to save the dog was stronger than his reluctance.

'Could you first call Marnie, John, to let her know we've got the dog?'

'Don't have a phone.'

'Oh. Right.'

Surreptitiously, Will eyed the old man. He was an unlikely ally but he didn't know that Will had his suspicions about him. And Will needed John if he was to have any chance of getting into the Big House and saving the dog. That was the priority. He'd worry about the role John might have played in Alice's death later.

'You'll have to carry it,' John said.

'Sorry?'

'The dog. I can't. My back's buggered.'

'Yes. Of course.'

John shut the terrier in the cottage kitchen and Will, carefully, picked up the larger dog. It seemed heavier now that the adrenaline in Will's blood had dissipated; it was a cold, dead weight in his arms. Following John, Will carried the animal out of the cottage, up the path and over the road. He only had the one boot which meant every stone and sharp edge pressed into the sole of his bare foot. John Morahan went ahead, marching up the drive to the Big House and rapping on the door like a sergeant major.

After a few moments, the door was opened by Mrs deVillars' nurse. 'Oh!' she exclaimed, when she saw the two men. 'I was expecting someone else!'

'Is Mr deVillars available?' John asked.

'He's popped out to get a prescription for his wife.' She looked at the dog in Will's arms and then at Will's feet. Will tried but couldn't muster one of his charming smiles.

'He won't mind if we use the boot room,' said John. 'It's an emergency.'

'Well, I don't know...'

'He'll be fine about it,' said John, stepping forward with such confidence that the nurse was obliged to step back.

With a glance of apology, Will followed him into the hallway, through the kitchen and into the boot room beyond, the same room where he and Marnie had brought Mrs deVillars before. Having established they didn't need her, the nurse excused herself and went back upstairs.

John switched on the radiator, then turned on the taps over the butler's sink, running his hand beneath the flow until the water ran warm. 'Bring it over here,' he said when the sink was almost full. Will did as he was told. Carefully he lowered the dog into the water.

'Gently. *Gently!*' John's voice softened as he leaned closer to the animal. 'There you go; there you are, my lovely. How's that? Is that nice, is it?' The water in the sink turned opaque as the mud came away from the dog, which slumped, too weak to support even the weight of its own head. Will kept his arms underneath it, kept its head out of the water, feeling the clots of mud softening beneath his fingers. 'Right,' said John. He took off his coat and put it over the back of the chair, rolled up his shirtsleeves. 'You hold it there. Clean off the mud as gently as you can. Top the water up as it cools; gradually bring it up to blood temperature, not too hot all at once. I'm going to find some towels. I'll be back in a minute.'

'We need to let Marnie know.'

'All in good time,' said John. 'First things first.'

He left the room and Will exhaled shakily; he'd been on tenterhooks every moment he'd been in John Morahan's company.

But something had changed. The dog, at last, was trembling, its shivers making tiny ripples in the cloudy water.

Will was so grateful and relieved that he felt something give inside him; as if some part of him had cracked; as if his heart had begun to work again.

'You're going to be OK,' he told the dog, speaking in the same confident tone that John had used to reassure the animal earlier. 'We're going to look after you. Everything's going to be fine.'

From the far side of the house he heard the doorbell ring.

62

'Thanks for coming,' the nurse said to Marnie. 'Camille's been asking for you and we don't have long before Mr deV comes back. Mind the mud on the floor. Camille's upstairs.' She glanced over her shoulder, towards the downstairs rooms, then ushered Marnie inside. 'Please hurry,' she said. 'I don't like Camille being up there on her own.'

Marnie followed the nurse up the staircase. Their feet were quiet on the carpet. The house was quiet too; as if it was waiting for something to happen. Marnie heard murmurs, male voices, somewhere below. She thought she heard her father and touched Zoe's arm.

'Yes, it's your dad,' said Zoe. 'He's fine. I'll explain after you've seen Camille.'

The nurse, always so calm and sensible, sounded nervous, and this worried Marnie.

'Camille's been in a funny mood all day,' Zoe said. 'She keeps asking for you and Mr deV keeps telling her she's being silly. He refused to call you. He's watching her like a hawk and she doesn't want him anywhere near her. In the end she was so agitated I sent him out to the late-night chemist and prayed you were free.'

They reached the first-floor landing and hurried to the narrow staircase leading up to the attic rooms. Zoe unlocked the door at the top of the steps and Marnie followed her along the narrow corridor with the sloping ceiling and into Mrs deVillars' room. It was as it had been before. Too warm, dark, with its uneasy slopes and shadows. A mirror in an ornate, Gothic frame reflected the lamplight. Camille deVillars was sitting in her armchair, her hands on her lap. She was dressed in an ankle-length, powder-blue dressing gown. Her hair had been drawn into a bun on top of her head; she was wearing a dash of pale lipstick.

She looked up and said: 'Hello, Denise. Thank you so much for coming.'

'It's not Denise,' said the nurse. 'It's Marnie. You've been asking for her all day, Camille, remember?'

'Marnie? Come here, dear, so I can see you properly.'

Marnie stepped forward. The old woman reached for Marnie's hand and enclosed it between hers, reversing their roles the last time they met. Her skin was cool and dry. Marnie remembered this woman's myriad kindnesses to her as a child and felt a strong affection. She smiled warmly. Her lips made the shape of the word: 'Hello.'

'It's difficult for me, Marnie,' Camille said. 'The thoughts come and go, and I have trouble holding onto them.'

'We don't have long,' said the nurse. 'Your husband will be back soon.'

'The three of you were so alike. You, Denise, Alice. I get muddled.'

Zoe moved to the window, pulled back the curtain, looked out.

The old woman's lips moved but no words emerged. She was

struggling to form a sentence and Marnie, who had struggled too, understood how she felt and was full of sympathy.

'Be quick, Camille,' said Zoe.

Mrs deVillars tried, but it seemed an age before she managed to speak.

'I'm sorry, Marnie,' she said. 'I only understood these last few days. Before then it was all a puzzle.' She hesitated. 'I'll go back to the beginning...'

Zoe exhaled in frustration.

'I was walking by the estuary one day,' said Camille. 'I used to love it down there. All that water. I used to think of my father on his ships and...' Marnie urged her on with her eyes, willing her to get to the point. '... and I saw Denise sitting on the slipway, looking out to sea.' She glanced at Marnie. 'Your mother. She was Denise, wasn't she?'

Marnie nodded, and Mrs deVillars continued. 'She was sitting there and I thought I'd never seen anyone look so sad. I didn't know her well. She didn't often come over to the park and I thought, well, she's a private person, I don't want to intrude, but that day... oh, she looked so unhappy. So I sat down next to her and asked her what was wrong and she said her situation was impossible. "What situation?" I asked and she said: "I can't tell you, Mrs deVillars. I can't say." "Is it to do with your husband?" I asked. "Is he being unfaithful? Is he drinking too much?" "Oh, no," she said, "no, it's nothing like that. John is a good man." She wouldn't tell me what it was that was bothering her. I said we should go and get a cup of tea and we walked back together. We talked about you, Marnie. She told me how proud she was of you. And she said something odd. She said she'd made a mistake a long time ago and that she was paying for it now.'

Marnie could see the two women in her mind's eye so clearly

that she wondered if she might have seen them together, that day, if the memory was locked away somewhere inside her too.

'I was going to take her over to my house,' the old woman continued, 'but Denise said the cottage was closer. She said: "I'll make the tea. We can sit outside and watch the birds," and I said that would be lovely. But when we got there, there was a bouquet on the doorstep, lovely flowers all wrapped in Cellophane. I knew they weren't from John – he'd never spend money on something like that – so I said: "Oh, Denise, looks like you've got a secret admirer!" It was supposed to be a joke but the blood drained from her face like she'd heard some awful news and she picked up the flowers and threw them over the hedge and she was saying: "He won't leave me alone! He's always sending me bloody flowers!" and I understood. Because having a man after you when you don't want him after you is a dreadful thing, Marnie. Especially when you can't get away from him.' She paused and sighed.

Zoe was watching intently, her eyes flicking from the window to the women, and back again.

'I still didn't understand,' Camille continued. 'If I'd known what was going on, I'd have helped her. I'd have given her money, at least, or...' she trailed off. 'I should have done more for your mother, Marnie. If I'd worked it out I would have helped her, properly helped her. But I didn't understand. And I can't believe now I was so stupid because afterwards, when I read the letter... Marnie, dear, she wrote a letter before she died. A letter to me. A confession, or a warning – call it what you will. And it was all in there, everything except his name. Perhaps I didn't see it because I didn't want to see it. I don't know. Sometimes, the closer something is to you, the harder it is to see it clearly.'

Lights from outside moved across the ceiling.

'It's Mr deVillars,' Zoe said urgently. 'He's back already. He's turning into the drive.'

Camille's lips moved but once again, no words were spoken. Marnie was breathing fast.

Don't stop now, she prayed. Keep going! Get to the end of the story.

The old woman beckoned Marnie closer. 'I might not have another chance to tell you. My mind might not be so clear again. Edward tells me things to confuse me and then he says I don't know what I'm saying. He says I can't trust my mind, that it plays tricks on me, but I'm not stupid. I know I get things wrong, but—'

'He's getting out of the car,' Zoe said, from the window. 'Hurry, Camille.'

'They looked so alike,' Camille said, 'Alice and your mother. I should have worked it out.'

Marnie's breath was coming quickly now. She needed to speak. She wished she'd brought the photograph. She tried to shape the words of a question to which she was certain she already knew the answer: 'You're saying Alice was my mother's daughter?'

They came out oddly, wrongly, gobbledegook; like a record played backwards. Camille couldn't untangle them.

Marnie tried again, more slowly but again the words didn't work.

'Sign it,' said Camille. 'Talk to me with your hands.'

Was Alice my mother's daughter?

'Yes, that's right.'

Zoe was staring out of the window. 'He's patting his pockets, looking for his house keys.'

'Denise was fourteen,' said Camille. 'She'd fallen in love with a boy who came into her father's bookshop.'

A hammering on the door downstairs.

'He can't get in,' said Zoe.

'When she fell pregnant, the boy's family took him out of the school, whisked him away, found him a job and a suitable wife.'

Male voices downstairs. Marnie could hear her father's voice clearly now, calling: 'All right, all right! I'm coming!'

Camille leaned forward, closer to Marnie. 'He was obsessed with Denise,' she said. 'He never stopped wanting her.'

From a distance, Mr deVillars' voice exclaimed: 'John! What are you doing here?'

'They stayed in touch, you know, him and Denise, right up until she married, and then she told him she wanted a new start. She didn't want her past to interfere with her present. But he couldn't let her go. He wouldn't. He found out where they lived, even when they moved to the back of beyond. He found her and he would go there to pester her when John was out, always turning up trying to make her love him again, spying on her...'

There was a mechanical clunk; the sound of an engine turning.

'The lift!' Zoe hissed.

'Then when John found him lurking about on the farm track outside their home one night, he made up some story about the car breaking down and made friends with John and tricked him into bringing Denise here. Her and you and—'

'He's coming up,' Zoe said.

Mrs deVillars leaned forward towards Marnie, her eyes wide. 'In the letter, Denise told me that he was threatening to tell John about her past if she didn't take up with him again.'

A whirr as the lift rose.

'Either she did as he said or he would destroy her marriage.'

Sounds from the hallway outside; the lift mechanism unlocking.

Who, Mrs deVillars? Marnie signed. *Who? Say his name!*

Zoe, frantic, hovered by the door. Footsteps were approaching. Mrs deVillars looked over her shoulder.

Tell me, please!

The door swung open.

'Here I am!' said Mr deVillars. He stopped when he saw Marnie, caught his breath: 'Oh.'

Marnie was looking at Camille deVillars. She was watching the old woman's hands. Mrs deVillars didn't look at her husband. She held Marnie's eyes.

She signed: *It was Edward.*

Edward was Alice's father?

Mrs deVillars gave a small nod, and signed something else, panicky now, her hands rushing, tripping over themselves.

He said he'd gone fishing the evening she disappeared but his rod was in the boot room all night.

The evening Alice disappeared?

I knew he was lying so I went to her caravan the next morning and she wasn't there.

He killed her?

'Camille, what are you doing, darling?' asked Mr deVillars, stepping forward, approaching his wife. Marnie didn't take her eyes off Mrs deVillars' hands.

He was responsible for your mother's death and he killed Alice too. He will kill me next, she signed, *and then he'll blame me for Alice.*

63

John Morahan came back into the boot room.

'That was Mr deV,' he said.

'Does he know I'm here.'

'I didn't mention it.'

'What did he say?'

'Nothing. I tried to explain but he was anxious to get back to his wife. How's the patient doing?'

Will washed warm water over the dog's back. He could see the shape of its spine through the blue-grey pelt.

'I think it looks a bit better.'

John came round to get a better view.

'I reckon you're right. She's a girl. Pretty little thing.'

'Do you think she'll make it?'

'If she doesn't, it won't be through lack of trying. Is she warming up?'

'A bit.'

John ran his hands over the dog. 'She's definitely better than she was. Breathing stronger too. Bring her over to the heater. We need to persuade her to drink something, to warm her up from the inside.'

Will reached down into the sink and lifted the dog out, soaking himself again as he did so. He placed her carefully into the nest of towels John had made and wrapped her up, so that only her snout and her eyes peeped from a hood made of towels. She looked at Will and he felt as if she was looking right into his soul.

I almost let her drown, he thought and swallowed back his shame.

'Bring some warm water and a spoon and let's see if she'll take it,' said John.

'This is like the old days, John,' said Will. 'You telling me what to do.'

'Ha,' said John. 'Someone bloody needs to.'

64

Mr deVillars turned to Marnie. The benevolent-old-man mask had slipped. His expression was angry, his posture threatening.

'What was she saying? What was she signing?'

'Nothing,' said Zoe. 'She moves her hands like that all the time. It doesn't mean anything.'

Mr deVillars' eyes studied the faces of the three women in the room and settled on Marnie. Marnie was used to making herself unreadable and gave nothing away.

'Why are you here?' he asked her.

'Marnie's father's downstairs,' said Zoe without missing a beat. 'She kindly popped up to say "hello" to Camille.'

'That was good of you,' said Mr deVillars coldly.

'Camille was pleased to see her.'

Camille's face had blanked when her husband came into the room. Her eyes had become unfocused, her expression neutral. She was picking at something invisible on her lap. Either she was a good and practised actor, or she really had slipped out of lucidity.

'It's late,' Mr deVillars said. 'Camille needs to settle.'

Surreptitiously Marnie signed: *Will you be all right?* but Camille wasn't looking and there was no indication that she had understood.

The nurse touched Marnie's arm.

'Don't worry. We'll be fine.' She hesitated, then said in a low voice: 'Could Maya stay with you tonight? That means I can sleep in this room, with Camille.'

'There's no need for that,' said Mr deVillars.

'To be on the safe side,' said the nurse. She turned back to Marnie. 'Tell Maya she can pick up her school things in the morning.'

Mr deVillars said: 'Zoe, show Marnie out, will you?' but both Zoe and Marnie saw the panic in Camille's eyes at the prospect of being left alone with her husband. Marnie indicated that she could find her way down the stairs perfectly well on her own.

* * *

In the ground-floor hallway, she paused. She could hear her father's voice, and Will's in the boot room on the other side of the kitchen. Apart from that, all was quiet. She listened for a moment and then crept across the grand wooden parquet floor and pushed open the door to the living room. The walls were lined with paintings, the bookshelves busy with photographs. Marnie eyes scanned them until at last she found what she was looking for: a school photograph, a cricket team; two rows of floppy-haired young men sitting outside an imposing pavilion; sweeping green countryside behind.

She read the caption. 'St Aubin's School U-19s' Cricket First Eleven'. The players were listed by name. The batsman in the centre of the picture, the one with his arms folded and one leg crossed over the other was Guy deVillars. The picture had been taken in the same location as the picture in Alice's tin. The poses were almost identical and the faces of the young men were similar but the picture in the tin had been taken decades earlier. The man in the centre of that picture was not Guy deVillars, but his father, Edward.

Camille was right. Edward deVillars was Alice's father.

65

'You saved a life tonight,' said John Morahan.

Will cradled the dog's head on his lap. She gazed up at him sleepily.

If he'd listened to his first instincts, she'd be dead by now; a minuscule speck in that massive expanse of water. Marnie would never have known what had happened to her. She'd have carried on searching, worrying, hoping. Will could never have told her what he'd done; his shame would have been too great.

For the first time in more years than he could remember, Will was proud of himself. For once, he had done the right thing.

The boot-room door swung open. It was Marnie, pale as a ghost. She gave a gasp of relief when she saw the dog and joy flooded her face. She came over to Will, crouched beside him, lifted the dog's head between her two hands and kissed her snout. Beneath the towel, the dog's tail twitched. Marnie looked at her father for an explanation.

'She's OK,' John told her, 'thanks to our friend here. She was stuck in the mud but he dug her out.'

He clasped Will's shoulder.

'She's just taken some warm water,' Will said, doing his best to sound casual. 'We think she's going to make it.'

Emotions flickered over Marnie's face: shock, relief and gratitude. Yet as soon as she'd convinced herself the dog was all right, her agitation returned. She signed to her father, urgently.

'What is it?' asked Will.

'She says we need to get out of here.'

Will was up for that.

'Hold on,' said John, 'we can't leave the room in this mess.' There were puddles on the floor and the area around the sink was wet and clodded with mud. 'We can't just walk out with Mr deVillars' towels.'

Marnie shook her head, frustrated. She signed some more.

'But, Marnie, I need to talk to Mr deVillars, I need to—'

Marnie gazed at her father pleadingly. He gazed back at her. As Will watched, they came to some understanding without another word being uttered.

'OK,' said John Morahan. 'We'll go together.'

Will's clothes were soaked. His socks were wet and his bare left foot was cold and sore. His back ached from carrying the dog.

He didn't care.

He gathered the dog up into his arms once again, and followed Marnie and John Morahan back through the downstairs of the Big House. Upstairs he could hear a murmur of voices; it sounded as if the nurse and Mr deVillars were arguing.

They went outside into the bitter cold. Marnie trotted ahead.

'She's going to fetch the car,' said John. Will held the dog close, like a baby, still wrapped in her towels.

They were almost at the end of the drive when they heard Edward deVillars calling. Will looked back to see the old man standing framed by the open door, illuminated by the hall light, tall and thin with his head jutting above a tortoise-skin neck and his kindly face, the hook nose and fluffy white hair. He was wearing his trademark baggy corduroy trousers, an old jacket with patches at the elbow. He had less of the film star about him that night, more the air of a retired schoolteacher.

'I say, John!' called Mr deVillars. 'What's going on? Come back and have a whisky with me!'

John looked towards his old friend and hesitated, torn between his desire to do right by Marnie, and affection and respect for his oldest friend.

'Come on, old chap,' called Mr deVillars. 'You've time for a catch-up, haven't you?'

'Marnie wants us to leave,' Will reminded John.

John came to a decision. He raised a hand. 'Thank you, Mr deVillars, but not tonight,' he replied. 'Right now, I need to take care of my family.'

66

Marnie's car headlights – one of them held in place only by duct tape so its beam was skewed – illuminated her father and Will standing at the end of the drive to the Big House. She pulled up beside them. Will climbed into the passenger seat with Luna while John fetched TT from the caretaker's cottage. Marnie conducted a hasty three-point turn, then drove home.

Lucy and Maya were thrilled to see Luna safe. While they questioned Will about her rescue, Marnie texted Gabriel.

I'm sorry, but I can't collect Mister. Can he stay with you tonight?

The reply came at once:

No problem. We're making friends.

* * *

John opened a beer and filled in the girls about Luna's adventures, and Will and Marnie went upstairs to find some dry clothes for

Will.

While he changed, Marnie wrote a brief explanation of what had happened in Camille's room on her phone.

She showed it to Will who stared at the screen for a long time, reading and rereading what Marnie had written. Then he laid the phone down and sat on the edge of the bed with his head in his hands. After a while he looked up into Marnie's eyes.

'I thought it was Guy,' he said. 'All this time I believed Guy was responsible for Alice disappearing and then, for a while I thought...' He trailed off. Marnie waited.

'Are you sure,' Will asked, 'that what Mrs deVillars told you is right and not just her blaming her husband to protect her son?'

Marnie nodded.

I'm sure.

Still Will couldn't quite accept it.

'Why didn't she say anything to anyone before?'

She didn't know that Alice was dead.

'Do you think it's true? Do you believe that Mr deV was responsible for Alice's death?'

Yes.

'He killed his own daughter? That respectable old man? Jesus! Why? To stop her telling the truth?'

Marnie shrugged.

'It's not like she'd have wanted anything from him. She didn't care about money. All she ever wanted was to be part of a loving family.'

Even as he spoke, Will realised that he'd read Alice wrong from the beginning. He had misinterpreted her words and actions because he'd never tried to see the world from her perspective. He hadn't understood. Of course she'd wanted to get to know Guy: he was her half-brother! When she'd said there was nothing 'like that' between them, she'd been telling the truth! And he'd been jealous of her interest in the deVillars family, jealous of her going to Camille's birthday party. He'd been so blinded by his own insecurity that he'd got every single thing wrong.

Will stood up, paced the small room, turned back to Marnie and noticed, for the first time, how distraught she was.

'Hey,' he said, 'it's OK.'

He reached out his arms, put them tentatively round Marnie, not really touching her. She leaned forward so that her face was pressed against his chest.

'Marnie, it's OK,' Will said again. He held her close. 'It's OK.' He patted her back awkwardly. 'Out of everyone you're the one who shouldn't be feeling bad. You gave Alice what she wanted. She came here looking for family, and she found you.'

Marnie put her arms round him. She held onto him. Everything was clear to Will now.

'Alice knew that you loved her, Marnie,' he said. 'She *knew*.'

* * *

They sat side by side on the bed, leaning against one another, Will's arm round Marnie's shoulder.

'Is it my fault that you don't speak?' he asked her.

She frowned.

'That time in your bedroom, when I came, I told you not to say a word to anyone. I made you promise.'

She shook her head.

'You mean, it wasn't my fault?'

Marnie said: 'No.'

* * *

Will wanted to tell the police everything, but Marnie didn't see how they could do that without making Mrs deVillars' situation even more precarious.

She was unlikely to be able to repeat what she'd told Marnie, and even if she did who would believe her given her confusion? Would anyone seriously believe Mr deVillars posed a serious threat to the wife he made such a point of adoring? Only the day before, the police had witnessed his tenderness to her when they laid the flowers for Alice.

'We have to let the police know something's going on,' Will said, 'so that if anything happens...'

He tailed off. He could hardly believe he was having to consider these dreadful possibilities. Yet Edward deVillars had proven himself to be ruthless and Camille's behaviour was unpredictable. The old man would be anxious to make sure she did not cause any more trouble.

As a compromise, Will used Marnie's phone to call the police and told them he'd recently gone past Blackwater House and heard an argument taking place inside – a man's voice raised in anger, making threats. Beside him Marnie fidgeted. She didn't think this was the right tactic.

Next, Will messaged Emily, who gave him Guy deVillars' phone number. Will called Guy but Guy didn't want to listen.

'First you threaten and accuse me and now you're turning on my father!' he cried. 'Why should I believe a word you say? Why should anyone?'

'I was wrong about you and I'm sorry but—'

'It's ludicrous to suggest that my father would lay a finger on my mother. He worships the ground she walks on! I've never known a couple so close.'

'Please,' begged Will, 'if you wake up tomorrow to find out there's been some accident at Blackwater House and—'

'Fuck off, will you,' Guy said. 'Leave my family alone. Don't you think you've done enough damage?'

He cut off the call.

*　*　*

Will and Marnie decided there was nothing for it but to make sure Camille deVillars was safe themselves for the coming night. After that they'd have time to come up with a better plan.

Will borrowed John's shoes, which were a little on the tight side, but then so were the clothes that Marnie had lent him. They left John with the girls and dogs and went back to the Big House. Marnie parked on the verge, in a place where they could see the house and its windows through the gateway. There were no street-lamps on that road. If anyone should look out, they would be hidden by the darkness.

Lights shone in the living-room window, in the hall, stairs and landing, and in the attic windows. The curtains were drawn across the barred window beneath the main gable; the window of Mrs deVillars' bedroom.

After a few minutes, lights approached from the direction of the town and a police car turned into the drive.

'Bingo,' whispered Will.

Two police officers climbed out of the car, went to the front door, knocked and were admitted inside. Moments later, Guy's Jaguar followed. Guy let himself in to the house with his own key.

From the patterns of shadows and movement, it was clear that the police and Guy were talking to Mr deVillars in the living room. The curtains were open and at one point Guy came to stand by the window, looking out, a tumbler of whisky in his hand. At another Mr deVillars stood with his back to the window, gesticulating in an exasperated fashion.

Then the shadows stilled and for a while nothing changed. The rain was fine but persistent; clouds covering the moon. The night was dark. Nobody came to the living room window. Marnie and Will's eyes became tired from watching.

At last the front door opened, light spilled onto the steps and the police officers emerged, walked across the drive and got back into their car. There was a delay before they started the engine. Guy stood at the door until they had driven away, their car sweeping past Marnie's.

'At least Guy is still there,' Will said, but a few moments later the front door opened again and, after embracing his father, Guy left the house and he drove away too.

'Mr deVillars must have convinced them that everything's all right,' said Will. 'Still, he won't do anything now, will he? It would be too risky.'

Marnie stared at the house, frowning.

She was thinking about what Camille had told her, and how vulnerable the woman was. How easy it would be for her to have an 'accident', to fall down the stairs, to slip under the bathwater.

Too easy.

'Shall we head off?' Will asked.

Marnie shook her head.

'You want to stay?'

'Yes.'

Will considered for a moment, then he said, 'OK. We'll stay together.'

Marnie texted Zoe to let her know that she and Will were outside the Big House.

If you need us or if you're worried, call me or text.

Up at the window beneath the gable, the curtain moved. Marnie flashed the car headlights and Zoe responded with a wave. She didn't text to say their presence was unnecessary. She didn't suggest they went back to Marnie's cottage and that she'd call them there if there was a problem. She must have her own grave concerns.

Marnie and Will sat together in the cold car. They couldn't put the radio on because the battery was on its last legs. They were cold and uncomfortable. The rain sometimes fell heavily, sometimes lightly. Will told Marnie the story of how he'd rescued Luna from the mud. He elaborated, said that the tide was washing round his ankles before he managed to free the dog; made out that he'd been genuinely afraid for his own safety. Marnie listened. From time to time, she nodded or widened her eyes. It was a good story. Will looked forward to telling it to his London friends. It put him in a good light.

He left out the part where he'd considered walking away and leaving the dog to drown.

After that he couldn't think of anything else to say, but it was OK, they were comfortable together. They settled back into their seats. For a long time, nothing happened apart from the configuration of the lights in the Big House changing as Mr deVillars moved from room to room.

Eventually, the lights in the attic were dimmed; now only a nightlight cast a faint glow at the gable window. Shortly after, the living-room light was extinguished, and after that the hall light and then the first-floor landing light as Mr deVillars made his way up to bed. At this point, Will and Marnie decided to take it in turns to sleep, an hour at a time, using the clock on Marnie's phone as an alarm. From 11 p.m. to midnight, Will slept. He was tired and fell asleep easily, but it was painful dragging himself awake again so that Marnie could sleep the next shift. By the time he woke her, Will was so cold and hungry that he knew further rest would be impossible.

He nudged Marnie, yawning beside him.

'Hey,' he said, 'let's drive to the service station to buy some coffee and food.'

Marnie shook her head, but she passed the car keys to Will before opening the door at her side. Cold air rushed in.

'I'm not leaving you here on your own, Marnie.'

She made a shooing motion with her hand.

'OK,' he said, 'I won't be long. Coffee and a pasty?'

'Yes.'

Will shuffled into the driver's seat.

'Are you sure you'll be all right?'

'Yes!'

* * *

Marnie watched the car disappear along the road, the wonky head-lamp casting its off-kilter light. Then she turned back towards the house. Her eyes scanned the walls, from bottom to top and down again. She went forward, to the gates, then stepped inside, keeping to the lawn where her movements wouldn't make any noise. As she came closer, she noticed a light moving in one of the attic rooms: the bathroom behind Mrs deVillars' bedroom. From its jerky motion she guessed what she was watching was someone holding a torch.

Perhaps Zoe was using the bathroom and hadn't wanted to disturb Camille by turning on the lamp.

Marnie crept forward through the rain. She didn't mind being alone in the dark like this, knowing the only person she had to fear was inside the house in front of her. She could hear the call of a pair of owls, the rustling of a fox as it moved along the hedgerow. The person with the torch had left the bathroom now, but the light wasn't extinguished as it would have been if it was Zoe and she'd gone back to bed. Instead the light was in the attic corridor, moving towards the staircase. As it passed the window, Marnie glimpsed the silhouette of a tall, hunched figure: Mr deVillars. She only saw him for a moment, then he disappeared.

She realised she'd been holding her breath.

Mr deVillars had been on the prowl.

It was probably nothing. It wasn't as if he'd stopped by the bed to hold a pillow over Camille's face.

Only it didn't feel like nothing.

Marnie put her hand in her pocket to call Zoe. The phone wasn't there. She'd left it in the car.

Frustrated she turned and paced the other way. Then she turned back.

She didn't know how long Will would be. She couldn't wait for him.

She ran towards the house, staying on the lawn. The gable window was two storeys high; too high for her to throw pebbles with any accuracy and there was no way to climb up.

Instead, Marnie ran light-footed round to the back. It was dark, but she knew the house well. She tried the back door; it was locked. She hesitated but only for a moment before she picked up one of the ornamental plinths in the garden, hefted it to her shoulder and heaved it at the boot-room window next to the door. The glass shattered and fell. Marnie held her breath, expecting someone to call out, to hear a voice raised in fear and anger, but she heard nothing.

She pulled her coat sleeve over her hand and punched out the exposed shards before reaching inside to turn the key to open the door and within moments she was back inside. The floor was slippery. It still smelled of estuary mud and wet dog.

Marnie crept forward.

The clouds had moved and now moonlight fell through the windows, casting a dim, blue light and deep shadows. The big old house creaked and shifted. It felt to Marnie as if the house was observing her, aware of her footsteps, knowing exactly where she was. She heard a scuttering: mice perhaps or rain in the chimneys. She went into the hallway, reached the foot of the grand stairs, put one hand on the banister, one foot on the bottom step. By moonlight, she began to climb. She was almost halfway up, when she heard a door open above her, and the sound of Mr deVillars clearing his throat.

Marnie turned and jumped down the stairs. She darted through an open doorway into the dining room and pressed herself against the wall. Mr deVillars came down the stairs and switched on the hallway light. Marnie waited for some exclamation, some cry of anger or a gasp of alarm when he noticed something was amiss, but none came. He'd gone into the living room. She heard the chinking of ice against glass, the sound of something being poured. He was fixing himself a whisky.

This was her chance! Marnie nipped round the door and ran up the stairs, her footsteps muffled by the carpet. She scooted along the landing, and trotted up the steep stairs to the attic. The door was open and the nightlight glowed dim orange in the corridor. Marnie knocked gently on the door to Mrs deVillars' room. There was no answer. She tried the handle. The door was locked.

'Zoe!' she called, but her voice was weak and the word a croak, not loud enough to rouse anyone.

But there was another way in. Marnie tried the next door along and that opened into a small bedroom. Zoe's coat was hooked on the door, her possessions tidily organised inside. The connecting door to Camille's room was closed. A towel had been lain along the bottom of it, cutting off any draught. It took Marnie a moment to notice masking tape was sealing off the other cracks.

She crossed to the door; pulled away the towel, went down on her hands and knees and sniffed. She smelled a faint, chemical odour: exhaust fumes.

Marnie peeled away the tape, letting it drop onto the floor behind her. She turned the handle, half-expecting it to be locked, but it wasn't and the door swung open towards her. She was assaulted by a gust of overwarm air that smelled of motorway, that stung her eyes and caught in her throat. She pulled her jumper up over her nose and mouth and went into the bedroom. The glow of the nightlight was dim, but she could see the heads of the two women, Camille and Zoe, beside one another on their respective pillows on the bed. She could not tell if they were still breathing.

She went forward to rouse them, and suddenly felt herself pushed from behind. As she fell onto her hands and knees, something heavy hit the back of her head. For an instant there was pain, then there was only darkness.

68

First she felt the thudding ache, creeping around her skull, tightening like a vice. Then she became aware of the carpet beneath her cheek; the gritty air in her lungs. She could see blurred shapes in the darkness. Her eyes were sore. She lifted her head a fraction. She remembered where she was.

Marnie summoned her willpower, turned and crawled towards the crack of light beneath the door, reached for the handle, turned it; no use. The connecting door through which she'd entered had been locked. Marnie was trapped inside Mrs deVillars' bedroom with the old woman and her nurse.

Through narrowed eyes Marnie scanned the room for something heavy enough to batter open one of the doors. But they were substantial and anything with which Camille deVillars might conceivably hurt herself had already been removed.

Marnie dropped down low again, where the air was cooler and cleaner. She knew it wouldn't be long before she lost consciousness but she didn't know how long she had. A few minutes maybe. She crawled to the side of the bed and tried to switch on the bedside lamp, but it didn't work. Somewhere in the house,

Edward deVillars had disconnected the power supply to the bedroom.

Marnie felt the first stirrings of panic. She pulled herself up to the side of the bed, took hold of Zoe's shoulders and shook the woman.

Wake up, please!

But Zoe was limp. Marnie heaved her down onto the floor and turned her on her side. Then she went round to the other side of the bed, and pulled Mrs deVillars down too. If they were still breathing, she hoped this would give them a few more minutes. She patted around the bedside tables, trying to find Zoe's phone, but it wasn't there. Mr deVillars must have taken it. He would have seen her earlier message, known she and Will were outside. And she understood, now, that he must have been looking out of the window, waiting for her car to drive away before he made his move.

He thought there were no witnesses to his cruelty but he was wrong.

She crawled to the window, and looked out: there was no sign of Will, or the car. She pressed her hand through the bars as best she could but they were close together; there was no way of breaking the glass pane beyond.

Be calm, Marnie told herself. Think.

She could not break her way out. She had no way of calling for help. There was no obvious way to ventilate the room. Her only chance was to find the source of the fumes and block it.

She held her breath and listened, concentrating heard. She could feel a faint vibration through the boards beneath the carpet and heard a gentle chugging sound, almost like a heartbeat. Marnie was the caretaker's daughter. She knew about plumbing and heating systems. She knew what was making the noise. It was the boiler.

She set off again, crawling across the bedroom, round the

corner of the partition wall and into the bathroom. It was windowless, pitch-dark.

She patted her hands along the side of the wall until she felt the plaster change to wood; a cupboard door. The vibrations and the fumes were stronger here. Marnie knew what she would find in that cupboard. Her father had a similar set-up in his bungalow. It would be a combi-boiler installed to provide hot water and heating to the attic rooms and it had been rigged so that the fumes were being pumped into the bedroom instead of out through the ventilation pipe that ran through the bathroom wall.

Marnie could sort this if she could stay conscious for long enough.

She lay down again and took a deep breath of ground-level air, then stood and opened the cupboard door. Warmth enveloped her. The boiler was burning hot; it must have been pumping away for hours. She reached out, burned her hand on the metal, withdrew it. She tried again, then ran out of breath and had to drop down to breathe for a moment or two. This time, when she stood up, she felt the brush of a towel against her cheek. She grabbed the towel and used it to protect her hand while she groped for the bottom of the boiler. From there, she found the gas intake pipe. The handle to cut off the supply had been disabled. Never mind. She followed the pipe into the boiler, felt her way to the emergency cut-off, pressed it. Waited.

Nothing happened.

She tried again.

Still nothing.

She tried pulling at the pipe to break it free, but it had been soldered into place. She couldn't move it. Still the old boiler chuntered away, hiccoughing, pumping its carbon monoxide cocktail into the rooms.

69

Marnie was tired. She could barely keep her eyes open.

She'd done her best but she couldn't turn off the gas. She needed to sleep.

She would rest for a little while, just a few minutes, then she'd try again. She crawled back into the bedroom, to be closer to Zoe and Camille. She didn't want to sleep in the bathroom on her own.

Marnie lay down on the carpet next to Camille deVillars. She took hold of the old woman's hand. Her eyelids were heavy. She couldn't remember ever feeling so tired. Lights moved across the bedroom ceiling, as they had done before. A car had turned into the drive. The lights were parallel so it wasn't her car. Guy maybe. Perhaps he'd come back.

Marnie closed her eyes.

The room was tilting and spinning, like a fairground ride, like the floor in the fun-house. She felt as if she might slip off. She remembered an evening a long time ago, climbing out of her bed in the caretaker's cottage, looking out of the window, seeing someone throw something into the sea. She remembered that the man on the shore turned towards her and the moon came out from behind the clouds and she saw his face.

It was Edward deVillars.

She remembered now, but it was too late. She was so tired. She was slipping; she was falling. She let herself go.

Nothing hurt any more.

It was her turn to sleep.

She drifted away.

She was on the estuary shore, looking towards the bridge. In the distance, a hazy figure waved: it was Alice. She was with Denise, standing side by side, so close together that they were touching.

I'm coming, Marnie called. *Wait for me!*

She tried to push herself up, but it was an effort; she was so heavy, so tired.

We're here, sweetheart, Alice said. *We're always here for you!*

Other voices; nearby. Male voices. A discordant noise.

'Don't wake your mother, Guy, she needs the rest.'

'It's locked!'

A rattling of the door handle. It was distracting. Marnie wished it would stop.

'Where's the key, Father?'

Marnie tried to shut the voices out. She looked back to where she'd seen her mother and sister; they were further away.

No! Wait! Don't go without me! she called, *don't leave me behind!*

'The nurse insists on locking the door from the inside to stop your mother wandering.'

Alice looked back. *Wake up!* she called. *Wake up, Marnie! Let Guy know you're there!*

'The nurse is in there with Mother?'

'Yes.'

Marnie's eyes snapped open.

Call him, Marnie, Alice told her. *Call out to Guy!*

Marnie lifted her face from the carpet. She opened her mouth. She cried: *Help!*

It was nothing, a faint croak; barely audible to her own ears.

'Go home, old chap,' Mr deVillars said. 'I'll call you in the morning.'

HELP!

She couldn't do it. She couldn't make a sound loud enough to save her life.

You can do this, Marnie. Do it for Lucy! Call him!

'Help!' Marnie cried.

On the other side of the door, Guy deVillars asked: 'What was that?'

'It was nothing.'

Louder, Marnie! Louder! Go on!

'HELP!'

'There it is again! Didn't you hear it, Father? Somebody's in trouble!'

70

ONE WEEK LATER

Marnie opened the door to the caretaker's cottage and stepped inside. She walked past the ugly dresser, climbed the creaky old stairs and went to the door of the master bedroom.

She remembered being nine years old, running up the stairs, calling, 'Mummy! Mummy!' and throwing open this door. Denise was on the bed, curled under the quilt with her dark hair spread about the pillow, looking as if she was sleeping.

'Mummy?'

Marnie remembered reaching out and touching her mother's shoulder. 'Mummy, wake up!'

But Denise had been beyond waking.

The week before she died, John had cut some early roses for Denise and she'd been delighted by them. She'd declared their perfume 'perfect' and had put them in a vase on the living-room window ledge. They were delicate blooms, the outer petals pink, the inner ones yellow. The roses had made Denise happy.

Marnie never told her father about the other flowers, the ones that didn't make her mother happy: the extravagant arrangements that used to arrive at the cottage, the 'big flowers' that Denise always threw away. If John had known, perhaps everything would have been different. Perhaps he'd have seen the true colours of Edward de Villars.

The memories were close as Marnie went into her parents' old bedroom. She sat on the bed, and she opened the locket that Denise had hidden under Marnie's pillow all those years earlier. She held it on her lap, the pictures of herself and Alice keeping one another company, always.

Outside, the rain fell. Drops ran down the window. Marnie heard the faint roar of the bulldozers on the building site.

Alice knew Denise was dead before she came to Severn Sands, but she must have hoped her father would receive her with open arms, take her in and that his love would make up for the unhappiness she'd experienced with the Langs. She had a fairy-tale idea of what family life should be and could not have conceived of a world where Edward deVillars would not be thrilled to be reunited with his long-lost daughter. She wasn't to know that her existence threatened the stability of the life he'd so meticulously built. She could not possibly understand how precarious his world was; how viciously he guarded it.

She could not have known that her mother had taken her own life when she realised there was no escaping his will.

* * *

After Guy had forced open the door to Camille's bedroom and found the three women unconscious inside, the police had been called. The women had been taken to hospital by ambulance. When she was well enough, Marnie had told the police everything she knew. Edward deVillars had been questioned yet still he denied murdering Alice. He blamed Camille, as she had predicted he would. He said Alice had come demanding money to keep the secret of her parentage quiet and Camille didn't have the money so she had killed Alice. But Alice wouldn't have done that and Camille never hurt anyone in her life.

Edward's story was a typical construct of those with the kind of psychopathy he exhibited. He was transposing his actions to Alice. Marnie believed *he'd* tried to buy Alice's silence, offering her money to keep quiet and go away, and when she refused he had killed her.

He was an arrogant, proud man who did not want his reputation or his perfect life ruined by a scandal, the fact that he'd impregnated and then abandoned a teenager when he was still at school. He was used to manipulating women. He hadn't expected Alice to stand up to him, but that's what she would have done.

* * *

Marnie heard a knock at the front door, and then it opened and a voice called up the stairs, 'Marnie? Are you there?'

She closed the locket and slipped it back in her pocket, went to the top of the stairs. Will was standing in the hallway.

'Hi,' he said, 'how's the head?'

'OK,' Marnie said.

'Good.' Will held up a bottle of cider. 'Fancy going down to the estuary and sharing this with me for old times' sake?'

She smiled.

* * *

They went together, the two of them, and they sat by the shore and watched the waves coming in. The water was almost black in colour. Still it was beautiful.

'I'm leaving today,' Will said. 'Getting the last train out of here. Going back to London.' He took a drink of cider. 'You're welcome to visit any time. You and Lucy and the dogs. You can even bring your father, if you must.'

He passed the bottle to her and she took a drink.

They gazed out across the sea.

'That night,' Will said, 'when I went to the service station and the car wouldn't start...'

'It wasn't your fault.'

'I ran all the way back. I wouldn't have left you.'

'I know.'

She passed the bottle back to him.

'Will you be all right?' Will asked.

'Yes. You?'

'I'll be OK,' he said. He sniffed. 'Only I think I'm coming down with something. My partner, Saoirse, she's had a bad cold. I must have caught it off her.'

'Is she nice?'

'Saoirse? Yes. Very nice. Only, you'll find this hard to believe, but I've behaved like a bit of a dick towards her. Ignored her messages, didn't consider her feelings, that kind of thing.'

Marnie picked up a pebble, turned it between her fingers.

'I texted her to apologise,' said Will.

'Did she reply?'

'Yes.'

'What did she say?'

'She told me to fuck off.'

Marnie smiled and threw the pebble into the sea.

71

AFTERWARDS

Will went back to London and he started writing his book about Alice.

He immersed himself in his writing. He lost himself in memories, found details he'd forgotten, revelled in Alice and his memories of her. He worked every day, from 6 a.m. to 6 p.m. and after that he switched off his laptop and he called Saoirse. Sometimes she agreed to go out with him for a walk, or a run, or a drink. If she wanted to visit an exhibition, or go to the cinema to watch a film, or if she'd heard about a new arty-farty vegan restaurant and wanted to see what the food was like, even if she'd agreed to meet up with some of her friends, Will went with her without moaning or pulling faces or getting drunk. He put his flat up for sale. He hoped, one day, that he and Saoirse could buy a place together.

First, he needed to finish the Alice book and second, make it up to Saoirse. Or vice versa.

He stayed in close touch with Marnie, who had the biggest heart of anyone he'd ever known. He knew he didn't deserve it, but she seemed to have found it in herself to forgive him.

* * *

Mr deVillars was charged with the murder of Alice Lang and was granted bail on condition he stayed in Guy's flat in London and didn't go near Severn Sands. He had to undergo the humiliation of being electronically tagged. Guy wanted nothing more to do with his father. He stayed with his own family at their house in South Gloucestershire and visited his mother every day.

* * *

Camille, Zoe and Maya continued to live in the Big House. They moved out of the attic and down into the main rooms. Without Edward's bullying, Camille's condition stabilised and then improved. Marnie, Lucy and John Morahan went to see her often. Camille was particularly fond of the little grey lurcher dog, Luna. Trip Two made himself useful keeping vermin at bay.

* * *

John Morahan was badgered into enlisting as a volunteer helper at Jenna's animal sanctuary. They were always needing something fixing, or something building, and he became invaluable and spent a great deal of time there. The other volunteers asked his advice about problems they had with their cars or their lawnmowers or their cameras. John became something of a legend.

* * *

Angharad Jones promised to come and visit John – he being unable to visit her because the sanctuary wouldn't manage without him – as soon as the weather improved.

'I can't be doing with all that greyness,' she said. 'I like my sea blue these days.'

In the meantime they stayed in regular contact on Face Time, reminiscing, she drinking port and lemonade in Majorca with her sister, he on the whisky in his bungalow in Severn Sands. They laughed a great deal, they lifted one another's spirits and they looked forward to their reunion.

* * *

John visited the churchyard each day. He stood over his beloved wife's grave and he talked to her about this, that and the other, how proud he was of Marnie and Lucy, how much he missed her still, and Denise, quiet as always, listened.

He'd been at the churchyard the day Alice disappeared. He'd been to talk to Denise because of the girl who'd come, who looked so like Denise used to look. He told Denise that the first time he saw Alice he thought she was Denise, returned to him somehow.

'You could have told me about your troubles,' John said. 'We could have sorted things out together.'

But Denise hadn't been one for talking about the things that worried her. John knew this. Still he wished it wasn't so.

* * *

Gabriel Romanescu and his new dog, Mister, spent more and more time at Marnie's cottage with Marnie, her daughter, Lucy, and their two dogs, Luna and Tessy. Together they watched the spring come in, celebrating the lengthening of the days, the proliferation of wildflowers, the arrival of the first swallows. Marnie practised talking and it became a little easier every day. By the end of May, she and Gabriel could hold entire conversations without either of them faltering.

Marnie and Gabriel walked along the side of the estuary, watching the light changing in the sky and over the water, the foreshore reflecting the sky like a mirror. Hundreds of wading birds fed in the shallows; a flock of lapwings fluttered above, their wings making a sound like rain falling. The dogs stayed close.

Mister was wary of puddles, stepping carefully, lifting each huge, stubby paw in a pernickety manner like a ballet dancer. He was more confident these days. He was unconcerned by Luna – who had forgotten her ordeal – bounding about like a baby goat, spattering the silt, chasing after imaginary playmates, careering this way and that. Tessy stayed close to Marnie as always.

Marnie knew they should turn round or risk losing the light but she loved being out here, with the sea and the wind. With the dogs. With Gabriel.

They sat for a while on a tree trunk washed up on the shore and watched the birds. The glare of the setting sun was blinding. Marnie thought of all that water moving, the pull and tug of the current dragging it back out into the Atlantic; the creatures in the water drawing with it, the pebbles and shellfish turning over below; elvers and salmon and sea trout and bass.

The estuary was a purer colour than Marnie had ever known it and she could see further into Wales than she'd ever seen before. She didn't know if it was the change in the weather, or a change in herself.

For many years, she was afraid of coming close to the estuary, particularly at daybreak or nightfall, afraid that she might see something of Alice, her spirit caught in the mist, or something more substantial: a dead girl rising from the shallows. She was no longer afraid. She would have regretted those years of secrets and silence if it wasn't for Gabriel telling her that regret was a useless emotion.

Even so... All those years of being afraid for entirely the wrong reasons. She wasn't going to waste another minute of her life.

Mister came to Gabriel with a rope of seaweed in his mouth. He dropped it at Gabriel's feet and stood in front of him, stumpy tail wagging, staring hopefully at the weed.

'Thank you,' said Gabriel.

He threw the weed for Mister and then put his arm round Marnie's shoulder. She liked the weight of it. She liked the feeling of belonging. She understood how Alice had wanted to belong to someone. She would always be in Marnie's heart.

'Are you happy?' Gabriel asked.

'Yes,' she replied. 'Are you?'

'If you're happy, then I'm happy,' said Gabriel.

He kissed her and she kissed him back.

They were at the beginning of something that was going to last.

Marnie had a feeling it would be something good.

ACKNOWLEDGMENTS

Thank you to Sarah, Yvonne, Rose, Becky, Nia, Ellie and everyone at Boldwood Books. I'm so proud to be part of this amazing team.

Thank you to Alison, Marianne, Vicki and Pat for all that you do and for being wonderful.

Thank you to the book community: authors, bloggers, librarians, booksellers, reviewers and especially readers. I couldn't ask for a kinder or more supportive crew.

Thank you to Martin for agility training – any mistakes in this book are my own – and to all my crazy, brilliant agility friends and their dogs. We have so much fun together!

Thanks as always to my family and friends.

This story was inspired by a visit to the real-life town of Severn Beach in South Gloucestershire.

Although it's situated approximately in the same location, Severn Sands is nothing like Severn Beach and is entirely fictional. The geography to either side of this made-up town also does not represent what's there in real life but is an amalgamation of different stretches of the coast, from the fossil cliffs at Aust to the beach at Berrow and everywhere in between. Most of the places on which the fictional locations are based exist, but not where they're found in this book. I hope people familiar with the area will forgive me.

READING GROUP QUESTIONS

1. Do you think the story of The Scarlet Dress is driven more by plot, or character? Or is it a combination of both?

2. Referring to the holiday park staff, Angharad Jones tells Will: 'We were like one big family.' How important is the theme of 'family' to this book?

3. The present day action takes place in February, at a time when the town of Severn Sands is fading, but the characters look back to a long, hot summer when the holiday park was in its heyday. Why is this dichotomy relevant to the story?

4. What does Will Jones have to learn over the course of the action in order to become a more rounded human being?

5. Why was Denise unable to tell her husband about the untenable situation in which she found herself? Should she have told him the truth earlier? What might have stopped her doing so?

6. Several of the characters have difficulty communicating what they really need to say. Why is Marnie's muteness particularly significant?

7. Alice Lang has been dead for almost a quarter of a century before the story begins. Is she still a valid character in her own right?

8. Why do you think animals are so important to Marnie?

9. The inevitability of change is key to this story, yet neither Marnie or Will has been able to move forward since Alice's disappearance. Why not?

10. We only see Mr and Mrs Lang through Will and Marnie's eyes. What do you think of the couple? Could they have done anything differently to help Alice come to terms with her situation?

MORE FROM LOUISE DOUGLAS

We hope you enjoyed reading *The Scarlet Dress*. If you did, please leave a review.

If you'd like to gift a copy, this book is also available as an ebook, digital audio download and audiobook CD.

Sign up to Louise Douglas' mailing list for news, competitions and updates on future books.

http://bit.ly/LouiseDouglasNewsletter

The House By The Sea, another chilling and captivating novel from Louise Douglas, is available now.

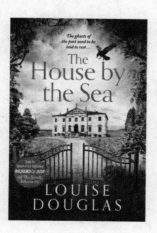

ABOUT THE AUTHOR

Louise Douglas is the bestselling and brilliantly reviewed author of 8 novels including *The House By The Sea* and *Missing You* - a RNA award winner. *The Secrets Between Us* was a Richard and Judy Book Club pick. She lives in the West Country.

Follow Louise on social media:

facebook.com/Louise-Douglas-Author-340228039335215
twitter.com/louisedouglas3
bookbub.com/authors/louise-douglas

ABOUT BOLDWOOD BOOKS

Boldwood Books is a fiction publishing company seeking out the best stories from around the world.

Find out more at www.boldwoodbooks.com

Sign up to the Book and Tonic newsletter for news, offers and competitions from Boldwood Books!

http://www.bit.ly/bookandtonic

We'd love to hear from you, follow us on social media:

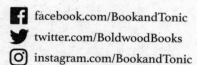

facebook.com/BookandTonic

twitter.com/BoldwoodBooks

instagram.com/BookandTonic